Praise for *Whispers of Love*

". . . as sensual as a Sandra Brown romance, as riveting as a Clive Cussler thriller. Love and espionage at its best."
—Michael Lee West
Author of *She Flew the Coop*

"Whispers of Love will tug at your heart, then send it soaring. A compelling read from Shirley Hailstock, one of this genre's fastest rising stars."
—Susan Connell
Author of *Rings on her Fingers*

"A perfect love is shattered in this emotionally-charged roller coaster of espionage, intrigue, and romance. Not to be missed."

"From whispers of love to whispers of heartache when an assassin stalks—and a choice must be made that no woman should have to face."
—Joanne Pence
Author of *Too Many Cooks*

"Watch this writer, read this writer—she's going places, and readers will be glad they were there from the beginning!"

"[*Whispers of Love*] should be marketed as a story for all readers regardless of color or race."
—Garda Parker
Author of *Blue Mountain Magic*

A SCHOOLTEACHER'S LESSON

"You said you wanted to talk to me?" Clara asked.

Luke took her arm and pulled it through his. Clara noticed how pleasurable it felt to have it there.

"It has to do with Miss Emily and her constant attempts to throw us together."

"Yes," Clara commented, caution in her voice.

"Miss Emily has been playing this game with me and I think it's time I taught her a lesson. I want you to help me."

Clara stopped and stared at him. This part of the path was tree-lined and secluded. The moonlight turned the road into a bright ribbon and bathed Luke's face in a soft glow.

"What do you think we should do?" Clara knew she wasn't going to like Luke's plan.

"Pretend."

"Pretend to fall in love?"

Luke nodded. "If you don't want to set your sights on the man of your choice, rest assured, Emily Hale *will* find you a husband. You're willing to try it?"

"I might be."

"With whom?"

Clara looked Luke steadily in the eye. "You."

SHIRLEY HAILSTOCK

CLARA'S PROMISE

P

PINNACLE BOOKS
KENSINGTON PUBLISHING CORP.

PINNACLE BOOKS are published by

Kensington Publishing Corp.
850 Third Avenue
New York, NY 10022

The P logo Reg. U.S. Pat. & TM Off. Pinnacle is a trademark of Kensington Publishing Corp.

First Printing: June, 1995

Printed in the United States of America

To my children, Ashleigh and Christopher, who give me support and love greater than I ever thought possible.

Prologue

Clara stared at the advertisement. She'd folded and unfolded it hundreds of times since Janey Willard had abandoned the *Richmond Planet* on one of the dining hall tables. Janey's rich cousin in Virginia had sent her the newspaper read by nearly every person in Richmond's colored society. Clara Winslow had watched with envy from another table as Janey and her friends had turned up their noses and giggled over the absurdity of teaching in the ice-cold wilderness of Montana.

Clara grasped it as a lifeline.

One

Lifting her head, Clara closed her eyes and let the sun touch her full on the face. Then, shielding her eyes, she squinted and panned the landscape. The vast Montana sky was a new world for her. She smiled, feeling the warmth spread through her like dark brandy. She felt girlish, not like the twenty-one-year-old woman she was. She wanted to run, jump up and down, kick her heels up, and capture some of the freedom the openness afforded her. No buildings, crowds, or shops; no one screaming from windows, disturbing the stillness of the afternoon—just open space and clean air. She could stare at it for hours and not get tired. Clara sighed, knowing she had a purpose for her trip today. And she'd better get to it. Picking up the picnic basket, she lifted her cotton skirts and went down the three steps of Hale's Boardinghouse. The gate hinge creaked as she opened and closed it. Emily Hale's house was big and roomy and ringed by a waist-high white fence. Flowers bloomed in the July sunlight. Clara stared at the sky again. Since leaving

Union Station in nearby Washington, D.C., she'd spent a lot of time gazing at the heavens. She could make a case that she had time to daydream these days, whereas in her home in Virginia there had been too much to do to take time out and notice the sky.

Following the path around the back of the rooming house, Clara struck out at a steady pace. She hadn't been this way before, but Aunt Emily felt poorly and she was running an errand for her.

Waymon Valley wasn't nearly as big as Arlington, Virginia, but everyone was friendly. Clara looked forward to school's beginning. Soon her own house would be ready and she would finally be completely independent. She had never thought when she answered that advertisement that she would actually follow through with her decision, but here she was and here she would stay. She tilted her chin an inch higher, as if confirming her decision.

The tapping started before she reached the rise in the hill. There were trees ahead and she couldn't see what was causing it, but by the steady sound and because Aunt Emily had told her it was a building site, Clara knew someone was hammering. She expected the place to be running over with men. Yet the sound was singular. The basket of food she carried was heavy, enough to feed a crew. Clara hadn't expected to find only one man.

He was on the roof, nailing sheets of blonde-colored wood to the beams that formed the skeletal structure of a very large house. She watched him for a moment, one hand extending the brim of her plumed hat. He was large and muscular. The sun glinted off his shirtless back, polishing the sheen of sweat on his golden skin. Clara swallowed, not taking her eyes off him. She watched the way he held the hammer, the way he swung with purpose and sureness. She'd seen men working before, had witnessed them raising barns and finishing houses. Yet, today was the first time she'd ever seen a man so at one with his work that the division between him and the roof was indefinable.

What is Aunt Emily up to? she thought. "I'm feeling a little poorly, Clara," she had said. "Would you mind taking the lunch pack out to the building site?" Clara couldn't refuse. Aunt Emily had provided her with food and shelter since her unannounced arrival in Montana two full months earlier than her appointment called for. Emily was Clara's aunt on her mother's side. The older woman had come west on the Overland Trail en route to Oregon before Clara was born. She'd taken her niece in like a lost child. Now, however, Clara wondered.

In the two months she'd been here, Emily Hale had done nothing but talk about how every woman needed a man in her life. Clara didn't need a man and didn't want one. Yet looking at the way muscle covered bone on the body above her head, she knew she could be tempted. Aunt Emily must have known, too.

Squaring her shoulders, she pulled her thoughts back and called to him. "Hello."

The hammering continued. He hadn't heard her. "Hello," she called again, waving her free arm. The hammer stopped in mid-arc. He peered at her.

His face was shadowed, but Clara could see his features screw into an unmistakable frown. "Miss Emily sent your lunch." She held the heavy picnic basket up as proof, its red-and-white gingham cloth concealing the mouth-watering contents beneath.

He climbed down slowly. At least she thought it was slowly. His actions seemed to follow the pace of her breathing. Clara, watching his ease of movement, was unable to take her eyes from him. She'd seen men without their shirts before. In the refinement of her teachers' college, the other girls would have been appalled at how she'd lived and what she'd seen; but farm life was different from the velvet-tufted parlors of Washington where she'd attended school. Seeing men in the fields take off their shirts in the heat of the day had never been out of place in her mind. But seeing the tall, muscular man walk to where she stood, she felt her body respond to his presence. He was much taller than she'd thought from seeing him perched so high. He seemed as tall as a mountain. His eyes were dark and fringed with long black lashes. His shoulders were wide and strong. Clara had never seen such a magnificent man. She swallowed again. His gaze was sure and steady, and she found herself tearing her eyes from his.

"Miss Emily sent you something to eat," she repeated, needing something to say. Sweat congealed between her breasts and she felt a trickle slip down the center of her back. She glanced up, attributing the heat to her exercise. He was a powerful man, his skin colored dark by the sun. His hair, a rich brown, was cut close and neat. His eyes were penetrating, black and piercing, but Clara saw something in them she couldn't identify. He had a strong chin and square jawline. Clara wondered how his face would transform if he smiled. She offered a smile of her own in hopes of having it returned.

"Why did she send you? She usually comes herself."

His tone smacked her. She was stunned by the anger in his voice, as if she were a poor substitute for the older woman. It had been a long time since anyone had spoken to her like that. Teachers' college had trained her to keep her voice controlled and to be courteous to everyone, especially those who did not deserve it. Wade had treated her like a fifteen-year-old and she wouldn't allow it here. She would not stand by and let this man, no matter how much of a giant he was, intimidate her.

"Miss Emily isn't feeling well today." Clara struggled to keep her voice controlled. "As a favor she asked me to bring this." She lifted the basket, willing her arm to hold it and not fling its contents at the man before her. "And now that I've performed my duty, I trust you'll return the dishes and basket at your convenience."

Clara set the basket at his feet and turned, taking several purposeful steps in the direction she'd come.

"Do you always perform your duties, schoolteacher?"

She stopped, her hands balled into tight fists, her back ramrod straight.

"We usually eat over there." He pointed toward a plank table with one long bench in the shade of a large tree.

She turned back, ready to give him the benefit of her scathing tongue, but what she saw took her breath away. He took a step toward the shade tree, grabbing a towel and wiping the sheen from his naked torso. Clara stared at his movements, watching the towel as his powerful hands brushed against his skin. Her throat closed off, stopping the air in her lungs from its normal course. He dropped the towel and shrugged into a dark shirt that hung in the juncture of the tree where the towel had been.

"Sit down . . . please." His voice was low.

Pulling herself out of the trance that gripped her, Clara stared at him.

"Aunt Emily might need me. I think I'd better go back."

"Miss Emily will outlive us all," he said dryly. "Please, eat first. I'm sure she had a purpose in sending you out here."

His manner told her there was a reason other than his lunch that had prompted the older woman to ask her help today. Clara secretly agreed with him. "What does that mean?" she asked. He was confusing her. From the moment he had frowned from the roof of the unfinished house, she'd felt as if he were magnifying her, looking for the tiny nicks in her armor, some unrevealed reason for her being here. The thought scared her.

"It means I've known Miss Emily a lot longer than you have."

"Of course you have." Clara stated the obvious. "I've only been here for three weeks. Emily is my aunt, but she and my mother separated when they were young girls."

The giant man in front of her only shrugged, not explaining anything. Although Clara's mother had always spoken of her sister with affection, they hadn't met face to face until Clara arrived to accept the post of teacher. Before her mother died, a childhood likeness of her aunt had graced the parlor wall for as long as Clara could remember.

Picking up the basket, Clara came forward. She set it on the table. When she turned back, he stood directly in front of her, blocking her path. She felt trapped. For a moment she was back in Virginia. Fright clenched her heart, pushed her back, and she sat down on the bare bench, one hand stealing to the ruffles at her throat.

"Wou—would you like me to set it out for you?" she stammered. What was happening to her? She shouldn't be frightened of this man. She wasn't in Virginia anymore. She'd left that life behind, run from it; and out here she would make things different, better.

"Miss Emily usually shares the meal with me," he said when she opened the basket.

Clara stared at him, not moving. Was he asking her to stay and eat? Her throat was so tight she didn't think she could swallow anything. She turned back to her task, her movements mechanical and awkward. She spread the gingham cloth over part of the table and lifted several covered dishes from the basket. He walked around and reached inside to help her. His hand brushed against hers. Both of them snatched their hands away as if they'd been burned.

Clara stared at her own hand as if it were somehow different from its brief encounter with his.

"It's the air," he explained. "Static electricity builds up and snaps all the time."

Clara nodded, apparently accepting his reason. Her training had taught her about static electricity. It was rare to have it on a warm July afternoon and she had not seen or felt any spark, yet something about him had touched her core.

He finished unpacking the basket and set two plates and tumblers next to each other on the table, taking her acceptance of a meal with him for granted.

"You're Clara Winslow, the new schoolteacher." He stated the information as fact.

Clara took a seat and nodded. "I suppose everyone in town knows who I am. I apologize for not knowing everyone's name." She loosened the ribbons on her bonnet and set it on the bare part of the table. Her hair was pinned up, but she felt less restricted without a head-covering.

"Time will correct that," he said, helping himself to several pieces of fried chicken.

His speech was intelligent, schooled. She lifted her eyes, accepting the bowl of mashed potatoes he passed her. She filled her plate as he'd done his and found she was ravenous.

"What is your name?" she asked, daring to glance at his penetrating eyes.

"Miss Emily didn't tell you?" His eyebrows rose

as if his identity was common knowledge in three counties. "I'm Luke Evans."

Clara had heard his name mentioned but knew very little about him. Only that Emily Hale liked and respected him enough to make the trip to this site to have lunch with him. Yet in the time she'd been in town, she had not seen him.

"What are you building?" she asked, shifting to look at the structure behind her. The movement made her brush against his shoulder. The spark she'd felt before skittered through her blouse and snapped against her arm. Quickly she adjusted her position on the bench so she would not touch him.

"It'll be a house when it's done."

Clara could see that. When finished, it would be a three-story colonial with a center hall and a wide staircase. "Who's it for?"

He hesitated as his eyes looked at the bare bones of the unfinished building. "This one is mine."

His voice was a whisper, almost a prayer.

Clara's breath nearly caught in her throat. She envied him his skill: the house would be magnificent when complete. She thought of the small building that would soon be hers. Her position as teacher came with an unfurnished three-bedroom house across from the school. A house which would have been ready to receive her had she arrived at the appointed time. Luckily, Emily Hale had taken her in.

"It's very large," Clara commented. "You must have an awfully big family."

She felt more than saw the change in him. She could almost have said his body closed up, retreated inside itself, like a wounded animal fearful of a remembered injury. What had she said to cause him that kind of pain?

They completed the meal in silence. Clara began replacing the soiled dishes. Luke rose and watched her. She stopped, feeling his stare as if it were tangible.

"Would you like to see it?" he asked.

Clara was sure he offered due to the number of times her head had turned toward the large edifice. "I'd love to," she answered, unable to keep the smile off her face.

He extended his arm, allowing her to precede him. Quickly, she replaced her hat and tied the long ribbon on the left side of her chin. She felt him watching her as he'd done from the roof when she'd approached. The walkway leading to the giant building had been carved out and angled to receive carriages as they arrived for parties or receptions. She wondered if Luke planned to entertain.

Inside, the beams were up and the rooms outlined. They walked silently, smelling the freshness of the sunshine and the pine wood he used as building material. Clara looked up and counted. "Seven bedrooms!" she exclaimed. She couldn't remember ever being in a house with that many rooms. Of course, Emily's boardinghouse had six bedrooms, but that was a boardinghouse. This would to be a private residence.

"What are those tiny rooms off to the sides?" She pointed.

"Bathrooms," he said.

"Inside the house?"

For the first time, he laughed, throwing his head back and letting a hardy sound escape. Clara liked it. She hadn't heard a man laugh in a long time. Wade had always been too tired after working all day, and they had had few friends and never entertained. Luke's face did change when he laughed. It softened to a boyish charm. His eyes twinkled as the humor reached them.

"Yes, Clara," he answered finally. "Inside the house."

"Are you a rich man, Luke?" she asked directly.

"Rich? Why would you think that?"

"It's going to take quite a staff to maintain a house this size. You need people just to carry water up and down the stairs to service all those bathrooms."

Again he laughed. Clara didn't know whether she liked it the second time. She hadn't intended to make ignorant comments, but obviously she had.

"Water will be pumped into the bathrooms," he explained and, to forestall another question, he answered it before she asked. "It will also be drained out. There will not be the need to carry it up and down stairs."

Clara had heard of such things. While she was at the teachers' college, one of her friends' mother had worked at the White House and they had had many bathrooms there.

"I am impressed, Luke. It will be a grand house."

Clara turned all the way around. She imagined herself dressed in a fancy ball gown, twirling and laughing under the lights of a chandelier. She almost smiled, wondering what Janey Willard would say if she actually did attend a ball here—in the ice-cold wilderness of Montana.

"I'm glad you like it."

He walked her back through the framed doorway and to the path she'd take to return to Aunt Emily's. Thinking of her aunt reminded her of something Luke had said earlier. She turned back to him. "Luke, what did you mean earlier about knowing Emily a lot longer than I have?"

He shifted his weight in an uneasy fashion. Clara could tell he was deciding if he'd answer her question. "Emily Hale has been throwing women at me for three years."

"You think that's why I came out here?"

He spread his hands, letting his silence speak.

"Well you're wrong, Mr. Luke Evans." She rounded on him, looking him directly in the face. "My trip here was to fulfill the request of a sick old lady. I do not now, nor in the future, I assure you, have any designs to jump the broom with you or any other man." Clara was angry, angrier than she'd ever been. She brushed by him, leaving the basket and its contents on the table. She practically ran back to the path. When she was out of Luke's sight, she stopped to catch her breath. Why was she so angry? She knew Aunt Emily hadn't been ill. She'd even wondered why her aunt hadn't just asked her to go to the site. But manipulation, the thought had never crossed her mind. She wasn't a prize for Luke or anyone, and she wouldn't have Emily marrying her off. Retracing her steps to the

boardinghouse, she determined that she would
have words for the sick old lady when she got
there.

   Luke saw the anger in Clara's walk. Her white
skirt caught around her legs, hampering her efforts
to make strides. He was struck by his feeling of
surprise. She hadn't known why Miss Emily had
feigned sickness. It was an old game, and he and
the old woman had played it many times. Clara
was a pawn and obviously one who didn't take
kindly to the role. The other women had known
(some might have even suggested it), but he was
determined he needed neither wife nor child—ever
again.
   Clara's dark head disappeared over the hill. She
hadn't glanced back over her shoulder. That was
the cue he was looking for. All the women Miss
Emily threw at him had one trick or another, but
the act that proved they weren't angry was the turn
back to check if he were looking at them. Clara
hadn't done as expected.
   Luke let his breath out in a long sigh. She did
affect him, he admitted. On the roof, he'd been
surprised to find her slim body standing below
him. Her dress had clung to her in the breeze, and
the white color highlighted her dark skin tones.
He'd seen her coming up the hill, but hadn't let
on. She'd moved with a quiet poise that had caught
him off guard. During the meal, he'd studied her,
trying to find a reason for her being there, but
unable to. He couldn't tell what she was thinking.

One moment he didn't think she was aware of Miss Emily's ploy; the next, he was sure she was.

Schoolmistress. She didn't look much like his teachers, he chuckled to himself. She was beautiful, with dark brown hair that looked as soft as cotton coiled in a loose chignon and piled in the center of her head. Her brown eyes were as large as saucers, and her smile undid his insides.

He went back to work. Clara Winslow's face ran through his thoughts. He told himself it was useless to think about her, even if her skin did remind him of the dark cherry-wood furniture he'd ordered for his bedroom. It should arrive sometime next spring. By then, maybe Clara Winslow would be gone.

Two

Luke stood outside the dining room door, pulling at the tight collar that choked him. He hated dressing up. His work clothes were much more comfortable than this get-up, but he certainly couldn't pull a chair up to Miss Emily's dinner table dressed in wranglers and a flannel shirt.

The old woman stood at the end of the room when he slid the doors open. Her hand rested on a silver-handled cane, but Luke knew she had the constitution of a stone bridge. The table was set for the evening meal, fresh flowers in the center, crystal glasses at the head of every plate. Soon the entire household, miners mostly—men who scratched and picked at the underground copper veins—would arrive, as clean and starched as he was, for the planned ritual. Before that happened, Luke had a few words for Emily Hale. He stepped inside and pulled the doors shut behind him. Emily Hale stood like a queen reigning over the ceremonial chamber, her pearly-colored hair swept up and anchored by silver combs, as much her trademark as the monogrammed napkins standing like praying hands on the bone china plates.

Miss Emily was waiting for him. She had known he would come to dinner and that she'd sent Clara with lunch. Since the schoolteacher's arrival, he'd been absent from Hale's Boardinghouse, and Emily Hale had taken matters into her hands.

Until tonight, he'd avoided the house, knowing Emily would find ways to throw the community's latest maiden in his path. The old woman, whom he loved as dearly as his mother, made no pretense about the state of his bachelorhood. She lived to get him married. It was like a continuing card game between the two of them. Before meeting Clara, he had felt he'd won all of the hands; but today Emily had played a trump and Luke could only fold and re-deal.

"I want you to stop, Miss Emily," Luke told her, his voice menacingly quiet.

"She got to you." Emily smiled. She took a step toward Luke, her cane making an emphatic thud on the rugged floor. "I knew it the moment she set foot in this house. She's the one for you, Luke."

"You know my feelings on wife and family."

"Yes, I know them." She stamped her cane. Luke was familiar with the gesture. "They don't make sense, Luke," she continued. "You buried Peg. You can't bury your life with her. It ain't right. The Lord didn't—"

"Emily Hale!" he stopped her, his arm raised, palm out. "Don't spout the Good Book at me." He went toward her, knowing the old woman would stand her ground. Predictably, she did, raising up to her full height and challenging him with her stare. "It's my life, my decision, and I want you to stay out of it."

"Luke, I felt as you do once. I came to Montana en route to Oregon. I was going to settle there, begin a whole new life."

Luke knew the story. They didn't discuss Miss Emily's past often, but he knew her very well.

"After my man and my boys . . ." she paused, taking a moment to swallow. "After they died, I pulled up what was left and joined a wagon train."

He could have cut her off, but Emily Hale presented such a strong face to the world that there were times when she needed to unload some of the heaviness in her heart. She had come west from Tennessee, where midnight riders had killed her husband Jimmie along with their two sons. Their farmhouse had been set on fire and, by morning, the then-thirty-year-old woman had had nothing left in the world except her determination to begin a life somewhere else.

"Coming west, I saw families torn apart by Indian raids, cholera, disease, and accidents."

"I, too, traveled on a wagon train to get here, Miss Emily." Luke reminded her of his own trip from Illinois to join his father in an untamed country. Emily Hale didn't appear to hear him. She was lost in time, back on the Oregon Trail where she had left one life and begun another. Luke knew the point of her story, but he wasn't ready yet to forget everything. He didn't know if he'd ever be ready. He'd begun the house as a way of setting his mind on something for the future. A future he would live without his wife and child. Life was hard enough; death was even harder to take. And without Peg . . .

"If anything could stop a man or woman from wanting to live, it would be losing everything," Miss Emily continued. "Being the one left to bury the dead, rebuild the house, replant the crops—it's harder to go on being brave when all you want is to crawl into a hole and pull it in after you."

Emily's voice pulled Luke away from his thoughts of Peg.

"People are stronger than that, Luke. When someone dies, the rest of us have to go on. We can't bury ourselves in a bottle of whiskey, behind shuttered walls, or in the building of a house. You can't bury yourself, Luke Evans. Peg is dead. I'm sorry about that, but Clara is alive and she's here."

"Miss Emily," Luke began in a soft voice. Somehow he wasn't angry any longer. He knew the old woman thought of him as a son, and how could a son remain angry with his mother, especially when she hadn't really done anything to hurt him? It was his best interest she had at heart. Even if the concern were unwanted and misplaced. "There might come a time when I feel as you do about beginning again," he told her gently. "But not now and not with Clara."

"Why not Clara?"

Luke regretted he'd said that. Emily Hale's blood flowed through Clara Winslow's veins, and the old woman would fight anyone who attacked her family.

"Hold it, Miss Emily. I don't mean any disrespect to Clara. She's a fine young woman. I am just not in the market for a wife."

Emily smiled, her eyes twinkling. "What did she say when she came out today? You were angrier tonight than you were when Edwina Riley set her sights on you, or when Marsha Reeder came to town to visit her sister. That tells me I was right in sending her. It also tells me why you've been absent from this household since her arrival—"

"It tells you nothing." Luke cut her off. "I've been working, Miss Emily."

"You've worked before. You've worked as far away as Butte, yet you found time to get home each evening."

"I've been doing more lately. You know the winters around here. I'm trying to get the house done before the weather turns. I've got other jobs all over the valley. That's kept me away, not Clara and not your undisguised matchmaking games—for which I have no time. When I'm ready for a wife, I'll make the decision as to whom and when." Luke's voice was positive, but he felt his explanation was shallow. In the back of his mind he knew Clara Winslow *had* done something to him. She'd tested him. She had walked into his project and tested his convictions. And the old woman standing in front of him, as if she had the right to overrule his wishes, had sent her.

"Then explain it," Emily teased. "Explain why you've come in here like a raging bull, if Clara had no effect on you." Luke didn't get a chance to answer before she continued. "I can see it even if you can't. She dented that thick skin of yours.

And . . . you . . . don't . . . like . . . it." Emily peppered her words with jabs to his chest.

"You're wrong, Miss Emily," Luke told her. "Clara's effect on me is as minimal as the other prospective wives you've thrown in my path. All I ask is that you stay out of my life. I am capable of running it without you."

Emily Hale gave him a searching stare, then turned and resumed her regal position at the head of the table. Luke knew she hadn't listened to a word he had said. He'd lost this battle and it bothered him. He wasn't even sure he'd wanted to win. Peg *had* been dead a long time. There were nights he'd wake reaching for her, but more and more her face faded in his mind. He found himself going to her photograph to relearn her features. In the past he hadn't cared about Emily Hale's undisguised Cupid techniques. He didn't understand why this time was different.

When Clara had walked up the hill this afternoon, he'd been shocked at the jolt to his senses. And Emily Hale, no doubt, saw the change in him.

Clara breathed in the night air, pulling her knitted shawl closer around her slim shoulders. She *had* to get out of the boardinghouse. The atmosphere at the dinner table had been as thick as the steak Aunt Emily had put on her plate. She didn't know what had happened between her aunt and Luke, but she was sure they'd had words. Their actions were polite to the point of being stilted, but if the other roomers noticed it, they were too polite to say anything. Aunt Emily and Luke conversed warmly, but Clara could feel the underlying malevolence between the two. Whenever she glanced at either Aunt Emily or Luke, she'd felt as if she were being cross-examined. Aunt Emily watched her with a bit of humor, but Luke's glare was hostile.

Clara had tried to collar her aunt that afternoon for sending her on a husband-hunting trip, but the older woman had merely shrugged off her concerns, claiming she was overreacting. She knew she hadn't handled the situation in the best manner.

As soon as the men went off to smoke and the few women retired to their embroidery, she excused herself to get some fresh air. Outside, she walked toward Main Street, where a few other people were also enjoying the pleasant evening. They smiled and said hello; some stopped for a curious chat.

Waymon Valley had a lifestyle all its own. In the capital there was always activity—carriages racing down the cobblestone streets, people crowding the sidewalks as they made their way to the markets, children playing games as they scampered through the alleyways. On the farm something always needed fixing or mending, food needed preparing or canning. Here there was quiet, an easy atmosphere, a place where people could stroll down Main Street instead of hurrying to get out of the way.

"How do you do?" A man and a woman stopped her. They looked familiar. Clara recognized Mrs.

Carter. The couple was well dressed, probably prominent citizens of the valley.

"Fine," Clara smiled.

"We're the Carters, Marlene and Joe," the woman explained.

"You run the store in town." Clara remembered her as one of the many people she'd seen at the boardinghouse. Mrs. Carter looked pleased. Clara was glad she remembered, feeling it was better to be on the right side of this woman than the wrong. "I'm just out for some air," Clara told them.

Mr. Carter checked the darkening sky. "It's warm for evening. Enjoy it while you can." He nodded and they continued down the boardwalk.

"Seems like a nice lady. She'll make a fine teacher."

Clara overhead Mr. Carter as they walked away. They were out of range before she could hear what Mrs. Carter had to say.

Clara strolled. The dinner incident was beginning to recede as she passed the general store and headed toward the church at the end of town. Lamps burning inside cast a welcoming glow to anyone wishing to enter. She heard voices lift in song. Off key, she thought, then winced as someone missed a high note.

The church was the tallest building in town, freshly painted and identifiable by the large bell-less steeple. A wide stairway led to a central door that stood open to the night. Next to it and connected by a canopied walkway was a smaller structure that Clara had found out was the children's nursery.

She walked toward the church. During her six-day trip west, she had passed many towns. In some of them she'd seen buildings that could hardly be called churches, yet long lines of people gravitated toward them to praise the Lord. This building was different. It was framed and raised with painted slats of wood worthy of any establishment she'd seen in the nation's capital. As she reached the steps, she thought of Luke and the house he was building outside of town. She wondered if he had built this church.

The same voice she'd heard miss the high note a moment earlier missed another one as Clara entered the lamp-lighted structure. She stood at the back, listening to the choir of men and women sing without benefit of piano or organist. At the left of the raised platform, where a minister would preside on Sunday morning, was a piano. An organ sat on the right, but no one played either instrument.

"I think we need to rest awhile, Reverend." A dark man with a bushy mustache and tight collar spoke.

"I think you're right, Brother Wilson. Why don't we think about what we're trying to do and resume in a few minutes," the preacher agreed.

Clara heard the collective sigh of the choir members at the affirmation of the director. They quickly left their positions, gathering in small groups to talk, and conversation buzzed as friends and neighbors smiled and traded confidences, many of them glancing at her. The pastor spotted her and came forward. He was a square man, short and solid as if he both worked and ate in equal portions. His hair was cropped close on the sides, leaving the top completely bare.

"Welcome, sister," he greeted her, using a large white handkerchief to wipe the sweat from his brow. "I'm Reverend Reed."

Clara smiled. "Clara Winslow." She extended her hand before she remembered she shouldn't. The Reverend Reed took it. His fingers were as thick as sausages, but his smile was genuine. Clara liked him immediately.

"Have you come to join the choir? We can always use another voice."

"Oh, no." She shook her head as he let go of her hand. "I was out for a walk and heard the singing. I didn't mean to interrupt."

"No interruption." He glanced over his black-clad shoulder at the choir members behind him, then in a conspiratorial whisper said, "We're without our pianist and tonight's practice is more like penance."

Clara covered her mouth as she shared a smile with the minister. "I think I'll just sit here." She indicated the last pew, taking a step toward it. "This is a very beautiful church."

"It is. It's a surprise to most folks who aren't from these parts. They expect the standard prairie building."

Clara had seen some of those buildings, slatted wood or logs with gaps between them, flat roofed and windowless. Yet people gathered and worshiped without regard to comfort.

"We're very lucky to have Luke in our congregation," the minister continued, "although he isn't much for attending the service."

"Luke?" Clara's voice was a tone higher than usual. "Luke Evans?"

"His daddy built this town." The minister nodded. "Taught Luke just about everything he knows. Luke planned this building from the pulpit to the three crosses on the front lawn. Of course, everyone pitched in, but it was Luke that oversaw the details."

Clara pictured Luke as she'd seen him this afternoon, his shirt off, his body glistening with sweat, and a hammer in his hand. Her body warmed at the thought and she shook off the image.

Several people left the front of the church and walked up behind the minister. He turned as Clara's gaze was directed over his shoulder.

"Dora Davidson." A stout woman with trusting eyes and a sincere smile introduced herself. "I'm sorry I haven't been able to get to Emily's to meet you."

"Good evening," Clara said, knowing they all knew her name.

Reverend Reed introduced her to the rest of the choir members. She nodded at them, memorizing their names as they were pronounced. They were mostly miners or the wives of miners. All of them apparently had children and were glad she'd come to teach them.

"I had better get back to the practice." The minister broke into her thoughts. "Are you sure you won't join us?"

Clara shook her head. She didn't know many of

the people in the front and at the moment they frightened her a little. She'd tried to join in with Janey Willard's friends when she had first gone to teachers' college, but had been pushed aside and labeled the "scholarship girl."

"Stay as long as you like." Reverend Reed glanced at the choir members.

Clara sat down.

"I look forward to seeing you for service on Sunday." He smiled and, using the white handkerchief, went back to his task. The break had done nothing for their voices. Individually they might be all right, but collectively they were not inspiring. Clara did not stay long.

Her mind was clearer after her talk with Reverend Reed, and she thought of going back to the boardinghouse. Most of the women would be in the front parlor talking and snacking on the sweet cakes Aunt Emily had made that afternoon. The men would be playing cards in the back parlor. If Clara entered through the kitchen, she would not have to pass anyone on the way to her room.

Outside, she took notice of the three crosses. Painted white and lighted by the door, they cast giant shadows on the ground. Clara stood in their glow, reflecting that Luke had put them there. She wondered about him. The pastor had said he wasn't a church-going man, yet she recognized his hand on the crossed pieces of wood. They were simple, unadorned lines, like those of the house Luke had shown her. The same style had been evident in the skeleton of the house where Luke would live.

Would he be alone? she wondered, turning to-

ward the boardinghouse. He said he didn't want a
wife; but when she thought of the size of the structure, she couldn't see him wandering through all
those rooms with no one but himself. Clara suddenly smiled. She wondered what it would be like
to have a house of her own. She'd lived in her
parents' house until they had died. Then it was
Wade's house. The small house next to the school
belonged to the community. She wanted her own
space. She sighed, knowing that dream might not
come true.

A sudden peal of laughter snapped Clara's attention from the house and Luke. Turning toward
the sound, she faced the children's building.
Thoughts of Luke immediately crowded to the
forefront of her mind as the laughter broke out
again. She smiled at the innocent sound, her heart
filling with her love for children. It was why she
had decided to become a teacher. Thank God Wade
had agreed. Although agreed might be too kind a
word. What he'd agreed to was that his dinner still
had to be on the table when he came in from the
fields, the children had to be cared for, and none
of the farm animals could be spared to give her
passage into the District. Consequently, Clara had
prepared meals at night after doing her studies so
that the next day they'd only needed reheating.
Miss Picket, down the road, had agreed to watch
the girls and Clara had walked the ten miles into
D.C. each morning and again home each night.
Wade hadn't liked the stubborn streak in her, but
he hadn't fought her determination either.

She'd repaid him by leaving. A pang of guilt

asserted itself, but Clara squelched it. She'd done the right thing. This was her life. The laughter rang out again, and Clara went toward the sound, a smile in position as she entered the open doorway.

Luke sat in the middle of the large room, a circle of children gazing up at him. He lifted one arm, pushing up the sleeve of his suit coat to reveal the ruffled cuff of his starched white shirt. With practiced ease, he did the same with the other arm. Then he smiled at a little girl with long black braids while he pulled a shiny new penny from behind a lanky boy's ear and presented it to the girl. The crowd laughed and clapped.

Clara held her breath. She'd never seen a magician before, and Luke had completely fooled her with his production of the coin. How had he done that?

"Do another one, Mr. Luke," a child with two french braids coming untangled asked. The child reminded her of Lisa Rose, back in Virginia, whose braids never stayed unless she banded the ends with twine.

At that moment Luke saw Clara. She leaned against the doorjamb, her folded arms pulling the fabric of her dress tight across her breasts, a wide smile highlighting her face and emphasizing her high cheekbones. Luke's heart pounded. How could she do that to him by simply entering a room?

"Mr. Luke! Mr. Luke!" Alice pulled at his sleeve. "Make some more magic." Luke turned his attention to the five-year-old. Alice smiled, showing the vacant space where her new front tooth would grow.

Luke lifted Alice on his knee and turned his gaze to Clara. "Children, have you met your new teacher?"

A chorus of "no's" echoed off the bare walls of the small room.

"Well," Luke stood, placing Alice on the floor and taking her hand. He also took Jimmie's and led the small crowd to Clara.

She straightened as they approached, her smile never leaving her face, her attention riveted on the children.

"Miss Clara." Luke's gaze swept over his entourage. With the exception of one girl of about sixteen, the tallest child stood only waist-high to the man. "I'd like to introduce some of your pupils. Jimmie Jones . . ."

"Here, ma'am," the smiling youngster piped up, his hand raised. The group laughed. Luke goodnaturedly grabbed Jimmie's face and pushed him to the back. The child reveled in the attentiongetting tactic.

"Joanne Wilson . . . Martha Ames . . . Wendell and Mike Carver, and Alice Mildred Davidson." Each child raised a hand as Luke pronounced their names in roll-call fashion, except Alice. She stood, shyly peeping out from behind Luke, her small hand curved around his leg.

"Hello, Alice, Martha, Jimmie, Wendell and Mike and Joanne."

Luke was impressed by her memory; the chil-

dren's mouths gaped open as she looked at each
and repeated the correct name.

"Are you all ready for school to begin?" Clara
asked.

Another chorus of "no's" sang out on a better
note than the choir had maintained.

Clara dropped to eye level with the small congregation. She addressed Alice. "You don't like
school?" she asked in a conspiratorial whisper.

The child stepped further behind Luke, obscur-
ing half her face, and gripped his leg tighter.

She shook her head slowly, causing the only visible braid to slap back and forth.

"Have you ever been to school?"

Again the child, whose eyes were large and
bright, shook her head.

Clara smiled. "Well, we'll have to make sure we
have plenty of games for you to play."

"Games?" Wendell questioned. "We never
played games before."

"I'll tell you a secret, Wendell," she said in a
hushed whisper. The children moved a step closer,
and even Alice's whole face was visible. "You're
going to be my first class, and I have lots of sur-
prises planned for you."

"Yeah—" the chorus screamed.

"Can you do magic, too?" Joanne ventured,
pulling on her loosened hair, when the noise
abated.

"I'm afraid not." Clara glanced up at Luke to
find him staring at her.

Luke averted his gaze, surprised by her—and by
himself. He liked the way she talked to the chil-

dren and got them to trust her. He was sure they would be glad to enter her classroom on the first day of school.

"Mr. Luke does a lot of magic." Mike seemed proud of the announcement.

Clara stood up.

"Does he?" She stared at Luke.

"Mr. Luke, please do another trick," Wendell pleaded.

"Just one more," he agreed with the least amount of persuading.

The children stood back, taking positions that would give them a good view. Again Luke pushed his sleeves up, showing he had nothing to hide. He held out his empty hands, palms up and palms down. Then he reached into Mike's trouser-pocket and pulled out a red rose. Clara couldn't prevent the exhale of air from escaping. With a gallant bow, Luke presented her with the flower. She took it and smiled.

"Another one, I want a flower, too," Joanne called, but at that moment the choir practice ended and the parents came in to claim their children.

Clara wished the children good night before they left. She was still smiling after everyone had gone.

"I think you've won over the kids. Must be that charm you exude so well."

Clara ignored the hint of an insult in his comment. She held the rose higher and smelled its erotic fragrance. She felt like crying, but didn't want Luke to know it. She wondered what Wade William and Stephen were doing now. Did they miss her? Leaving Wade was one thing. The children were another story.

"Do you often watch the children during choir practice?" Clara asked, pushing her thoughts away from dangerous ground. She didn't want to be so homesick she'd return to Wade.

"No, that's Aunt Lucy's job, but she didn't feel well tonight. Martha Ames, the tall girl—" Luke raised his hand about five feet off the floor to demonstrate "—she was filling in."

Clara had met Aunt Lucy. She was a spry woman of ninety who bragged of being the second family to settle in the valley. Everyone called her Aunt Lucy and she had a genuine love for children.

"Another woman who didn't feel good today. I wonder if something is going around?" Clara turned toward the door, leaving Luke to get the real meaning of her words. Luke extinguished the lamps and followed her.

Together, they turned toward the boardinghouse. "How did you learn the magic tricks?" Clara asked when they reached the main road. "The children loved them." Clara lifted her rose and smelled its fragrance, hiding the fact that she too enjoyed the illusion.

"My mother taught me."

His voice sounded tight. Clara glanced at him. Had she stepped on hallowed ground again?

"My brothers and I left Illinois with only our mother and a wagon train," Luke continued, his gaze fixed straight ahead. "It was a long, boring trip. To entertain us, my mother practiced magic tricks using a book her father had brought home. As she learned, I learned."

"Where are your brothers now? Do they live in the valley, too?" Clara had been in Waymon Valley long enough to know that nobody who lived there called it anything else. Even the Butte residents referred to it as *the valley*.

"We lost them all."

"I'm sorry," she whispered. She remembered losing her parents. The pain had dulled over time, but she still felt their loss.

"Matthew and Mark died of cholera soon after we left St. Louis. John was crushed under a wagon wheel and lost his legs three days before we arrived here. He lingered in pain and fever for nine days before he died."

Clara swallowed the tears gathering in her throat. Matthew, Mark, Luke, and John. Clara listed their names, a method she used to remember people. His family had used the Bible to name children. It was a common practice. Clara had been named after her great-grandmother, but her mother's name was Ruth and her father's, Joshua. Both had come from the Old Testament.

Clara touched Luke's arm. "I understand what it means to lose someone you love. My parents died when I was fifteen, and my sister—" She stopped.

"It's all right." Luke covered her hand with his. "You don't have to finish."

Clara nodded, allowing him to misunderstand her meaning. She hadn't lost a sister, but a sister-in-law.

They continued walking more by mutual agreement than conscious decision.

Clara's gloved hand merely rested in the crook of his arm. She wasn't pulling him or clinging to him, yet Luke felt every single impression of her delicate fingers. Why had he mentioned his brothers? Why had he told her about them? She hadn't asked, yet somehow it felt natural to talk to her. It had been years since he had allowed himself to remember the overland trek from Illinois and the cost that decision had brought to his small family. Whereas most of the neighbors he remembered, from twenty-plus years ago, had had large families, his had been relatively small. Only the four boys and a stillborn sister he'd never seen. She'd been buried almost immediately after delivery.

It had probably been the death of Mary—his mother had insisted the baby have a name to go to heaven with so she could be found when eventually they all met for the final reward—that had made Melinda Evans pack her children, their eight horses, and three cows and set out on a two-thousand-mile journey to meet their father.

Clara reminded him a little of his mother: delicate, soft-spoken, and unable to resist a child. He'd seen it in Clara's face as she'd watched the children, especially shy little Alice. In a matter of moments, she'd drawn the child out and had her talking. It had taken him weeks just to get her to move from her position by the door, where she could run to her mother at the first sign of a problem.

As they stepped off the boardwalk, Luke helped her down. He could feel the warmth of her hand through his jacket. He knew gossip would flow like quicksilver if anyone saw them as intimately attached as this, but he did nothing to change the situation. He knew he should, especially after his discussion with Miss Emily. But he didn't want to push Clara away. He wanted to move his arm and encircle her with it, pull her body into contact with his and find out if the excitement she sent through him would explode.

Stealing a glance at her, he watched the single curl she allowed loose from the tight pull of her hair. It bounced in the moonlight, pulling up and down like a spring. He tightened his grip, locking his elbow against his side to keep from reaching up and playing with that curl.

He knew now why he'd stayed away from Miss Emily's and why he'd argued with her over Clara. His normal reaction to the women Miss Emily sent was silence. But Clara had changed that. And it scared him. He didn't want her holding his arm, yet he didn't want her to let go either. He didn't want her intruding into his orderly life, yet she made him feel as if the world were a new place. In a way, she was like the children she'd talked to tonight; for her, everything was new and each discovery was wonderful.

She *was* an enigma. One minute she made him angry and the next he wanted to see that smile again—the one which lit up her brown eyes, raised her high cheekbones . . . and melted his insides.

Maybe he'd check on her furniture tomorrow. If it arrived sooner than expected, she could move to her own house and leave the room next to his unoccupied. If not, it was going to be a long summer.

"Did you enjoy your visit with the good Reverend Reed?" Luke asked, needing a distraction. He'd seen her enter the church before he'd gone in to the children and found them alone with only Martha Ames to watch them. "Thinking of joining the choir?"

"No, I don't sing much." Luke felt her suppress a laugh. He knew she'd heard Dora Davidson using her voice to reach for the heavens and missing the clouds. No wonder Alice was such a quiet child; her mother more than made up for the child's shyness with her exuberance.

Luke looked at Clara. Her face went from a quiet smile to a wide grin. Luke's heart stopped, then pounded in his ears. They were no longer walking, but were staring into each other's eyes. He couldn't drag his gaze away; and what surprised him was, he didn't want to. He *wanted* to devour her with his gaze and he wanted her mouth fused to his.

Clara's smile faded, but her eyes didn't leave his. In them was desire, passion. He recognized the emotions, knowing his own eyes reflected the same yearnings. He leaned toward her, and she raised her chin in anticipation. He was going to kiss her; he had to. And she wanted him. . . . She was leaning toward him. The night took on a tangible dimension, wrapping them in a sheath of fabric that pulled them closer together.

Suddenly, Luke straightened, clearing his throat and remembering where they were. He took a deep breath and began walking again. Clara missed her footing, and he swung around and caught her. His hands held her waist. Her arms clutched his shoulders and her eyes locked with his, dark pools of wonder staring at him. For the space of a heartbeat he held her, her body warm against him, her heart pounding against his own.

"Clara," Luke whispered, "I'd like nothing better than to kiss you right here and now. But we're standing in the middle of Main Street."

For a second his words failed to register. "Oh," she said, stepping back. "Oh!" She adjusted her dress, dusting herself off as if she'd fallen in the road. Her gaze darted up and down the street as if the eyes of the town were trained on them.

Luke watched her react. He wasn't sure he was glad or sorry they were in full view of the town. He wanted Miss Clara Winslow and he hated himself for it. Miss Emily had been right. Clara Winslow had an effect on him. But he'd fight her. He had no need for a wife—ever again.

Thank God they were alone, Clara prayed. She hadn't thought much about losing her job, but being discovered kissing a man on the main street could be grounds for dismissal and she had yet to hold her first class. What had happened to her? She had never acted like this before. Luke could have kissed her. She'd actually invited him to kiss her . . . and on a public road! She hadn't felt any revulsion about Luke. When Ian Watson had tried to kiss her in the barn, she'd fought with all her strength. But in Luke's arms, she had no strength. Her bones were the consistency of churned butter and her body wanted him against her.

"Why are you here, Clara?" Luke broke into her thoughts as he fell into step beside her. "Why did you leave the civilized East to come fifteen hundred miles to teach people you don't know?"

"I answered the newspaper advertisement, and the committee sent me passage." She paused a moment. "I also needed a job."

"You say that as if you were running away from something."

Clara tensed. She tried to pull her hand free, but Luke kept it pinned to his side. She was glad it was too dark for him to see her expression. "If you think I've committed some crime and the law is after me, Mr. Evans, your mind can rest in that respect. I have had no encounters with the law, and no lawman is looking for me."

She chose her words carefully to keep Luke from the truth. He eyed her levelly, but didn't comment. Clara knew she'd over-explained. In her quest to avoid suspicion, she'd only made herself suspicious. There *was* no lawman looking for her, but there was Wade. She thought of Wade with his unassuming ways, his gentleness for a man of his height and bulk. A pang of guilt attacked her for what she'd done. She had run away from him. She wondered how he was coping with the farm and

the children. Miss Picket would give him a hand.
Hadn't she helped her during her years of schooling? It would be no hardship for her to continue.
Still she thought of him, wondering what he was
doing now. She was sure he was too busy to look
for her. It was precisely the reason she'd chosen
to leave months ahead of her appointment.

They had reached the gate to Hale's Boardinghouse, and Clara turned to Luke.

"What are *you* running away from, Luke?"

"What makes you think I have anything to run
from?"

Clara eyed him carefully. "Everything about
you. The way you stand back when people are near
you." Clara had been an observer all her life.
While in school she'd had plenty of time to be on
the outside looking at the way people talked and
reacted with each other. Luke was alone even in
a crowd. "You told me about your family, your
brothers' dying, the pain of losing them. Does it
keep you from ever wanting that to happen
again?"

Luke stared at her. She didn't know how close
to the truth she'd come. Peg had been the one person who had pierced through his skin, and he'd
married her only to have her and his child die
within days of each other. Losing them had been
more than he could stand. If it hadn't been for
Miss Emily and Ellen Turnbull, he probably would
have died. He didn't like to think about that time
in his life. It still made him feel as if he should
have done something. They should never have had
a child. Peg had known it was dangerous, but she

hadn't told him—not until it had been too late to do anything about it.

"Like you, Clara," he replied finally, "I'm not running away from anything." He was trying to resolve losing so many people he'd loved, but he wasn't leaving Waymon Valley. He'd stay here and, eventually, like Miss Emily, he'd be able to love again. Looking at Clara, he was sorry the timing was wrong. She was beautiful, delicate, and everything he could want in a wife, but he wasn't in the market.

Clara entered the quiet house. The gaslights had been turned down, bathing the pathway to the stairs and beyond in a dim light. It was warmer inside. Clara heard the card party in full swing in the parlor and she knew Aunt Emily had an after-dinner snack on the dining room table. It usually consisted of a confection with a sugary sweet taste and a smell that wafted through the house along with a carafe of coffee or strong tea. Clara would have liked some tea. She thought it might calm her jangling nerves, for she still shuddered at her actions in Luke's arms.

Luke was beside her. If she went into the dining room, she was certain he would follow and she didn't know how much more of his company she could endure without embarrassing herself.

Turning to Luke, she offered him her best smile. "Thank you, Luke, for escorting me back," she said. She should have offered her hand, but she knew his touch would jolt her again and she wasn't ready to handle that yet. "Good night," she muttered.

"Good night, Clara."

Her name sounded like a caress on his lips, and she couldn't keep her head from coming up. He smiled at her. Clara forced her gaze to the floor, lifting her heavy skirt and starting up the stairs. Luke followed her. On the landing was a large cut-glass window that, during sunset, spread prisms of colored light across the double stairways that led east-west to the sleeping rooms. Clara threw Luke an inquiring glance as she faced the eastern stair-case and found Luke at her back.

"May I inquire, Mr. Evans," she paused, "just where you are going?" Her faced flamed. Only the dim lighting prevented Luke from seeing the expression change on her flawlessly dark complexion.

"To my room, Miss Winslow." He answered her in the same formal language she'd used. "I live here, too."

Clara's heart pounded in her ears. "You-you live he-here?" she stuttered.

Luke nodded. "I don't always use my room, but I reserve it just the same."

Clara hadn't known where Luke lived. She hadn't seen him since she'd arrived. Frequently, there were extra dinner guests. Aunt Emily always prepared enough food to feed the 10th Cavalry, just in case they showed up at supper time. She considered it ill-mannered if anyone in residence at the time did not have enough to eat. So Luke's presence at the dinner table was not surprising, but his declaration regarding a room and his presence at her back was disconcerting.

There were only four rooms on this side of the house. Clara knew two of them had storage chests in them, because her own boxes occupied space there. The room she'd considered unoccupied was next to her own.

A gasp feathered its way to her throat, but she swallowed it and turned to proceed up the steep set of stairs. The heat seemed more and more stifling with each step. By the time she'd climbed the fifteen stairs, her dress was as sticky as warm taffy.

Clara walked down the hallway, which appeared as long as a church aisle. At her door, she turned. Luke stood at his own door, watching her. They didn't speak, but the air between them was like a bond.

"Good night, Miss Clara," he said. Then he opened his door and went inside.

Clara let go of her breath and put a hand to her face. It was hot. She slipped into her room and immediately found herself staring at the common wall as if Luke could see through it. Her bed rested against that wall.

There was something wrong with her. In all her years, no man had upset her as Luke did. He was taller than Wade and just as muscular. When she'd tripped and he'd held her, she'd felt safe in his arms. She wondered what it would have been like if he had kissed her. Bringing her hand to her lips, she rubbed them slightly.

Luke lay in the darkness. His bed was made of heavy brass with a high headboard. He knew

Clara's was carved wood with a headboard that reached to the ceiling. He closed his eyes, listening, imagining her in that big bed alone. No sound came from her room. He'd occupied this room for three years. In that time, many men had slept next door and he'd heard them dropping boots, banging chifforobe doors, and falling onto the bed with its rusty springs. Clara, he presumed, must be standing still. He wondered what she was thinking. Were her thoughts on him as his were on her? Her near fall on Main Street had taken everything he had to keep him from crushing her soft body into his.

He'd known Emily Hale would give her the room next to his the moment he'd heard she was in town. Emily made no pretense of her matchmaking, and to date Luke had been only slightly put out. Clara was different. She was beautiful and innocent and behind those huge brown eyes was a fear that he didn't quite understand.

There had also been a fear in Peg's eyes when he had first kissed her, but it had quickly died. He knew the moment they met at the church social while she was visiting her cousin that she would be his life-mate. Luke rolled over with a groan. The pain of losing his wife and child and the plans they had made that would never see fruit was too much to risk. He'd been an idealist. He was sure their love was the forever kind, sure they'd have children and grow old together. Her death shattered his ideals. Luke knew how tenuous life could be, how much pouring his emotions into a relationship could hurt him. He knew there were no guarantees, that life dealt you a hand, but he wouldn't play

this one. He'd keep his heart intact. He'd never
marry again. He'd never go through that pain
again. Not for Miss Emily and not for Clara.

Three

The music reached Clara before she descended
the second staircase. The smell of bacon, eggs, and
warm syrup filtered through the air, reminding her
of her hunger. Ignoring her stomach, Clara went
toward the sound of Brahms. It was played quietly,
but beautifully, as if the player didn't want to disturb the rest of the household.

When she opened the door, she found Martha
Ames at the piano. Her fingers moved across the
ivory keyboard with the same ease with which she
breathed. Clara stood and listened as the girl ef-
fortlessly moved from one song to another without
benefit of sheet music. Her fingers knew the
sound, and it came through in glorious praise.

Martha sat erect, her elbows close to her body
and her head bobbing with each inflection of the
music. This morning she had her hair down. It
reached her waist like a jet-black waterfall. When
she had finished, Martha pulled the cover over the
keys and stood up.

"Martha, that was beautiful," Clara said when
the young girl faced her. "You have a real talent
for music." Clara remembered her own piano train-

ing before her parents died, but she hadn't touched the instrument since she had gone to live with Wade.

Martha smiled and dropped her head in embarrassment. "I like the piano," she said.

Martha was about fifteen. Her body was on the brink of developing into womanhood, and Clara envied her. She had her whole life ahead of her to decide what she wanted to do and whom she wanted to marry.

"Have you had breakfast yet?" Clara asked.

"I was about to go in."

"Why don't we eat together?" Clara invited.

The two women were the last to enter the dining room. Most of the miners had eaten and gone hours ago. Clara didn't know whether Luke was up yet. After tossing and turning for most of the night, she'd finally dozed off as the sun had begun to tinge the horizon. If Luke had wakened and left, she'd never heard him. She was usually a light sleeper; but since her night hadn't been the best, anything could have happened.

Clara made a cup of coffee and dug into the flapjacks Emily placed in front of her.

"What have you got planned for today?" Emily asked as she took the seat at the head of the table and lifted her coffee cup.

"I thought I'd go to the schoolhouse and check on the supplies. If there are things I need, I'll have to order them now if they are to arrive before the first bell." Clara needed to have something to do in case Emily asked her to go to the building site again. She didn't want to see Luke unless she had to.

Emily nodded. "The committee was pretty thorough in setting up the school, but there isn't any harm in your taking inventory." Emily paused, breaking off a piece of sweet bread and popping it in her mouth. "What about you, Martha? How are you going to spend your day?"

"Do you need my help, Miss Emily?" Martha kept her eyes averted. Emily reached over and lifted her chin.

"No, honey. The girls in the kitchen have everything under control. And the rest of the staff have their duties. You're free to do whatever you like."

Clara didn't understand the underlying sympathy in Emily's voice.

"I would like to go for a ride. Do you think I could use one of the horses?"

"Anyone you like." Emily smiled. Clara saw her features soften as she waited for the girl's response.

Martha's face lit up. "I like Starfire."

"You be sure to let Zeke and Aaron know where you're going. We don't want to have to send out any search parties."

"I will," Martha promised.

"Do you ride a lot, Martha?" Clara asked. "It's been a long time since I was on a horse."

"I usually go out before breakfast, but today I helped out in the kitchen."

"Maybe one day we can ride together."

"I'd like that." Martha finished her meal and left to change for her ride.

"She's a very nice young lady," Clara commented when Martha's eager step had hurried around the corner and could be heard thumping up the stairs.

"Yes," Emily agreed. Clara saw the mist in the old woman's eyes when she looked at the place Martha had vacated.

"Why does she drop her eyes and stare at the floor?"

"She doesn't believe anyone wants her."

"Why?"

"Martha's mother died in an accident only a year after she was born. Her dad was the only parent she has ever known. They lived in a small cabin near the mining company. Last year he died when the shaft he was working caved in." Clara noticed the catch in her aunt's voice, but said nothing about it.

"She's Indian, isn't she?" Clara had never seen an Indian. She'd expected them to have red skin and straight black hair. Martha had the hair, but her coloring was like the walnut shells Clara used at Christmas time to make decorations for the tree.

"Half-Indian." Emily got up and refreshed her coffee. Her hands shook as she lifted the silver pot. "Would you like another cup?" she offered. Clara passed her cup and saucer to her aunt. "Martha's mother came from the reservation. She brought blankets they weaved and sold them in town. Garret Ames saw her one day, and they were married within a month. I never saw two people more in love than those two."

Emily had resumed her seat. She was staring off

into space as if she'd lost track of time. As if she were remembering the past and memories that were somehow bittersweet. Clara wanted to go to her.

"The two of them built that little cabin they lived in, and then the accident left Garret alone with Martha. When he died, she came here." Her face looked younger when she mentioned Garret Ames. Clara realized Garret must have meant something special to her Aunt Emily.

"Doesn't she have other family?" Clara felt an affinity with the young girl. Their lives paralleled in many ways. They had both lost their parents before adolescence and had had to live with strangers. Clara understood Martha better now.

"None that would take her." Emily snorted her disdain. "She has uncles and aunts at the reservation. Few of them will even acknowledge her. There is one she goes to see when she rides. He teaches her some of the Indian ways. It's good for her to know her history."

"When she had nowhere else to go, you took her in," Clara stated. Hadn't her own residence at Hale's Boardinghouse happened in nearly the same manner?

"She couldn't stay at the mine by herself, so I offered her a room here."

Emily was lost in thought. Clara wondered how long Emily had been in love with Garret Ames and whether his child was the one Emily had always wanted but never had?

"Martha left almost everything behind," Emily continued. "Except that old piano. Sometimes she spends hours playing it. The child has talent. When

Garret was alive, he'd listen to her in the evenings and praise her playing. He loved that child better than any man I ever saw except—"

"Good morning, Miss Emily . . . Miss Clara." Luke's voice startled Clara. She dropped her cup in the saucer, its contents sloshing over the edge and spilling onto the lace tablecloth.

"Good morning," Clara whispered, using her napkins to mop up the spill.

"I thought you were long gone, Luke." Emily rose as Clara slipped her hands into her lap, hoping to prevent her aunt from seeing that they had begun to shake when Luke had entered. "I'll have some food heated for you."

"Don't bother. I have to go into Butte this morning. I'll get something to eat there."

"Are you sure? It's no trouble."

Luke got a cup of coffee and sat across from Clara.

"Is there anything you need me to pick up?" he asked Emily.

"I have an order at the Emporium. If you'd bring it back, it would save Zeke a trip. And there's mail at the post office."

"Consider it done."

Luke looked well-rested, Clara thought. He must have spent a better night than she had. Secretly she hated him for his ability to turn her world upside-down and then go calmly to sleep as if nothing had happened.

"Clara," Emily said from behind her. "You haven't been into Butte since you arrived. Why don't you ride in with Luke? You could do some shopping, see the town. I'm sure Luke wouldn't mind the company."

Clara stared at Luke. She saw his body stiffen at Emily's suggestion.

"I have plans and I'm sure Luke doesn't need me along."

"Nonsense." Emily discounted her refusal. "The school can wait another day."

"Luke—" Clara appealed to him for help.

"I'd be honored to escort you, Miss Clara."

In minutes, Clara had changed from her day dress into a traveling suit of bright green linen and was seated next to Luke in an open buckboard. The single-horse-drawn wagon bumped and jostled her along the rough road as she tried to maintain her distance from the man next to her.

The mountains loomed ahead of them. In most directions Clara looked, she saw the Rockies. Landscape was so different here. She enjoyed the openness, even the vastness of the distances. She'd never thought she'd be able to see anything more than the fields of the farm in front of the house she'd occupied with Wade. Had she never gone to the Teachers College of the District of Columbia, she'd never have met Janey Willard or her snobby friends.

She wouldn't have known how unsatisfying her future looked without hearing the young girls speak of marriage and futures full of party dresses, young soldiers, and children of their own. Clara had tried—unsuccessfully—to imagine herself in a brightly colored brocade gown, dancing at one of the Washington balls. She had found nothing that

Janey had described within herself, and her future had looked dark and empty. As for going to a ball, Wade wouldn't have allowed it. She had had no party dresses and there had been no money to buy frivolous things. Wade had said that enough times. Even if she had wanted to make the dress herself, as she did all her clothes, he wouldn't have approved purchasing the fabric.

That had brought her here to this open country where people could live and be free of the burden she'd carried since she was fifteen years old.

"You're mighty quiet, Clara." Luke broke into her thoughts. "If my company was unwanted you could have said so when Miss Emily asked."

"It isn't your company. I was thinking of something else."

"Your past?"

"Why do you say that?" Clara asked, her stomach tensing as she attempted to keep the suspicion out of her voice.

"No reason. It's normal for people new to the area to think about things that happened before they came here."

Clara let her breath out on a slow sigh. "I *was* thinking of my life back East," she confessed.

"What did you do there?"

"I was a student. I went to college and studied."

"Weren't you kind of old to be in school?"

Clara didn't hear any censure in Luke's voice. She had not been older than the other students, but she hadn't been like them. When she should have been acting like a schoolgirl, she had been busy running a house and taking care of Wade's

children. It had been years before she'd approached
him about enrolling in college.

"Not especially. Most of the girls were close to
my age," she told him. Annie Pearl, her best friend,
had been a year older. But she'd had to drop out
a year to care for her father.

Clara had been bright enough and poor enough
to get the school to allow her to attend without pay-
ment of the standard fees. For that she had been
ridiculed by the other students when they'd found
out. Few of them had included her as a friend.

"Out here schools are different. Back East . . ."
Clara couldn't believe she'd actually said that. Was
she already losing her roots? "Back East, we have
secondary schools. They go to twelfth grade."

"Twelve years in school seems like a mighty
long time. Most women are married and have children by then. Didn't you want that?"

Wanting a future was what had led her here. She
did want to be a wife with children of her own,
but that wasn't in the cards for her. She'd have to
settle for teaching.

Clara's face grew warm. "I wanted to attend
school. I wanted to learn." The ten-mile-walk into
town and back to the farm each day had been
proof of her perseverance.

"It must have been hard," Luke stated, "seeing
all your friends marry and leave."

Clara couldn't help looking at Luke. How did
he know that? Several of the girls had married the
day after graduation. She'd been happy for them
and envious of them and their dreams of what the
future offered.

"When I graduated, I applied for the position here, and the committee accepted me."

"This will be the first time you've ever stood in front of a class."

"Yes," Clara said. "I understand children can be cruel to each other and that they will test my abilities as a teacher, but I plan to win that contest."

"Good for you." Luke smiled, patting the hand she had laid in her lap.

His touch, although brief, made her stomach flip-flop. She'd never had this feeling before. Was this what Janey had meant when she'd talked about the boys she'd danced with or met at coming-out parties? Clara wished she'd attended those parties. She wished she'd had more experience with men.

"What are the winters like here?" Clara asked, steering the conversation away from anything personal.

"They come early and stay late compared to the ones in the East."

"Have you been to the East, Luke?"

"For a short time. I went to school in Philadelphia."

"You did?" she asked, surprised that he'd been farther East than the continental divide.

"It wasn't a real school. I was more of an apprentice to an architect. I attended classes in drafting and mathematics and learned the proper methods of design and building. Most of what they taught me had to do with the classical styles of ancient Rome and Greece. My father taught me the practical methods we use here in the valley."

Clara could compare the two. She had walked

past the monstrous office buildings in the District of Columbia. In the valley, their gleaming marble facades would look as out of place as the mountains would as a backdrop to the White House or the Capitol Building.

Clara leaned over to see the ground below them. It was dusty and without cobblestones. Ruts, from years of passage, had cut deep grooves into the hard ground.

"Don't do that!" Luke grabbed her arm and pulled her back onto the seat. "You could lose your balance and fall over the edge." His voice softened a bit, but the hand that gripped her arm was strong enough to break it.

The expression on his face was hard. "I'm sorry," Clara said, adjusting her position. Luke dropped her arm, needing both hands to drive the horse.

They were coming into Butte. The town was busier than the valley. The dirt streets were gone, replaced by paved roads. Trolley tracks ran down the center of the main boulevard, and many more buildings made up the frontier town. Everywhere, people seemed to be selling things: dresses, boots, books, picks, and shovels. The sidewalks in front of the buildings were crowded with people— mostly men. Clara compared the dresses of the few women she saw to her own. Every variety from the richest fabrics to meager muslin was represented. Men wore everything from wranglers to silk top hats and finely tailored suits. Every type of carriage rolled along the boulevard, and noise assaulted her from all sides. Dogs barked; people hawked their wares; children played in and out of the shop doors.

Luke stopped the wagon in front of the post office. "Stay put," he ordered as she prepared to get down. He came around and held his hands up to her. Grasping her waist, he set her lightly onto the ground. At eye level he said, "I was driving the wagon when John fell over the side."

Clara looked into his eyes, remembering the story he'd told about his brother. She wanted to reach up and comfort him, but she knew better. "I understand," she said, her voice as low as his. He was still holding her waist, and his hands trembled slightly. Clara felt the heat around them.

"I'm just more careful now."

"It's all right. I didn't mean to lean so far over the side."

Luke hesitated, then stepped back, releasing her. The spell surrounding them snapped with his movement.

"I have to take care of some business. Suppose I meet you back here at noon and we'll have lunch?"

Clara looked up and down the street, but saw no clock. "Does the church bell ring on the hour?" she asked.

Luke looked confused. He shook his head. Then, as comprehension dawned, Luke took his pocket watch out and opened it to check the time. He snapped it closed and pressed it into her hand.

"I'll see you at noon." With the back of his hand, he brushed her cheek and turned toward the general store.

Clara stood looking after him, her hand covering the spot where he'd touched her. Why was it every time she was with him he brought out feelings she didn't know she had?

Clara meandered through the shopping district. She lifted silk fabric that flowed across her hands like a spring breeze. She found books by Longfellow and Mark Twain. Any miner could be outfitted with everything from wool underdrawers to specialized equipment for panning gold, although copper was the main mining industry in Butte. Some of the boardinghouse residents worked in the many mines that surrounded the city.

It took Clara an hour to make the complete tour of the shopping center. She had nothing else to do before meeting Luke and, according to his watch, she still had another hour before the appointed time. Passing a shop, she paused to stare at a dummy dressed in a starched white blouse with leg-of-mutton sleeves and a black skirt with a waist the size of a small melon. The mannequin wore a large hat with frills of bows, flowers, and dyed feathers. Clara recognized the Gibson Girl trademark.

Turning away, she noticed Starfire tethered to the hitching post in front of the shop. Whirling completely around, she looked for Martha. She must have decided to come into town when Aunt Emily said it was all right for her to go for a ride. Quickly checking the shop, she was disappointed the young girl was nowhere to be seen. Clara wished she could find her so she would have someone to talk to until she met Luke.

The trolley passed Clara. She'd never been on a trolley car, and the ride seemed like fun. She would like to do it one day—maybe after she had begun teaching and received her salary, she could get a ride into town and try the trolley car.

Across from the post office was the Emporium Aunt Emily had mentioned. Clara ventured toward it, drawn by a beautiful bonnet in the window. It was made of yellow felt and had feathers circling the crown and a large purple plume angled toward the back. Clara couldn't possibly afford it, but it was the most beautiful thing she'd ever seen.

Continuing up and down the streets, Clara retraced her steps, looking into the same shop windows until it was time for her to meet Luke. She found her way back to the wagon and waited. Ten minutes later, he came out of the Emporium and crossed the street.

He glanced into the back of the wagon. "No packages?" His eyebrows raised.

"I didn't see anything I liked."

Luke gave her a long look, then asked, "Are you ready for lunch?"

Clara nodded, glad he didn't pursue the matter. He tossed a leather bag with U.S. Mail burned into its side into the open wagon.

"I checked the bag." Luke indicated the mail. "I thought you might be looking for a letter from home by now. Sorry."

"It's all right. There's so much to be done back home, people don't have much time for writing."

She hoped she kept the nervousness out of her voice.

Why hadn't Clara thought about mail? Had Aunt Emily noticed she hadn't received a single letter since she'd arrived? Naturally a person would *want* to hear from friends they'd left behind, but no one knew where she'd gone. She'd left Wade a note, but he couldn't read. Although it had seemed useless, she hadn't been able to just walk away without saying anything.

They walked in silence to a small restaurant on the main boulevard. Luke turned toward the door, but Clara hesitated instinctively, her eyes silently questioning his choice of eating establishments. Luke's hand reached around her, pressing against the small of her back, and guided her through the door.

"Luke!" a voice shouted. Clara tensed immediately, knowing they were about to be publicly humiliated.

A red-haired waitress in a starched black-and-white uniform made her way toward them. "It's been a long time since you've been in here." She hugged Luke to Clara's obvious surprise, and he returned the brief embrace. "And with a lady." She turned to Clara, her bright eyes sizing her up and approving of the choice. "News of this will be back in the valley before you finish lunch," she tossed at Luke.

He frowned. "Miss Clara Winslow, meet Miss Ellen Turnbull. She owns the place."

"How do you do?" Ellen said with a smile that never left her face.

"Fine, thank you." Clara returned her exuberant smile.

"You two just follow me, and I'll get you a table."

She sashayed across the room. Clara glanced at Luke before she followed the woman. The room, done in shades of red, was crowded. Clara heard Swedish dialects and the guttural sounds of Norwegian miners as she passed. Just as the street displayed a wide variety of affluent styles, the restaurant catered to a diverse population. Bearded Germans with dark hair and skin gave way to the redheaded Scotsmen and the sunshine gold so characteristic of the Scandinavians.

Ellen led them to a table near the window. Clara relaxed, observing the mix of people calmly conversing with each other as could be done nowhere in the East. Martha Ames waved from across the room. She sat with a man who must have been the uncle Aunt Emily had mentioned. His hair was long and loose, and he wore a necklace of beads and feathers.

Montana had only been a state for ten years. Maybe the ground that had to be clawed at to get it to give up its ore and the devastating harshness of the winters had forced people to give up their differences and work together, accounting for the harmony she felt in this room. Clara saw this small area as a whole world. Maybe it *was* possible to live and work together. She looked from Luke to Ellen, but neither of them seemed to realize the revolution she was seeing unfold before her.

Ellen handed them a menu and pulled her pencil

out of her order book. "What have you been up to, Luke? It's been months since I've seen you. You still building that house?"

She didn't give Luke much of a chance to answer before she followed one question with another.

"The house is coming along," Luke told her.

"And you, Clara? You're new in the valley. Kin to Miss Emily, I hear."

Ellen was obviously not a woman to stand on formality. She immediately jumped to the use of first names. Despite that, Clara liked the talkative waitress.

"I'm the schoolteacher," Clara got in before Ellen asked another question.

"I heard about that. It's about time the valley got a permanent teacher. I told Luke here—"

"Do you think we could get something to eat before the dinner hour ends?" Luke interrupted.

Ellen laughed and poised her pencil. "Sorry, Clara," she apologized. "I sling hash most of the day, then I teach piano in the afternoons."

"Oh, I listened to Martha Ames playing this morning."

"Wonderful child. I used to teach her before her daddy died in that accident."

"Ellen." Luke's voice was stern although both women knew he didn't mean it.

"Keep your britches on, Luke. The kitchen ain't gonna close before you get your steak; and from the looks of you, you certainly ain't gonna starve." She turned her attention to Clara. "What can I get you, honey?"

Clara ordered the soup and a small steak. Ellen wrote the order and replaced her pencil.

"Luke always orders ice tea. What would you like to drink?"

"Tea will be fine."

With the shake of her head, Ellen left them, her energetic walk carrying her across the room.

"She must be a lot of fun." Clara smiled as she brought her attention back to Luke.

"Yes, but if you're not careful, she'll talk you to death." He laughed tempering his comment. "She's buried one husband and is working on a second."

Clara looked at Ellen again. She darted around the room checking on her tables as if she were the hostess of a party making sure her guests were having a good time.

"How do you two know each other?" Clara asked, her gaze on the happy woman. Clara had watched Luke hug her. She could tell they were good friends.

"I'll tell you about Ellen another time," Luke said.

Clara turned back to him. *Had they ever been lovers?* The thought struck her like a lightning bolt. Her heart lurched at the thought. She clutched her chest at the pain that rent through her. Why had that happened? Glancing at Ellen, Clara discarded the thought.

"Why didn't you buy anything today?" Luke brought her back to the present.

"I told you."

"I left you alone for two hours, and in that time you found not even a trinket you wanted to buy?"

"That's right." She tried to keep her gaze direct, but found she couldn't hold his stare.

"When you lie, Clara, the small vein in your neck beats enough to be seen."

Involuntarily, her hand came up to cover the point he identified. "I'm telling the truth."

"There are only two reasons a woman goes shopping and doesn't buy anything. One—" He raised his hand and ticked off one finger. "—she has absolutely everything money can buy. You arrived with one suitcase and a hat box, so we know you don't have everything money can buy."

"My trunks will be along soon," she lied.

"Two—" Luke's second finger joined the first, and he continued as if she had not spoken. "—she has no money."

Clara stared at her hands, feeling trapped. "I forgot it," she explained. "When I went to my room to change, I picked up the reticule that matched my suit, but I forgot to put money in it." She clutched the drawstring bag that lay in her lap.

"Why didn't you tell me? I would have loaned you some money until we got back to the boardinghouse."

"It doesn't matter. Not having any money saved me from buying something I don't need." She remembered the yellow felt hat in the window of the Emporium.

"Here you are." Ellen slipped a bowl in front of Clara and set two glasses of tea on the table. The tomato soup smelled delicious. "Be careful, it's hot." She added a bread basket with several bread sticks in it and looked at Luke. "Your steak will be right out."

When she left, Luke turned back to Clara. His expression was solemn. "Last night, Clara."

"I don't want to talk about last night." Her knees turned weak, and she found if difficult to swallow as images of herself falling into Luke's arms flooded her memory.

"When I asked if you were running away, I was half-joking," he said, ignoring her request. "Now I'd like to ask that question again."

"The answer is the same," she answered quickly.

"I don't believe you."

"It doesn't matter whether you believe me or not. It's none of your business."

Luke stared for what seemed an eon. Clara wanted to drop her head, but she knew he expected it of her.

"Clara, the reputation of a schoolteacher needs to be almost as impeccable as that of a preacher. If there is someone looking for you, it could cost you your job."

Luke's voice was quiet as he spoke to her. She'd forgotten about her position. She hadn't stood in front of a class yet, and it was difficult to remember she had the credentials to be a qualified teacher.

"Luke, I promise you, I haven't done anything wrong. I haven't broken any laws."

"Then why did you arrive two months ahead of your appointment?"

"The notice I got said to report in July."

"That's a lie. I sent that telegram myself, and the telegraph officer made no mistake."

"You can't know that."

"I was there, Clara. I stood in the office while he tapped out the code."

"And I suppose you know Morse code?"

"You're damn right I do."

The air between them was solid with accusation. Luke glared at her. "And why don't you have any money?"

"I explained that."

"You lied again, Clara. I saw you looking at that yellow bonnet in the window of the Emporium. You stood there a full ten minutes. You never went in the store, and you wanted it. You wanted that hat so much you could taste it."

"There were other things in the window."

"Name one?"

Clara hesitated. She could think of nothing. "Leather shoes, a package of handkerchiefs . . ." she groped.

Luke shook his head slowly. "You're wrong, Clara."

"Hey, hey, hey." Ellen arrived with plates in her hands. "What's happening here? The two of you want to speak a little louder? There's got to be a miner or two on the seventh level who hasn't heard you."

She set the plates of steaming hot food in front of them.

"I apologize, Ellen. I didn't mean to cause a scene," Clara stated, averting her head from curious stares.

"I know Luke is a hard man to get along with, but he's usually a gentleman in public."

"It won't happen again," Luke told her.

They ate the meal in a silence that made Clara feel even guiltier. Luke had seen through her and she'd only met him twenty-four hours ago. If she continued to see him, eventually she'd have to tell him about Wade—and she didn't want anyone to know about him. It could cost her her job, and she had to hold onto that.

Damn, Luke cursed himself. What was wrong with him? He didn't want to be involved with Clara Winslow. He didn't want to feel sorry for her or be part of her plans. Yet he'd almost kissed her on a public road and then he'd picked a fight in a crowded restaurant. If word got back to the valley (and he knew it could arrive before they did), *he* could be the reason for Clara's losing her job. She could be telling the truth about the money, but somehow Luke didn't think she was.

He *had* been in the telegraph office when the cable had been sent to her. There had been no mistake in what the officer had done, and there was no mistake because the officer on duty hadn't sent the message. He had.

He had been in a hurry that day. The final inspection on the Terrill job was scheduled for that morning and he needed to get there on time. Henry Terrill hated to be kept waiting.

Jess Crawford, the telegraph officer, had run headlong into him as he'd reached the door. His wife had been giving birth to their first child and Jess, on his way out, hadn't even closed the office. He had shouted something about sending Matt over to cover for him, but Luke hadn't been able to wait that long. Since he'd learned the system of dots and dashes and had tapped them out more than once, he had felt perfectly competent to send the message himself so he could leave on time to meet Terrill and save himself another trip into town with no one the wiser. Certainly, when Jess returned, he'd have no memory of Luke's having been there. Sitting in front of the ticker switch, he had confidently tapped out the message, paid the required fee, and closed the door as Jess would have done had he been in a rational state.

Clara Winslow was hiding something, and he wanted to know what. He refused to ask himself why it was important or even to admit that it was important. Hadn't he told Miss Emily he wasn't interested in Clara? He didn't want to be, but her eyes were so large and trusting. She was like an innocent child, although at her age she should have been married and holding two or three babies of her own. If she had been, she wouldn't be here, making him feel things he didn't want to feel. She made him angry, mostly with himself, and she disturbed his sleep because he couldn't get the thought of the way her body felt against his out of his mind. Worse, he didn't want to remove the memory; he wanted the reality more than he dared to admit.

Four

"That's right," Martha called to Clara. "You're doing fine. Just press your knees in a little closer. Horses take their direction from the way you use your body."

Clara rode Red Wind, a spirited mare who'd been named for her rich, dark color and her temperament. It felt good. She hadn't been on a horse for the sport of riding since she was fifteen. Work on the farm was far too demanding for sport. But the knowledge hadn't left her. It was buried inside her head and surfaced when she needed it.

She slowed the horse to a walk and stopped in front of Martha. "Why don't we ride up there?" Clara pointed toward the distant mountains. "I'd like to see some of the country from that angle."

Martha, perched on Starfire, let her eyes follow the direction in which Clara pointed. "All right, but we might need a lunch. It's farther than it looks."

"How about tomorrow morning? We'll get Aunt Emily to give us a picnic basket and we'll ride into the mountains."

Martha agreed, but cautioned her they wouldn't

be able to go very far. They had been riding together for over a week. Early each morning, Clara
would meet her at the stables, determined to stay
out long enough for Luke to leave the house before
she returned for breakfast.

She hadn't seen him, except at dinner, since
they'd returned from Butte ten days ago. When
they had finally left the restaurant, followed by
several pairs of prying eyes, Clara had found the
wagon loaded with goods. Luke's statement, "Miss
Emily's order," were the only words he had spoken
to her for the entire trip back the boardinghouse.
Without waiting for him to help her, Clara had
jumped down and fled into the house and to her
room.

She'd avoided him since. He rarely appeared for
the evening meal, and at night Clara retired to her
room before he returned. He did continue to sleep
there, she knew all too well. Each evening, while
she lay only a wall away, Luke would enter his
room and complete his nightly ritual before going
to bed. She could hear him dropping his boots to
the floor and splashing water from the pitcher into
the bowl. She imagined him naked to the waist as
he washed himself of the day's dust. Finally, after
all sound ceased in the next room, she'd drift into
a fitful sleep.

"What's it like in the East, Clara?" Martha
called her attention back to the path they'd been
walking in silence. "I should like to see it one day.
Do you think I'll ever get the chance? To ride a
train and walk the street where you can see an

ocean so big it connects to a foreign country?"
Martha's animated face underlined her words.

"Hold on." Clara stopped her. Clara realized she
seldom saw the girl in any mood other than subservient. Out here she had a different personality.
Maybe that was why Clara liked her so much—she
reminded her of herself and how she had been before she had come to the valley. "You can't see
the ocean from the capital, 'though you can see
the Potomac River. It divides the District of Columbia from Virginia, but you can see across it."

"It must be the most exciting place in the
world."

Clara could argue that. She had lived in Virginia
and spent a lot of time in the District, but she had
always had a purpose to her trips. She had either
been going to class or working on the farm. Occasionally, she'd visited Annie Pearl, but she'd had
little time for excitement. In fact, that was what
had brought her to Montana.

"It seems so wonderful to be part of the place
where they make laws and all the presidents live—
and the pictures of the monuments are so beautiful.
We got a paper once that said they were building
a giant monument to the father of our country.
Have you ever seen it?"

"They were building it while I was in school,
and they're still working on it. But when it's complete, I hear, you'll be able to go all the way to
the top and look out over the entire city—as if
you were on top of a mountain." Clara looked up
at the green trees that covered the Rocky Mountains.

"It's hard to see down when you're up there," Martha said, her face falling a bit.

"There are no mountains in Washington, Martha. And the monument will be so tall you'll have a clear view of the whole city and parts of Virginia."

"Will I be able to see the part where you lived?" An eagerness showed in her eyes and body.

Clara nodded. Arlington was visible from the capital.

Martha stopped her horse and dismounted, and Clara followed suit. They tethered the horses to a bush and sat on a boulder.

"Do you miss it much, Clara?"

Clara stared at Martha, sensing that the young girl asked more for future reference than out of curiosity about Clara's present state of being.

"Sometimes," Clara whispered. "I miss places I used to go and some of the people. I miss the children."

"Did you have many friends?"

"No, not many." She thought of Abigail, her sister-in-law. She was the closest thing to a friend Clara had ever had, but Abigail had died in childbirth. Annie Pearl was her closest friend from school. If it hadn't been for her and her father's carriage, Clara couldn't have escaped and come to Montana.

"Did you have a . . ." Martha hesitated, dropping her chin in the fashion becoming more and more familiar to Clara.

"A what, Martha?"

"A boyfriend? Did you leave someone behind to

come here?" She voiced the question tentatively, a near-desperate quality underlying her words.

"No, Martha," Clara spoke slowly, regretfully. "I didn't have a boyfriend." She had never had a boyfriend. She could hardly describe Wade as a boyfriend. At forty-one he was much too old to be a boy and he'd never treated her like a friend.

"How about you?"

"Me?" Martha raised questioning eyes to her.

"You're the right age. Girls like you should be thinking about boys and parties."

"You mean it's . . . all right?" She hesitated on the last phrase.

Clara remembered what Emily had said about Martha's mother's dying and her father's being the only parent. Martha had no guide to help her form relationships. Clara certainly didn't feel qualified.

"Martha, has Miss Emily forbidden you to go to dances or talk to the boys at church?"

"No. Miss Emily is very kind to me."

"Is there someone special?"

Martha dropped her eyes, playing with the strings that held her hat secure on her head. Clara knew the answer before the girl spoke.

"There is one, but he never talks to me."

"Boys are shy, too, Martha. They feel just as scared and unsure of themselves as girls do." Clara had found that out at one of the few dances she'd been to before her parents had died and she'd been forced to leave the finishing school she'd attended.

"They do? Why?" Martha's eyes were wide with unconcealed surprise.

"Well," Clara began, "they have big bodies and

girls think their bulk protects them from heart-
break; but under all that muscle, their hearts are
just as fragile as ours."

"You mean they get scared and breathless and
feel like their legs aren't going to hold them up,
too?"

Clara nodded with a smile and held her hand.
Martha was a precious jewel. "They also have to
deal with rejection. At a dance, it's the boy who
comes over and asks you to dance. He's afraid
you'll say no." Annie Pearl's brother had told her
that.

"But I—" she stopped, putting her hand over
her mouth. "He did ask me to dance. I was so
frightened I couldn't."

"Next time, say yes."

"But what about my legs?"

"Don't worry, they will support you. If they
don't, he will hold you up."

Martha gasped at Clara's risqué words. Then
they both burst into laughter, and that was how
Luke found them.

As soon as his horse mounted the incline, Luke
saw Clara and his heart thudded involuntarily in
his chest. Martha sat on the grass in front of her.
Clara's back was to him, the sun highlighting the
dark brown hair that hung loosely about her shoulders, unraveled by the wind. He knew she'd pull
it up and secure it before she went into breakfast,
but just now it flowed like raw honey, dark and
thick. He had a sudden irrational need to thread

his fingers through the soft masses. As he approached, he could hear her soft laughter at something Martha said. Neither of them noticed his approach.

He'd been avoiding Clara since their trip into town. He knew she didn't want to see him either. So why wouldn't his mind leave her alone? Why had he let Emily Hale volunteer him to find Martha, when he knew the two women rode together each morning? It was for this and no other reason that he came: He wanted to see her. He wanted to hear her quiet drawl as she spoke his name.

Luke could have kicked himself for badgering her in the restaurant. Her finances weren't his concern. In fact, Clara Winslow wasn't his concern. But he'd acted as if she were. He'd acted like a husband admonishing his wife for going out without enough money to do the shopping. And in that he'd had no right.

"Morning, ladies," Luke spoke, cutting off their conversation. Both women turned to look at him. "Miss Emily asked me to find you, Martha. She wants you to help her with the silver for tonight's dinner."

Martha immediately jumped to her feet and searched for Starfire.

"You don't need to rush, Martha." He tried to slow the young girl down. He knew she felt as if she owed her life to Miss Emily and she rushed to do anything the old woman asked.

Martha smiled as she mounted the palomino. Turning the horse toward the house, she was off with a wave.

Luke looked back at Clara, who hadn't moved from her position on the ground. For a moment neither of them spoke. Just looking at her was enough for Luke, and he remained on his horse.

"I'm glad you stopped by." Clara got up and walked toward him. Tipping her head back, she shaded her eyes from the eastern sun.

"Why is that?" he asked, dismounting and standing in front of her. His body completely blocked the light, and she dropped her hands. "I thought you were avoiding me."

Clara shot a glance at him. "Why would you think that?" she asked.

"Since our trip to Butte, I haven't seen more than the back of you, not that that isn't a pleasant view." Luke watched as she shifted her weight from one foot to the other. "Every morning you're up at daybreak, riding with Martha. And directly after dinner, you flee to the sanctity of your room. What else am I to think?"

"You haven't actually been present in the boardinghouse either."

"I thought you wanted it that way."

"And you're willing to bow to my wishes?" she asked, dropping her chin and raising an eyebrow in question.

Luke pondered her question. The thoughts going through his mind and the possibility of answers that sprang forth would probably have turned her hair as silvery white as Miss Emily's.

"I'll save the answer to that for a more appropriate time."

Clara stared at him, her expression a mixture of

innocence and knowledge. Innocence won. She had no idea of the innuendo in his statement or her face would have changed from wonder to horror.

"Last week—" She paused. "—I forgot to return this." Clara pulled his watch from her pocket, turning it over in her hand. She pressed the tiny button on top of the case and the cover flipped open; then she offered it to him as if he'd asked for the time.

Accepting the watch, he snapped the cover closed and stuck it in his pants pocket, but he could still see the timepiece clearly in his mind. On the back was an inscription from Peg. She'd given it to him the Christmas before she died. Inside was a small reproduction of his dead wife. It had been there so long, Luke had forgotten about it. Now he felt as if he'd betrayed Peg.

"She was your wife." It was a statement.

"Margaret," Luke nodded. Everyone's life was open to discussion in the valley. "She was a wonderful wife, could handle anything except—" He stopped.

"I'm sorry," Clara paused. "Aunt Emily told me how she died."

Luke swallowed and changed the subject. He didn't want to talk about Peg. "Would you like to ride somewhere?"

Although confused by his abrupt mood-swing, Clara didn't let it bother her. "I wanted to go into the mountains," she stated with confidence.

"It can be dangerous up there if you don't know these hills." He glanced at the thousand-foot bluffs in the distance. They weren't hills by anyone's standard, yet no one but an outsider called them mountains. "They aren't very friendly to the tenderfoot. The air is thinner, which makes it hard to breathe. There are freak storms, falling rocks, and bears and wildcats who live in those hills and wouldn't take kindly to your disturbing them."

Clara's eyes flashed at him. "I won't be a *tenderfoot* forever, Luke Evans. One of these days I'll know this country as well as you do. And I'll be able to handle anything." Pulling the tether straps free, she swung her body into the saddle and rode away like an accomplished horsewoman.

"Damn," Luke swore as he watched her. "She's as volatile as nitro." She rode with confidence, hugging the horse and shifting her weight to accommodate the twists and turns in the rugged landscape. She had a good seat, better than most women and some men he knew.

"Clara!" In one fluid movement, Luke jammed his foot into the stirrup and swung his huge body across the flank of the massive horse. Digging his heels into its sides, he took off after the retreating woman. "Clara," he shouted, then rode with the wind until he was close enough to snatch the reins from her hands and slow the horses to a stop.

He dismounted quickly and yanked her from the saddle, backing her up against a nearby tree. "What's the matter with you? You had no call to run off like that—unless it's your intention to break that beautiful neck of yours." He shook her slightly, and Clara stared at him, defiance in her eyes. She clamped her teeth together and refused to say anything, leaving Luke to wonder why she was so angry. He attributed capriciousness to women in general, but for some reason Clara Winslow didn't strike him as one of the many stamped-out creatures he'd met since Peg had died. He dropped his head and let go of her arms, afraid that if he didn't he would gather her close and tell her how she'd frightened him with her wild ride.

Clara couldn't understand what came over her when Luke was around and she had no control over her feelings when he walked into a room. He didn't have to speak to her. He didn't even have to face her but, as Martha had described, she couldn't breathe, her knees turned to water, and she felt as if she were going to fall.

Taking a deep breath, Clara calmed herself. She had overreacted. Luke did that to her.

"Well?" He waited for an answer.

Pushing herself away, Clara began to walk and Luke fell in step next to her. "It was not my intention to fall," she sneered. "I'm no tenderfoot."

"I agree," he said.

She stopped, opening her mouth to retaliate before his words sank in. "You agree?"

"After that ride, I take it all back."

Clara searched his face for signs of mockery, but found none.

"Martha didn't teach you to ride like that." He stated it as fact.

Martha hadn't. Clara resumed her walk. Riding had been one of the skills she'd acquired at finishing school, but she'd really learned to control a horse on the farm. Carrying food back and forth

to the field and reaching ranchers had meant she
had had to be ready for any emergency. She'd had
her share of adrenalin-pumping rides across the
flat fields and through the dense woods to reach
a doctor or to get to a dying sister-in-law, but in
the past four years she'd hardly been on a horse.
Her studies and Wade's passive resistance to her
schooling had been enough to keep her away from
the farm animals.

"I learned in Virginia," Clara told him.

"Then you're letting Martha teach you so she'll
have someone to talk to."

Clara looked up at him, unsure if she wanted to
reveal the unspoken secret between herself and the
half-Indian girl.

"I can see the answer in your eyes," Luke said
in a low voice.

She dropped her eyelids. "Martha needs a
friend," she explained. Clara linked her fingers together and stared toward the hill in front of her.
"My parents died when I was her age," she began.
"I had no one to tell how I felt about their leaving
me alone. I know how she feels." Clara thought
of her fate—the accident that had claimed her parents, leaving school, the local gossip that had
forced her into Wade's life, and finally her flight
from him to a secret life in the open spaces.
Martha had Emily looking after her physical needs,
but she didn't have anyone to be her friend. Neither had Clara when her parents had died.

"You're right. Martha does need a confidant.
You two were so engrossed when I found you, you
could have been friends forever."

Clara smiled, remembering. "We were talking about traveling East. She wants to see the ocean." She looked east as if she could see the cresting blue waves from her position on the Montana hillside.

"It is a beautiful sight," Luke reminisced. They sat down on a grassy patch of ground, Clara still facing east. "I especially liked the smell of salt in the morning air and the sound of the water lapping against the shore. It was peaceful."

"That's the way I feel about the mountains." Clara lifted her gaze to the high peaks in the distance. "They break up the land, give you a feeling of definition, of belonging." Suddenly, she felt she'd said too much. She studied Luke's face, but found no indication that he found her words revealing.

"Like the ocean, Clara, the mountains are deceiving. In the distance they're vast and mysterious, but they are as unforgiving as a leaky raft two-thousand miles from shore."

Clara stared at the hills. She wondered why they fascinated her. Never having seen one before could be cause for wanting to discover what it was like to stand on the high peaks and look out. That was probably the motivation for building the high monument in Washington. She was no different from the men who envisioned the city from a space eight-hundred feet in the air.

For her, the motivation seemed to be the unknown. If someone had asked her to describe herself, she would never have thought to include explorer in the list of attributes. Yet her trip west

had shown her so much she had never expected
to see, and she'd found that the mountains were
an attainable goal. They were large and powerful
and mysterious. Suddenly she turned her stare to
Luke.

He was like the mountains, large and mysterious,
but was he attainable?

Five

"Children!" Clara clapped her hands several times. Martha looked up from the boy and girl she was physically holding apart. "Children!" Clara grabbed Mahlon Edwards as he darted across the chaotic room in pursuit of a long-haired girl. His legs flailed in mid-air without the traction of the wooden floor. "Children!"

In an instant everyone stopped. The room was as quiet as if it were empty. The small bodies froze in place—all except Mahlon. He was still swimming through the air. Clara set him on the floor and let go.

"Gee, she's strong," Mahlon said as he rubbed his arms and joined his friends.

"Does anyone want to tell me what's going on?" Clara asked, using her stern taskmaster's voice. Everyone spoke at once, filling the room with incomprehensible noise. Again she clapped her hands, and order was restored. "Joycelyn, why don't you begin?" she suggested. Joycelyn Edwards was Mahlon's ten-year-old sister. Their father was the valley blacksmith.

"Well, we were playing hide-and-seek. Jimmie,

over there—" She stopped to point toward a boy of seven or eight with his shirttail hanging out and shoes that must have been handed down by an older brother. "—he was it. Then Chucky Boy grabbed Linda's ribbon and . . ."

"No, I didn't," Chucky Boy, as he was known to everyone, protested loudly.

"Yes, you did," Linda accused, her hand holding her tangled braid.

"No, it wasn't me, Miss Clara." Chucky Boy appealed to her.

A chorus of "yes it was" rose, combined with a "no, I didn't." The chants threatened to revive the noisy room Clara had entered.

"That's enough," Clara shouted, raising her hands to ward off any further comments. Obviously, the children needed something to occupy their time while their parents practiced. "Why don't we try something all of us can do?"

Her question was greeted with suspicious stares. She was their teacher. They probably thought she was going to make them learn their times tables.

"Good." Clara took their silence for assent. "Boys stand over here." She walked to the middle of the room. The boys joined her, threading their way through the girls to form a small crowd around her. "One line, please."

Immediately, they shifted positions to stand according to height.

"All right, girls, here in front." She pointed to an imaginary line in front of the boys. Clara stood back as the stamping of feet on the uncovered floor deafened her. Martha joined the group as if she were one of the young ones.

"What are we going to do?" A smiling six-year-old standing on the end of the line asked.

"We're going to sing."

"Awww." The boys' voices were stronger than the girls', but equally as disappointed by her suggestion.

"Don't dismiss it out of turn."

"What does that mean?" the six-year-old asked.

Clara dropped to eye level with the small child. "It means give it a try before you decide you don't like it."

"I like it," she said.

Clara smiled. "What's your name?"

"Mercedes Dawson."

"When's your birthday, Mercedes?"

"September 9th. I'll be seven years old."

Clara wanted to laugh at the proud child. She'd obviously memorized the correct response in case someone asked the question.

"Why can't we do something else?" Jimmie asked. "Singing is girl stuff."

"Do you have a suggestion, Jimmie? Something we can all do?"

"Yeah, we could play baseball."

The boys laughed, but concurred.

"I don't know how to play ball," Clara admitted.

"We could teach you," Mahlon offered.

"Aw, you don't know how to play, Mahlon."

"I do so—"

Clara stopped the argument before it got out of hand.

"We could ask Mr. Luke to teach us to play," Mercedes said, her small voice innocent.

"Yeah," Jimmie grinned. "Mr. Luke knows everything."

"Can we ask him?"

The room quieted as every eye focused on Clara, waiting for her approval. She didn't want Luke around. He destroyed her equilibrium, and she had no idea how to regain it with him beside her. To deliberately invite him to teach them baseball was asking for trouble, and yet the children obviously welcomed his presence.

"Please, Miss Clara," Linda appealed. "I know he'd do it."

"You want to play, too, Linda?"

"Yes, ma'am."

Clara looked at each of the girls in turn. They all nodded.

"All right." She shrugged, then raised her hands to ward off the noise.

"One practice we sing, the next one we play—agreed?"

The group accepted the compromise with misgivings.

"All right, let's get started. You all know 'Happy Birthday.' Let's try singing it for Mercedes."

"I don't wanna sing that." Chucky Boy frowned. "I wanna sing 'Charlotte The Harlot.' "

"I don't know the words," Linda said.

"Me neither," Jimmie concurred.

"I don't think everyone knows the words to that," Clara said. "We'll let you teach them another time." She didn't act surprised, certain that the boy had only suggested they sing the bawdy saloon song to see her reaction. "Will that be all right?" She solicited his agreement, allowing him to save his reputation in front of his friends. Chucky Boy smiled and nodded.

"All right, everybody, look at me." She raised her hands, baton-style, and counted, "One, two, three." They started on a cacophony of sour notes. Clara let them get through the entire verse, then she began rearranging the children according to the sounds she'd heard.

"This time I only want to hear Linda, Jimmie, Mercedes and Charles." Chucky Boy frowned at the use of his given name. Clara counted and the children sang. She raised her hands higher and, instinctively, their voices followed her. "Good," she said when they finished. The four smiled as if they'd done something of importance.

She repeated the procedure several times, allowing everyone to sing in a quartet. After changing the arrangements twice, she raised her hands again.

"This time we'll do it all together. Everybody remember their parts?"

"Yes, Miss Clara," the group assured her.

Clara hummed the four notes and then counted. When they sang this time, it was better. She smiled at the end. Two boys elbowed each other, proud of their accomplishment.

"Would you like to try another one?" she asked.

"Do we have to?" Jimmie screwed his face into a frown.

"Well, I suppose that's enough for tonight."

They screamed "yeah" and scattered from the regimented ranks in which Clara had assembled them. For several minutes they played in noisy pandemonium before the practice in the main building ended and the parents began to arrive.

As each one found his or her mother or father, they said good night and left. Clara picked up a hat which had been forgotten by one of the children and placed it on the table, which she pushed back into place.

"Clara, is it all right if I leave now?"

Martha stood behind her, a curious expression of fear and anticipation on her face.

"Do you have someone to walk you home?" Clara asked, showing concern. She knew it was fine for Martha to walk alone, but she wondered if the young man Martha had mentioned was waiting out of sight.

"Yes," Martha whispered.

"You'll go straight to the boardinghouse?"

"Of course," Martha said, her voice a little high.

"I think I can put everything back. Go on. I'll see you in the morning."

Martha grinned and left, her long hair swinging as she rushed out.

Clara continued straightening the room. There were wooden toys and dolls in various degrees of disrepair. She wondered who had donated them to help keep the children entertained during the hours of church and the long choir practices.

Finally, everything was in place. She took one more look around before getting the ladder and climbing it to blow out the lamps. The fixture hung from the middle of the ceiling. It was high, and her foot caught on her skirts as she climbed. The room took on a strange quietness as she doused the light.

She began her climb down, carefully placing her feet and holding her dress; she didn't want to fall. When she was halfway down, a pair of hands grabbed her waist. Screaming, she fought blindly. *Not again,* Clara thought as her legs kicked the air and into the man holding her. Again she screamed.

"Clara!" Luke called her name. "Stop it!" He caught her arms and pinned them to her sides while trying to dodge her kicks. "What is the matter with you?" He set her on her feet.

Turning, she found Luke behind her. "What are *you* doing?" she asked, her heart beating wildly.

"Preventing a young lady from falling on her rather beautiful behind. At least that's what I thought I was doing."

Clara gasped and stepped out of the circle of his hands.

Luke closed the step ladder and repositioned it against the wall. "What did *you* think I was doing?"

"I was just frightened by your sudden appearance." Clara took another step away from him. Her heart pounded, but she knew there was another reason—Ian, a ranch hand back in Virginia. He had come upon her as quietly as Luke had and grabbed her from behind, but his intention hadn't been to prevent her from falling. He'd pulled her against him and kissed her. She still remembered his smoky breath, his sweaty smell, and the revulsion that went through her at his actions.

She had none of those feelings about Luke. He smelled manly—not sweet, like some of the men she'd seen at the Sunday meeting, but like the outdoors, as clean as sunshine and as fresh as the woods. Yet when he'd surprised her, she hadn't thought of his smells; she'd remembered only the terror Ian had instilled in her.

"Miss Emily sent me to walk you home," Luke interrupted her thoughts.

"Why? I don't need an escort." Clara remembered their last walk home. She was glad it was too dark for Luke to see her expression.

"You know Miss Emily." He shrugged. "I would like to talk to you, too."

Clara picked up her shawl and hung it over her arm, then together they left the building. The full moon made the clear sky bright and silvery. Clara opened the lace coverlet at the rush of the cooler outside air and swung it over her shoulders. Luke assisted her, innocently tugging at the sides to give her maximum coverage. His hands on her shoulders triggered a heat that seemed to fan out over her back and make her breath come in small gasps.

This couldn't go on, Clara told herself. Every time Luke came anywhere near her, her body reacted as if it had its own heat source. But he didn't want her around. He'd told her that, and so she had no right to be close to him. Besides, even if he had wanted to court her, she would have been forced to refuse his attempt.

"You said you wanted to talk to me?" Clara

asked when her breathing was restored enough to speak calmly.

Luke took her arm and pulled it through his. The last time she had had her arm through his had been an unpremeditated act. Tonight, however, she wondered, although the closeness was pleasurable. "It has to do with Miss Emily and her constant attempts to throw us together."

"Yes," Clara commented, caution in her voice. She wondered how long it had taken her aunt to send Luke for her tonight.

"Miss Emily has been playing this game with me, and I think it's time I taught her a lesson. I want you to help me."

Clara stopped and stared at him. They had passed the last town building and had yet to come in sight of the boardinghouse. This part of the path was tree-lined and secluded. The moonlight turned the road into a bright ribbon and bathed Luke's face in a soft glow.

"Why should I do this? Emily is my aunt and she's been very good to me."

"You are as involved in her plot as I am. More so."

"Plot! You make it sound as if she's doing something awful. All we have to do is ignore her, and everything will be fine."

"You don't know that old lady as I do. She gets a bee in her bonnet, and nothing can prevent her from waging a campaign to get what she wants."

"Why should she want this? She has nothing to gain by my marriage to you."

"She has immortality at stake."

"Aren't you being a little melodramatic?" Clara attempted to laugh, but feared that Luke was about to tell her something traumatic.

"Perhaps, but you, Clara Elaine Winslow, are Emily Hale's sole relative on this planet. She wants a grandchild or whatever the association with a blood relative would give her."

"I don't believe you. Emily is my aunt, but she wouldn't want me to marry a man—" Clara hesitated.

"A man you're not in love with just to provide her with a continued bloodline." Luke laughed. "You obviously don't know the will of that woman."

"What does that mean?"

"It means, Clara, that your appointment as teacher in Waymon Valley is no accident."

Clara pulled her arm free and stood back. "Explain that. Are you trying to tell me that I was given this job for reasons other than my qualifications?"

Luke dropped his shoulders in a defeated gesture. "I didn't mean to imply that you're unqualified. Quite the contrary. The committee who selected you had no problem with your credentials."

"Then what did they have a problem with?" She lifted her chin, ready to take whatever he threw at her.

"Your marital status and your age. But Emily Hale campaigned for you, and nothing could get her to change her mind. You were picked over three men, Clara. One of them had fifteen years' experience, a wife, and three children."

"Because I am unmarried and I'm twenty-one, the committee didn't want me?"

"That's not what I said."

"You said if not for Aunt Emily, I would never have been selected for this position and I'd still be in Virginia." Clara almost shuddered at the thought.

"I'm afraid that part is true."

"And all of this is because Aunt Emily wants me to marry you?"

"It isn't that simple. As much as Miss Emily puts on the strong matriarchal front, behind that is a very vulnerable woman. She left one life and came here to begin another. Before coming to Montana, she lost her husband and children. Marriage and children out here never happened for her. The one man she loved above all others married someone else. You're her only living relative. When she insisted we hire you, no one realized she was your aunt. She wants to be able to hold a child in her arms before she dies."

"Aunt Emily isn't dying." Her reply was more a question than a statement. She admitted she didn't know her aunt very well; but from her observations, she didn't think Emily Hale had been sick a day in her life.

"No, but she's not a young girl either. Without you, there is no one."

"But why you? Why didn't she pick Jake Harris or Pete Chapman or any of the other single men in town?"

"For her, I'm a special case. I was married and I lost my wife and my child."

"I know." Clara raised her hand to her throat.

"My wife died three years ago. Miss Emily thinks I should remarry."

"What do you propose we do?"

"I think we should give Miss Emily what she wants."

Clara gasped. "You think we should get married!" Clara took a step back. "I'm sorry Luke. I don't need a husband."

"Good, because I don't want a wife."

Six

"Then what do you think we should do?" Clara knew she wasn't going to like Luke's plan. She was already practicing one deception. She didn't think she could add another one. Luke must have taken leave of his senses.

"Pretend."

"You mean like a play? I should pretend to fall in love."

Luke nodded.

Clara shook her head. "I can't see how that's going to do anything except lose me a job I don't even have yet." She could also see herself actually falling for this bronze man with shoulders as wide as the Montana sky and arms as round as small trees. She knew already she found him attractive. He was the best-looking man she'd ever seen. And she'd already been mesmerized in his arms. Falling in love with Luke couldn't happen. She had no right to fall for him or any man. And as much as she might like a future like the one Janey Willard had outlined, with a white wedding gown and babies of her own, it wasn't in the cards. She was destined to become an old-maid schoolteacher, but that was better than living the empty existence she'd had for the past six years.

"If I play-act at falling in love with you—"

"Not with me!" Luke interrupted. "Miss Emily is no fool. She'd know something was not right if I suddenly took a liking to you."

"Then whom do you suggest I throw myself at?" Clara's anger got the better of her. What was wrong with her that he didn't find her attractive? Many of the men in the valley had shown an interest in her. She had skillfully avoided being alone with any of them, a technique she'd only heard Janey Willard whispering about, but it had worked.

"I didn't mean that the way it sounded." Luke softened his voice. "Emily Hale is a very astute woman. Her goal is immortality. She'll forget about me the moment she thinks you've found someone else to your liking."

And suppose I don't? Clara thought but didn't say.

"That doesn't seem very fair. I pretend to fall for someone, who has no knowledge of Aunt Emily's plan or your reluctance to adhere to it, and then—"

"It need not be that way. There are at least three men in the boardinghouse who can't take their eyes off you and more than that in town."

"I don't care if every man on earth thinks I'm the best thing that's come along in decades; I won't pretend to fall for someone I have no feelings for."

Luke sighed. His shoulders dropped in defeat. "I guess it wasn't such a good idea."

"It certainly wasn't," she concurred.

"After all, it's *your* problem."

"Mine?" she stared at him. "I didn't propose this plan."

"Miss Emily is going to find a husband for you somewhere."

"Me?"

"She'll drop me soon. We've butted heads for three years. She knows I'm not in the marriage market. And she'll stop her attention toward me to devote it full-time to you."

"I'll just tell her to stop her actions, that I am not in the market for a husband."

"You don't have much of a choice."

"I don't have to agree."

Luke was already shaking his head before Clara finished speaking.

"You don't know the determination of that old woman. What she wants, she gets, and she . . . wants . . . you." He slowed his voice, leaning closer to her as if she might miss his words. "So if you don't want to set your sights on the man of your choice—" Luke paused. "—rest assured, Emily Hale *will* find you a husband."

"I don't want a husband."

Clara couldn't believe she was having this conversation. And with Luke! If either he or Aunt Emily knew about Wade, they'd leave her alone. But if she told them, she could pack her bags and return to Virginia.

What was she to do? She couldn't pretend to fall for one of the men in town. Suppose they fell for her and wanted her to marry them? She couldn't do that. If Luke were right, and she had suspicions he knew what he was talking about, she would have to satisfy her aunt that she was absolutely against marriage and provide a valid reason why or she'd have to find a man.

That man could only be Luke.

An idea came to her. Could it work? Suddenly she doubted herself. She'd also doubted herself when she'd thought of answering the advertisement from the *Richmond Planet*. But she'd done that, and maybe she could do this, too—if she could get Luke to agree. Clara slipped her hand through his arm and began walking again.

"I suppose it isn't a bad idea to give Aunt Emily a little of her own medicine." Clara hadn't liked how she'd felt when Luke had accused her of being part of Aunt Emily's matchmaking efforts. To quiet her aunt, she could agree to part of Luke's plan.

"What do you mean?"

"Your plan might have a few holes in it, but it can work—to both our advantage."

"Then you're willing to try it?"

"I might be."

"With whom?"

"You."

"Oh, no," Luke stopped, pulling away and turning to face her. "I told you Miss Emily is no fool."

"Well, it was *your* plan, and I refuse to be part of a scheme in which the man doesn't know what's going on. So if it's not you, whom do you suggest we include in this conspiracy?"

Luke paused thoughtfully. Clara knew she had him. She wanted to smile, but feared such a response would cause him to back off.

"We're perfect for this," she went on. "Neither of us expects anything from the other, and both of us are aware of Aunt Emily's hopes. We're the only two who can do this."

"How long would this charade have to go on?"

"A month, maybe two," she answered. "Then we could let it be known we just weren't compatible. Aunt Emily would leave you alone and I'd move to my own house, taking me out of her immediate influence."

Luke raised an eyebrow. "It might work," he said slowly as if the plan had a flaw but he couldn't quite find it. "We're going to have to be convincing in both the attraction and the incompatibility."

"I know," Clara said, her eyes straight ahead. "Then you'll do it?"

Luke stared at her for a long moment until she thought he was about to refuse. As more time elapsed, she became sure of it. "All right," he said. "But remember, this isn't real. It's play-acting."

"Of course, it isn't real," Clara told him, but at that moment she wondered if her plan to draw him into the deception hadn't backfired. The way he looked at her, the way she felt whenever he was near, how was she going to pretend? Again she'd let her mouth get her into trouble. Being in Luke's company might take more acting than she was capable of.

Laughing voices greeted Luke when he and Clara walked through the door of Hale's Boardinghouse. Usually there were games going on in the parlors after dinner, but tonight the house seemed more alive than usual. Mrs. Laurie Andersson, whose husband was foreman at the Whitney Copper Mine, sat at the ornately carved upright piano playing a lively tune. Her blonde hair, which hung to her shoulders, bounced as her head bobbed with the beat of the music. She often entertained in the evening.

She'd once told Luke of her dream to go on the stage, but her family in Oslo hadn't thought it respectable. Bowing to their wishes, she'd stayed home until she'd met Swen Andersson. Then, defying them, she'd married the burly man and crossed the open sea to settle in the Montana wilderness. Laurie Andersson said she'd never been happier and, since she wouldn't leave her husband, she satisfied herself with playing the piano and occasionally singing in the evenings.

Antonia Morrison, Miss Emily's oldest friend and the valley's vessel on moral conduct, sat next to Jamison Sanders. The man, no doubt, was being subjected to one of her lectures on the do's and don'ts of the valley.

Miss Emily waved them forward, moving over and indicating seats. Luke and Clara took the offered chairs, and Miss Emily poured cups of coffee for them.

"How is the choir, Clara?"

"I didn't go into the church. When I got there, a small fight was going on in the children's wing, so I went in to help Martha." Clara looked around for the young girl. "She did get here all right?"

"She came in a few minutes ago and went to her room." Miss Emily smiled. Luke knew about Martha, and he knew about Frank Crabtree, the young boy she liked. He and Miss Emily had never discussed it, but he knew she was aware of it, too. There were few things Emily Hale didn't know about.

"Did she tell you about the children's choir?" Clara asked.

Emily leaned forward. "She didn't have time. When she came in, she had a big smile on her face. She said good night and went upstairs."

"Well, the children needed something to do while their parents practiced. I thought it would be a good idea to have them have their own choir rehearsal."

"And how did that suggestion go over?" Luke asked.

"Less than enthusiastically."

Miss Emily laughed.

"But," Clara went on. "We agreed to a compromise."

"What was that?" Luke asked.

"Something I need your help with," she hedged.

Luke saw the imperceptible change in Emily Hale. He gave his attention to Clara, wondering if she'd already begun the game.

"What would you like me to do?"

"The compromise was to rehearse during one practice session and play baseball during the next. I don't know how to play baseball, and the children were sure you'd agree to coach them."

"That's a wonderful idea," Emily chimed in.

Luke knew she'd agree for him before he got the chance to refuse.

"Will you do it?" Clara asked. Her eyes were wide and pleading, as if it were important to her that he help out. Luke felt his insides melt again. Why could she do that to him with just a look?

"Of course he'll do it." Miss Emily again took the decision from him.

"Mrs. Hale," Luke warned, calling her by her formal name, a practice he only followed when she was overstepping her bounds. "I can answer for myself."

The old woman sat back, quiet, but not defeated. She was never defeated. Luke knew it was why she'd survived the harsh trip west; dust storms, disease, even raiding Indians were no match for Emily Hale. Clara didn't know what a favor he was doing for her.

"A team usually consists of nine boys—"

"Not only boys," Clara interrupted. "The girls want to play, too."

"Oh, no," Emily objected. "It's not proper for girls to play such a rough sport." Luke watched her glance go to Antonia. Still engrossed in conversation, the other woman had not heard Clara's declaration.

"It's very good for them," Clara disagreed. "It will make them stronger and teach them how to get along with others."

"Is this a progressive idea from your schooling?" Emily asked. "Because it won't go over with the parents or the folks in the valley."

Luke knew what Emily was getting at. Clara

didn't. He'd only alluded to her tenuous position tonight. She was on trial, and the people of the valley were very strait-laced about their traditions. He knew he was going to hate himself, but he had to do it.

"Miss Emily, the girls will probably have fun playing and, since Clara's already got the boys to agree, let's see how it goes."

He looked at Clara for confirmation. He didn't know if the boys had agreed; but if their plan were to work, they had to convince Emily Hale they were on the same side.

"The boys didn't seem to mind playing with the girls," she said. Luke watched her for signs. He was sure Chucky Boy had objected. He was too playful not to. But Clara must have sidestepped his concerns.

"Of course there have to be rules," Clara explained. "The girls won't be expected to play like the boys, and they won't have to get dirty. But they really do want to play."

"Then it's all right with me," Luke agreed. "Emily?" Luke appealed to his friend. Deep down, he didn't want to do anything to get Clara in trouble with the townspeople. Emily had fought hard for Clara's appointment and, since the younger woman was aware of only a small part of the conflict, Luke would guide her away from any pitfalls.

"I suppose it's all right," Emily conceded, staring directly at Luke.

Clara smiled, and Luke's heart skipped a beat.

Seven

"Luke . . . Luke?" Clara whispered outside his door. Her bravado outside the house last night had turned to terror in the isolation of her room. What had she agreed to? Deception was foreign to her; she still felt guilty about running out on Wade. She'd left him at the busiest time of the year, when she'd known he wouldn't be able to follow her. She's taken the coward's way out. She was a coward.

She'd been up all night gathering the courage to walk the twenty paces to Luke's room. Finally, in the early morning before the household had begun to waken, she'd taken the plunge and knocked.

Her excuse was honest, even though it didn't ring totally true inside her head. She needed to talk to him and he was frequently gone when she rose for breakfast or to meet Martha. She wore her riding pants, brown, loosely fitting and split in the middle. They were the easiest outfit to put on, and she could meet Martha later.

"Luke, please wake up." She knocked quietly, looking about the darkened hall, hoping no one would see her. She and Luke were the only boarders on the third floor, but Clara felt as if every door would suddenly open and the eyes of the boardinghouse occupants would be upon her.

Luke didn't answer, and she didn't hear anything. Maybe he wasn't there, she thought. He'd come in last night. She knew that. Maybe he'd left already, but she didn't think so. She was a light sleeper and she'd been awake most of the night. If he'd risen, surely she would have heard him.

She looked at the doorknob. Should she try it? Her hand suddenly grew clammy and her heart beat in her throat. Clara reached out. The handle felt cold against her sweaty palm. It turned easily, not like her own door, which was heavy and slightly off center so that she had to lift up on it as she pushed or pulled it open. A scant turn, and Luke's door swung inward.

Luke slept on his side, his back to the entry. Clara stepped into the room. Quickly, she closed the door, making sure to keep the sound to a minimum. She took a deep breath, her hand at her chest, trying to slow her thundering heartbeat. The windows were curtained but without shades. Moonlight streamed in, making it easy to see the outline of the furniture in the room.

"Luke!" she whispered again.

He stirred.

How could he sleep so soundly? He wasn't even snoring. Walking as slowly as if she were treading in the ocean against the current, Clara made her way to the bed. She called Luke's name again. His eyes opened and he stared at her, then blinked. He rubbed his eyes.

"Luke, wake up. I need to talk to you."

He bolted upright, then quickly grabbed for his sheet. "You're not a dream," he stated.

Startled, Clara wondered briefly if he had dreamed about her.

"What are you doing here?" He looked at the door. "Get out." He pointed toward the exit, but didn't move, and Clara realized he was naked.

She turned quickly as if she had seen him. "We need to talk, Luke. Would you meet me on the ridge?"

"Give me ten minutes," Luke said. "Now get out of here."

Clara sped to the door. She cracked it open and peered into the hallway. Sure nothing was amiss, she nearly ran through the corridor, down the stairs, and out to the stable.

Taking no time to think, she saddled her horse and rode to the hill where she and Luke had last talked. She climbed down from her horse, pulling her jacket closer around her and watching her breath congeal and become visible. Moments later, Luke arrived.

"Clara," Luke reined in his horse and swung his huge body to the ground. "What is so important you need to discuss it before sunrise—and in my bedroom?" He was angry. She'd wakened him and she'd broken the boundaries of propriety by coming into his room. But Clara refused to be intimidated. She knew she shouldn't have gone to him, but she hadn't had a choice. She needed information if they were to successfully pull off this farce.

"I don't know how to act," she said.

"That's an understatement." Luke snorted.

"I mean . . . this agreement to pretend. What does it mean? I don't know how to show Aunt Emily I am attracted to you."

Luke frowned as he tethered his horse to a nearby branch.

Clara sensed she'd said the wrong thing. Did he want her to be attracted to him? He said he didn't want a wife, but that didn't mean he was telling the truth. *Men frequently say one thing when they mean something else, especially when the matter involves the heart.* Janey Willard's voice sounded in her head. Clara remembered her saying that during one of her many morning discussions on life and its lessons.

"Just do what comes naturally, Clara." Luke had turned back to her.

The mist rose over the grassy hill like a coven of ghosts fleeing the coming daylight. Clara stared at him. She didn't know what came naturally. She knew she had feelings for Luke—feelings that were different from any she'd ever experienced. But to court a young man! She had no clue what to do. And there was no Janey Willard around to eavesdrop on and learn from her comments on how to snare a man.

"Clara, you must have had a boyfriend back East," Luke continued. "Someone who took you to parties and dances. Just do what you did with him."

Clara couldn't. She'd never had a boyfriend. She had gone to two dances at teachers' college, but she had gone with Annie Pearl. And as for finishing school—she hadn't thought much about boys then, except when the situation warranted it—like dancing class. After her parents died, she went to Wade.

"I understand," she said, her voice unconvincing to her own ears. This had been a mistake. She should have talked to someone else, but whom? Annie Pearl was back in Washington, and Clara couldn't very well go to Aunt Emily for advice. "I suppose if we spend some time together . . . when . . . when Aunt Emily is aware of it." She rushed into breathless speech.

A lazy smile stole across Luke's face. He was laughing at her. "Yes, we could do that," he agreed. "Where do you suppose we could spend this time?"

Clara swallowed. Her ears had grown warm, and she felt that Luke was baiting her. "There's coaching the baseball game." She grasped at the first thought that came to her.

"And I could come to the children's singing rehearsals and walk you home."

"Yes." Clara smiled, grateful.

"And I could kiss you good night at the door."

A shiver of horror ran through her. Then she thought she'd misunderstood. "On my forehead, like a brother or father."

"No, Clara." Luke shook his head, a glint of mischief in his eyes. "Full on the mouth, in plain view of Emily Hale. Nothing would please her more."

"You're making fun of me." Clara's back stiffened as it always did when she felt the joke was at her expense.

Luke didn't reply immediately. The sun tinged the horizon, outlining the bluffs in shadow as the sky behind them turned to cracked gold. Luke's eyes had a dark and dangerous light that seemed both concealed and open. Clara's throat went dry. She wanted to say something, but no words would come. She wanted to flee from the influence of those mesmerizing eyes, but her feet refused to move.

"Clara," Luke whispered. He stepped forward, his hands going to her waist. Clara looked up, her lips parted in surprise, but her exclamation of surprise died before it made it past the lump in her throat. She attempted to move away, but he held her too tight.

"Luke, no," she rasped through parched lips. She knew the revulsion would come, the horrible trapped feeling that had overcome her when Ian had grabbed her in the barn.

Luke hesitated. His face closed the tiny distance until she felt his warm breath on her skin. Unconsciously, she wet her dry lips with her tongue. Luke gasped, and Clara swayed closer to him, feeling no revulsion at all. Luke crowded out the bad memories, filling every space in her mind with his presence.

"Luke, there's no need for this." She could barely speak. "Aunt Emily isn't here and—"

Luke cut conversation short with his mouth, covering Clara's with his. His lips, soft and warm, touched hers lightly, but the sensation prickled through to her toes, leaving Clara awkward and unsure. She didn't know where to put her hands or even if she should stop Luke. She didn't want to stop him. She'd never felt like this before, as if they were the only people on earth, as if pressing herself against him were the right thing to do.

Then Luke deepened the kiss, drawing her into him, wrapping her in his arms as if she were a soft doll. Clara's arms grabbed at his muscles, then traveled over his shoulders to connect behind his neck. Opening her mouth at Luke's persistent pressure, she joined him in a sensual tongue-dance. Luke's arms tightened then spread out over her back and hips with the same deliberate slowness with which his mouth moved over hers. Clara wore only her riding pants, with no petticoats to act as a barrier between their aroused bodies. With only her split-skirt between them, she could feel the outline of Luke's hard body and quivered at his touch.

Clara didn't find the sensation unpleasant. In fact, she actually liked what Luke was doing. She wanted it to go on, but Luke abruptly pushed her away and took a step back. She stumbled at the unanticipated need to support herself alone.

"Why do women do that?" Luke asked, his voice breathy and hoarse.

"Do . . ." Clara cleared her throat. "Do what?"

"Go all limp and boneless." Clara heard his anger. She couldn't deny it. In Luke's arms she'd been as pliant as soft gold. She'd felt weightless, as if she floated in the clouds without the need for a solid foundation. Luke had been her anchor, but now she felt ashamed—as if she had done something wrong.

"I—" She stopped herself. Her immediate thought had been to apologize, but strength of will came to her and she refused. "I will not be sorry," she said, only realizing the way her words could be interpreted after it was too late to stop them.

Luke glared at her. "I know now that what comes naturally will not be a problem for you, Clara." Luke grabbed the tether straps and pulled himself into the saddle. Turning the massive horse toward her, he looked down. "Don't ever come to my room again."

With that, he rode off. Clara stared after him, stunned. She hadn't invited his kiss. She'd thought she'd be kicking and scratching to get him to stop. How could she have known her body would melt the moment he touched it. And why had he felt it necessary to kiss her? She supposed he'd wanted to teach her a lesson.

But which one of them had learned it?

Eight

The object seemed to be to hit the ball with a three-foot cylinder and run around a formation Luke called a *diamond,* striking three planks of flat wood that had been laid at equal distances on the hardened ground, before returning to the home position.

Clara stood between Aunt Emily and John Streeter as John's daughter Cynthia approached the plank. In the previous games, Cynthia had missed all three pitches and been called *out* without having the opportunity to run the bases. Running seemed to be the most fun, and all the other boys cheered loudly for the runner. Using the bat, the small girl drew a large rectangle on the ground and stepped up behind it.

"You can do it." Clara heard John whisper as if he and the girl at the plate shared some form of communication concealed from her. Looking at him, she found his stare riveted to his offspring. His fists clenched and unclenched as tension marred his normally calm demeanor into a scowl. Cynthia threw him a worried glance, and Clara noted the slight nod of his head. The child had obviously been coached. Clara hoped it would help her. The other kids ridiculed her because she was afraid of the ball and often closed her eyes before swinging.

Cynthia's short red hair was a mess. Fortunately, the child was not nearly as unruly as her hair, which, no matter how she brushed it, tended to stand up like patches of disorderly soldiers. She wore a bright yellow dress, black stockings, and laced boots. Her stance reminded Clara of a proud rooster: Cynthia spread her feet, stuck out her behind, and lifted the bat out in front of her. The boys burst into laughter, and Clara ignored the commotion, training her attention on Chucky Boy, the pitcher for the opposing team.

Clara was proud of the girl. She wasn't falling apart in front of everyone. A few short weeks ago, she'd gone home crying and had done so each time the game was convened.

A wide grin split Chucky Boy's face as he stared at the mere girl imitating the boys. He checked both sides of the backfield, where satisfied smiles beamed on the team's smudged faces. Secretly rooting for the tiny girl, Clara caught the look which passed between the boys and knew that Chucky Boy was about to throw an unfair pitch.

They'd agreed that just as it was unfair to pit the boys against the girls, it was also unfair for the boys to throw the same pitches to the girls that they dealt each other.

Clara took a step forward.

"Leave it," Luke said, appearing by her side.

The ball left Chucky Boy's hand before Clara

could reply. All the force of his adolescent shoulder was behind the small white object. Cynthia eyed it. With her left foot she stepped into the rectangle she'd drawn on the ground and met the missile head on.

Cr-rack! The sound of a single buckshot accompanied Cynthia's swing. The ball rose in the air. The girl dropped the wooden club and ran. Chucky Boy's mouth dropped open, and he watched in amazement as the ball flew over his head. Aunt Emily, along with several women holding parasols to block out the sun, rose in disbelief at Cynthia's feat.

No one seemed to notice the redhead until she'd passed the first plank and headed for the second.

"Throw me the ball," Edward shouted, breaking everyone out of the surprised trance Cynthia had created.

Jimmie rushed backward. Kathleen came from the other direction, both intent on the same ball. Cynthia passed second before they reached it. Two pairs of eyes, focused on the tiny dot falling from the sky, didn't see each other.

"They're going to run into each other," Luke predicted just before boy and girl smashed young body into young body. The ball fell silently in the grass behind them.

"One more, honey," John Streeter shouted over the melee as he rooted for his daughter. "Come on," he called along with the crowd that had gotten behind the young girl.

Cynthia's black-booted foot stomped third. She glanced over her shoulder. Mikey Peterson had the ball and threw it toward home. The pint-sized child didn't slack her pace.

Luke had measured off sixty feet between the third plank and the one he called home. Chucky Boy had explained a regulation field would have ninety feet between each base, but since the girls were allowed to play they had decreased the size of the diamond.

Cynthia had covered half the sixty-foot distance when the ball snapped into Chucky Boy's glove and in one fluid movement he turned, lined up Agnes Wheatly, the catcher, and threw the ball toward her. Agnes was the only girl in a family of eleven brothers. She ranked fourth in the chain and had learned the game as she learned to walk. Clara had no doubt the ball would make contact with her glove as sure as mountain goats scaled the distant hills.

"Slide," someone shouted.

Clara held her breath, unconsciously squeezing Luke's forearm.

Cynthia didn't slide. Instead, she propelled her body up and made a missile of herself. She flew through the air like a July 4th rocket, her dress and hair as colorful as a starburst. The crowd inhaled collectively when Cynthia hit the ground, exploding the earth in a brown cloud a second before the ball connected with Agnes' glove.

"Safe!" John Streeter usurped Luke's position as referee and shouted the call.

The crowd went crazy. John rushed past Luke and Clara in pursuit of his daughter. Clara didn't see him reach Cynthia or notice Chucky Boy's ex-

pression of incredulous disbelief. She had thrown
herself into Luke's arms and hugged him. Luke's
arms spanned her tight waist and lifted her off the
ground. A loud shout came from his deep throat
as he swung her around. Clara bent her knees, feeling her dress flare to one side as the wind whipped
through it. She slid her arms around Luke's neck
until they met at his collarbones, squeezing herself
closer to him. He twirled her around and around.
Her hair came loose of her bonnet, and she pressed
her cheek next to his.

The action changed her. Suddenly the sound
around her ceased and she went into that private
world she seemed to create each time she found
Luke's arms about her. Luke stopped the swinging
motion, but pressed her against him. Clara warmed
at the feel of his arms crushing her to him. Her
cheek lay against his, and she smelled his male
scent mingled with sunshine and the faint aroma
of shaving cream. The mixture was heady, making
her want to turn her face and press her mouth to
his hot skin.

Blood shot through her system at the bold nature
of her thoughts. Her heart pounded so loudly he
had to hear it. For a moment Luke kept her sus-
pended; then, with a final squeeze, he buried his
face in her hair. She felt his mouth brush the skin
behind her ear before he slid her down his hard
length and set her on the ground.

Luke hadn't touched her since their early-morning
encounter six weeks ago, but his seat at meals had
been placed next to hers and that was no surprise.
Clara knew her aunt was responsible, and both of

them accepted the change without comment. Luke came to baseball games and choir rehearsals. He was courteous and kind in Aunt Emily's presence, but until this moment his hand had never even brushed against hers.

Luke's eyes were warm as they raked over her, taking in her disheveled hair and face.

With his hands still on her waist, he held her gaze. For the first time, his eyes were unshaded and full of passion, and he looked steadily at her. Then he dropped his hands and stepped back. Breaking the personal contact between them brought the field back into focus, and the noise crowded in on Clara like a rushing wave. An embarrassed heat rose to her face as she realized that she was in plain sight of the town spectators, especially Antonia Morrison, who Clara felt had a strong dislike for her. Her hands went to her hair, feeling for its disorder. She turned, checking for the stares she was sure she'd find.

Thankfully, everyone was still congratulating Cynthia for her spectacular finish, except Aunt Emily. The older woman smiled and waved at her, then turned back to her friend as if she'd seen nothing. But Clara knew better.

Luke had left the sidelines, heading for the center of the crowd, and Clara sank down on the bench near the head of the diamond. Her knees gave out at the thought of what she'd seen in Luke's eyes. No man had ever looked at her like that. She was breathless and frightened and she'd never felt better in her life.

She stared at Luke's back as he crossed the

dusty field. Had he meant anything by the way he'd held her? Or had it just been the excitement of Cynthia's winning the game? She could feel his arms crisscrossing her back, his cheek against hers, and the look in his eyes when he'd set her on the ground. She shivered slightly in the warm breeze. The hot gaze in his eyes had taken her by surprise, and Clara took a deep breath. Her heartbeat had nearly returned to normal. She liked the way Luke had looked at her, and a smile tilted her mouth. She wanted him to do it again.

Then she remembered Wade. As if she'd been caught in a sudden shower, a coldness ran through her. She couldn't let Luke look at her like that again. She had no right to want his attentions.

"Emily Hale, I can't believe you're letting this happen." Antonia Morrison crossed thick arms over her full bosom and humphed. "It's downright indecent. Why whoever heard of girls playing baseball?"

"Antonia, they're children. And this is the fifth game they've played. They have fun and, other than you," she raised her eyebrow as she faced her oldest friend, "the town seems to have accepted the progress of women."

"But what will they become? Running around like savages." She sneered, her nose etching a notch upward.

"They've got time. In a few years, the girls will discover they like boys for something other than playing baseball. By then, this game will be only a memory. A good memory, I might add." Emily stared at her friend. "Who knows? Maybe they'll understand each other better than we did."

Antonia rocked back and forth. It was a habit Emily had come to know well after nearly forty years of friendship with the church-going Antonia Morrison.

"It ain't decent, Emmy. It ain't decent."

"Stop saying that. What the children are doing is having fun. You wouldn't want them running wild, causing trouble, and fighting with each other, would you?"

"This is *her* doing."

Emily's back went up.

"I knew we should have accepted Marcus Smith and left her back East. He had a family to feed and needed the job, but you wouldn't hear of it. And once you get a burr in your—"

"Antonia, don't start with me. Marcus Smith had all the qualifications. He also had a history of beating children who didn't conform to his idea of proper behavior. Don't you remember how his own children behaved when we met them? They acted more like scared soldiers than young'uns. Clearly, Clara was the better choice."

"I don't know. She's awfully young and look how the men in town drool over her."

Emily knew that part was true. Clara was a beautiful woman; and it was strange that at her age she had not married and produced children of her own.

"Why, even Luke can't keep his eyes off her," Antonia continued.

Emily's head came up at Antonia's remark. "Luke?"

"Don't tell me you haven't noticed how often he manages to be in her company? You told me yourself, he shows up at supper time now more often than he used to. And she got him to coach this team, despite the fact it would include girls. Now why would a man do that if he weren't interested in a woman?"

Emily searched for Luke. Ellen Turnbull had him locked in a one-sided conversation near the punch bowl. Clara sat alone on the bench next to the playing field. Emily eyed her closely. She didn't look well, and her gaze was trained on Luke.

"Peg's been dead three years, Antonia." Emily turned back to her friend. "Luke's a healthy man. He has to find someone sometime."

"Emily Hale," Antonia turned as slowly as she pronounced Emily's name. "You're planning something, and I have the feeling Luke isn't going to like it."

"You know me, Antonia. Luke is like my own son. I'd never do anything he wouldn't like."

Antonia glanced at Luke, then at Clara before returning her attention to Emily. "She's gonna be trouble, Emily Hale. I knew it the moment I heard she was coming. She's gonna be nothing but trouble."

"When I heard the girls were going to play, I said, Luke and Clara must be out of their ever-loving minds. This will never work. The folks out here will run her back East faster than a rattler can strike." Ellen Turnbull stated her piece between bites of tea cakes. "But the girls couldn't be happier and the boys are thrilled Cynthia won the game for them." Ellen paused, but only briefly. "You two have been the talk of Butte since word reached us you were coaching a team."

"That's why so many people show up for the games." Luke surveyed the crowd. Since they'd begun regular play, the adult choir practice tended to end in time for the first pitch and the games had become organized events. When Clara held singing sessions with the children, only a few people ever came to hear them.

"To tell you the truth," Ellen continued, "they came the first time to see Clara make a fool of herself. Some people still wonder why she was chosen for the job."

It wasn't like Ellen to use unnecessary words. Luke knew she had something she wanted to tell him. "Say what you mean, Ellen."

"You know how people in the valley can be. It's hard for them to trust anyone who hasn't lived here since the hills were too small to obstruct view from the center of town clear to Wyoming. She has new ideas, and out here they might not play as well as they would where she comes from."

"So how's she doing?" Luke told himself he didn't want to know. He didn't care if she were doing all right in the eyes of the town or not. She meant nothing to him. He didn't want her to mean anything. Yet he'd asked the question and so the answer somehow became important.

Clara didn't know the town. She thought everyone was friendly and had no idea how vicious gossip could be or how it could affect her position here.

"She's still on tenterhooks, and you're not helping her cause."

"I haven't done anything. I avoid Clara if at all possible."

"The way you avoided her that night on Main Street." Luke stared at her. "I saw you." She paused. "And I saw you a few minutes ago on the playing field."

Luke glanced away from Ellen's direct stare, and his eyes encountered Clara. She sat talking to Martha Ames on the very spot where he'd held her in his arms. His heart lurched.

"Luke, you're a man; Clara's a woman. The most natural thing in the world is that you two are attracted to each other."

"I'm not attracted to her. She's just so green out here that she needs someone to help her find her way."

"And you've elected yourself her guide. This doesn't sound like a man who doesn't want to be involved."

"Ellen, you're jumping to conclusions."

"Luke, where you're concerned, you always get the benefit of the doubt. If you say you're not interested in Clara, I'll believe you."

Ellen turned to look at Clara and Martha. The young girl and young woman laughed together as if they were best friends. At length, she turned back to Luke.

"Tell me you're not interested, Luke."

He wanted to say it. He wanted to look Ellen in the face and tell her Clara meant nothing, but he couldn't. He didn't know when or how it had happened. Maybe it had been that first day when she'd walked onto his site or the nights he'd watched her lead the children in song or guide them during the baseball games. Whenever or however, she was dear to him now, and there was no going back.

He'd denied it long enough. Somehow the woman had gotten under his skin. He couldn't say she meant nothing. It wasn't true. Luke's fist clenched and unclenched with internal turmoil. Clara's quiet manner had invaded his impenetrable shell. He stared across the playing field, chagrined. He couldn't tell Ellen a lie. Outside of Emily Hale, Ellen Turnbull was his best friend, and even if he could lie to himself, he couldn't lie to her.

Ellen was still staring at him, waiting for an answer. He said nothing, and eventually she left him standing alone. Luke turned to follow her, but then he saw Clara with Martha. His heart skipped a beat at the way she looked. She was the perfect picture, sitting on the bench in a grey, lacy summer dress, its folds falling softly along her legs. Her grey hat sat atop her head, contrasting with the soft darkness of the hair she had swept up under the wide brim.

How had she done it? In the three years since

Peg had died, he'd frozen his heart against any female, especially those Emily Hale threw like sugar cubes into his path. But Clara wasn't a sugar cube. Maybe that was what he liked about her. If she got her back up, she would stand fast on any issue. She was smart, and the look in her eyes turned him inside out.

Luke wondered what it would feel like to really hold her, without the crowd of the baseball game, without his own reservations—with just undisguised feeling for another human being. Would she turn all sugary and sweet? She looked at him. His gaze locked with hers, and he couldn't move. His arms could almost feel her, his mouth taste hers. He swallowed. This was getting out of hand. Way out of hand.

He couldn't let this attraction continue. If he continued to court Clara, he'd have to marry her, and he knew what marriage meant. Losing Peg had been too painful. He couldn't take burying another wife.

Nine

The sun finally dropped behind the distant mountains. Darkness enveloped the landscape, leaving only the huge peaks outlined against the fading purple of the sky. Clara sat on the window seat in her room, watching the play of color. She smiled, remembering the game and Cynthia's spectacular finish. Clara hadn't been keeping score on whether her presence was being accepted in the valley, but tonight's show had proved the girls equal to the boys at baseball.

She had seen Aunt Emily talking to Antonia Morrison, and she knew Antonia felt it was her job to uphold the conscience of the valley. She wondered what the old woman had had to say about her and about the girls. Her ears should have been burning at tonight's gossip; yet when everyone had returned to the boardinghouse, they had talked of nothing but Cynthia and how well she'd done. Many people had congratulated Clara on allowing the girls to play, saying it was a wonderful idea.

Clara's cheeks still burned with happiness. Putting her hands up to her face, she could feel the

warmth. It was going to be all right here; she was
safe. No one knew where she was except Annie
Pearl, and Annie Pearl—who had graduated first
in their class—had been asked to teach one of the
freshman classes at the college.

Annie Pearl had glowed with happiness when
she'd rushed into the dining room to tell Clara.
She had hugged her and asked her to apply for a
position at the college, too; but since Clara had
already received the acceptance letter from Montana, her friend had helped her carry out her secret
plan. Annie Pearl had been the only person to hug
her and wave goodbye from the lonely train platform as she'd headed for Waymon Valley, Montana.

Clara left the window bench and went to the
desk. She needed to write to Annie Pearl. She
should have written before this, but she hadn't
wanted anyone to know how to find her, not even
her best friend. But Luke had mentioned mail
when they'd gone to Butte weeks ago, and it could
look suspicious if she neither sent nor received
mail. Pulling a sheet of paper toward her, she
dipped her pen in the India ink and wrote.

July 27, 1899

Dear Annie Pearl,
    *I apologize for the length of time that has
elapsed since I last saw you. My only excuse is
that things have been more different here than
I expected and I have been very busy.*
    *You're probably wondering what it's like in
Montana. You really need to see it to believe*

the vastness. The mountains are higher; the sky is bigger; even the stars appear larger than they did from your room overlooking the Potomac.

My aunt runs a boardinghouse full of miners. Some of them are married and come from places as far away as Norway, Germany and Sweden. All day they work hard in the copper mines near Butte. In the evening my aunt makes us dress for dinner. Her table is prepared with china and crystal she packed in flour barrels and brought all the way from Tennessee nearly forty years ago. Here, I look forward to dinner, but then Janey Willard isn't here to look down her nose at me and remind me that as a scholarship student, I was no better than a charity case. I suppose it was good training.

I enjoy listening to the stories everyone tells of where they're from and what they do in the mines. Some of the miners' wives are also here. Other boarders include a builder named Luke and a half-Indian girl, Martha, who plays the piano. She and I have become friends. Her classicals remind me of hearing you and your brothers playing Chopin and Brahms. I smile each time I hear a familiar song. On occasion I've heard her experimenting with songs I don't know. She's like two different people. One of them is quiet and subservient, the other free and happy. Her parents are both dead, and I think she's a little lonely.

I want to hear about you and home. Write

me soon and tell me when you begin to teach.
And have you and James decided to marry yet?
*   I miss you.*

                                        Clara

Clara read the letter over, then slipped it into an
envelope. An unfamiliar warmth came over her.
When she addressed the envelope, Clara realized
how much she missed Annie Pearl and her home
in Virginia. With Annie Pearl she had had someone
to talk to, share secrets with, even laugh with. Here
she had no one. She'd have liked to have had
someone to tell how she felt about Luke. Even
Janey Willard didn't seem too bad right now. Janey
always knew the right things to say and do. She'd
probably know exactly why Clara had felt so happy
in Luke's arms when he'd swung her around after
the baseball game, why she had been elated for a
moment when Luke's suggestion of marriage was
misunderstood, and why she'd been lost when he
kissed her.

Suddenly she heard Luke's door close. She
started the way she did every night when she heard
his door open and close. Her body went cold, then
hot. She'd been thinking of him, and his sudden
appearance made her feel as if she were naked and
he could see through the wall and straight into her
heart. She stood, facing the common barrier, a
small obstruction between the two of them. One
boot dropped and Clara jumped, scraping her chair
across the bare floor. A moment later, the next one
fell. Clara listened. Everything was quiet. Minutes
passed and no sound came from the room next to

hers. Had Luke gone to sleep without splashing water into the bowl? He never did that. For weeks she'd listened to his nightly ritual before falling asleep.

Tonight she wanted to talk to him. The time they spent together was always in a group and she rarely got to see him alone. This courtship wasn't what she'd envisioned. Although everything was for show, at times she looked at Luke and remembered the kiss on the hill. She smiled, wondering what it would be like to have a real courtship, but quickly doused the thought. She had to keep to a procedure; without plans she was lost. Maybe she could talk to Luke before he went to bed. She took a step toward the door, then stopped. Suppose he was already undressed? An image of him without his shirt slid into her mind, causing her stomach to tighten into a knot. Hadn't he told her never to come there again? Suppose she went to him and he invited her in? Her heart suddenly beat too loud for her to think clearly. Maybe she'd better think about this a little longer. This was a situation even Janey Willard's etiquette manual would not explain.

Ten

Luke stared from the tree stump to the structure. He should have been further toward completion. Of course he'd revised the plans several times in the past few weeks, adding a new wing to the left side of the house. He'd gone to work with renewed determination since the final baseball game and his talk with Ellen. Work seemed to be the only thing that could keep his mind off Clara. He had fought the way he felt about her, but talking to Ellen had confirmed his suspicion that Antonia Morrison had Clara on trial and the least infraction would have her packing. The baseball games had been a strike against Clara, although she didn't know it. Their false courtship would be another, so Luke had avoided her.

August brought a change in the weather. The ground was harder to dig with the drop in temperature. In a few weeks, snow would blanket the landscape and all construction would stop until spring.

Looking up, Luke spied Miss Emily, but didn't give the matter a second thought. He'd seen her lavishly blossomed hat bobbing as she'd come over the rise in the hill. The red flag was out, and she knew the drill. She'd wait until he gave her the all-clear signal. Two additional trees on the eastward side of the property stood in the way of his planned revision. He'd hated to cut down plants that had weathered more lifetimes than any man on earth, but they were in the way of the new parlor and he needed the space vacated.

The trees had been felled, logged, and boarded into neat stacks which would be used to raise the additional rooms. Today he would dynamite the stumps. He'd already set one charge and the other was almost done. He'd thought he'd experiment and get both stumps in one blast, but the job had taken more time to set up than he'd anticipated. Still, in the long run it would save time.

He glanced at the hill. Miss Emily was closer, and his mouth watered at the thought of the delicious food they would share in a matter of minutes. She'd been having lunch with him since he'd begun this project at the end of last winter. He'd wanted to do it alone, driving every nail, plumbing every plane, carrying every piece of wood, framing every door and window. At the end, it would be the completion of a dream—his father's dream. Waymon Evans had wanted to build a house with his own two hands—one that could match the best houses in the East—and he'd wanted to do it totally alone. He'd died without accomplishing that dream, but he'd passed the desire along to his son.

Although his crew had volunteered to help him, he'd refused their offer, using them to work on paying projects. This, plus the changes in the plans, had delayed his date until he was staring another winter in the face. Finishing the school and Clara's house plus his other jobs for new constructions and repairs had all cut into the time he'd allotted for his own project.

Luke lined up the two stumps. Satisfied with what he saw, he bent down and scraped a match against the side of a stone. Fire ignited as he cupped his hand around the flame, protecting it from the extinguishing breeze. The acrid smell of sulfur filled his nostrils. Cautiously, Luke touched the match to the single wire in front of him. Several feet ahead the wire branched, separating into two thick cords and flowing like black rope in a north-south direction. He was careful with dynamite; it was as dangerous as a coiled rattlesnake. A bright spark flashed as two wires travelling in opposite directions ignited. He knew the speed would increase and in seconds both stumps would fly as high as a trapeze artist before crashing to the ground several feet away from the skeletal building.

Luke waited, crouched on the ground, a safe distance from the impending blast and its devastating invisible thrust. Shielding his eyes, he watched for the explosion. Then he saw *her,* walking toward the two stumps. On the path she treaded, her steps would bring her into the center of the holocaust. What was wrong with her? Didn't she see the red flag?

"Damn fool," Luke cursed, scrambling to his feet. He looked again at the flower-brimmed hat, but it wasn't Miss Emily that he saw. "Clara!" he cried in shocked horror. It was too late to stop the blast. He could get to one maybe, but he'd set two and there was no way he could stop one, then turn and stop the second. His only recourse was to try to reach Clara.

In a flash Luke raced across the clearing as she, unknowingly, walked to her death, waving to him. Luke gritted his teeth. How could she not see the sparks racing across the ground? The bright light rushed as fast as Luke, and he prayed he'd be in time. A wide smile curved Clara's mouth as she moved without a hint of acknowledgment that both of their lives might end in the next second.

"Stop!" Luke shouted. "Go back." But like a woman who always does the opposite of what is expected of her, Clara lifted her face and began to run towards him, closing the distance between life and death at a faster rate than she knew.

Luke continued, his lungs bursting from exertion, pushing on, hoping there was time to reach her before the fire found the two sticks of dynamite he'd shoved into the dug-out tunnels under the stumps.

Luke was ten steps away from Clara when his luck ran out. The eruption lifted him off the ground and sent him flying toward his intended mark. His six-foot-two-inch, one-hundred-eighty-pound body slammed into Clara with the force of a sixty-mile-an-hour hurricane. The blast blew them to the ground, leaving Luke no time to break his fall. Clara took his running weight.

Together they skidded like a sleigh on snow over the green, grassy, rock-strewn ground. The skin was scraped from Luke's knuckles as he held tightly to Clara in an effort to protect her from the jagged rocks. In a mass of arms, legs, and petticoats they rolled over the rough surface. Rocks cut into Luke's naked back, ripping his flesh and scoring him with rivulets of blood. They skidded along, each helpless to stop the invisible hands that dragged them like marionettes. Their forward roll smashed into the red warning flag, snapping the stick that held it and doing little to impede their progress. The rush of wind pushed them onward until their movement was halted by a large boulder placed strategically at the beginning of the path. A place where Miss Emily would have stopped and waited until he'd signaled her everything was safe. A place Clara did not know about.

Dirt and rock rained down on them. Luke instinctively covered Clara and bowed his head, warding off the falling debris. He coughed through the thick cloud of dust enshrouding them. Luke groaned as the boulder knocked the wind from his lungs and dug into his injured back. He didn't think of his hands or the pain in his back. He held Clara close while his breathing calmed and the dust settled. She lay limply against him, not uttering a word. He should be angry with her, but knowing she might be hurt robbed him of ire. There was something so innocent about her—some happiness inside her that she appeared to hide, not wanting anyone to know of its existence. Unconsciously, Luke pulled her closer, burying his hands in her loosened hair, hugging her. She came without resistance. Clara hadn't known about the dynamite. He'd never told her the reason for the flag, and she'd only been at the site once.

Luke leaned her back against his arm, his heart pounding suddenly, seemingly wanting to jump from his chest. Clara was unconscious and bleeding.

Clara heard her name called softly. Someone stroked her forehead. She moved, then was paralyzed by pain rioting in her head. She raised her hand to touch her face, but was stopped by someone she couldn't see, someone who was calling her name. She tried to open her eyes, but the blinding pain forced her eyelids closed. Her eyes felt heavy, as heavy as the pain in her head.

She moaned, trying to move, turn, sit, roll over, anything that would help the aching in her head. Nothing seemed to relieve it. What had happened to her?

"Clara, open your eyes."

Luke! She recognized his voice. It was soft as he spoke her name. She tried to open her eyes. The pain was stabbing, but she finally opened them.

"What happened?" Her hand came up again, but Luke took it.

"There was an explosion."

"My head hurts."

"It probably will hurt for a few days," he told her. "I tried to warn you, but you didn't stop. Then the explosion came and I was thrown into you."

She remembered him running toward her when

suddenly a light had flashed behind him and he'd hit her as hard as a rock. "Am I going to die?" She felt as if the weight of the mountains were pressing down on her.

"No, Clara." He still held one of her hands. He pulled it back to his unclothed chest. Clara felt his heart beating fast. "You have no broken bones," he continued. "You do have some cuts that need attention, and I imagine you'll have bruises in places you won't want anyone to see."

Clara's eyes opened wider, but the effort caused the pain in her head to increase and she immediately closed her lids with a moan. She hurt everywhere. Luke had said she had no broken bones, but every movement she had tried had hurt.

"Where are we?"

"Inside the house."

That must account for the brightness, Clara thought. None of the rooms were enclosed. She felt the sunlight slanting across her.

"Do you think you'll be all right until I get back?"

"Where are you going?" Fright replaced the pain. She gripped his hand with the one he still held. She didn't feel as if she could help herself if he left her alone.

Luke squeezed her hand. "I won't be long. I'm going to get some water to wash away the blood."

"Blood!" This time Clara's hand did reach her head only to come away red and sticky.

"It's not as bad as it looks." Luke stopped her fear from escalating. "You hit your head on a rock, and we skidded across the ground before crashing into a boulder."

"That accounts for the pain in my side."

Luke nodded.

"Am I bleeding anywhere else?" She sat up with Luke's help, her teeth biting into her lower lip.

"No."

He leaned her against two beams and sat back on his heels. For the first time Clara noticed his wounds. He had brush burns and cuts on his shoulders, and Clara thought they must hurt. Yet Luke seemed more concerned about her pain than his own. She knew he often worked without his shirt and guessed that their slide across the ground must have been just as bad or worse for him.

"I'll only be a moment," he told her. "Don't go away." He smiled reassuringly.

Clara tried to return his cheeriness. It was strange how he could make her feel better with such a small gesture. Luke stood and walked away, and Clara gasped when she saw the ripped skin on his back. Flogging couldn't have done his back any more damage.

The pain she felt suddenly didn't seem as bad. She explored her head and arms, finding a gash in her forehand and another at the back of her head. Her legs and arms were covered with raw skin, and her slips and petticoats had soaked up the blood. Still, she thought Luke needed more attention than she did.

As promised, he came back within minutes carrying a bucket of water and the picnic basket.

"I'm afraid lunch is gone, but the towels can be

used." He took one from the basket, wet it, and squeezed the excess water out. Clara watched the ripple of muscle under his torn skin. When he came toward her, she took the towel away.

"Your wounds are worse than mine." With an effort, Clara raised herself to her knees. "Turn around."

Luke sat on the floor and presented his back to her. Clara frowned at the cleaved flesh. Grass and rocks were embedded in the drying blood. "You must be in a lot of pain." Luke's only reaction was a shrug, yet Clara knew his gesture was all show. She found a piece of clean, flat wood and gave it to him.

"Put this between your teeth."

Luke did as he was told. Clara carefully washed the blood down his back. Then she located one of the knives in the picnic basket, cleaned it, and used it to remove the stones and grass from Luke's rented flesh. He sat still, holding in his pain, his only outward display of emotion the tenseness Clara felt in his shoulders.

She didn't see any sign that he needed stitches, but he did need an antiseptic to prevent infection. Clara worked as quickly as she could without causing undue pain. She dipped the towel in and out of the water so often it turned a murky pink.

She finished his back. "Turn around," she said. Luke hesitated only a moment before complying. The expression on his face was masked. "The worst is over," she told him.

His chest was unscathed, but his shoulders had been skinned. Clara used the wet towel to cool the

pain there, although touching his dark skin sent
shivers through her. While she worked on his back
she detached herself from any feelings; but facing
him, she was close enough to feel his breath on
her cheek. Luke's hand came up and brushed one
of her dislodged curls over her shoulder.

Swallowing hard, Clara concentrated on his
shoulders until Luke reached for her hand. Clara
stopped the motion of washing out the wound.
Luke took the wet cloth from her unresisting hand,
and her gaze slowly turned to meet his. Her
breathing stopped at the dark passion she saw in
his eyes. For the space of a lifetime, they stared
at each other.

"Let me clean the blood from your face," Luke
said. "We can't take you back to Miss Emily looking as if you've been in a dynamite blast."

Instead of feeling cold water, Clara felt the heat
of Luke's fingers. The sensations slicing through
her took her breath. Her hands felt lost, out of
place. They wanted to grab hold of his arms. She
felt as if she were going to fall, yet she sat next
to Luke on the uncovered floor. Her heart pounded
as he carefully wiped the cloth across her head.
Then, feeling in her hair, he separated the strands
and dabbed at the mass of blood that caked behind
her head. His fingers were gentle, yet her blood
roared through her system like a runaway train.

Clara couldn't stand it any longer. It felt good
to be close to him. She wanted to be closer. She
slipped her arms around him, forgetting his back.
His cry of pain was like a bucket of cold water

thrown in her face. Her hands snapped back like a door on a strong spring.

"Come on," she told him. "We've got to get you to a doctor."

"Clara, are you all right?" Emily Hale rushed into Doc Pritchard's surgery, the tension in her face adding years to her age.

Clara nodded. The pain in her head had been eliminated by a powder the doctor had given her, and her arms and hands had several bandages on them. "I'm fine, Aunt Emily. Luke got the worst of the explosion."

"What happened?" Antonia Morrison asked, her bulk crowding the room.

"Luke was removing some tree stumps when I arrived. I didn't know about the dynamite signal." Clara looked directly at her aunt. "He saved my life."

Emily Hale took Clara's hand. "Is he going to be all right?" Her voice sounded unusually low and strained.

"The doctor is looking at him now."

The small waiting room filled up quickly as word reached the citizens of the valley that Luke Evans had been hurt. Ellen Turnbull came through the door like a ball of fire. She was out of breath as if she'd run all the way from Butte. She scanned the room in one quick glance and came to Clara.

"How is he?" she asked without a greeting.

Clara took her hands. They were cold. "He'll be fine," she assured the small woman. Ellen seemed to expel all her breath in a single gasp, and Clara helped her to a chair. Again she wondered what had endeared Luke and Ellen to each other. She no longer thought they had been lovers, but they had a relationship that went deeper than most friendships.

When Doc Pritchard opened the door to the waiting room, everyone stood. He found Clara and addressed her. "You did a good job, young lady." He smiled. "Cleaning his wounds and removing the debris probably prevented infection."

"How is he?" Ellen asked, clutching her shawl as if the room were below freezing.

"He'll be fine," the doctor assured them. The room sighed. Aunt Emily's hand went to her breast and even Antonia looked relieved. "He'll need to rest for a few weeks before tackling that house again . . ."

"I'll see to it," Aunt Emily interrupted.

"He won't like that," Antonia told him.

"Like it or not, I had to put stitches in his back and I don't want them broken until I personally cut them out."

"You don't have to worry about that, Randy." Aunt Emily knew everyone in the valley and addressed the doctor as if she'd known him from birth.

"I have a carriage outside," Antonia said. Clara noted that her face had softened. Maybe she wasn't the ogre Clara had been led to believe.

"I think it best if he's kept flat," the doctor told her. "Does anyone have a wagon?"

"I've got my buckboard," a man in the back that

Clara only knew as Aaron spoke. He managed the horses at Hale's Boardinghouse. All eyes turned to him.

"Good," Doc Pritchard said. "He's asleep. I gave him a powder, so I'll need a few of you to get him in the wagon."

The women moved aside to let the men through. When they carried Luke from the doctor's examining room, several of them gasped and tears ran down Ellen's face.

Sunlight slanted across Luke's eyes when he woke. Throwing his arm up, he blocked the offending brightness. Clara was in the room. He could smell the lilac scent she always wore, and knowing she was there made him feel better. She pulled the shade, and he was able to open his eyes, but couldn't see her. She stood in front of him, silhouetted against the window, and her image weaved in and out of focus. Holding his eyes open took most of his strength. He closed them and opened them, each movement taking what seemed to be a lifetime.

His body hurt. Every joint and muscle was filled with pain, and he couldn't remember ever feeling this bad. His throat was dry and parched as if he'd been in the desert, and swallowing didn't help his thirst.

"Here, drink this." He recognized Clara's voice. She was all right. He'd saved her. He tried to speak, but couldn't.

Her arm slid under his head, and she lifted a

cup to his mouth. He swallowed a few drops of water, then she pulled the cup away. He tried to follow it with his head, but the pain stopped him. A moment later, he felt the cup against his mouth again. A few more drops slipped between his lips before his head lolled against her arm and she laid him back against the pillows.

He groaned as he tried to turn over. Breathing hurt his chest and his back felt as if it were held by a tight belt. His arm fell across her legs, and he slid it up to her waist.

"Don't move," Clara cautioned. She pushed his shoulders back into the pillows, preventing him from shifting, her fingers warm on his skin.

He turned his head to look at her. She was a dark blur in a room of indistinct images. Then his eyes focused, but it was painful to keep them open. She had a bandage above her right eye and gauze covered both hands; only her fingers were not shrouded in white. He couldn't tell how far the bandages went up her arms, but her sleeve buttons were undone and the gauze disappeared into the white eyelet blouse. Even with the blemishes to her skin, she was still the most beautiful woman he'd ever seen.

She sat down on the bedside. "The doctor said you weren't to move around. He put stitches in your back," she explained.

My back, he thought, blinking several times. Clara moved in and out of clarity.

"Luke, are you all right?" Clara asked.

He stared at her again. Her voice held concern. When his eyes cleared, his brain seemed to clear, too. He knew why he felt as if he had a restriction on his back.

"How are you?" he asked.

Clara smiled. "I have a slight headache; but other than that, I'm fine."

"You must be bruised." He indicated her hands. Clara nodded.

"You shouldn't be wearing that corset."

"Luke!" Clara's eyes grew to the size of apples.

"Blame it on my state of pain," he told her. "A moment ago, I had my arm around your waist. I felt it. I understand your pain and you shouldn't have that thing on. It's got to hurt."

"Only a little," she admitted, but Luke knew she was lying.

"When you leave, take it off." Clara nodded. She looked embarrassed at the discussion of underwear. Luke decided to change the subject. "Sorry about the dynamite."

Clara clutched his hand in hers. He felt the pressure she exerted on it. "I'll know better next time."

Luke lifted his arm and caressed her face. She didn't push him away. Her hand came up to cover his, and she smiled at him.

"You caused a lot of people concern," she told him. "Aunt Emily sat up with you most of the night. We had to force Ellen to go home, and even Antonia Morrison wouldn't leave until after midnight."

"What about you?"

His heart slammed into his chest. He hadn't meant to ask that, but it had slipped out. The hand that held his tensed and slipped free of its hold on

him. She looked down. When her gaze came back
to him, fear darkened her eyes. Luke had seen it
before: It crept up on her whenever she started to
let herself go, to show how she really felt. Luke
wondered who could make her feel like that and
why.

"I've never been so scared in my life." Anguish
showed in her voice. Tears sprang to her eyes.

"Please don't cry," Luke said, taking hold of her
hand.

Clara blinked several times, then her tears
stopped. "I didn't think I could get you to the
wagon. You collapsed just before we reached it."

Luke remembered walking toward the wagon.
The day had suddenly gone grey and threatened
to become night. Then he'd been falling, clutching
for something to hold onto. He'd found Clara and
grabbed her just before everything went black.
When he'd opened his eyes, Doc Pritchard had
been looking down at him.

"I'm sorry," he apologized.

"I'm the one who should be sorry. You saved
my life," Clara told him. "If it hadn't been for
you, I'd have walked into the center of the explosion. And you were the one who got hurt." A tear
rolled down Clara's face. "Oh, Luke, I'm so sorry.
I promise I won't—"

"It's all right. It's all right," he told her, hoping
it would stop her tears. Her pain sliced through him
like a hot knife. "We're both going to be fine." He
squeezed her hand. "I'll be up in no time."

"Oh, no! The doctor said you needed to rest for
a couple of weeks."

The way he felt right now, Luke wouldn't argue about staying put. Although the pain in his head had eased and his vision cleared, he still felt lethargic. Lying around for a couple of weeks seemed like heaven—especially if he could have Clara as his nurse. She looked tired, though, he observed. She probably needed rest, too.

"What did Doc say about you? Your bruises?"

"He said I'd be stiff, my head would ache worse than I ever thought it could, and I'd have bruises everywhere. I don't think I'll ever be able to sit down again without several pillows under me."

Luke smiled at her comment. She'd delivered it in whispered tones. For Clara, talking about her body was like pulling up her skirt and showing him her legs. How her ears would burn if she knew he'd checked her cuts before she'd regained consciousness. He knew how long and shapely her legs were, how her breasts felt crushed against him, how soft her hair was, and how he longed to taste her mouth again. He couldn't believe that now, in his weakened condition, he was thinking of kissing Clara.

Luke tightened his grip on Clara's delicate hand and eased her forward. She stared innocently at him. How he loved that.

"Luke, you're awake." A smile beamed on Martha's face. He immediately released Clara, and both of them turned toward the voice. Martha came through the open doorway holding a silver tray. "Miss Emily sent me to relieve Clara. She gave us all a good scare last night, too."

Luke flashed a glance at Clara. "You said you were all right."

"I am. I'm just a little tired and I have a headache. You told me I was going to have a headache," she reminded him.

"I brought you some tea." Martha addressed Clara. "Miss Emily says you're to go back to bed."

"And no one argues with Miss Emily," Luke joked.

"Are you going to sit with Luke?"

"I don't need a sitter," Luke was quick to point out.

"Mrs. Turnbull just came back. She's waiting for Miss Emily to finish Luke's tray, then she'll be up." Martha looked at Clara. "I'll take this to your room and turn down your bed. Then I'll come back to help you."

She left them. Clara tried to rise, but Luke's hand reached for her arm, proving he had more strength than she thought. She stopped. Clara's eyes traveled from his hand to his face, her gaze locking with his. Her stare held him, making his heart hammer and cutting off his breath; he was helpless to break the contact. The pressure he exerted on her arm pulled her forward.

"Luke," she whispered, "I'll lose my balance."

"Good," he said, aware that if she hadn't been hurt and hadn't been wearing that damn corset she could easily have risen. As it was, he had her at his mercy.

Clara glanced toward the door. No one was there. "Someone might see us." She fought him. He knew she was afraid, and he should have taken that into consideration; but his emotions were flying and he wanted, *had,* to kiss Clara now.

"Only Ellen," he said, dismissing her concern.

She lost her balance, her free hand pushing into the pillow next to his head. He released her arm to thread his fingers into her hair. She had a lump the size of a goose egg on the back of her head, and she winced when he touched it.

Being careful not to hurt her, he edged her closer until her mouth touched his. He'd meant to be gentle, probing, wooing, but something inside him raced the moment his lips found hers. In seconds he'd dug his tongue into her mouth and fought for all the pleasure she had to give. Clara released her hold on the pillow and hugged her arm around his head. He circled her waist and pulled her onto the coverlet until she lay across him. Her weight felt good, and he wanted more; the cover between them impeded his effort to feel her soft curves against his. He lifted her head for a moment to gaze into her eyes. They were heavy-lidded and dark with need. *God! He wanted her.* He took her mouth again. This time the fervor between them was like an open flame. Neither of them was concerned about their injuries; neither of them was aware of their injuries. They were only aware of each other—the feel, taste, and touch of man and woman. Unwilling to let go, Luke held Clara, his mouth fused to hers, his hand skittering down her back and up again in a frenzied effort.

Luke wanted her and he wanted her *now.* Forgetting everything except his need for her, he

kicked the covers back and tried to turn over. The
action abruptly ended the kiss as pain gripped him
and tore his mouth from hers with a gravelly
groan. They held onto each other, his ragged
breath mingling with her strained efforts to control
hers.

"I told you if you ever came to my room again
I wouldn't be responsible for what happened." He
pulled her forward, his mouth only a breath away
from hers, when a startled sound erupted from the
doorway. Antonia Morrison, her hands planted on
her ample hips, a scowl marring her pudgy face,
stared at them.

Eleven

Ellen could tell something had gone wrong by the way Antonia descended the stairs. Her heavy bulk, which usually swayed from side to side like a Baptist choir marching up the center aisle of a church, took the stairs as if the weight of the world was carried on her shoulders.

Emily Hale saw her friend and sat down as if she were bracing herself for bad news. Ellen sat with her. Both women stared as Antonia made her way to the bottom of the steps.

"I don't know what happened, Ellen," Emily whispered, "but I think I'm going to need your help."

"What can I do?" the redhead covered her mouth in case Antonia looked up from her single-minded purpose. "She doesn't like me."

Antonia stomped into the room, her chest heaving up and down.

"She's got to leave, Emily Hale," she announced, winded. "I won't have another thing to do with your niece."

Emily took a deep breath. Ellen sat still, wondering what Antonia perceived Clara guilty of.

"Calm down, Antonia." Emily got up. "Take a chair and let me get you some tea."

"I don't want any tea. I want that *harlot* out of the valley."

"Mrs. Morrison," Ellen said, her voice calm. "What happened?"

"They were in bed together. I found them."

Ellen and Emily exchanged glances.

"Whom are you talking about?"

"Luke and Clara, kissing and carrying on. Why if I hadn't come along, they would have . . ." She stopped, exasperated. "She has got to go. She's not fit to teach children. I told you, Emily—"

"Sit down, Antonia." There was no doubt of the command in Emily's voice when she interrupted her angry friend. Antonia took a chair across from Ellen. Her face was as closed as her mind. If Clara were to survive Antonia's accusation of misconduct, Emily would have to reason with her, but Ellen didn't know how she was going to do that. Antonia and Emily rarely butted heads, but since the board had decided to hire a teacher and the applications had come in, neither woman had agreed on the candidates. Clara, unfortunately, stood in the middle of these two strong-minded women.

"Ellen, would you excuse us?" Miss Emily asked. Ellen stared at her for a moment. She had asked her to stay. Did she really want her to leave? "Why don't you get Luke's tray?" the older woman urged. "It must be ready by now."

Ellen left the dining room without a word, closing the door behind her. She didn't envy Miss

Emily. When Mrs. Morrison went on the warpath, everyone in her line of fire moved aside to make room for the raging tide. Ellen hefted the tray from the kitchen and, skirting the back staircase, took the left wing which led to the top floor, stopping first at Clara's room.

"How is she?" she asked Martha.

"I'm fine," came a teary reply.

"I'll have her drink her tea and go to sleep," Martha said.

Ellen nodded, knowing there was a mild sleeping potion in the tea. Clara would rest and that was best for her at the moment. Balancing the silver tray on her hand, she knocked on Luke's open door. He turned his head as she advanced into the room.

"I don't suppose you're hungry?"

Luke pushed himself up in the bed. Ellen set the tray down and helped him. She wasn't used to seeing him in pain, and it tugged at her heart.

"Is she crying?" he asked when he'd settled comfortably against the huge headboard.

"Yes," Ellen told him. She poured a cup of tea, added sugar, and handed it to him. "What happened?" she asked, taking the chair next to his bed.

"I kissed her."

"According to Antonia you did more than that. She's downstairs now demanding Clara be rail-roaded out of town."

"Ellen, you can't let her do that," Luke jerked forward in the bed. "Clara didn't do anything wrong. It was all my fault."

"Don't get upset. Emily Hale is going round for round with her."

"I certainly hope she wins." Luke slumped back against his pillows.

Ellen stared at him for a long time. There had been desperation in his voice. What did Luke really feel for Clara? He wasn't the kind of man to love 'em and leave 'em. When he'd met Peg, they'd fallen in love immediately, and in their few years of marriage he hadn't looked at another woman. Then Peg was gone and she appeared to have taken Luke's heart with her. Until Clara had come to the valley, Luke had resisted all other women, even though Miss Emily had thrown them at him like hot biscuits.

She thought of the woman downstairs. Why was Antonia so against Clara? She'd been hell-bent to have her replaced since the moment the committee had approved her acceptance.

Antonia had grandchildren, but they lived in Wyoming and attended school there. Everyone in the valley seemed to have embraced Clara, especially after she had proved such a likable person— and the children loved her. Yet Antonia had remained distant and opposed to anything the young woman did.

"Ellen?" Luke called her.

"Luke, why do you suppose Antonia is so against Clara teaching in the valley?"

"Antonia is against everything."

Ellen nodded. "But with Clara she seems on an absolute crusade."

Luke gave her his undivided attention. "What are you getting at?"

"I don't know. The valley is different from Butte, the people more closely aligned to each other. Clara has won over most of the families in town. Even the baseball games helped win her acceptance among the townspeople; but Antonia is so set against her, it seems there has to be some secret she knows that no one else does."

"If she does, I have no idea what it is. She was so upset when she found us, she could hardly talk."

"Antonia has seen people kissing before. You're both over twenty-one and unmarried. Why would that upset her?"

"Clara is the schoolteacher, and her reputation needs to be spotless. I'm afraid I've tarnished her in front of the worst person in town. If it hadn't been for the pain in my back, Ellen, Antonia would have really gotten an eyeful."

"Well, you *can* take the sting out of Antonia's words."

Luke didn't ask how, but Ellen could see the question in his eyes. He had been fighting his feelings so long, it had become second nature with him. Since Peg's death, every woman who'd showed an interest in him came up against the promise he'd made his dying wife. Luke would politely excuse himself from any further association, no Sunday teas or afternoon carriage rides. Clara, however, had gotten under his skin, even if he wouldn't admit it to himself. With her, he was doing the pursuing. It had been so long, Luke probably didn't recognize the symptoms. He was in love with Clara and he didn't know it.

Ellen took her time pouring herself a cup of tea. She passed on the sugar and squeezed a lemon wedge into the hot liquid. Taking a sip, she waited for Luke to voice the solution to his and Clara's dilemma. As stalwart as a mule, he remained silent, staring at her. Lowering her cup, Ellen leaned forward and answered the question Luke refused to ask.

"Marry her," she said.

Emily Hale circled the dining room. For the past several minutes, Antonia had spewed vile comments about what she had seen when she'd gone to check on Luke. Emily let her rant. She seemed to be calming down, which could have been due to the powder Emily had slipped into her tea—not as much as she'd given Clara and Luke, who needed rest, but enough to make her relax and listen to reason.

Emily knew she could suggest any number of reasons why Clara appeared to be in Luke's bed kissing him, but secretly she was glad to hear Luke's crusted shell had been penetrated. Somehow she had to convince Antonia that both of them were fully clothed and it was only a kiss.

"Have you finished?" Emily asked, taking a seat across from her.

"I want to know what you plan to do about her or if I should let the committee know what I saw?"

"Antonia, school begins in less than a month." Emily paused, checking Antonia's reaction. "If

Clara doesn't retain her post, we'll have no one to teach the children. We have agreed the only way children have a chance in this world is if they have a decent education."

"I know that is necessary, Emily. I just don't think your niece is the woman for the job."

"We're not going to discuss her qualifications again. You know she's qualified, and you've seen how the children react to her. From our own experience, we both know how much that can motivate a child."

"Emily, what kind of example can she set?" Antonia slapped the table with the heel of her hand. The centerpiece, a fine crystal bowl of flowers, danced precariously before resettling on its base. "We don't know when she and Luke—"

"Antonia, they were only kissing. You act as if you'd never seen two people kiss before. And Luke and Clara aren't adolescents."

Antonia's eyes widened, her eyebrows nearly reaching her hairline. "Emily, it was more than kissing."

Emily was determined to squelch this line of discussion. Having known Antonia for forty years, Emily was aware her mind would embellish what she'd seen until it bore no real resemblance to the truth. When Antonia went on a crusade, nothing veered her off course.

"I'm not going to defend what they were doing; I didn't see them. But there is something I did see." Emily stopped. She hoped Antonia would remember and relent.

"What was that?"

"Antonia, isn't it about time you went to visit your friend in Colorado?" Emily's abrupt change of subject was a ploy not lost on her friend. Antonia sat up straighter and stared directly in her face.

"Emily Hale," she said in a voice low and cautious. "I haven't been to Colorado in nearly forty years, and you know it."

"Yes, I do," Emily admitted. "I remember a very young woman who went to visit her relatives in Colorado and fell madly in love with a ranch hand named—"

"Don't say it," Antonia stopped her. "Please don't remind me."

Emily watched her friend's eyes. Hurt replaced the fire that had been there.

"I only suggest that people make mistakes," Emily said quietly.

"Emily, you know I wasn't aware he was married."

"Of course, I know that." Emily softened her voice. "When you found out, did it make a difference?"

"I loved him."

"I know you did. And he told you he loved you. You believed him, because you wanted to believe him."

"I never thought you'd throw this in my face." Antonia's eyes filled with unshed tears. Her chin quivered, but she fought the inclination to succumb to tears. "I thought you were my friend."

"I am your friend, Antonia. After Colorado, you

made morality your cross and you want everyone to bear it."

"You mean all these years—"

Emily nodded. "All these years I've stood by you, knowing what a hardship it was for you to finally realize the man you loved didn't really love you."

"I didn't really love him either."

Emily knew she was lying. If Johnny Rainsford walked through the door today, Antonia would react the same as she'd done at twenty. "Well you certainly put on a good show."

The two women stared at each other until the beginnings of a grin creased their lips. It burst into a full smile and then into hearty laughter. When they finished, both were dabbing their eyes with the corners of linen napkins.

"Leave them be, Antonia," Emily stated, thinking of Luke and Clara. Luke needed a wife and Clara was perfect for him.

"You can't mean you approve of her being in his bed?"

"I'm not saying I approve. I will reserve my opinion until I've had time to talk to the two of them. But if she was there voluntarily, it may just be that they are attracted to each other." Emily paused, remembering her own past. "We both know what it's like to be in love."

Antonia didn't say a word. After her fiasco with Johnny Rainsford and the scandal it had created in Colorado, she had never visited again.

The worst possible outcome: she had carried Johnny's child away with her. And from that day, she'd spent her life repenting for her sin: falling in love.

Antonia looked defeated. Emily hadn't meant that. In fact, she was angry with both Clara and Luke. She wanted them together, but she also wanted them to follow the rules of propriety, especially under her roof.

"Antonia," she suggested. "Why don't we go into Butte? I could use a new hat, and we haven't been shopping in a long time."

"What about Luke and Clara?"

"They're probably asleep in their own beds." She lifted her teacup and drank. "I put a powder in their tea."

Antonia smiled.

"Ellen will be here for a while, and Martha is taking care of Clara. They won't let anything happen."

"I think a new hat is just what I need."

Twelve

Five days! Clara thought, throwing back the quilts and climbing out of the huge bed. She had been cooped up in her room too long, and she wouldn't stand for it another minute. Dressing herself, she walked into the dining room and poured a cup of coffee before taking a chair at the highly polished table concealed under a lace ecru tablecloth. Surprise showed on Aunt Emily's face, but she didn't order her back to bed as she'd done Luke when he'd tried a similar tactic the day after the Antonia Incident. Mrs. Andersson and Mrs. Hauserhoffer sat at the table.

Clara's side didn't hurt anymore, but her bruises looked worse today than they had the day after the explosion. Ugly purplish blemishes marred her dark skin. The only good thing about them was they no longer hurt. Although she wasn't ready to sit a horse yet, she did feel better. Lifting her cup, she wondered how Luke was feeling. She hadn't seen him since she had turned and found Mrs. Morrison's disapproving countenance in the doorway. Clara had pushed herself free of Luke's hold and run after the retreating woman, but Antonia had refused to listen to her shouts of explanation. She'd rushed down the stairs to tell her aunt. Clara knew she'd have to leave now. For a kiss her world had collapsed. She'd be forced to return to Virginia and to Wade, if he'd have her.

Then Luke had appeared at her side, weaving and threatening to fall. Martha had run to the two of them, helped him back to bed, and insisted that Clara return to her room.

Clara was ashamed of how Antonia had found them, ashamed she'd let Luke kiss her, ashamed that she'd wanted him to. He must have felt the same, since he hadn't tried to see her in the five days of their forced hospitalization. Somehow Aunt Emily had smoothed Antonia's feathers. The woman had returned, apologizing and helping her to stop the flow of tears that threatened to completely soak her feather pillow.

Aunt Emily hadn't come until nightfall. She'd asked her to explain. With puffy eyes, Clara had told her most of the truth, how she'd lost her balance when Luke pulled her forward, how she hadn't intended to kiss him—it had just happened. Although she had promised her aunt it would never happen again, she had admitted to herself that whenever she was in Luke's presence she wanted to be in his arms.

The older woman had listened without judgment, but asked her to remember her reputation. Clara had agreed, knowing that what she did reflected on her aunt.

"You look a lot better," Mrs. Andersson said with a smile. "How's your head?"

Clara forced herself not to touch the patch of puffed skin on her forehead. She'd tried to comb her hair over it. "Better," she told the blonde woman. "Although I don't think I'll be doing any riding for a few days."

Mrs. Andersson laughed. "You take it easy. After an accident with an explosive, your insides might need a little repairing."

"I'll be careful," Clara said.

Aunt Emily set a plate of hot cakes in front of her, and Clara reached for the syrup. It was strange to have someone wait on her. For years she had been up at daybreak, fixing food and preparing meals for the farmhands. Now she only needed to step into the dining room and someone served her.

"Clara, you must be looking forward to school's beginning soon," Mrs. Hauserhoffer addressed her.

"I am." Clara took a bite of her hot cakes. She needed something to keep her mind off Luke. School, teaching, the children; it should be enough to fill her days. In the evening, she'd have papers to correct and choir practice. Soon it would be too cold for the children to play baseball any longer. "I thought I'd go over to the school this morning."

"No, you won't," Aunt Emily contradicted her. "Your first day out of bed, you'll not go out in the cold."

"Aunt Emily, I'm not a baby. Most of my problem was bruises. I didn't need to stay in bed, and the exercise will be good for me."

"I don't think you should go out so soon."

"Why not?" Clara had to have a good reason. Going back to her room, with Luke next door, wasn't something she wanted to do. She needed to be away from him because she really wanted to go into his room again and he'd told her not to come.

"You've had a bad turn. You need to rest more, heal."

"I've healed all I'm going to. Now I need sunshine and work. There is plenty I still need to do to prepare for the first day." She'd been to the two-room building three times. She looked forward to beginning teaching. Whenever she thought of it, she smiled.

"All right, but Martha will go with you." Aunt Emily gave in.

"She's right," Mrs. Andersson said. "You shouldn't go out alone after an extended rest. You'll tire easily."

Clara knew she was outnumbered. Although Mrs. Hauserhoffer had two other children and was pregnant with her third, all three women seemed to be in a mothering mood.

"Fine, I've missed Martha." Clara told the truth. Martha had spent many hours with her, but she missed their morning rides and their evenings at the church. "Where is she?"

"Where she always is," Aunt Emily said. "Out riding Starfire. The Indians believe people can become the animals they love. If that is true, I swear that child is going to turn into a horse."

Clara finished her breakfast and got a jacket. She thought she'd walk to the stables and see if she could find Martha. It was cold outside. She found it hard to believe the temperature could have dropped so much in the one week she'd spent in bed. At the stables Zeke told her Martha had been gone about an hour.

"She should be back soon," he said, then flatly refused to saddle a horse for her to ride out and find the young girl. "Miss Emily's orders," he told her.

Arguing would have been futile, so Clara made her way back to the house. Before reaching the kitchen door, she looked up. Luke stood in the window. They stared at each other for an eternity before he put his hand up to the windowpane, touching it as if he were touching her. Her hand came up to her cheek, and Luke walked away.

Hypnotized, Clara remained in place. When, finally, she walked around to the front of the boardinghouse, she found Doc Pritchard's carriage at the street. She went quickly inside.

"I don't know how much longer I can keep him in that room," Aunt Emily was telling the doctor. "It's like having a caged lion in the house."

"I'm removing the stitches this morning. I'll talk to him, Emily."

He smiled at her, nodding slightly, and disappeared up the center staircase. Clara went into the parlor and sat at the piano where she often found Martha. Clara liked Doc Pritchard: His manner was soothing, and he spoke quietly and made her feel as if everything would be all right.

She ran her hands lightly over the keys, and sound tinkled in the room, reminding her of Annie Pearl. Thinking about Annie Pearl made her wonder about Wade and the children. How were they?

The fields would be bursting with color now. In a few weeks the harvest would begin. From then on, no one would have time for anything. Then the winter would set in and planning for spring would start. Farming was a hard way of life; but for some, it was the only way to survive. Wade was one of those people.

He didn't ask much from life. A tear caught in her eye. When she compared Wade to the few men she'd ever known—her father, Luke, Annie Pearl's brother, Ian—Luke was a giant. Her heart ached at what she'd done to him.

And the children! What must they think of her? Did the girls even remember who she was? And the twins, they'd be eleven now.

"Clara!" Martha's voice called her back from her reverie, and she wiped the tears from her eyes. "You're up." Martha had been a constant companion during her resting period; now she ran forward to hug her, then quickly stepped back. "I didn't hurt you?" she asked tentatively.

"No." Clara grinned. "I feel great."

"What about Luke? I saw Doc Pritchard's carriage."

"He's with him now, removing the stitches." Clara didn't want to talk about Luke. Her face got hot every time someone mentioned him. "How was your ride?" she asked instead.

"Fine." Clara watched the girl transform again into the animated creature she had grown to love. "I love this time of year. The air is crisp and wild, like a frisky horse. It bites your face, grabs your hair, and makes your eyes tear." She wiped at the moisture gathering in the corners of her eyes.

"That sounds romantic. I'll be glad when I can go riding again. Being forced to stay in bed is something I'm not used to."

"School will be starting soon."

"Yes, I'm going there this morning."

Martha frowned, her glance darting toward the door.

"Aunt Emily has given her permission." She paused. "As long as you go with me." Suddenly it occurred to Clara that Martha would make a wonderful assistant and she wondered if the committee would hire her. She'd ask Aunt Emily about it.

"I didn't know you could play," Martha said.

Clara laughed. "After hearing you, what I do can't be called playing."

Martha sat down next to her. "Here, let's play something together." Martha ran an arpeggio up the keyboard, then launched into *The Last Rose of Summer.* "Do you know this?"

"Not well enough to play."

Martha sorted through the stack of music on top of the upright piano. Finding what she wanted, she spread the sheets across the stand.

Clara studied it. It had been too many years. She couldn't read music anymore. "I can't play that," she said. "And besides, this isn't a duet."

"Just play the left hand," Martha instructed. "Like this." Reaching across Clara, she demonstrated a repetitive sequence of three notes that changed every fourth measure, then returned to the same keys. At Martha's prodding, Clara tried it. Her fingers stumbled at first when the sequence changed; but after a few tries and watching Martha point to the notes on the music sheet, she got it. "I'll play the introduction, you come in here."

Clara took a deep breath and nodded. Martha's fingers skated over the black-and-whites without hesitation. Clara counted silently and came in on time. She continued keeping time as Martha played on. Halfway through the first stanza, Clara smiled, liking the sound, liking how Martha modified it for two people. While Clara couldn't read the music as well as she could when she was fifteen, she knew that what Martha was playing wasn't on the pages in front of them.

When they finished, both women stared at each other, then burst into laughter. "That was good," Martha complimented. "Let's do another."

"I think I'd better quit while I'm ahead."

Clara moved her hands from the keys, but Martha continued, her hands at one with the piano. Clara stared at her fingers, recognizing the song she was playing, but not really being able to place it. She finished one and went into another. Several measures later, Clara's face grew hot with embarrassment. Martha was playing *Roll Me Over In the Clover.* She had so cleverly disguised it, even Aunt Emily wouldn't recognize the bawdy saloon song.

"Where did you learn that?" Clara whispered, sneaking a glance at the archway which separated the parlor from the central hallway.

"Mrs. Turnbull," she whispered back.

"What's this one?" Clara asked when Martha went into another melody.

"Empty Bed Blues." The deep voice behind them snapped their heads around as if they'd been caught doing something wrong. Doc Pritchard stood in the doorway.

"I—" Martha stammered.

He came toward them, setting his black bag on the sofa. "I wouldn't play too many of those," he told her. "Emily will certainly recognize them sooner or later."

Conspiratorially, they all laughed.

"How are you doing, Clara?" he asked in his best doctor manner.

"I feel much better," she told him.

"Your bruises?"

"They look worse." She raised the hair off her forehead to show him. "But they don't hurt anymore."

"Good. Just take it easy for a few days."

"How's Luke?" Clara asked.

"As stubborn as a bull." For a moment his face was serious, then it softened into a mischievous grin. "I told him he could spend a few hours a day downstairs, but he still needs rest. In another week, he should be able to resume work, but slowly."

"Do you think he'll do it?" Clara asked. Luke was a virile man. She knew that firsthand. Keeping him indoors was like caging a mountain lion. She'd heard him prowling his room late at night.

"If I know Emily Hale, she'll find a way."

"Find a way to do what?"

Luke stood in the place where Doc Pritchard had been when he found them.

"Luke!" Martha called.

Clara's heart flopped. His face was clean shaven, water still glistened in the short hair at his temples. His eyes bore into hers as if she were the only person in the room.

"Good morning," he said, walking toward the small group at the piano. Clara had the feeling he was concentrating on proving he could walk without limping or bending over since Doc Pritchard had just removed the stitches. Clara knew from experience that he could still be in pain from flesh not completely healed.

"One hour, Luke," Doc Pritchard warned. "Or I'm instructing Emily to tie you to the bed."

Martha laughed, and Clara knew she was imagining Luke tied to his bed. Clara's imagination went a step further and had her there with him. Her mouth suddenly went dry.

"And you know she'll do it," the doctor told him. "Now I'm going to talk to her. Good day, Clara . . . Martha."

With a smile, he retrieved his bag and went toward the dining room. The room was quiet when he left. Luke didn't say anything, and Clara stared at her hands, afraid to let Luke see her feelings.

"Luke." Martha stood up. "Miss Emily made apple fritters. Would you like some?"

"I'd love some," he told her. "And coffee." Martha darted out of the room, and Luke stared at Clara. She couldn't hold his gaze. "You didn't come back after Mrs. Morrison saw us," he said.

She winced. She'd been too ashamed. "You told me not to come to your room." She had tried to be flippant, but it didn't come off.

"What happened with her?"

"I'm not sure. Aunt Emily mentioned something about her going to visit her daughter in Wyoming." Her aunt hadn't told her why Mrs. Morrison felt it time to go away, but Clara felt there was more to the story than she'd ever know.

"I missed you, Clara," Luke said quietly.

Clara's breath caught in her throat. She'd missed him, too. She hadn't known it could hurt just to look at a person, but not seeing Luke had been as painful as sitting across the room and not being able to go to him. Right now, Clara questioned her decision to come to Montana. If she'd stayed in Virginia, she wouldn't have met him. Everything would be simpler, not this awful tightening around her heart every time she saw him and not this constant need that pooled in her stomach and made her thoughts anything but pure.

"Clara?"

Her head came up.

"Didn't you miss me?"

Oh God, Clara thought. How she had missed him! Then a worse thought struck her.

She was in love with him.

By the time Martha reined in the horses and helped Clara down from the wagon, Clara was tired. The school was painted white with a red door, and a cupola on the top reminded her of the one on Founders Library at Howard University. Howard stood adjacent to the Teachers College of the District of Columbia and had been a goal to strive for when she'd walked up the hill to her classes.

"Why don't we check the house?" Clara suggested, and Martha followed her as they passed the schoolhouse and went toward the three-bedroom residence building that came with it. From what Luke had told her, Clara knew the committee had had a man with a large family in mind when they'd planned the house. Clara's boots echoed on the bare floors.

"This is going to be wonderful." Martha spun around in the empty room that would be her parlor. "I'd give anything to have my own house."

Clara suddenly found the prospect of living alone frightening. She'd only lived alone for a few days after her parents' death. Then she'd gone to Wade's. In all her years, this would be the first time she'd be completely by herself. Shivering at the thought, she entered the small room next to the parlor. This she could set up as an office where she would correct papers and prepare tests. She considered placing a desk near the window.

"My father used to have an office like this," she said aloud, not really meaning to.

"What did he do?" Martha asked.

Clara turned back to her. "He was a doctor." She smiled. "When I was small, I used to hide under his desk." A giggle escaped her as if she were a child again. "He'd come in and sit down, and his feet would bump into me. Then he'd get

down on his knees and say, 'Is this my little girl,
my beautiful little girl?' And he'd pull me out and
set me on his knee, and I'd stay there until I fell
asleep."

Martha's footsteps on the polished wood pulled
Clara's attention back to the present. Turning, she
saw Martha at a near-run as she went through the
door.

"Martha," she called. The young girl kept going.
Clara ran after her. "Martha, what's wrong?"

She caught up with her as she reached the
wagon. The young girl grasped the sideboard so
tightly Clara thought she'd get splinters in her fingers.

"What did I say?" Clara asked.

"Nothing." Martha shook her head, but kept her
face averted from Clara. "It's not you. It's just that
I miss him so much . . ." Her voice cracked, and
she broke down in tears.

Clara took her shaking shoulders and hugged
her. "I understand how you feel, Martha."

The young girl seemed to pull herself together
and pushed away from Clara.

"I lost both my parents in the same accident. I
miss them still," Clara explained, understanding
what Martha felt.

"I don't remember my mother, but my dad . . .
my dad—" Martha paused, swallowing hard. "He
was always there. The day of the accident, I had
just finished my lesson with Mrs. Turnbull. The
sound of the explosion rocked the windows; plates
crashed to the floor, and Mrs. Turnbull's clown col-
lection was smashed to bits. I knew he was dead,

even before I got to the mine. He was on the seventh level. There's lots of gas down there. He'd told me about it, saying smoking wasn't allowed and that an unexpected spark could start a fire. It wasn't the explosion that killed him, but the gas."

"Martha, maybe you shouldn't remember this."

Martha ignored her. Clara wasn't sure she'd even heard her. The young girl had a faraway look in her eye, as if she were reliving each awful moment.

"They brought his body up after three days. His face had turned black and old. Doc Pritchard said he must have been leaning against one of the mine walls when he died. His body was stiff, like a wooden carving. His arms bent at his sides as if they were resting on a chair."

"Martha, stop!"

She faced Clara. Her face was devoid of all feeling as if the story she told had happened to someone else. Martha had insulated herself inside a cocoon where the hurt couldn't get to her, but it wasn't the right thing to do. Clara knew that firsthand because she'd done it, had held her pain in for years until she'd met Annie Pearl and finally been able to voice her feelings. They had rained out one day in a steady flow of words Clara had been unable to stop, and it was then the healing began. Maybe today was Martha's day for healing.

"After that, I had nowhere to go. Everything we owned belonged to the mine. After the funeral, they barged in, breaking everything, throwing things around that were precious to me. Mrs. Turnbull came and made them leave. She took me away and had her husband get everything I wanted out of the house that afternoon. I never went back."

"Since then you've been at Aunt Emily's?"

Martha nodded.

"What about school?" Clara glanced at the building behind them.

"After my dad died, I helped Miss Emily."

"Didn't you want to go on, learn a skill?"

"I wanted to teach music, like Mrs. Turnbull. I wanted nothing more than to spend my whole day playing tunes as if no one has ever done it before."

Animation was returning to her face. This was the Martha Clara knew. "What about a music college?"

"I can't go to college."

"Why not?"

"It costs a lot of money. And around here, Indians and Negroes don't go to college."

Being here had made Clara forget the prejudices. Everyone lived and worked so well together. Ellen was her friend, and Mrs. Andersson lived at her aunt's boardinghouse. Going to college didn't seem so farfetched. Then Clara's idea came back to her. "Martha, suppose you had a job?"

"Doing what? No one would hire me."

"I would."

"You?"

"Yes." Clara felt the excitement flowing through her. "I haven't approached the committee yet, but I'm sure I'll have Aunt Emily's approval." Clara knew how her aunt felt about Martha, even if Martha didn't. "I want to ask them if they will hire you as my assistant. With so many children in the class, I could use the help. And since you play the piano, we can teach them songs and lessons."

"Do you think they'll do it?" Martha's eyes lit up like Christmas candles. "Oh, Clara, a job! I could actually do something more than be a maid."

Aunt Emily didn't treat Martha as a maid, but that must have been how the young girl saw her future. Clara's heart went out to her. Martha reminded her so much of the person she had been— the girl who had grasped at a future better than the one she'd thought had been designed for her.

"Clara, I'll have my own money," she told her on a whispered note as if all the breath in her body were expelled on the realization. Clara only smiled.

"Why don't we go into the school and see what you can do."

Thirteen

Her first day out had been exhilarating, but tiring. Clara was looking forward to a long nap when Martha stopped the wagon in front of the boardinghouse.

Luke was no longer in the parlor when she passed it. She hadn't expected him to still be there, but it was her last memory of him. Maybe he was back in his room.

"Clara."

She whirled around, standing erect on the bottom step. Aunt Emily came from the kitchen.

"You got a letter." The old woman held the envelope toward her.

Clara recognized Annie Pearl's handwriting. Her heart lightened at the thrill of having her friend answer.

"Thank you," she said, taking the letter.

Aunt Emily smiled her understanding. "Go on to your room. There's a surprise there, too."

Clara almost ran up the stairs. Three trunks, taking up almost all of the available floor space, sat haphazardly about her bed. "Oh, Annie Pearl, thank you," she said to the sunny room. With An-

nie Pearl and her brother, she had sneaked her
mother's trunks out of Wade's storage shed.

Pushing the door shut, but forgetting it didn't
close unless she lifted up on it, she tore open the
letter.

August 5, 1899

Dear Clara,

*Thank God you wrote. Forgive the absence
of a preamble regarding the state of your
health, because what I have to say is of great
importance. Clara, you have to write Wade.*

*When you didn't come home, he went to the
school. They sent him to me because they knew
we were friends. He's beside himself with worry
over you. Clara, I've never seen a man cry, but
I actually thought he was going to break down
in my parents' living room.*

*I didn't tell him where you were, but my heart
felt so heavy withholding the knowledge. If he
comes back, I don't know if I can prevent myself
from speaking the truth. James says it isn't
right. We should never have planned such a
childish prank. I know we didn't say it was a
prank; but after speaking to Wade, I felt like a
thief stealing something that was his. I know
when you left it was your intention to remain
in Montana; it is only right to let him know that
you're all right and that you will not return. He
needs to understand your feelings as I understand them. Clara, he seems a fair and reason-
able man and, knowing that you want change
in your life, I can't see him standing in your*

way. Put yourself in his place. Think how you would feel with all the scandal he's having to endure.

On a more pleasant subject. I've shipped your mother's clothes. Because James is away at medical college, I have plenty of time. I used that time to alter the clothes. I hope you don't mind, but we are the same size and there were beautiful gowns in the trunks. I knew you could use them.

Your letter told me much about life in Montana, your aunt, and even Martha. The one-line mention of your neighbor Luke tells me more than the actual words in your letter. Is he the one? Have you found someone to love as you could never love Wade? I'm sure these dresses will come in handy if I'm reading you right.

James and I have set a date for our wedding, but it won't be until he completes medical college next summer. By then, you'll have come to terms with Wade and can stand up for me as my maiden of honor.

As far as news, you'll never guess who Janey Willard married. As much as she talked, you'd think some African prince was waiting to escort her down the aisle. As it is, she and Jeff Cobb eloped last month. Can you imagine Janey married to a butcher? Her mother came into the school to bring Mrs. King some library books. She told her the whole story.

I miss you, too, Clara. Please remember what I said about Wade. I've enclosed some money.

*I know by now you can use it, and I know you
wouldn't let a soul know what state you're in.
Your faithful and loyal friend,*

Annie Pearl

Tears rolled down Clara's face when she finished
reading. In the envelope she found several twenty-
dollar gold certificates. She hadn't thought of how
Wade would take her disappearance. Gossip would
surely spread about her, but it would pass. She'd
left Wade a letter, but beyond that she'd never
thought he'd go so far as to try to find her.

She supposed Wade loved her in his own way.
She supposed she loved him, too, but she knew
living under his roof the rest of her life was like
being sentenced to prison.

"Bad news, Clara?"

She looked up, her vision blurred by the tears.
She wiped them away with her fingertips. Luke
filled the space in her doorway. Not now, she
thought. Why did he have to come in now?

Luke knew Clara's footsteps by heart. He'd listened to them come up and down the stairs leading
to her room hundreds of times. Today she'd
bounded up them, a light happy lift to her step.
The letter Zeke had brought from town along with
the trunks must have been the reason.

He'd listened quietly when she'd entered. Then
everything had stopped. He'd assumed she was
reading the letter and imagined a happy smile on
her face. News from home had made him smile

when he'd been away in Philadelphia. Then the quiet had stretched into minutes and he'd realized that something was wrong. She should have been throwing the trunks open and inspecting the contents.

It had taken every bit of resolve he had not to rush to her when he'd pushed her door open and found her sobbing into her pillow, the letter clutched in her hand.

After he spoke she changed, retreating into her private world. He admired her strength, her ability to handle her own problems, but there was a time when she needed another person to help carry the burden. From the look on her face, this was it.

Luke didn't think he'd moved, but he found himself next to her, cradling her in his arms. He felt her warm tears burn into his neck and her body shake against him.

He didn't tell her to stop or ask the reason for her pain. He'd learned to let the course run until it ended. Then she would talk. Until then, he'd just hold her, feel her softness, let her cling to him.

He brushed her soft hair. It was tightly curled and flattened from being crushed under her hat. Loosening the ribbons, he stripped them from her neck and threw the hat on the bed cover. Then he hugged her again. Her tears reduced to hiccuppy sobs, and she pushed herself away from him. Using a handkerchief she pulled from her sleeve, she dried her eyes and blew her nose.

"Do you want to tell me about the letter?"

Clara shook her head. She folded the sheets of paper back into their predefined creases and fitted them into the envelope. "I was just a little home-sick," she explained.

"Your tears were more serious than homesick-ness." He waited for an answer.

"They had to do with a promise I made once."

"A promise you didn't keep?"

"I thought I could keep it when I made it. I was fifteen, and I didn't know what it really meant."

"What did you promise?"

Clara hesitated. "I can't tell you."

"Whom did you make this promise to?"

"I can't tell you that either."

"Can you make up for it?" Luke kept his voice quiet. Her emotions were so fragile, a wrong com-ment would have her retreating to her glass shell.

"It would mean leaving here and going back to Virginia—forever."

The desperation with which the last word was spoken cut through him. What could she have promised? She'd sworn no one was looking for her.

"What's in all these trunks?" Luke asked, chang-ing the subject.

"My mother's gowns," she sniffed.

"Your mother's?"

"Yes," Clara confirmed, her eyes dry. "You may as well know the truth. I haven't had any clothes for years. Annie Pearl's letter said she altered my mother's gowns and sent them to me. She also sent me some money."

He'd been right when he'd accused her of having no money. The knowledge didn't make him feel good. It made him feel as if he'd invaded her pri-vacy.

"Annie Pearl is . . ."

"My best friend. We went to school together. She's teaching there now."

"Did you live with her?"

"No, she lives in the District. I lived on a farm in Virginia." Clara paused. "You're wondering why she had my clothes."

Luke gave her a noncommittal stare.

"She helped me escape."

"Escape?"

"I ran away, just as you suggested that day in Ellen's restaurant."

"You said no one was looking for you."

"I said I'd committed no crime and no *law* man was looking for me."

"Then who is looking for you?"

"Someone I left in Virginia."

"A man?" His voice was quiet. Clara thought it was somewhere between a whisper and a prayer.

"A man," she confirmed.

Luke forced himself to breathe normally. When he'd found Clara crying, he'd never imagined it would lead here.

"Are you in love with him?"

"No, but I owe him a lot. When my parents died, he took me to live with him. He fed me and gave me a roof over my head."

"And you made a promise to him?"

Clara nodded. "But I can't keep it. I'd die if I had to go back."

"You were only fifteen, Clara, a child. No one would expect you to keep a promise you made that long ago."

"This one they will. I may have been fifteen, but I was old enough to know right and wrong. I knew what I was promising, but six years is too long. I can't go back, Luke. I won't go back."

"Don't worry," he told her. "You won't have to."

Luke slipped his arms back around her waist and pulled her forward. He knew he couldn't let her go. Even the episode with Antonia Morrison couldn't keep him from seeking her out. In the future, Luke knew he'd have to stay away from her. She didn't want to go back to Virginia, and he'd already participated in a scene that would see her returned to a world she feared and a man she wasn't ready to face.

At dinner that night, Clara had none of the residue of the afternoon's tears. The alterations had done wonders for her mother's gowns and each one fit her as if it had been made to her specific measurements. Annie Pearl had removed the flounce necessary for the bustles of the 1880's and replaced them with straighter lines; some of the dresses had a small train. The one she wore tonight was a deep-wine creation that tapered down her bodice to end at a tight waist before flaring out in a skirt with long lines that stretched to the floor.

Martha was the only occupant in the dining room when Clara entered. "Oh, Clara." Her hands went to her face. "You look great! Like one of those Gibson Girls."

Clara had heard of Gibson Girls. She'd seen drawings of them in magazines left in the school dining room. Everyone wanted to look like them. Tonight her own reflection in the bedroom mirror had been a darker reflection of the much-photographed models. All she needed was a hat to complete the picture. Since she wouldn't be wearing one in the dining room, she'd threaded a ribbon through her curls. Now that Martha had been surprised by her, what would Luke think?

Fourteen

Clara swung down from the saddle and patted Red Wind's neck. She held three sugar cubes to the horse's mouth. Red Wind's square teeth grabbed them from her gloved hand as she snorted her approval.

"I'm sure Aunt Emily wouldn't approve of your eating the sugar she puts on her dinner table," she told the red mare. The horse whinnied as if she understood. Clara smiled and tied the tether straps to a bush. The landscape sprawled before her. It was beautiful, she thought, staring at the peaks in the distance. They weren't snowcapped yet, but they were imposing. Pulling her jacket closer around her, she knew it wouldn't be long before snow covered everything she could see—the distant hills and all the grounds.

For a brief moment, Clara closed her eyes, trying to imagine a world covered with powdery flakes. It rarely snowed in Virginia; and when it did, the fields looked like rows of black-and-white feathers. The snow never covered them completely, and it was gone in a few hours. She'd heard Mrs. Andersson talking about two feet of snow falling during a single day and drifts as high as the second-floor windows. Clara couldn't imagine anything like that. She thought Mrs. Andersson was making good-natured fun of her ignorance, but she didn't take it as unkindness. Mrs. Andersson had only been friendly with her.

The wind whirled, grabbing at her hair. She wore no hat or pins to hold it in place. Even her clothes were looser, a split-skirt and full-sleeved blouse under her jacket. She found the openness gave her freedom here. She was convinced she'd made the right decision in coming. In time she'd get used to the differences between this country and the Virginia she had left. In time she wouldn't think of the people she'd left behind and in time, hopefully, she'd gain some resolve over her feelings for Luke.

Walking up an incline, she panned the landscape. High hills and vast valleys in all shades of color from deep gold to graduated shades of purple took her breath away. She had known the mountains would be like this. They'd beckoned to her from the moment the train had crossed the continental divide.

Mesmerized, Clara watched the sky, following the rise of the hill until it topped out at blue sky. The noise of the wind rushing and the quietness of being alone surrounded her. The air brushed her skin, the river rushed in the canyon below, an eagle squealed as it soared above her; yet she still heard the small pebble that rolled against her booted foot.

Luke Evans stood several feet away, the leather tether straps to his horse held loosely in his hand.

Clara stopped the gasp that nearly escaped her throat. The sun behind him shaded his features, but his surefooted gait drew her attention to his denim-covered legs.

"You're an awfully long way from home, Clara." Luke took a step toward her, then stopped. "If the sun set, at this level you'd never find your way down."

Despite the cool air, her body warmed. She couldn't move her eyes from him. A short buckskin coat with fringed arms, pockets, and hem accentuated his broad shoulders and heightened his deep, golden coloring.

"I suppose I'll have to take care that I'm not here when the sun sets." Her smile took the sting out of her words. She was so glad to see Luke she didn't want to argue. Since the day Annie Pearl's letter and the trunks had arrived, she'd seen little of him. It was apparent he was purposely finding reasons not to come to the boardinghouse when she was there.

"You've been avoiding me." Clara's stare was direct.

"I have." Luke's response was immediate. He hadn't even taken a moment to lie or even stretch the truth.

Clara's courage was stabbed by his direct reply. She wasn't used to challenging people, and Luke's stare had thrown her off balance.

"May I ask why?" She sounded like a proper schoolteacher.

"After Antonia walked in on us and you received your letter, I thought it was what you wanted."

It was what she should have wanted. She knew that. She should have wanted as much distance between them as possible, but missing him this last week had torn her apart. "We're supposed to be making Aunt Emily think I'm falling for you." She said the first thing that came to mind.

"I've been thinking about that, and I'm not convinced it was the best plan. I thought you might want to call the deal off."

"Is that what you want?" Clara held her breath, not sure of which answer she wanted to hear. Clasping her hands together, she waited. She didn't want them to stop seeing each other. She wanted to see more of him. She wanted to see him all the time, be with him all the time. She wanted that out-of-breath feeling that accompanied his presence, to laugh with him.

"In the light of your position and Antonia's crusade, it seems a wise course. You're still the schoolteacher. In Antonia Morrison's eyes, your reputation's been damaged and I'm the cause. Another act she deems improper and she'll have you on the next train out of here." His voice sounded strained, as if he weren't comfortable with the words he had to say.

He was right. She'd already grown too close to Luke. Suppose by some miracle he felt the same way about her as she did about him. Suppose he changed his mind and he did want to marry her. She couldn't marry him.

"Don't you think Aunt Emily will continue her campaign?"

"We'll just have to convince her there's nothing between us."

Isn't there? Clara wanted to ask.

"She'll only find someone else. You said so yourself. That will put me exactly where I am now."

"It might. We'll have to take that chance."

"Did I do something wrong?" Anger enveloped her. "I have tried to—"

"Clara!" He came a step closer before halting. "It's not you. It's the valley. People here have lived a certain way for too long. If Antonia decides to spread her news, you won't have a chance; and I don't want that to happen."

Suddenly Clara wondered if he would miss her if she were forced to leave. Would he fight Mrs. Morrison to keep her in the valley?

"Why not?" she had to ask. "Why should it matter to you? You've told me you don't want a wife. You were reluctant to help me deceive Aunt Emily. Why should my being sent away matter? It would appear to solve all your problems."

Luke stared at her, indecision apparent on his face. He was fighting with himself. Clara waited wondering which side of the argument he'd win. "It would matter, Clara," he admitted. "I didn't want it to. I fought you and Miss Emily. But you're a good woman, a proper woman. You have good manners and you're beautiful—inside and out."

Clara's heart soared.

"You deserve a man who'll bring you flowers and take you to church socials, a man who's as proper as you are." Luke paused. Clara waited. "When I'm around you, Clara, I can't act proper."

Clara swayed forward, then caught herself before she ran to him. She turned and stared at the horizon, letting Luke close the distance between them. His hands took her shoulders and turned her around, and her breathing slowed. She'd never been so weak; she hadn't known this could happen. A mere touch turned her strong body into a boneless mass. Being close to him was all she wanted; having his arms around her would be heaven.

"Luke, my knees are turning to water. You didn't seem to like that the last time it happened."

He ignored her words, pulled her body in contact with his, and bowed his head. Clara lifted her mouth, anticipating his kiss, wanting it.

"This is not why I came looking for you." His hands came up, cupping her face. His mouth touched hers gently. Clara's eyes closed as she went up on her toes.

A gladness ran through her. Luke had come to find her. "Why did you look for me?" Clara slipped her arms inside his jacket, circling his waist.

"To tell you we need to end this farce." He kissed her eyes, her cheeks. Heat poured into her ears as her heart thundered.

"What farce is that?" she asked, her voice seductively low. The coolness around her was no match for the furnace that radiated from within her.

His mouth took hers passionately, and Clara responded immediately. She molded herself to him, giving and receiving as much as she got, as Luke's arms crushed her against him. Clara had never thought kissing a man could make her feel like this. Everything about her tingled—her feet, her arms—and inside her was a need that Luke had pierced. He stood with his legs apart, fitting her frame into him. His hands rubbed over her back and down to her hips, then up again. Sensation rocked her as the unmistakable bulge in Luke's pants pressed into her. Her hips rotated against him, setting her on fire.

"Clara." Luke's voice was thick with emotion when he tore his mouth from hers. "We'd better stop now or I'll make love to you in these hills."

Clara leaned against him, her breath coming in ragged gasps. If Luke couldn't act properly around her, she'd proved she couldn't act properly around him either. He was right. She knew it, but she didn't want it to be that way. A moment ago, she'd been telling herself she needed to resolve her feelings, and now she was in his arms, drowning in his kisses.

Stepping back, she looked at him. His eyes were dark with the aftermath of passion. What would they look like if he really made love to her? Right now, she could think of nothing she wanted more than to make love with Luke, but doing so would change her forever. She didn't know if she could ever give him up then. She wondered if all the books were right, if Janey Willard's stories had been right. Luke had made such a difference in how she felt: He made her happy. She smiled around him, liked talking to him and hearing the sound of his voice. Making love with him seemed the most wonderful thing in the world; yet it wasn't to be.

"Luke, I think you were right," she said, turning her back to him, her conscious mind completely footed in reality. "Deception isn't something I'm cut out for." She was a greater deceiver than he would ever know. Her whole life was nothing more than a lie, beginning with the promise she'd made to Wade. She had lied about that; and by not telling her aunt the whole truth, she'd lied to her. Now she was lying to Luke. He had said it was the best thing for them. She couldn't deny the truth of that. She turned back to him, a smile planted on her face. "It's good we decided to end this deceit before things get out of hand."

Luke's eyes narrowed as she spoke. She wondered if she were convincing him or if he'd seen through her thin disguise.

"If that's what you want."

Of course it was what she wanted. Why did he ask that? He was the one who'd suggested they call it quits, why now did it appear he had changed his mind?

"I guess this means there is no need for us to avoid each other at Aunt Emily's," Clara said, biting her lip.

"We won't be at Miss Emily's."

Clara stared at him. Her body stiffened as she waited for his explanation. Was he moving, finding a room at another boardinghouse? Did he know how she felt? Was his conviction that he would never remarry forcing him to put a physical distance between them?

Luke walked toward her. She was too scared to move. He stopped close enough for her to smell his clean scent, and his eyes searched her face. Clara held her breath as Luke's eyes darkened with passion. She wanted to touch him, to tell him she hurt as much as he did, but she didn't. She let her eyes say it.

Raising his hand, Luke pulled a large paper rose from behind her ear and held it out to her. "Your furniture arrives tomorrow," he said.

Clara accepted the magical long-stemmed beauty, dipping her head to hide the mist that gathered in her eyes. Luke wasn't leaving the boardinghouse; she was. With her furnishings in place and school scheduled to open in a week, there was no need to delay her moving. She had things to get in order, and she needed to get used to living alone. She needed to get the children's books sorted and prepare for the first class. There were a hundred things she needed to do. Moving would be good, she told herself. It would give her space away from Luke. He wouldn't be on the other side of the wall, and she wouldn't wait to hear him come in at night or listen to his boots fall to the floor.

There would be no temptation to repeat the scene that had taken place in his bedroom, and she wouldn't have to see him every day. This would be better. Sniffing the papery smell of the rose, she repeated, *this would be better.*

* * *

Supervising her move was more emotional than Clara had expected it to be. She imagined Luke picking out each piece of furniture, designing the room around what would be placed in it. She could see his style in the mahogany table, feel his presence in the four-poster bed. She felt as if his eyes looked at her from every room, every wall. Yet like forbidden candy, she couldn't touch or talk to him.

When the final piece was set in place, she was left with more than her feelings. Luke's presence permeated the room. Pulling herself together, she banished her thoughts. She'd come to Montana to begin again, to have independence, and to teach. Falling in love hadn't been in her plans, but it *had* happened.

Clara would spend one more night at Hale's Boardinghouse, one additional night sharing a common wall with Luke Evans. She closed the door of the house and got in the wagon to go back to her aunt's.

The ride didn't take long. The closer Clara got to her aunt's the more she thought of Luke. Would he be at dinner tonight? Could she remain distant and friendly across the white-lace expanse of Aunt Emily's table? Questions tumbled in her mind like bouncing balls, each colliding with the other.

She needed some time alone, time to think over what she'd do and how she'd act. She longed for the sanctuary of the barn in Virginia, her escape room when she needed a place to gather strength and push herself forward. At Aunt Emily's there were few places where she could be alone. Her room—next to Luke's—offered no peace.

She scanned the sky. Clear, cloudless blue invited her. A ride in the mountains came to her like a revelation.

She thought of Martha. The two of them usually rode together. When school began she'd be far too busy for morning rides, but today Clara wanted to be alone with her thoughts.

Martha was out when she arrived, but Zeke saddled Red Wind and the afternoon beckoned to her. She rode higher than she had ever gone before. Higher than she'd gone the morning Luke had come looking for her. He wouldn't come today or any other day.

The air was unusually warm for this time of year, but it cooled as she went higher. Dismounting, she walked through the hills, marveling at their beauty. She found them calming. There was such a quiet elegance about them that they humbled her. Sitting down near the end of a precipice, she watched the play of color as the sun began to set. It would be dark in an hour, Clara thought. She only had a few minutes to relax before she'd have to start back.

Leaning against a boulder, she swept her eyes over the horizon, drinking in the sheer awesomeness of the hills. If Mrs. Andersson were right and there would be massive amounts of snow, these hills would be beautiful draped in white. Clara tried to imagine it, and it was the last thought she had before drifting into a light sleep.

At the first drop of water, Clara's eyes flew

open. She sat up, propelled forward, trying to focus. Where was the sun? Why was it so dark? She closed her eyes, hoping the darkness would disappear and the sun would be where it had been before she'd fallen asleep. She hadn't meant to doze off. The valley had been so peaceful and the breeze such a delight that she must have closed her eyes. And now the sun had set. By the feel of the wind and the coldness of the rain, she guessed she'd been asleep for hours.

Darkness consumed the big sky. In front of her stretched the inky blackness of a photographer's studio. Only the stars, far away and providing no light, offered any dimension to the vastness before her. She jumped to her feet, immediately reaching for a support to hold onto. Her hands clutched empty air as she lost her balance and plopped down on the rocky ground.

Another drop of rain hit her, followed by several more. It was going to storm. Clara's heart pounded. She had to get back to Aunt Emily's. But which way? Her eyes darted back and forth, searching for anything that would keep her mounting fear from breaking into a scream. The rain matted her hair to her head and soaked through her dress, wetting her skin. Slowly she stood, her dress heavy and clinging. Gripping the face of the mountain, Clara eased her feet forward. She remembered the valley she had thought was so beautiful while the sun had shone on it. Choosing the wrong direction would mean she could pitch over the edge and wind up with a broken neck. The thought froze her in place. Rain

pelted her cheeks and arms. Fear choked all but
a strangled cry from her tight throat.

Why hadn't she told someone where she was
going? Luke had warned her to be careful of these
hills. How angry he would be to find out she
hadn't heeded his warning.

She'd needed some time alone and had wandered
off looking for solitude. She had often done this
in Virginia; but there wandering off had meant
climbing into the barn loft and watching the sky
through a small, square opening. Out here she
didn't see a piece of sky, but the entire galaxy that
spanned the horizon.

Lightning flashed with a sudden brightness that
blinded her. She squeezed her eyes closed and
gripped the rugged surface more securely. Her wet
fingers slipped, and her feet anchored in mud. Falling to her knees, she scraped her cheek on a rough
wall of rock. Clara knew no one was going to find
her. She had to get down and back to Aunt
Emily's—alone.

Rubbing her eyes with the back of her hand, she
pulled her resolve into place and stood up. She
had to do this. No one knew where she was; no
one was looking for her. She'd gotten herself into
this situation; she would have to get herself out.

"One step at a time," she said to the howling
wind which chanted like voices in her ears. The
Indians had stories about the wind and the rain.
She wondered if they were true. Concentrating on
these, she moved one foot, then the other. How far
had she climbed this afternoon? Above the tree
line, she was sure.

Clara stopped. Where was she going? She could be heading for a cliff and not know it. She found Red Wind and hugged her neck. At least she wasn't alone, but what could they do? Clara stood under the tree where she'd tied Red Wind. Only a little of the rain didn't reach her there. She pulled her jacket closer, trying to keep her fear at bay. Luke's words came back to her. There were mountain lions in these hills, bears and snakes. She knew snakes only came out during warm periods. As cold as the rain was, she was safe from them. Bears hibernated, she remembered, but not all of them and not all winter. Technically, it wasn't winter yet. And today had been extremely warm. Bears could climb trees, and in this darkness she wouldn't be able to find her way.

She looked around. She had better find some dry wood she could use when the rain stopped. Gathering it, she piled it near Red Wind, using his blanket to keep it dry. Her teeth were chattering and her body was wet through to the skin, but the rain slowed and eventually stopped. She wondered what time it was. Had anyone missed her? Had Zeke reported that she and Red Wind had not returned to the stable? She hoped so; but even if he did, hampered by rain and darkness, no one could come out until morning.

"Cla-ra," Luke called over the howling wind. Where was she? When he found her, he'd break her beautiful neck. She knew better than to wander off like this. And Zeke should never have let her go by herself. The last time he'd found her, she'd been halfway to the old miner's cabin. Like the dynamite flag, she didn't know about the cabin, and it was unthinkable that she'd find it in the dark. Stumbling around, she could pitch off any one of a hundred cliffs and lie dead at the bottom of a ravine.

Luke stopped to peer in the darkness. "Cla-ra." The rain had stopped nearly an hour ago, and he still hadn't found a sign of her. Where was she?

Wild thoughts of her hurt and bleeding crowded in on him. He had to find her. Dismounting, he started up a steep incline. There was nothing above him now but rock and a few hardy bushes that defied the harsh winters.

"Damn, Clara. Where are you?" Luke admitted he was worried. When Miss Emily had told him she'd hadn't returned, he'd calmed the old woman, telling her Clara was smart enough to find shelter, that she was probably at the mountain cabin knowing it was better to stay put than to try to come down in the dark. Now he didn't believe that. Each step he took, he got angrier and angrier that she had gone off alone.

What was that light? He squinted, trying to see through the obstructions ahead of him. Was it a fire? Was Clara there?

"Cla-ra?"

Her eyes opened wide. Was someone calling her name? Clara sat up. She braced herself in front of the boulder she used as back support. Cocking her head, she listened. It had to be the wind. It was too dark for anyone to see, so no one from the valley would come out in this storm. Her mind was playing tricks on her.

"Clara?"

There it was again. She strained to hear what the wind tossed at her dazed brain.

"Clara, where are you?"

"Here," she whispered, unsure if she were really hearing her name. "I'm over here." Her voice was low, too low to be heard more than a foot away. She scrambled to her knees, then her feet, her head searching in the direction of the solitary voice.

"Can you hear me, Clara?"

Whoever called her sounded far away, elongating the first syllable as if he were singing her name.

"Over here!" she shouted. "I'm over here." She moved toward the sound.

"Stay where you are," he called back, as if he knew she'd run toward rescue.

"Luke," she cried. "Luke, you've found me!" Relief flooded through her like a sickle cutting a corn stalk. She gripped the gritty surface behind her to remain standing. Rescue sapped the life from her knees.

"Clara, talk to me," Luke called to her. "I need your voice as a signal."

His voice was so calm, it helped her remain tranquil when she wanted to shout hysterically. She had thought no one would find her, that she'd have to wait for sunrise to see her way clear of the mountain. She'd tried not to think of bears and mountain lions, knowing the meager fire wouldn't keep them from tearing her limb from limb.

"Here, there is a clearing," she instructed him. "Behind me is a large rock about eight feet high and five feet around. In front of me is a fire." She hugged herself, shivering at the small amount of light and warmth coming from the fire she'd started.

Something large broke through the trees. She crouched against the rock, poised to run if a wild animal threatened her, but her eyes focused on Luke leading his horse. He stopped as soon as he saw her. Clara pushed herself up slowly. Stepping around the fire, she hesitated. Later, she didn't remember taking a step, running across the clearing, or flinging herself into Luke's arms. She was just there, her arms around his waist, her cheek against the wet parka covering his broad chest. He was so big, she felt safe and protected.

"Thank God you found me," she whispered. "I was so scared."

Clara spoke, but Luke wasn't listening to her. She'd slammed her soft body into his. Her arms sought comfort, and he was helpless to withhold it. All the anger he'd planned to unleash at her foolishness dissipated the moment her form aligned to his. His arms rose instinctively, ready to wrap around her. Suddenly his brain kicked in and he hesitated as indecision, conviction, and common sense told him to step back. Ignoring all three voices and knowing he'd lost the battle, he encircled her small frame and crushed her to him. She buried her face against his chest, and his hands climbed to her hair. It was damp and plastered to her head, but felt soft like wet cotton. Pushing her head back, he stared into large, trusting eyes.

Of its own volition, his head bowed and his mouth brushed hers lightly. She was as addicting as morphia, and he wanted more. He kissed her again, deepening the union, releasing the pent-up emotions he'd staved off since seeing the sun glint off her bonnet as she'd walked up the hill to the building site. It was inevitable. Why had he fought against it? His arms were around her. She smelled like rain and lilacs, and the scent hit him like an aphrodisiac. He hugged her closer, his mouth devouring hers until the need to breathe forced him to lift his mouth. Still he couldn't let her go. He buried his face in her hair and breathed in the clean scent that was identifiable to this woman alone. A bubble rose in his throat and emotion rocked him. His blood coursed through his veins with the speed of lightning.

Luke didn't move. He was afraid. His body was as hard as hers was soft. Movement would have them on the ground, and he wouldn't be able to control his need for her. Just holding her wasn't enough! He wanted Clara. Despite his resolution that he didn't need anyone in his life, she felt too good to push away.

He held her closer, not allowing himself to break contact. She'd frightened him, more than he'd ever been frightened. Visions of her lying dead or hurt had taunted him. Finding her safe, he couldn't let her go; he wanted to hold onto her forever.

"I'm sorry, Luke." Clara leaned back and looked into his eyes. "I didn't mean to fall asleep. The valley was so beautiful, and the water rushing below was like a sedative. I closed my eyes for a moment. Then it was suddenly dark, too dark to try finding my way home, so I built a fire to wait out the night. I'd have come down at daybreak."

"You had everyone worried. There are men all over these hills looking for you. Miss Emily was beside herself when you didn't show up for dinner."

"Do you think we can get down?"

Luke walked her back to the fire. "Sit down," he said, buying himself time. He needed it more than she did. "Most of the pathways have been turned into mud slides. It's too dangerous to chance trying to find our way tonight."

"So." She hesitated. "We have to stay here until morning."

Luke nodded, not trusting himself to say anything. She stared into the fire, shivering.

"The first thing we have to do is get you out of those clothes."

Clara's head snapped up, one hand going to her neck.

"Wet clothes," he explained. "Miss Emily thought you might have gotten caught in the rain. She sent you some dry clothes."

Luke went to the huge gelding standing at the end of the clearing and pulled a package from his saddlebags.

"Are you alone?" Clara stared at the parcel Luke offered her.

"There's no one with me. The others are checking other parts of the hills. I need to send them a signal that you're all right."

Luke stepped away from her and took a gun from his holster. Clara had never seen him wear a gun. In fact, none of the men in the valley wore guns. In Butte, everyone had one strapped to his leg. He fired the black instrument three times in rapid succession. She shied away from the sound, covering her ears at the blasts. Answering replies came from several different directions as four parties responded.

"They'll go back and let Miss Emily know you've been found."

When he turned back, Clara asked again, "Can we get down?"

Luke looked at the sky and then around them. He stared at the direction from which he'd come. "Not tonight," he told her. "If there were a moon to give us light, I might chance it; but in this darkness and after that storm, I'm not willing to test it."

Clara shivered at the thought of spending the night with him.

"How will the others get down?"

"Some of them are at lower elevations. The others will have to spend the night where they are."

Clara dropped her head. She didn't think she could feel any worse. Her foolishness had caused people to spend unnecessary time searching for her, and now some of them would have to stay the night in the cold.

"There's a mountain cabin not far from here,"

he told her. "We'll go there for the night and return in the morning."

Clara didn't move. She clutched the package to her breast.

Luke smothered the fire with dirt. Smoke rose as the small bit of light went out and plunged the area around them into pitch blackness. Clara could barely make out Luke's outline in the dark. "Come on," he said. "If we don't get you out of those clothes, you'll catch your death of cold."

Clara thought they had been leading the horses for hours before they came to a small house set high on one of the hills. It surprised her that the *cabin* Luke had mentioned was really a house.

"Who owns this?" she asked.

"It used to belong to a mountain man named Clem Kincaid. The story goes he hated people, so he built this cabin to get away from them. He said he never wanted to see another human being as long as he lived. He died twenty years ago, but this cabin still stands. No one lives here, but everyone knows about it for times like this."

"I caused a lot of trouble, didn't I?" Clara stared at Luke in the darkened light. She remembered how everyone had come to check on her and Luke after the dynamite. Tonight they were probably doing the same, and it was all her fault. She had known better than to go so high into the hills and to fall asleep so search parties had to try to find her. She wasn't proving herself very well to the people of the valley. Everything she did turned out wrong.

"They won't hold it against you, Clara. More

than one person has been lost in these hills. We find most of them." Luke smiled at her and touched her cheek. For a moment their eyes locked, then Luke led her through the door.

Inside was a large living room, a dining room-kitchen combination, and a single bedroom. No gas lines extended this high, and Luke lit the room using candles and hurricane lamps. He started a fire in the living room fireplace while Clara went into the bedroom and changed into dry clothing. Aunt Emily had sent her a dress, but she hadn't included a chemise, petticoat, or bloomers. Clara tugged at her wet undergarments, shivering in the cold room. Finding a towel on a rack near the washstand, she dried her frozen body and slipped into the dry dress. It felt good against her naked skin, but did not completely warm her. Her shoes and stockings were too damp to replace. Hanging her clothes in front of the unlit fireplace in the bedroom, she went to the door and studied Luke's back.

He worked at the fire. The candles and lamps gave the room a warm golden glow that invited Clara to enter; but she stood still, watching Luke, not wanting to disturb the moment—like the first day she'd seen him on the roof of the building site. The candles added intimacy to the scene, and Luke stoked the logs he'd placed on the hearth. Fire leaped up the blackened chimney as heat consumed her. She'd dreamed of being alone with him, had thought of all the things Janey Willard said happened between a man and a woman. She wondered if they were true. For all Janey's confidence, Clara was sure she was all mouth and had done none of the things she'd professed to know about.

"It's warm over here." Luke glanced over his shoulder as if sensing her presence, and indicated a chair next to the hearth. Feeling rather under-dressed, Clara crossed the threshold. He came to her, helping her as if she were an invalid. His hand, on the small of her back, guided her across the floor, and fingers of warmth spread up her spine. Clara's state of undress embarrassed her, and she glanced at Luke. When he had been sick from the explosion, a mere touch had told him she wore a corset. She had no doubt that now, in his full physical awareness, he knew she had nothing on under her dress.

Clara took the chair and set her naked feet on the bricks close to the flame. Luke grabbed a knit-ted blanket from the back of the sofa and draped it over her. Without a word, he sat in front of her, taking one foot and massaging it until it warmed and circulation returned; then he started on the other. Usually she was ticklish, but with Luke holding her feet in his hands, Clara closed her eyes, relaxing against the back of the chair. Elec-trical shocks skittered through her at the circular motion of his hard hands. She'd never thought of them before, but they were rough against her skin, making her breasts tingle and a strangled feeling pool in her stomach. She liked it, feeling liquidy, as if she'd melt. Like drinking brandy, his hands warmed her through and through.

Unconsciously, she slipped down in the chair,

imagining herself wrapped in Luke's arms, imagining him holding her and kissing her, and she warmed as fast as a pot-bellied stove. She wanted to slide off the chair and wrap herself around him.

Her eyes opened when Luke wrapped her feet under the blanket and moved away. "You must be hungry," he said. "Let's see what we can find to eat."

"I'll do that." Clara jumped up and went toward the small kitchen.

"You're still freezing," he said a little stiffly. "Go back and warm yourself."

"You're freezing, too. I'm dry now. You go dry off, and I'll fix us something to eat."

Luke looked at her for a moment; then, seeing the determination in her eyes, he nodded and went toward the bedroom.

Clara winced the moment he closed the door. Her underwear would be in plain view. Well, she shrugged, he had to have seen it before. Her face grew hot, but she didn't run after him. She turned to the storage cabinet to search for food. The cabinets were stocked, overstocked was a better word, with canned goods. Someone had carted preserved peaches, beans, corn, beets, carrots, even pickled pork up the hills and left it here. She wondered who?

"Clara." Luke stopped her thought processes. "Put these on." A pair of his socks sailed across the room. She caught them in one hand as Agnes Wheatly would have done at any of the baseball games. Her feet *were* cold. Without a thought to fashion, she sat down and slipped on the heavy woolens. Immediate warmth spread over her toes and up her legs. She thought of Luke wearing the socks, his feet next to hers. Her throat went dry and she swallowed.

"There's some food in my bag. It's by the door."

Clara found it. Inside, wrapped in a white cloth, were several crushed Parker House rolls. Also included were uncooked steaks, potatoes, carrots, salt pork, and enough mustard greens to feed a large family.

"Did Aunt Emily think we were going on a picnic or setting up house?" she asked the room. With all the preserved food and this cache, she and Luke could spend the winter in the cabin and never run out of things to eat.

"Did you say something?" Luke had disappeared into the bedroom, and Clara was glad he hadn't heard her. He returned several minutes later, having changed into dry denims and a flannel shirt, open at the neck. Clara had the sudden urge to cross the room and press her mouth there. God! what was wrong with her? She had never had these feelings before. Luke couldn't come within eyesight without her emotions going out of control.

"What's inside?" Luke asked. "Miss Emily pushed it into my hand while I mounted. All she said was it was food if we got hungry."

Clara tore her gaze away from Luke. She was hungry with a hunger she had never known existed within her; an inner turmoil had taken hold of her. Something was changing inside her. She could feel it, but wasn't able to stop or change it, and she didn't know if she welcomed the change. Suddenly, she wondered what she looked like. Her hair must be matted to her head. Any style she had had, had been ruined by the wind and rain, leaving her looking like a wet cat.

Bending to the oven to give herself something to do, she found wood already in place. While she lit it, she told him what she'd found. "I'll have this cooked in no time."

Opening and closing doors, she searched for pots and pans. Luke's presence stilted her movements. Outside, the temperature dipped and the wind picked up, howling through the canyons and around the hills like Indian calls. The sound unnerved her.

Luke took one of the two ladder-back chairs and straddled it, watching Clara work. He made her nervous, and her hands shook when he stared at her. A smile played at his lips. He liked that she was aware of him, and he was certainly aware of her. His body hardened each time he looked at her. The fact that beneath the thin material of her dress was only her cherry-colored skin had the bulge in his pants pressing painfully against the restriction of his denims.

He thought of Peg. He used to watch her in the kitchen. She would hum spirituals while she worked. He hated that he'd made her a promise. Clara had told him about a promise she had made that she couldn't keep. Luke knew as he watched Clara that he, too, would not be able to keep the promise he'd made his wife.

He had tried valiantly to stay true to Peg's memory, but her memory had faded without his doing anything. The pain of her loss lessened as he'd been told it would. He could have gone on believing that nothing mattered to him if it hadn't been for Clara.

Miss Emily had done her part to test his strength. Until Clara's arrival, everything had worked fine. But the day she had walked into his life, his convictions and beliefs had been irrevocably altered. He realized now how much of himself he'd buried with Peg. Emily Hale was right: It was time he got on with the business of living. And that business involved the woman standing three feet away from him nervously trying to prepare a meal.

But was Clara the woman to break his promise for? She was beautiful, that he couldn't deny. He liked her, liked how she felt in his arms. He spent his nights wondering what it would be like to hold her next to him, wake up with her in the morning, share her breakfast, her pain, her happiness. Marriage was what he was describing. What would it be like to be married to Clara? He shook his head, trying to clear the image the setting forced him to view. Here it was easy to see the two of them living together, but he'd sworn off ever marrying again.

"How do you like your steak?" she asked, breaking into his thoughts.

Luke stared at her. She had spoken but he hadn't heard what she'd said. Color seemed to surround her like a rainbow aura. Her skin glowed in its light, her dress streamed down her body in never-ending lines. He stood and walked to her, but she stepped back, unsure of what was about to happen. Luke cupped her face and stared at her. Her eyes were deep, dark pools of questioning radiance. Her cheeks glowed with renewed life, but her mouth, tinged with its own natural color, fascinated him. Luke stared at it. Her lips quivered slightly as he leaned toward them.

She didn't say a word, but he noticed the rapid fluttering of a telltale vein in her neck. Her breath was short, and her breasts rose and lowered in quick succession. He could feel her heat, feel the vibrations that came from her.

Slowly, tenderly, he kissed her mouth. He wanted her to know how much he valued her. His touch was the lightest he could muster—as if he held a child, newborn and unable to support itself. He held her that way for an eon. His eyes drank of her as if she would be his last sight before going blind. Sensation racked him, then he could hold his need in no longer. His arms slipped around her waist and he pulled her into hard contact with him. His mouth devoured hers, his tongue thrusting inside her mouth, sampling all the nectar she had to give. He tasted her, drinking in her essence as if they were the only two people on earth. His hands felt the softness of her back. He gently massaged her down over her hips. Without the rigid obstructions of undergarments, she was soft and pliable, and she ground her hips into his groin, sending pure sensation spiraling through him so violently he wanted to holler. Faster and faster, he rotated her hips, opening his legs to give her body access to the throbbing sensation she caused in him.

He wanted her now, naked next to him, touching him, kissing him, running her hands over every inch of his hot skin. He wedged her into him, his hands thrusting her thighs against his rigid protrusion. God! he ached for her.

Sliding his mouth from hers, he held her close, his arms hugging her back, his hands running up and down from her hips to her shoulders. He liked the way she felt, her softness, how she fit so perfectly into the groove of his body.

"Luke, make love to me."

He froze. Pushing her back enough to see her face, he said, "Clara, you don't know what you're asking."

Dropping her gaze to the floor, she fidgeted with a button on his shirt. "I'm sorry," she began, hesitantly. "I thought . . . I thought you wanted . . ."

"I do. God! you don't know how much." The anguish in his voice was evident to his own ears. "I'd like nothing better, but Clara, you're a *virgin*. You should love the man—"

"How do you know that?" She stepped back out of his grasp.

Luke felt embarrassed. He'd never had to explain this before; and with Clara, he felt he needed to be extremely careful with his words.

"It shows in everything you say and do, Clara. Each time I've touched you I can tell by your hesitancy, by your reluctance to be kissed or touched and the way your pulse beats in your throat whenever I stand too close." To demonstrate, he closed the one-step distance between them.

"Then you don't want to make love to me . . . because I'm a virgin?" she questioned.

"Not want to make love to you!" Luke glared at her. "This is how much I don't want to make love to you."

He grabbed her wrists and pulled her palms into contact with his groin.

Clara's eyes opened so wide her eyelashes fanned out like half-moons; her mouth dropped and her head snapped up in one jerky movement, but she didn't move her hands. She'd never touched a man there before.

Luke was hot and throbbing. She could feel his heart beating, or was it her own heart she felt through her hands? She didn't know. She knew she liked the way he felt, and her hands moved involuntarily. Luke grabbed her shoulders and squeezed, and she heard the strangled groan that accompanied each movement of her fingers. It was wonderful to know she did this to him, that she could make him as weak as he made her.

"Clara." Luke's voice was barely audible. "The first time you make love . . . should be with someone you love, someone whom you'll marry if you . . . don't marry him first. I'm not that man."

She brushed her hands over his denims, sliding her fingers between his legs.

"I'm not asking you to marry me," Clara said, her voice unrecognizable. She'd accepted her lot in life. Clara Winslow was going to be an old-maid schoolteacher; but if she were to have only one chance of finding out what it was like to love a man, she wanted it to be with Luke.

Moving her hands upward, Clara slid them over Luke's massive muscles. Raising herself to her toes, she pressed her mouth to his. Luke resisted for a split second before she felt his resolve snap.

He crushed her to him, his mouth seeking hers as if he wouldn't live through the next second without her. Losing all reason and control, all sense of right and wrong, he knew only that he had to have Clara; he had to assuage this pain she had created in him. He had tried to calm himself, tried to pull back, tried to stop the tide of emotion that filled him when he had her in his arms, but he could no longer. He slid his mouth to her neck, and Clara's head dropped back as she accommodated him. He couldn't get enough of her. Following her collar line, he kissed the pulsating beat at the base of her throat, then moved onward to the front opening of the cotton dress. His hand deftly unfastened the first button, then another and another until her bare breasts were exposed to his mouth. He took one dark bud full into his mouth and sucked. Clara let out a gasp, then instinctively grasped his arms and held on.

The heat around them from the fire, the oven, and the room full of candles only added fuel to the furnace of their escalating passion. He felt her hands in his hair, her mouth kissing his crown as he fully unbuttoned the dress and dropped it to the floor. She shivered, never having stood without clothes before a man. She was beautiful all over, her body strong and flawless, her breasts small and firm. Her even coloring extended down her frame to a tiny waist and over hips that were as round as small moons. Her legs were long and strong and ignited flames of desire in Luke. He thought all the air would completely desert his body if she didn't release him from this stranglehold of desire that spun around them like a spider's web.

He took her mouth again, and her arms went around his neck as she pressed herself to him. She was so smooth, so small, he could crush her frame, but he didn't want to. He wanted to make her laugh and sing. He wanted to be her first sight in the morning and her last at night. Lifting her feet from the floor, he carried her into the bedroom and laid her on the bed.

Clara's breath was almost nonexistent. She knew the moment couldn't last: It was too beautiful. If she blinked or breathed, this world would shatter into millions of crystals. Luke stood above her, pulling his shirt from his pants. He was a giant and she a small bird. She'd never seen a man undressed before, and propriety told her to close her eyes, look away, and remember her upbringing. Curiosity and Luke's magnificent physique forced her to keep them open.

His actions seemed to slow as she watched. His shirt fell in folds to the floor. He reached for his belt, undoing the buckle and pulling it free of the loops. His hands on the buttons of his pants drew her gaze to the spot where he bulged hard, where he'd held her hips against him, and where her hands had been. She gasped at the sensations rioting through her at the thought of his hardness.

He lowered his pants, underwear, and socks, pulling them over his feet. He was magnificent, like the pictures of Greeks she'd seen in books. His sex was fully erect as he joined her on the double bed.

"Luke." She hesitated. His body was hot to the touch. "Will it . . . hurt?"

"A little," he whispered.

"I'm scared."

"I'll try not to hurt you."

He kissed her then. His body touched every inch of hers, yet he made no move to cover her. Clara had never been touched by a man, but she'd seen enough animals to know how people made love. She'd also heard enough stories about the pain on the first try to be frightened. But with Luke she would risk the pain. She believed he wouldn't hurt her if he could help it. He was so large, yet his big hands could be so tender. They held her as if she would break in his arms, making her feel as if she were the most special woman on earth. No one had ever made her feel like that.

Luke stroked her arms, his work-roughened hands moving over her as if she were more precious than the copper ore the miners risked their lives to extract. His hands drew circles over her stomach making her relax. His thumbs flicked back and forth over her nipples. Biting down on her lower lip, she attempted to hold back the whimper of pleasure that rose in her. It escaped as a low moan. Then he reached over her, kissing her shoulders and her breasts. Her stomach tight-

We've got your authors!

If you seek out the latest historical romances by today's bestselling authors, our new reader's service, KENSINGTON CHOICE, is the club for you.

KENSINGTON CHOICE is the only club where you can find authors like Janelle Taylor, Shannon Drake, Rosanne Bittner, Sylvie Sommerfield, Penelope Neri and Phoebe Conn all in one place…

…and the only service that will deliver their romances direct to your home as soon as they are published—even before they reach the bookstores.

KENSINGTON CHOICE is also the only service that will give you a substantial guaranteed discount off the publisher's prices on every one of those romances.

That's right: Every month, the Editors at Zebra and Pinnacle select four of the newest novels by our bestselling authors and rush them straight to you, usually *before they reach the bookstores*. The publisher's prices for these romances range from $4.99 to $5.99—but they are always yours for the guaranteed low price of just $4.20!

That means you'll always save over 20% off the publisher's prices on every shipment you get from KENSINGTON CHOICE!

All books are sent on a 10-day free examination basis, and there is no minimum number of books to buy. (A postage and handling charge of $1.50 is added to each shipment.)

As your introduction to the convenience and value of this new service, we invite you to accept

4 BOOKS FREE

The 4 books, worth up to $23.96, are our welcoming gift. You pay only $1 to help cover postage and handling.

To start your subscription to KENSINGTON CHOICE and receive your introductory package of 4 FREE romances, detach and mail the card at right *today*.

We have 4 FREE BOOKS for you
as your introduction to
KENSINGTON CHOICE
To get your FREE BOOKS, worth
up to $23.96, mail the card below.

FREE BOOK CERTIFICATE

As my introduction to your new KENSINGTON CHOICE reader's service, please send me 4 FREE historical romances (worth up to $23.96), billing me just $1 to help cover postage and handling. As a KENSINGTON CHOICE subscriber, I will then receive 4 brand-new romances to preview each month for 10 days FREE. I can return any books I decide not to keep and owe nothing. The publisher's prices for the KENSINGTON CHOICE romances range from $4.99 to $5.99, but as a subscriber I will be entitled to get them for just $4.20 per book or $16.80 for all four titles. There is no minimum number of books to buy, and I can cancel my subscription at any time. A $1.50 postage and handling charge is added to each shipment.

Name _____

Address _____ Apt. _____

City _____ State _____ Zip _____

Telephone (____) _____

Signature _____

(If under 18, parent or guardian must sign)

Subscription subject to acceptance. Terms and prices subject to change.

KC0695

We have
4
FREE
Historical
Romances
for you!

(worth up
to $23.96!)

Details inside!

KENSINGTON CHOICE
Reader's Service
120 Brighton Road
P.O.Box 5214
Clifton, NJ 07015-5214

ened and her breasts stood erect as if they knew
he wished their attention. Clara couldn't stop the
moans that erupted from her in guttural upheaval.
Luke's tongue slid down her body, sampling every
curve. His tongue dipped into her navel, causing
her to grasp his shoulders and dig her fingernails
into the soft flesh. His mouth went lower and her
head thrashed back and forth on the pillow as spi-
rals of sensation shot through her.

Her body was hot and flowing. Luke had turned
her into an erupting volcano. The pleasure-pain he
created in her was excruciating. She gasped for
breath, her legs involuntarily encircling his. He
looked at her, his eyes heavy-lidded and dark with
passion, then pulled himself over her. Clara felt
his hot, throbbing sex against that part of her no
man had touched. Her legs opened, instinctively
wanting him inside of her.

"Look at me," he grunted in a voice thick with
passion.

She opened her eyes. His were filled with a deep
longing that only she could fulfill. She wondered
if she looked the same way.

"I don't want to hurt you."

It wasn't a question, but he waited for her to
nod. Then he kissed her and rolled his full weight
onto her. His knee parted her legs and he pushed
himself gently inside her. Clara held her breath,
waiting for the pain she knew would come. What
she felt suggested pleasure, almost there, but not
quite. Luke pulled out. Was that it? It couldn't be
over so soon, Clara thought. Then he went in
again. This time he pushed further inside her, and

the sensation added a greater pleasure. She wondered how her small body could accommodate such a large man. He felt good, and she liked what his movements did, how his legs felt against hers, how her breasts felt flattened against him. Under him, she couldn't stop herself from joining in the rhythm he had started.

"Not yet," he told her.

As he continued his slow progress, Clara knew he was holding back. She touched his shoulders, drawing her hands down his back. He groaned, a low grizzly sound. Luke squeezed his eyes shut and pressed into her again. This time he met resistance. Clara resisted, but he pushed through. The pain was sharp and tearing. She cried out, stuffing her fist into her mouth to muffle the sound. Luke stopped, paralyzed, then he continued pressing further and further inside her.

"It's over," Luke said, moving her hand and replacing it with his mouth. He kissed her into submission before continuing the rhythm he'd begun. A moment later, the pain was forgotten and Clara's hips moved with Luke's. His hands grasped her buttocks and lifted her toward his thrust. Clara's legs came up, giving him full access to her inner core. She followed his lead, meeting him thrust for thrust, and sensation after sensation racked her. Brilliant color exploded before her as Luke led her through a new world of sensation that only a man and a woman could experience. Nothing but light and beauty dwelled in this world made for only the two of them.

An aura gripped her, taking her on a pleasure

trip she hadn't known existed. She felt at one with
Luke, the only man on earth who could make her
feel this way. He filled her, made her free to express everything, free to give her body, her mind,
and her soul to him. For the first time in her life,
she felt as if she could do anything, be anything,
as long as Luke was with her, as long as he kept
her in this world of rainbows and electrifying sensation. She heard him groan, a raw tortured sound,
and suddenly she was gripped with a radiating sensation of white pleasure. She reached toward it,
upscaling her undulations until she thought she
would die from the uproar of feeling flowing between them. Then the burst came, rocketing
through her, exploding like a giant balloon, tearing
Clara apart. Wave after wave of sensation flooded
through her, each one sending shocks of pleasure
greater than the one before. Balling her fist, she
stuck it into her mouth, but it was no match for
the scream that ripped Luke's name from her in a
final climactic shriek.

Luke's weight fell against her. Ragged breathing
came from both of them. He gathered her close
and held her as if she would run away, but she
had no strength to move even if she wanted to—
which she didn't. She never wanted to move again.
She wanted to stay here, warm and protected in
this private world where only love existed, for the
rest of her days.

"Are you all right?" Luke asked.

Clara cooed. "I'm fine."

* * *

Clara woke with the first light. Luke lay next to her, his golden-colored arm contrasting against her darker one. Clara ran her hand over his skin. The hair on his arms resisted her fingers, but still she tingled at being able to touch him. She'd been watching him for a long time, yet she didn't want to move. She wanted to wake this way every morning, curl her fingers around him, and kiss him awake.

The intimacy of last night making her bold, Clara pressed her mouth to Luke's chest. He shifted slightly. His arm came around her, pulling her closer to him.

Clara smiled at the feel of his body pressed thigh to thigh with hers. Heat started in her stomach and radiated downward. She stretched languidly, tangling her legs with his. Suddenly, his arms crushed her to him and his mouth descended on hers in a deep kiss, transforming her into a soft, warm liquid. She climbed onto Luke, deepening the kiss, pushing her tongue between his teeth and battling with him for dominance. Luke won, turning her over and quickly bringing her body to fever pitch. She tried to hold back, but couldn't. When he entered her, she was hot and ready. She felt a soreness but said nothing, and in moments the primal rhythm he'd taught her the night before was replayed and the same climactic scream achieved.

In the aftermath of their union, Luke cradled her to him. Last night, Clara proved a wonderful lover. This morning, she was a timid coquette, running her fingers up his arm and kissing him while she thought he slept. He loved the feel of her, the smell of her hair and her skin. It was a shame they would have to return to the valley and all its rules.

Fifteen

Red Wind stood ready for Clara to climb into the saddle. She stared from the horse, who had become a close friend, to the cabin where her life had changed.

"Got everything?" Luke asked, pulling the door of the cabin closed.

Clara nodded with a smile. Luke stepped onto the ground where she stood, and she stared openly at him. Finally, she felt she didn't have to conceal her true feelings, she didn't have to pretend she was falling in love with him. She *was* in love with him.

"I'm sure there's a welcoming committee waiting for us. You'd better mount up."

Luke dropped a kiss on her mouth and started to move away. Then, thinking better, he stepped back and pulled her against him, his mouth taking hers in a toe-curling kiss. Clara opened her mouth as his tongue sought entrance, and her arms climbed over his shoulders, her fingers touching the sensitive parts of his ears. She felt his sound against her mouth, a sound she'd become accustomed to during their long night of lovemaking.

Heat spread against her stomach as she felt him grow hard. His hands pressed the sides of her breasts and moved over her hips, then he put her soundly away from him.

"The other parties are probably all back by now. If we don't show up soon, they'll be out looking for us both." Luke's voice seemed tight, and Clara didn't trust hers to speak at all. She patted her hair down. She'd brushed it into straight waves that fell to her shoulders, since all her curls had been washed out by the rain. She had no mirror to check her reflection, and she wondered if anyone would be able to tell the difference in her. On the inside she felt a glow, knowing that Luke was responsible for this transformation in her. She wondered if the glow came through her and could be seen on the outside.

Luke mounted his horse and turned toward her.

"Do you need help?" Luke asked, preparing to dismount again.

"I can't ride." Clara's insides were sore and swollen. It was a wonderful feeling, especially when she remembered how she'd come to be in this state, but even the idea of mounting a horse brought pain to her tender flesh. Spending two hours in the saddle would kill her.

Luke swung down and stood in front of her. "Sore?" he asked.

She nodded.

"It'll pass." His voice held nothing that would embarrass her. He astounded her in his efforts to make her comfortable, to make her first encounter with lovemaking as pleasurable and as painless as possible. With Luke, lovemaking had been a beautiful experience. She had nothing with which to compare what had happened to her, but it was the most poignant and beautiful expression of life she had ever encountered. And with Luke it had been greater than anything she could have dreamed possible.

"Do I . . ." She hesitated. "Do I look . . . any different?"

Luke's gaze raked over her. Then, at a slower pace, he studied her expression from top to bottom.

"Yes," he said. "You're gorgeous."

Kissing the tip of her nose, he took Red Wind's reins and tied them to his horse's stirrup. Then he climbed onto the gelding and reached for her hand. Trusting him as she had never trusted anyone, she let him pull her onto the big horse in front of him. She sat sidesaddle, her back resting against his chest, and together they started for Aunt Emily's.

Luke negotiated the trail with practiced ease, and Clara felt comfortable sitting in front of him. She knew she was going to have to get down before they reached the boardinghouse; but for the time being, she was glad to have Luke to herself.

"Luke?" she asked when the ground leveled to a point where they didn't appear to be traveling straight down. "Who maintains the cabin? It was so clean, free of dust, as if someone had been expected."

"Ellen does it. She comes up twice a year to make sure it's stocked with food and to air the place out."

"Why? No one could possibly get up there during the winter, if Mrs. Andersson's stories can be believed."

"Believe them. When Clem was alive, he was like a squirrel gathering food for the winter. Once the weather turned, few people could make the trip up the mountain."

Clara had the distinct impression Luke was one of those people.

"Was Ellen related to Clem?"

"No, Ellen isn't one for the hills and Clem didn't have much use for the people in town. He died before she ever met him."

Clara shifted to look over her shoulder. "Then why does she keep his house clean and stocked?"

Luke didn't answer immediately. He guided the gelding's sure feet down another portion of the rocky incline. When they were again on level ground he remained quiet.

"The reason has something to do with the two of you," Clara prompted.

"It does," he sighed.

"And you're not going to tell me what it is?"

"It's a long story and I promised Ellen I'd never tell it to anyone."

Clara leaned her head back and kissed his chin. "I understand about promises. I wouldn't want you to break it either." She wouldn't ask Luke again about Ellen, but there was something she had to know.

"Were you two lovers?" she asked.

Luke's arms tightened around her waist and he laughed. For the second time since she'd met him, she heard him laugh from the depths of his soul. When he finally stopped, he answered her with a question.

"Do we act like lovers?"

Clara didn't know how lovers acted. Were she and Luke lovers now? How was she supposed to act? "I don't know," she told him. "You act like more than friends."

"Ellen is my friend, my very good friend. We've been that way since we were seventeen."

"Is that when it happened?"

"What?"

"Whatever you and she and Clem Kincaid's cabin have in common?"

"Yes," Luke answered.

They rode in silence for several minutes. He knew his comments had confused Clara and he chuckled at her question that he and Ellen could ever have been lovers. They were closer to sister and brother, at least as close as they could get.

Luke wanted to tell Clara the story. He wanted her to know everything. It had been twenty years ago, and there could be no harm now in anyone's knowing what had happened at the cabin between him and Ellen; but he had promised he wouldn't tell anyone. He had never broken that trust, yet somehow he wanted Clara to know the truth.

"Ellen was seventeen," he began several minutes later, not really expecting to say anything. "Her father ran the bank in Butte, and Ellen had everything she ever wanted. She went to the best schools. When she was in her teens, he sent her to a finishing school in Boston."

Clara leaned back, remembering her own fun-filled days before her parents died.

"She came home every summer. Her seventeenth year she decided to surprise her father by coming home for Christmas, but there weren't any trains then and her entire journey had to be made by stage."

Clara stiffened, instinctively knowing that whatever he was about to tell her would be painful.

"The weather that year was unusually severe. The snows came early and stayed late. Just this side of the valley, the stage was ambushed and everyone else was killed. I was hunting deer when I found her. Her face was black and blue, and she couldn't talk. They'd tried to choke her and she'd fought. Red bruises ringed her neck; her clothes were torn, and her feet were blue with cold."

"You took her to the cabin."

Luke nodded against the top of her head.

"How did you get up there with all the snow?"

"The first night we didn't. When she first saw me, she thought I was one of the people who'd attacked the stage. She screamed as much as her sore throat would allow, then she ran in the snow. She fought me like a wild woman. Finally, when she had little strength left, she realized I wasn't trying to hurt her. It hurt too much for her to talk. She had to write down in the snow what had happened to her. I wrapped her in the horse blankets and got a fire started. Then I told her we should go to town and alert the authorities, but she refused. She didn't want her father to see her. She was sure he'd hunt the men who'd attacked the stage and kill them in cold blood."

"They deserved to be jailed."

"They were found, tried, and convicted. But Ellen knew her father wouldn't give her time to explain if I walked in with her, especially if you could have seen the way she looked. More than likely, he'd have had me in jail. So I went back to the stage and gathered her bags, then we went to the cabin."

"Didn't anyone find the stage and the other people who were on it?"

"Telegraph messages sent to the last stop confirmed an on-time departure, so search parties were sent out. The stage was found, and within days, the men who'd robbed and killed the passengers were also found hiding in the mountains. They'd miscalculated how deep the snow was in the hills, one of them froze to death. The other two were found with the money and jewelry they'd stolen from the passengers."

"What happened to Ellen?"

"She spent the winter at Clem's cabin. I'd bring her food and make sure she was all right and report that no one had missed her in town."

"What about the school? Didn't they write when she didn't return after Christmas?"

"Ellen wrote the school a message and signed her father's name. I rode to Helena and telegraphed it. She asked them to store her belongings until spring, when she'd send them money to ship them home."

"What about her father? Didn't he wonder about her?"

"She also had me send a telegram to a friend she had in Boston, who wired her father she was staying there through the holidays."

"He believed that?" Clara frowned.

Luke nodded. "Her friend was from a very wealthy family. Ellen's father took pride in telling everyone his daughter was hobnobbing with the rich society of Boston, Massachusetts."

"I'm amazed she thought of doing all that!" Clara couldn't imagine thinking clearly after so traumatic an experience.

"She thought of most of it. Mainly she was terrified of her father and what he would do to me if he found out I was helping her."

"It could only have taken a few weeks for her bruises to heal. Why didn't she go home then?"

"The winter of '81 dropped snow every day for thirty-seven days. The hills racked up snow six to seven feet high. Getting to and from the cabin took hours. Ellen couldn't have made it down alone and she refused to allow me to escort her into Butte."

"Why didn't you take her to Helena and put her on the stage?"

"I thought about it, but Ellen had nightmares. Everything scared her. She'd jump each time an icicle fell or an animal howled in the night. She'd awaken screaming in fright and then she couldn't sleep the rest of the night. If she'd gone home it would be a matter of days before her father and the whole town knew the story. In 1881 people weren't as liberal as they are today. We spent many hours talking about our differences that winter."

"And you became the best of friends." Somehow Clara felt jealous of Ellen and her relationship with Luke.

"As you said, more than friends. Ellen is like the sister I never had."

"A sister in Ellen. Aunt Emily considers you a son. All you need is a wife and children to complete the family."

Luke stiffened, his hands grabbing her arms like steel traps."

"No wife and *no* children."

As Luke had predicted, a welcoming committee consisting of Ellen Turnbull, Martha Ames, Reverend Reed, Zeke, and every inhabitant of the boardinghouse waited as Luke and Clara rode up to the picket fence. Clara sat on Red Wind, having completed the last quarter-mile on her own horse.

Aunt Emily's arms reached up to her as they came to a stop.

"I'm fine, Aunt Emily," Clara began her explanation, taking hold of the older woman's hands. "I didn't mean to be such trouble." She sat straight-backed in her saddle. Getting down would be a problem. Her insides had felt each upward movement of Red Wind's walk.

For the first time since she'd come to the valley, Clara saw her aunt in a less than perfect condition. Aunt Emily's beautifully coiffed hair had tendrils dangling from it. Her eyes were tired as if she'd had no sleep. While Clara had been curled up warm and happy in Luke's arms, her aunt had been wide awake wondering if she were alive or dead.

Luke got down first and quickly came to her rescue. "Clara bumped her head on a falling rock. She may be a little dizzy," he lied. His powerful arms grasped her waist and lifted her off Red Wind. Clara realized his lie would give her reason to need help walking. Even without it, Martha Ames was by her side.

"I'll help you." The young girl took her arm.

"There's no need. I'm not hurt," Clara protested.

"Come on in, child. I have a hot bath waiting," Aunt Emily said.

"I'll take her," Luke whispered. Only Clara noticed the strange note in his voice. He picked her up and followed Aunt Emily toward the door, and the entourage followed Clara. On the porch stood Antonia Morrison. Clara stifled a groan; she would have to return from her visit with her daughter now. Her gaze took in Clara's appearance and Luke's arms around her, and Clara was sure that she knew that she and Luke had spent the night in each other's arms.

"Are you well, my dear?" she asked.

"Yes, ma'am," Clara replied.

Luke rode casually through town two days later. Not much seemed to have changed. Antonia's viper tongue had had enough time to spread her story to every family in the small community, yet he could see no visible difference.

Miss Emily had ushered Clara straight to bed
after her bath. Few effects of her ordeal were present, except the soreness only the two of them
knew about. Several people dropped by to make
sure she'd arrived home safely, and Doc Pritchard
checked her bruises and pronounced her healthy.

Clara had fully moved into her own house, and
school would begin in another few days. Maybe
he was wrong and Antonia had surprised him. If
she were going to have Clara run out of the valley,
this would be the best time to do it.

He supposed he'd have to wait and see what happened. In the meantime, he needed to talk to Ellen.

Living alone had it merits. It afforded Clara the
ability to do what she wanted, when she wanted
to do it. There was no one talking incessantly, no
card games going on in the parlor, no heated po-
litical discussions in smoke-filled rooms. Here,
there was peace and quiet. Clara hated it.

She'd been in the house she'd thought she'd
wanted for almost five days. Three days ago it had
begun to rain, and yesterday the leak in the ceiling
had begun. She knew all houses had their problems. In her time she'd been to many barn raisings
and newlywed house-building parties. She pushed
the desk aside and set a bowl on the floor. Luckily,
the drip was slow and wouldn't make too big a
mess before she fixed it.

Tonight the choir met, and Clara thought she'd
walk over and help out with the children. Since
the cold weather had set in, there were no longer

any baseball games and frequently the children needed another place to express themselves. Unfortunately, their expressions could be rather loud.

Donning a long coat, Clara slipped her arms into the sleeves, placed a hat on her head, and left for the church. She heard someone playing the piano long before she reached the children's building. It was early, and choir practice wouldn't begin for another half an hour. The playing sounded like Martha, but Clara didn't recognize the song and Martha rarely went into the sanctuary except on Sunday. Clara stopped outside the door and listened. She'd never heard Martha play this song. It had a wonderful melody and she could only think of being in love as she stood, listening. It was the most beautiful song she'd ever heard.

When it ended, she opened the door and stepped into the warm room. "Martha, what a beautiful song," she said.

The young girl jumped as if she'd been caught doing something wrong. "You're early," she accused.

"I finished up and set out bowls to collect the water. Listening to the drip was driving me crazy."

"Drip?"

"There's a leak in the roof. I'll have to fix it when it stops raining," she explained.

"You can fix a leaky roof?"

"Yes." Clara nodded, but she didn't want to talk about the roof. "What were you playing?"

Martha didn't answer. She stared at the floor, and Clara walked toward her.

"It isn't anything," she said. "I shouldn't have played it."

Clara had seen Martha nervous before, but never with her. They had always been friends, equals. "Is something wrong, Martha?" she asked.

"Oh, no." She tried to smile, but Clara wasn't fooled.

"Martha, it's a wonderful song."

"Do you really think so?" Martha sneaked a peek at her.

"Did you write it?" Clara lowered her voice.

Martha stared at her and nodded timidly.

"Why didn't you tell me?" Clara asked. "Are there others?"

"I have hundreds of them."

"Play another one."

Martha grinned. The color rose in her cheeks as she turned back to the keyboard and played another song with a similar style. It had a lively melody and made Clara want to tap her toe. At Clara's nod, Martha launched into another original piece.

"Have you written these down?"

"Yes," Martha told her, giving Clara an idea. She didn't want to tell Martha about it. It was farfetched and might not work, but if she were right Martha was going to have the surprise of her life. "Do you mind if I look at them?"

Martha shook her head. "I'll bring them when I come on Thursday." School would begin on Thursday, and Clara knew Martha was excited about the start of the term.

Behind them, the choir members began to file in and Clara greeted them cordially, sensing a hesitance in their response. In previous meetings everyone had been friendly, overly friendly, in fact; but after she'd returned from her ordeal in the mountains, things had changed ever so slightly. Clara recognized the signs. She'd seen them before, six years ago when her parents had died and she had gone to live with Wade. The gossip had begun and she was the reason for it; she made a mental note to talk to Ellen soon. Even though Ellen lived in Butte, she knew everything that went on in the valley. She'd be able to tell her what was happening, and maybe Clara could do something about it. She wouldn't let the same thing happen to her here as in Virginia. She wasn't fifteen anymore. She was a grown woman now and capable of making her own decisions.

Stopping to greet Reverend Reed, Clara observed the choir members before she and Martha moved to the children's wing.

"Good morning, Mrs. Carter." Clara walked into the store early the next morning. The citizens of the valley were early risers and several brightly clad women browsed about the mercantile. Clara noticed them turn their gazes toward her.

"Miss Clara," Marlene Carter's mouth was tight as she spoke. "Can I get you something."

"I need some ten-penny nails and some roofing tiles," she told her.

"Nails are over there in the barrel. I'll have Joe get you some tiles." She hesitated a second then walked toward the back of the store.

Clara bypassed the nails and went to the two women standing near a rack of ready-made dresses.

"Good morning, Mrs. Edwards, Mrs. Wilson."

They turned as if they hadn't noticed her arrival.

"Good morning," Mrs. Edwards said stiffly. "I suppose you're having Luke come by and fix something?"

Clara glanced over her shoulder. She knew they'd heard her order. Yet she said it as if Clara was conspiring to get Luke to her house. "I hadn't planned to ask him," she said.

"Then what do you need tiles and nails for?" Mrs. Wilson blurted out.

Clara had the impression the woman did not intend to speak. "I have a leak," she explained. "I can fix it myself."

"Surely that won't be necessary." Mrs. Edwards' sugary voice was getting on her nerves. "There are plenty of people who'd be willing to come by and fix the leak for you."

"Does that include Luke?" Clara challenged. The valley hadn't been the same since she and Luke returned from their night in the mountains.

Mrs. Edwards took Clara's arm. "Let me give you some advice," she whispered, turning her away from Mrs. Wilson. "The valley probably isn't as . . ." She hesitated, giving herself time to compose her words. "I suppose where you're from is more, shall we say, progressive than it is here."

"Mrs. Edwards." Clara stepped away, putting a display table of fabric in front of them and forcing the woman to drop her hold on Clara's arm. Mrs.

Wilson stood directly behind them, hanging onto every word the two were saying. "There's something you're trying to say. Please say it directly."

The older woman raised her chin and pushed her shoulders back. Her face stiffened as if her face muscles had suddenly gone into rigor mortis. "Quite frankly, my dear, there's talk in the valley about you and Luke Evans."

"What kind of talk?"

"What do you think people are saying? You two spent the night together."

"How do you know that?"

"You're not going to deny it?" Her pencil-thin eyebrows raised. "Why the whole valley knows he was with you in the hills all night long."

"The whole valley wasn't there. Did Luke tell you he spent the night with me?"

"No, but—"

"Have I told you that?"

"No."

"So it's conceivable that we didn't spend the night together, that we were both in the hills at the same time."

"I'm only trying to help you, Clara."

"How, Mrs. Edwards? By spreading malicious gossip? By telling a story you know nothing about? Luke Evans did find me that night. He quite possibly saved my life. But I can see it would have been better in your eyes if I'd died on that mountain. Then my reputation would be absolved."

"There's no need to get so upset, Clara. I'm on your side."

Clara almost laughed. This woman was a viper

if she'd ever seen one. "Well Mrs. Edwards *and* you, too, Mrs. Wilson, here's something you can spread around for anyone interested enough to hear. Whatever happened concerns only Luke and myself. If we wanted you to know about it, we'd make an announcement."

"But you're the schoolteacher," Mrs. Wilson addressed her.

"And I've done nothing to jeopardize my ability to teach. If the children talk about me, they could only have overheard the gossip said by their parents."

With that Clara turned and went to the back of the store. She filled a sack with nails and asked Joe Carter to stack the tiles in the wagon. She said no salutations to the women as she left. She was sure word of her encounter would reach everyone in town before the noon meal. Clara didn't care. She would not allow them to rule her. Her life was not theirs to model into a proper form. She and Luke had spent the night together, made love, slept in each other's arms and Clara didn't regret one minute of it. Even if she never taught a single subject, she wouldn't give up one memory they'd created during their night of rapture.

Easing the buggy to a stop, Clara climbed down and tied the tether straps to the hitching post in front of Ellen Turnbull's restaurant. She'd told herself she needed to come into town to run some errands, go to the post office, get materials for the roof, and find herself a decent horse and wagon.

Living alone meant she needed to be able to haul her own goods and to get around, but it was all an excuse. She was really here to talk to Ellen.

Without reservation about walking into a fashionable restaurant, Clara went straight to the door and pushed it open.

Inside everything looked the same. The lunch hour was nearly over, and most of the tables were empty. Clara had planned it this way. Without so many people to attend to, Ellen would have time to talk to her. The redhead saw her the moment she walked through the fringed archway.

"Hello." She smiled, and looked quickly behind her. "Are you alone?"

"All alone." Clara nodded, hugging Ellen as Luke had done on their first trip here.

"Lunch for one?" Ellen's eyebrows went up.

"I was hoping to have lunch with you, if you haven't eaten yet."

A wide smile replaced Ellen's surprise. "Table for two. Right this way."

Ellen led her to a table near the rear of the room. It was private and concealed behind a large plant. There they could see anyone who came in, but were almost hidden from view. Ellen took a moment to order for them, then sat down and gave Clara her full attention.

"What gives?" she asked.

Clara shrugged. "I needed to do a little shopping, so I thought I'd drop by."

"Well from the looks of you—" Ellen looked her up and down. "—you've done quite a bit of shopping."

"My clothes arrived from Virginia."

Ellen nodded. "Where did you live before Virginia?"

Clara stiffened. "How did you know I'd been somewhere else?"

"It's how you speak. When I was in school in Boston, I'd never have said my clothes arrived from Butte. I'd have said they arrived from home. So where is home?"

Clara needed to confide in someone, and she'd already chosen Ellen. She knew she could tell her the truth and not be judged for what she'd done, but she wasn't ready to tell everything. "We used to live in New York City. My father was a doctor there. When my parents died, I went to Virginia."

"Yet you never really considered it home?"

Clara shook her head. A waitress came and placed a bowl of soup in front of them. Clara smelled the tomato aroma and reached for a bread stick.

"I had to go there," Clara explained, "but it was never really my home." It had been Wade's home, Wade's farm, Wade's children. Everything about it had belonged to someone else, and she had had very little that was hers. Her parents' house had been sold, and Wade had saved most of the money. Some of it she'd used to supplement her scholarship at school; the rest she'd left behind in Virginia. All she had now were her mother's clothes. Her father's books and instruments were back at Wade's.

Ellen took a spoonful of soup and tasted it. "So why did you come to see me?"

Clara thought she'd never be any good at hiding anything. Ellen had already seen through her. "I came to ask what's happening in the valley."

"You mean the talk about you and Luke?"

Clara had hoped she'd been imagining things, that there hadn't been any gossip about her and Luke, but Ellen's question dashed that idea.

"You didn't exactly look like a woman who needed rescuing when Luke brought you down from the mountains."

"What did I look like?"

Ellen didn't answer immediately, and Clara felt uncomfortable under her stare. "You looked like a woman who'd bumped her head and been frightened half to death."

Clara didn't believe her for a moment. Ellen didn't have to tell her how she'd looked. She knew. Probably the whole town knew, too. "Was I that obvious?"

"It's obvious to me that Luke has feelings for you and you for him. That's all it takes around here for gossip to begin."

"But I didn't ask him to find me. I would have been all right on the mountain until morning. It was Aunt Emily who sent out the search parties."

Ellen kept eating her soup. Clara knew it didn't matter. The fact was, Luke had found her and they had spent the night together.

"Do you think there's anything I could do about this?"

"There's nothing *you* can do."

Clara eyed her carefully. "If I can't, who can?"

"Luke can declare for you."

"Declare?"

"It's a custom in the valley. A man makes a declaration, usually to the family of the woman he wishes to court, then the two of them are free to meet, hold hands, and go to dances and parties as a couple. In time, they are expected to marry."

"Luke would never do that. He doesn't want to marry again." Clara wondered why Luke hadn't mentioned this custom to her when they'd decided to pretend. Remembering that the couple would be expected to marry gave her the reason. He'd been clear about his feelings on the subject of marriage.

"He says that, but I see him look at you and those are not the eyes of a man who's buried his heart."

The blood coursed through Clara's system, and she wanted to jump out of the chair. But she remained composed, hiding her real feelings from Ellen.

"How does anyone know when this declaration is made?"

"In the valley everyone knows everything. With the amount of meetings, choir practices, parlor games, Sunday services—" Ellen rolled her eyes to the ceiling. "—word gets around."

"I can't ask him to do anything like that," Clara said.

Ellen began to speak, but stopped when the waitress took their soup bowls away and placed plates of southern fried chicken with candied sweet potatoes and snapped beans in front of them. Clara had sampled German, Swedish, and Danish foods since she'd arrived because Aunt Emily liked to make everyone feel at home by providing them with their native foods. Yet the smell of this meal stirred Clara's stomach juices.

"How do you really feel about Luke?" Ellen asked when they were alone again.

Clara thought about that for a long time. "I'm in love with him," she told her. "But he isn't in love with me. He's still in love with his wife."

"Did he tell you that?"

"No, he told me I deserved a man who was in love with me and he wasn't that man."

"Well, maybe it's time we showed him how wrong he is."

"No!" Clara said. "I can't marry Luke even if he wanted me to." Clara didn't explain since she didn't feel she could tell the whole truth and she couldn't ask Luke to deceive the entire valley, just to stop people from wagging their tongues, when she couldn't hold up her part of the bargain. "Maybe it won't amount to anything. Maybe something else will come along for people to talk about and they won't think about Luke and me."

"And maybe pigs will fly." Ellen bit into her chicken. "Luke was here at breakfast. I know he told you about our winter in Clem's cabin."

"I'm sorry he broke his promise. I won't tell anyone." Clara tasted her chicken. Ellen's cook had prepared it exactly as she would have.

"It's not likely to cause any commotion now." Ellen paused. "Of course, we have our die-hard conservatives. They'd try to start a scandal and keep people away from the restaurant, but I'm bet-

ting they'd be more interested in what's going on
here and now than something that happened eigh-
teen years ago."

"I would think they'd try to ruin Luke's business."

"That would happen, too, but he has an interest
in this place." Ellen opened her arms to encompass
the room. "It would be enough to keep him until
the gossip mongers found a juicier morsel."

"Luke owns part of this restaurant?" Clara lifted
her ice tea glass and drank.

"He didn't tell you about that?"

"No," Clara said.

Ellen leaned back in her chair. "A few years
after the winter at Clem's, I married Reginald
Adams, a man I thought I was in love with. He
turned out to be a fortune hunter only interested
in the fact that I was the banker's daughter and
likely to inherit a lot of money. He drank hard and
gambled away everything we owned. One night he
was killed during a card game when a man accused him of cheating, and that was when I found
out we didn't own the house we lived in. Reggie
had mortgaged it to a bank in Helena. A month
later, the night before a bank examiner was due
to audit the bank, my father committed suicide.
He'd been embezzling funds to maintain his own
extravagant lifestyle. I had nothing—no place to
live, no money, no relatives."

Clara felt a large lump in her throat. She wanted
to cry, but Ellen's eyes were dry.

"Luke came to my rescue. He paid the note on
the house and allowed me to live there. I started

giving piano lessons, but they weren't enough to pay for everything. Miss Emily suggested I open the restaurant, but I needed a loan."

"The bank gave you a loan?" Clara found that surprising since her father's crime had involved the bank.

Ellen shook her head. "Luke loaned me the money to get it started. It's been our secret all these years; even Miss Emily doesn't know where the money came from."

"So Luke owns half of this?"

"No." Ellen shook her head. "I tried to repay him several times after it began to earn money, but he refused. He wouldn't even let me change the deed to include his name. He said he owed it to me. Can you imagine that? First he saves my life in the hills, then rescues me from bankruptcy, yet he thinks *he* owes me."

Clara understood. Luke was a quiet man. He didn't have to shout messages to the world, but altered things without anyone's really knowing it. Ellen had helped him in a big way, even though she didn't realize it, simply by accepting him. She welcomed him in her restaurant, just as she accepted the Indians and Germans and Swedes. Clara knew prejudices had to be learned, and here she could actually see the difference it made when people weren't taught that one race was inferior to another. Luke had said Ellen's father would have jailed him, yet his daughter had openly befriended him.

A smile curved Clara's mouth.

"What are you smiling at?" Ellen asked.

"You don't know what you did for Luke and Martha or the rest of the valley's inhabitants?" she questioned. "My father used to take me to the hospital on Sundays after church," Clara told her. "I looked forward to going and wanted to be a doctor myself for a while."

Ellen looked at her, confused by the abrupt change of subject.

"One afternoon when I was twelve, we went into the big building and, as usual, we visited his patients, read their charts, and asked about their families."

Clara coughed, remembering the day she was about to describe. Taking a drink, she continued. "As we left, there was a commotion in the street, a carriage accident. Several people were hurt, including a pregnant woman. Of course, my father rushed to help, and nurses, orderlies, and doctors poured from the hospital doors with wheelchairs, gurneys, and medical bags. I felt in the way, but kept my eye on my father. He went to work immediately, trying to gauge the degree of need for each of the wounded passengers."

Clara paused. The lump that always came to her throat when she remembered that day lodged in place. She swallowed it and went on.

"I stood on the curb, watching as he went to the pregnant woman. Blood flowed from a cut on her head, and her husband nearly covered her. My father tried to pull him away to check the woman, who clutched her swollen belly and wailed in pain. The man pushed my father's hands away when he approached his wife and wouldn't let him touch her. She moaned louder, then started to scream. My father asked her questions about her pain, but her husband prevented her from answering by shouting for him to go away and leave them alone. Then some of the other doctors came over, each of them trying to get the man to let his wife be examined, but it was no use."

"What happened? Why wouldn't he let them help her?" Ellen's eyebrows knitted together.

"My father was a Negro. The woman was white."

Ellen's hand went to her throat.

"When she moved her legs, the ground was covered with blood. No amount of reason could convince the man they could help her if he'd only let them. Suddenly, she started to scream, and it was so loud I had to cover my ears. My father whispered to the others, and they grabbed the man and pulled him away so my father could go to her. But by then it was too late and she died in the street in a pool of blood. My father told me later they could have saved her and her baby. But because a man thought a Negro doctor was not worthy to touch his wife, he lost both her and his child. She bled to death in front of a hospital and in view of at least three doctors and several nurses."

Clara finished and sat back against her chair. She'd never forget that day or the impact it had had on her as a child.

"You think because I open my restaurant to everyone that I'm changing the world?"

"Maybe not the world," Clara granted. "But you

have made a difference in Butte. You've been to Boston; you know how separate the races are there. Here, the dividing line isn't as strong. I'm sure it's because of you and Luke and the special friendship you share. Maybe one day he and I can have that kind of friendship."

Ellen smiled. "I don't think so," she said. "Luke's a good man, Clara, and he was hurt badly when Peg died; but he's had three years to recover. I've seen the way he looks at you, and it's not friendship he wants. If you're in love with him, maybe he should declare his intentions toward you."

Clara shook her head. She knew better than to even think anything could come of the relationship they had. It had no future. She was the school-teacher and she would always be that. Nothing more was owed her, and she could ask for nothing more.

Sixteen

Luke pushed his hat back on his head. He closed his eyes, shaking his head in frustration, but when he looked again, what he'd thought he'd seen was still there. Clara, a hammer in hand, knelt on the roof, nailing tiles near the left edge of the house.

"Woman!" The word was a curse. She had to have been put here to drive him crazy—and he was only a week away from getting there. Slapping his hat against the horse's rump, he rode swiftly, but slowed before getting near enough for her to hear his approach. She was dangerously close to the end of the roof and at a sudden sound might turn the wrong way. "Why the hell do you insist on trying to do everything?" he grumbled under his breath.

Luke covered the remaining distance on foot. Testing the ladder, he made sure it was secure enough to accept his weight before climbing to the top. Clara, finishing her chore, placed her hands on her hips and sat back on her legs.

Luke surveyed her work. She had done a good job, he had to admit. Each tile overlapped the one before, and her patch linked the roofing together in a seamless sea. Luke nodded. He couldn't have done better himself.

"Clara, what are you doing up here?"

Lightning couldn't have struck faster. Exactly what he had been afraid of happened. Clara jerked up, over-balancing. Hammers, nails, and loose tile scattered across the roof, spilling into the gutters with little tinkling sounds as he reached for Clara. His heart leaped to his throat and lodged there. *Don't let her fall,* he prayed. *I'll die if she falls.*

Leaning as far as he dared, he grabbed for her. His hand caught one of hers, and he scooped the other around her narrow waist. The ladder teetered as his weight strained it, and he didn't move, didn't breathe. He held Clara so tight he thought he'd break her. If the ladder lost its center of gravity, they'd both go over the edge.

"Luke!" Clara squeezed closer to him.

"Lean the other way," he muttered, his voice tense with his own effort to settle the shaky ladder. She couldn't weigh more than ten pounds over a hundred, but the shift of weight might save them both.

Clara obeyed.

The ladder righted itself and Luke exhaled a long, slow breath. His fingers and arms turned to water and he suddenly couldn't grip anything, not even Clara. He climbed onto the roof before his legs refused to support him. Holding Clara next to him, he waited until strength returned to his limp arms.

"Let's get down. I'll feel better when my feet are on solid ground." It was actually her feet he was worried about. Luke was careful when he worked. Safety was his prime concern, and his crews knew it. Every few years there was an accident in the mines, and someone's carelessness caused innocent people to die, children to grow up without fathers. His sites had few accidents.

"I'll go first." He helped Clara to the edge, making sure she was safely positioned before he stepped backward over the first rung. A few steps down the ladder, he motioned for her to join him. Together, they worked their way to the ground.

At the bottom, Clara hiccupped as she tried to drag the air into her lungs. After a few moments, reason seemed to return to her and she turned to him, suddenly angry. "Why did you do that?"

"Do what?"

"Scare me half to death. I could have been killed." Tears welled in her eyes, but she fought them. She didn't have time for tears now. She wanted to pound Luke into the ground.

"I saved your life."

"If you hadn't come upon me like a cat in the night, I wouldn't have fallen over the side and you wouldn't have had to save my life."

"That was what I was trying to avoid." Luke stopped. "What were you doing up there anyway?"

"Wasn't it obvious? The roof leaks. I was fixing it."

"And why the hell did you think you could do that? All you had to do was ask and I'd have come and fixed the damn thing."

"I didn't need your help. The house is my responsibility." Clara turned away. She was taking her anger out on Luke, but the truth was she was scared. For the second time she had been in a near-death situation, and she didn't like it. "This is my house," she repeated, reasonably.

She had been responsible for everything that happened in Wade's house. If the fire needed wood, she chopped it. If the cellar became unmanageable, she cleaned it. If water poured in from the roof, she went up and fixed it. Calling Luke had simply not occurred to her. "I didn't ask for your help. Why are you here?"

"Miss Emily sent me. You told her the roof leaked."

"I didn't," Clara said, then remembered she'd mentioned it to Martha and her indignation abated. She had spoken in anger and regretted her irritation. Luke had come to help her and he *had* saved her life. "Luke, I'm sorry. I should thank you."

Luke's shoulders dropped as if he, too, let go of his anger. "I don't want you on the roof again. If anything, *anything* needs fixing, promise me you'll let me know?"

Clara stared at the ground. Why was she having problems with this question? Hadn't she wanted this? Hadn't all the years of having the responsibility for the house, the children, and her schooling been enough? Wasn't part of her reason for leaving Virginia to make someone else responsible for everything? Why now did she think Luke was threatening her ability to be independent? Mrs. Edwards' words flowed into her mind. Luke's presence, no matter how innocent, wouldn't be looked upon as such.

"Clara?" Luke prompted.

"I promise," she said. Clara's hand went to her stomach. She felt sick. Thinking about falling off the roof made her close her eyes to control the sinking feeling that had her hot and cold at the same time.

"Are you all right?" Luke put his hand on her shoulder and touched her forehead with the back of his hand.

"I'm fine," she said weakly.

"Here, sit down." He lowered her to the third rung of the ladder and pushed her head down. "Don't move," he told her when she tried to raise her head.

"I feel better," she said after a few moments.

Luke helped her sit back. She tried to smile but felt her lips falter. "I guess I don't take nearly dying the way I should."

"You're doing fine," he encouraged. "Can you stand?"

Clara nodded and pushed herself up with Luke's help.

"Shall we go inside and see what the ceilings look like?"

Clara led the way. She tried to appear normal, but admitted to herself she was shaky.

"Most of the damage is in my den and the small upstairs bedroom." She entered the room, which was clean and neat and had all her papers organized. Everything looked in place except the brown stains across the ceiling and three bowls of water on the floor. "I'll get these." She reached for the first bowl, and Luke took it from her.

"Sit down," he said. "You're probably more shaken than you realize."

She took a seat in an overstuffed chair and pulled a shawl around her shoulders. "Would you like something to drink?" she asked over her shoulder as he surveyed the ceiling damage.

"I can't stay." Luke moved one of the other bowls and stood on a chair to test the damage on the high ceiling.

"I have to go over to one of the sites. I've got a crew trying to finish a house before the snow falls. I'll have to come back to fix this." He indicated the ceiling.

"I'm sure it won't leak anymore, and I can—"

"Wait until I get back to do it," he finished for her.

"I promised," Clara replied. "How's your house coming?"

"It'll wait until spring."

Clara hugged the shawl closer to her. "I slowed you down," she murmured, remembering the dynamite accident. If she hadn't come by that day he would have had time to finish.

"Tell me what happened?" he said.

"You've heard already?"

"I know something is wrong."

"I had an argument with Mrs. Edwards a couple of days ago. She indicated that my ability to teach has somehow been impaired by our night on the mountain."

"I'm sure she was much harsher than that."

"Yes, she was," Clara confirmed, dropping her head to his chest.

"Is that why you didn't ask me to fix the roof?"

"Not entirely."

"If there had been any way to get down from the hills, Clara—"

"I know, Luke. I don't regret anything that happened."

Luke's heart hammered when she said that. He didn't regret it either. He found it difficult to keep her out of his thoughts, despite his conscious decisions to do so.

Dropping his hands he stepped back. "I should be going now."

"Luke, we're not entirely innocent of most of the gossip. I think it would be best if we didn't spend any more time together."

Luke heard her words, but knew her heart wasn't in them. Yet he knew she was right.

He nodded then pulled her into his arms and kissed her soundly. "I knew if I did that I wouldn't want to leave." Clara's eyes darkened and she stared up at him. Her arms circled his neck, and he kissed her again. Passion flared between them as hot and fast as a flash fire.

"Push me away, Clara," he pleaded, his voice low and hungry. "I don't have the strength to do it myself." His mouth rained wet kisses over her face, her eyes, her cheeks.

Clara did the opposite of his request. She fit her body into his and pressed her lips against a mouth both soft and firm. Their union was a duel of lips, tongues, and heads. Clara's hands gripped his crown as she fought to keep him from ending the embrace. With ragged breath, they collapsed

against each other, hugging as tight as they could.
Luke knew the pent-up emotions he dealt with. He
could feel Clara's. Inside her were the same needs,
the same drives that kept him awake and wanting
her at night.

He had to go. If he didn't, he'd take her to bed
and make love to her for the rest of the afternoon
and long into the night. The thought had merit. He
wanted to act on it. He turned her toward the door
so he couldn't change his mind. With his arm
around her waist he walked back to the entrance.
"I'll come back soon and finish the ceiling. I'll
also make sure we're properly chaperoned."

"All right," she said. She had that nervousness
about her he'd recognized in the hills. She put her
hands behind her back at the entrance. Her eyes
held secrets when they met his. Luke fought with
himself over leaving. Dark brown eyes he could
drown in, he thought, looking at her. He wondered
what other secrets she had and whether he'd ever
be able to uncover them.

School began and the first major snowfall of the
season fell on the some day, but of the thirty students Clara expected, only one failed to showed
up—Mike Carver. His brother Wendell said he was
sick with a cold. The children tried to convince
her there was too much snow and that the other
teachers would always let them go home early, but
Clara disregarded their moans. She accepted this
as a test of her ability to control the situation. The
first day should set the tone, she thought, as she

and Martha seated them according to age and grade level. The former teacher had left records which Clara had spent hours going through to get her footing. She had been glad to see that some of the students had received very good grades. Her job was going to be to keep them motivated while she and Martha worked with the ones who needed extra help. Her newly appointed assistant passed the books out, then took the younger children to a corner of the room where she began reading them a story. Clara worked with the older group, doing arithmetic and history.

The day, which Clara had thought would drag by, flew away. By dismissal time, there were four inches of snow on the ground, more than she had ever seen in her life. Clara and Martha helped the little ones with their coats and scarves and sent them home with a chorus of goodbyes.

Martha, beaming with happiness, left shortly afterwards, and Clara checked the potbellied stove before going to her own residence. The snow topped her shoes, and she had to hold her skirts up to keep them from dragging in the wetness. She'd supervised the moving of her furniture and spent the week before school unpacking the trunks Annie Pearl had sent her, planning what kind of curtains she would make when she got her salary at the end of the month and spending some of the money Annie Pearl had sent on food supplies she needed to stock the kitchen.

On her own meant doing everything for herself, so she set about getting supper started. She lit the gas lamps in the kitchen and looked at the pages she'd left on the table this morning. She'd been trying to write to Wade, but no matter what she said, she couldn't explain why she could no longer live the same life she had lived under his roof for the last six years.

She realized now that saying it in person would be easier than writing. She didn't want to hurt Wade. He'd been too good to her for her to treat him this way. Running out and leaving only a letter behind, a letter he in all probability couldn't read completely, had been wrong—cowardly.

Clara was no coward. She had to go back. She knew that now. If she wanted control of her life, *real* control, she couldn't leave it like this. She had to face the consequences of her action; and if that meant returning to Virginia, she'd go there. As Annie Pearl had said, one way or another, she'd have to settle things with Wade.

She'd finish the letter tonight, she told herself. She'd explain as much as she could and let him know she would be returning when school ended. It was unfair of her to leave the valley without a teacher while she went back to Virginia.

Returning did not mean she would resume her life as it had been. When she'd left she'd known that that kind of life was not for her; and now that she been here for two months, she didn't want to go back. Luke had something to do with her decision, but even without his influence, her life as she had lived it in Virginia was at an end.

She set out the dishes for the dinner meal, feeling better. Having made the decision seemed to lift a weight she hadn't realized she'd carried. She would also have to let Aunt Emily know the whole truth. It might hurt her at first, but her only relative had been nothing but kind to her; she deserved to know the truth. Just as she lit the oven, she heard a knock.

"Hello, Zeke," she said, seeing Aunt Emily's stable hand standing at her door, covered in snow. His hat brim acted as a ledge, collecting the flakes and holding them. He touched it when she opened the door, causing a crack in the perfect mountain that had collected on his head. His mustache and beard contrasted starkly against the dark, ruddy color of his skin.

"You got another letter," he told her, reaching under his snow-dusted coat to pull out the white envelope, and she knew Wade had found her. Her breath stopped and she shivered suddenly.

"You're cold, ma'am. Better get inside. Winter can be mighty rough out here."

Zeke's voice reached out and steadied her. It was only a letter. And there was nothing he could do in a letter.

"Zeke, I was about to make some coffee. Won't you come in and have a cup?"

Zeke touched his hat again. "Thank you, but I'd best be getting back to the house. Good evening."

With that he was gone. Clara watched him leave for a moment before closing the door. She shivered again, looking at her name on the outside of the envelope. Written in a hard, scrawling hand, it was cryptic, as if a child just beginning to form letters had penned it.

Clara sat down in front of the fire in the living room and opened the envelope.

August 29, 1899

Dear Clara,

I don't know why you left. The children were very upset and I was worried. They want to know when you'll be coming home. I can't tell them. They need you, especially the girls. Stephen and William miss you, too, but they won't let anybody see how they feel.

Come home, Clara. We'll talk about whatever it is that needs changing. I'm sure your mama and daddy would want you to be happy, and that is all I want.

Wade

Numbness gripped her when she finished reading. The letter was short, many words had been spelled wrong, but it was Wade. He must have spent a long time writing it since he found it difficult to read and write. It ripped her heart out. What she'd done was wrong, not leaving him, but the way she'd left him—the coward's way. She hadn't confronted him with her feelings, but had left like a thief in the night, stealing her trunks and boarding a train in the early-morning mist. Wade deserved more than that. He'd provided much for her in the past six years and her actions had been unforgivable.

Stuffing the paper back in the envelope, she headed for the kitchen when another knock on the door stopped her. *Zeke must have changed his mind about the coffee,* she thought.

"Zeke, did you . . . Luke!"

Mesmerized, she didn't say a word, then the cold

air blew through her clothes and she remembered where she was. "Come in," she said. She couldn't leave him standing on the step in this weather. It was hospitable to invite a friend inside and offer comfort, even though the valley's tongues wagged about the two of them. What else could she do?

Slapping his hat against his hand and kicking one foot against the other to rid himself of the excess snow, he stepped across the threshold. With one hand he pushed the door closed.

Clara started across the room, but Luke caught her, turning her around and into his arms. He kissed her like a starving man, his cold mouth warming her and making her shiver at the emotional sensations that weakened her knees. Clara knew she should push him away. She should . . . but she couldn't. His mouth was too enticing. She wrapped herself around him, blocking out her thoughts. She didn't want to think of Wade or what she'd done to him. She didn't want to think of anything but Luke.

"I tried to stay away," he said, kissing her face, "but since you left, I can't stop thinking of you." His mouth found hers again and he kissed it tenderly. She was lost; once more, he'd taken her to that world where only the two of them existed.

Clara loved his roughness, when he held her tightly and ground her softness into his hard muscles. When he was tender, she melted, her throat so tight she didn't know if she could hold the tears back. No one had ever held her with such care, made her feelings so raw and so alive. No one had ever made her feel like a woman—except Luke.

He was the only man who could ever make her feel like this.

She hugged him, burying her face in his shoulder. Hot tears filled her closed eyes and spilled from under her lids. She stayed pressed against him, afraid to move until she could control the emotions that overwhelmed her.

"What are you doing here?" Clara asked. Four inches of snow covered the ground, but no one here seemed to take any notice of the white roads and hills, except her.

"I told myself I wanted to check to make sure you were all right." His hands curled into her hair, loosening it from its upswept style. "That everything was all right." His mouth touched her eyes. "The truth is, I wanted to see you, hold you, kiss you." His mouth found hers. His lips were soft, seeking, tasting. Her mouth opened, allowing him entrance. His tongue filled the space, absorbing her into him, battling with her in their quest to dominate each other.

Finally, weak with need for each other, they slumped together for support. Luke held her loosely, his hands running through her hair.

Thank God for Luke, Clara thought. She needed a man who wanted her. She hadn't known how starved she was for someone to hold her until Luke had pulled her into his arms the first time. She came alive when he kissed her and made love to her, and she didn't want to live without that kind of love. Yet as long as Wade remained in her past, she'd be forced to forget any thoughts of a life with someone else.

"Did the amount of snow surprise you?" Luke pulled her back to the present.

"Yes, and to think it will get worse! I can't imagine it. But everything is fine here." Clara was comfortably clasped against his chest. "I checked on Red Wind, made sure she had plenty of fresh water and that it wouldn't freeze. I closed the school, damped down the fire, and secured all the doors." She felt conscious of his presence. Her heart hadn't stopped the flips it did whenever she was with him. She took several steps back. "When I came here—" She indicated the room behind her. "I lit the fire and started dinner. Are you hungry?"

Luke's eyes swept over her in a slow trip that took her in from head to foot. "I'm starving," he said.

Clara swallowed at the baldness of his comment. Her body already tingled from Luke's kiss, and his watching her with such raw longing in his eyes threw her senses into overload. "Aunt Emily will be serving supper soon," she said. "Is she expecting you?"

Luke shook his head. "She thinks I'm in Helena picking up supplies."

She was relieved, although she shouldn't be. He could stay. She could spend a few hours in his company even though soon they would have to forget about each other. Luke had told her he didn't want a wife, and she couldn't be one. "Would you like to stay and eat with me?" she asked.

She thought Luke hesitated before he nodded.

"Hang your coat over there." Clara indicated the pegs on the wall near the door and hurried into the kitchen ahead of him. She gathered her unfinished letter from the table and tucked it—along with Wade's note—into her desk drawer. She met Luke on her way back to the cooking area.

"I hope pork chops are all right." Eastern Montana was cattle country, as was Wyoming to the south. She'd eaten so much beef since arriving, she looked forward to a change in diet.

"They'd be fine," Luke said. Turning a ladderback chair around, he straddled it, resting one arm along the top and touching the jar in the middle of the table. In it was the paper rose he'd given her the day before her furniture arrived. Clara glanced at his hand, knowing he was remembering their encounter on the mountain.

She fried the meat, boiled potatoes, chopped onions for the gravy, and reheated the collard greens she'd made the previous day. The silence between them stretched to the point where she felt she'd break under it. Luke's gaze made her nervous.

"What do you do in the winter months?" Clara asked, looking for something to say.

"Repairs mostly. People find leaky roofs or windows that are too drafty. Sometimes I do remodelling jobs if it's not too cold. How's everything here? Any work for me?"

"Since you fixed the ceiling and floor in the upstairs bedroom, everything seems to be settling fine." Clara placed a bowl on the table and sifted flour into it.

"How about you?" Luke asked.

"Me?" Clara tensed, buying time. The conversation was about to turn personal, and she didn't know if she wanted to deal with that at the moment. Wade's letter was still on her mind, and she'd found she often told Luke the truth when she spoke to him.

"Are you settling in fine?"

"Beautifully," she said with a smile, then turned to the stove to stir the gravy. Somehow Luke could look through her defenses and see how she really felt. "I suppose the winter will get much worse before spring comes."

"That's something you can count on in Montana. Winter comes and stays. You may find that being out here—" He paused. "—can get pretty lonely."

"I'll be fine," Clara told him. "I don't mind being by myself. I'll have papers to correct and plans for classes and programs at the school."

Removing the gravy from the fire, she went back to the flour. Making a valley in the mound, she grabbed a handful of lard and dropped it into the center, then added a cup of warm water and began kneading the mixture.

"Have you ever lived alone, Clara?"

She hesitated. "For a short while. After my parents died, I was alone in the house." She had stayed alone in that huge house on Maple Street before Wade came to get her. "It was quiet and eerie. The rooms were empty. I kept expecting to run into my mother as I dashed around a corner or hear my father come in from the hospital just before supper." She stared directly at him. "I'm not afraid."

Luke got up and walked to her. "I know you're not. It's one of the things I like about you most, your willingness to try anything, overcome anything."

"I want to be here," she told him. Since receiving Wade's letter, she wasn't sure if she could stay; but she wanted Luke to know that if she left, it wouldn't be because she had a choice.

"What are you making?" he asked, standing at her shoulder.

"Biscuits." Clara deftly blended the flour with the lard and water until she had a ball of dough. Instead of rolling it out and cutting it into circles, she pulled a ball from the larger one and fashioned it into a perfect circle, converting it quickly into a pan full of unbaked bread.

Luke had to step away for her to set the pan in the oven and attend to the rest of the meal. Clara was efficient and organized. She compensated for the fact that he was throwing her off balance by busying her hands. Luke grabbed one of her curls and pulled it, and her hand came up instinctively. He took her fingers and she turned around to face him. Heat seared through him, turning his insides to volcanic lava.

Someday he'd get used to her huge eyes and the wonder in them and the way she made him feel when she looked at him. Someday, he would be able to come upon her and not have this feeling of anticipation, not shiver at the sound of her voice. Someday, everything about her would be familiar and usual. Someday, none of the feelings that seized him and made his body as hard as a rock would be remembered. He hoped he wouldn't live that long.

He reached for her. He only wanted to hold her against him. He'd missed her in the past weeks. He knew he couldn't stay, but he wanted to smell her lilac scent and remember the way she fit against his body.

Clara snuggled against him. She felt light and boneless in his arms, and he didn't want her to know how much he loved it.

Suddenly, Clara smelled her bread. She quickly pulled away from Luke's arms and opened the oven door. The bread was golden brown. With two towels she lifted the pan from the oven rack and set it on an empty burner.

Luke was too close, and his heat cut her breath. If she moved, she'd be back in his arms, but she wanted to be there. She could have stayed in his embrace the rest of her life—except that tonight she'd made a decision about Wade. Until she'd truly severed her ties with the East, she wouldn't have a future here, even if Luke wanted one. So far his words had pushed her from him, yet his actions suggested a completely different story. Thank goodness dinner was ready!

"We'd better eat now," she said quietly.

Luke was hungry, but not for food. He wanted Clara. He stared at her, but her eyes confused him. Sometimes, like now, they said *kiss me* despite fear he could see lurking in their depths. He wondered if the fear had anything to do with the promise she'd mentioned. He didn't want her to be afraid. He wanted her protected and loved, her life filled with happiness and free of worry. Then his own promise asserted itself and he pulled back.

"Where are the dishes?" he asked. The moment was lost. Clara looked past his shoulder, then pointed to the cupboard above the sink. The look in her eyes was gone, replaced with a kind of relief. He got the plates and, together, they set the table. Conversation during the meal centered around her first day at school. She recounted the antics of the children and told him how well Martha had done with the little ones.

When they finished, Clara cleaned the dishes while Luke checked on the fire, which he had roaring when she entered with a tray and coffee. Luke stooped in front of the fire, overcome by her loveliness. Each time he saw her, he was surprised by his feelings. Her presence made him happy; the sound of her voice made him want to listen for the sheer pleasure the musical lift gave him. Standing, he took the tray and set it on a low table.

Clara poured two cups. She handed one to him, which he set on the mantel, keeping her hand in his. He turned to watch the fire, reminded of their time in the cabin and the warm glow of candles for just the two of them. How he wished they were there now, away from the eyes of the valley! He'd put his horse in the shed when he'd arrived, but that didn't mean he hadn't been seen. If he didn't leave soon, there was no telling what additional gossip would fuel the amount already running through the small community.

Clara hadn't mentioned it. He wondered if she were aware of the talk. He squeezed her hand, knowing she wouldn't say anything to him. She would try to deal with it herself, the same as she'd done with the roof.

Luke slipped his arm around Clara's waist. He just wanted to hold her for a moment before he went out into the cold. It might be the last time. He'd heard the talk, even if Clara hadn't. He knew he was dealing with dynamite. Staying around her could only cause an explosion which could hurt them both.

He drew her toward him, and she offered no resistance, closing her eyes before looking directly into his. A mixture of passion and anticipation fought for dominance. Luke groaned and pulled her closer. Just for a few moments, he told himself. He'd leave in just a few moments. It wouldn't make much difference.

Then he covered her mouth with his. He kissed her, tasted her, trying to hold back, trying to keep a rein on the thoughts that told him to crush her to him, to grind her body into his, and to feel every curve of her small frame. Her arms slid over his shoulders and connected behind his neck as her tight breasts thrust into his chest. He felt his body harden as he pressed against her.

"Clara, I have to go," he groaned against her mouth. "If I don't go now, I won't be able to leave at all." His hands on her waist rotated her against his hardness.

"Don't leave," she whispered, burying her face in his chest. "Not yet. Stay just a little while longer."

Luke looked at the top of her head. He ran his

hands through hair that felt like raw silk. He
wanted to look into her eyes, but knew what he'd
see there; trust, passion, need. It would be his undoing. If she looked at him, there would be no
way he could walk away.

Then she did.

Seventeen

Luke wasn't used to waking up next to anyone anymore. His effort to turn over had brought him up against a soft, warm body. His eyes flew open, and in the draped-darkness of midnight a single candle burned low. He saw the wispy waves rioting over her head and smoothed them back, but they had a mind of their own. Clara didn't move. He looked at her sleeping. Why hadn't he ever noticed her long eyelashes? They lay like dark fans against her cheeks.

Gathering her closer, he fit her shorter frame into his and pulled the cover over her arms. "I love you, Clara," he whispered into her ear, then went back to sleep.

Something woke Clara. She thought she was dreaming, but when she opened her eyes Luke was still there. She faced him, her arm around his waist and her legs entwined with his. The feel of his body next to hers sent heat flashing through her.

She could feel her breath in the limited space between his neck and her face. On impulse, she pressed her closed mouth to the hollow where his Adam's apple bobbed up and down. Luke's arms tightened around her, his legs pushing her back into the mattress. She hesitated, then her tongue came out to taste the spot she'd kissed.

Luke came awake instantly, enjoying the feel of Clara in his arms. Before Clara, he hadn't held a woman since Peg had died, but now his body was electrified. A stab of heat pierced through to his core when her mouth touched him. Slipping his hands into her hair, he pushed her back and turned her face to his. He kissed her forehead reverently, afraid anything more would have him melting in the heat that mounted between them. Silently, letting sensation push him on, he grazed her cheeks, then worked his way to her mouth, almost frightened by the contact. His body reacted violently to her wetness, and he gathered her closer, wanting to experience every inch her, and the agony in his groin told him how much he wanted to force her into the bed and bury himself inside her. Her smooth legs rubbed against his hair-roughened thighs until the pleasure was so intense he feared he would lose control.

Clara didn't care about the town right now. She didn't care about her job or what anyone would think, only the sensations that ran through her. Tonight might be her last time with Luke and she wouldn't give it up because of petty gossip. After tonight, they might only share friendship, politeness over coffee cups when they met at social gatherings; but she hadn't been able to prevent herself from touching him, and he'd responded by pulling her close. Clara readily gave herself up to

Luke's ministrations and the spasms of pleasure that bolted through her like greased lightning.

Luke's hands went to her waist. His mouth nuzzled her neck and shoulders as he sampled the luscious flesh.

"God! Clara. I want you." His voice was raspy.

His hands moved over her, slowly, methodically, as if he knew everything about her sensitive body. The smooth fabric of the sheet covering them, under the tutelage of his fingers, skimmed over her erect nipples. Clara clamped her jaw tight to keep from screaming, but lost the battle. She was exposed, naked to his inspection as he worked the sheet to her waist and further over her legs. He dropped the cover over the edge of the bed and, on his knees, he let his eyes drink her in.

She liked having him watch her. She felt beautiful, haloed by a glow that he alone was privileged to see. He was beautiful, muscular, and hard, his knees straddling her feet. His hands reached down and took her ankles. While his eyes watched her reaction, he ran his fingers up and down her legs, working closer and closer to the center of her throbbing need.

Clara's breath was a soft staccato. Her eyes closed and sensation washed over her. Her mouth called Luke's name and several unintelligible phrases he couldn't understand. She gasped when his fingers reached the small button of pleasure at the pinnacle of her sex. Her hands grabbed his shoulders and her nails dug into the tender flesh. She wanted him to continue and to stop at the same time. His fingers strayed downward until they found her opening and together ventured inside. Clara cried out at the pleasure that rocketed through her. She wanted to speak, to say something, but nothing came from her mouth but a whimpering desire for him to continue.

Her body grabbed at the tormenting delight his hands evoked. She pulled at his shoulders. She was ready, now!

"Not yet," Luke groaned, fighting against his own need to thrust himself inside her and find the release his body sought. But he continued drawing from her, deepening the well, heightening the pleasure-package until he could no longer stand the pain.

Clara arched toward Luke's hands. She was a body of flowing lava, the pent-up strain in her stomach near overflowing. Her grip on Luke's shoulders tightened as her teeth clamped down on her lip. She held on, but the racking convulsion of sensation that soared through her drained her of strength. Her head whipped from side to side as Luke lifted her legs over his shoulders and dug his fingers deeper into her. Clara cried out, not thinking he could take her to any higher planes, but he'd found a way. She could no longer control her reactions and she gave up the effort. Luke had free rein to do whatever he wanted. She could die in the midst of the euphoria he had created.

He let her legs down and, with agonizing slowness, allowed his fingers to slip out of her. Clara panted below him, her breasts rising and falling in rapid succession. Then he covered her body with his. His kisses were drugging and wet as they blanketed her face. Raising her hips, he slipped inside her.

Eruptions took her as she matched Luke's rhythm and the two of them found and danced the primal ritual. Clara wrapped her legs around him, continuing the wave of thrills that took her to the brink of rapture. She could feel it mounting in her. Dry, throaty, incoherent noises came from her throat as she and Luke entered the next level of excitement. Colors suffused behind her closed eyes. She heard a scream as the rolling thunder of climax engrossed her in a rainbow that seemed to vibrate and explode. Beneath him she rocked side to side, up and down, lost in the summit of physical uproar.

Luke didn't recognize the gruff sound coming from his throat as his. The release tearing forth was so intense, so powerful, he felt he could die from the massive impact on his senses. He struggled to maintain the height he'd reached, struggled to continue the poignant passion Clara summoned like a command to his obedient body. He climbed higher, taking her to the brink and over it. Time and again, he thrust into her soft flesh, unmindful of her tenderness, lost to everything except the need to fulfill, to find a release from the torment that had taken hold of him. Clara matched him. Thrust for thrust she met his strokes, her body liquid to his touch. He molded her around him, and she pulled and released to a music only the two of them could hear.

Climax seized Luke. It drove him harder and harder, his powerful thrusts rapid as if his life depended on seeing how much endurance he had. One last time he thrust himself into her, seeking the ultimate pleasure, then collapsed in solitary gratification.

Clara labored under Luke's weight. She reveled in the feel of him, her hands stroking his naked back along the angle of his spine to the smooth flank of his hips. She smiled to herself in the aftermath of their lovemaking. This is where she wanted to be, where she never wanted to leave. Happy tears rolled from her eyes and down the sides of face. She didn't move, only hugged him closer.

Clara noticed the roughness of his unshaved jaw next to the smoothness of her face. His mouth touched her warm skin and she turned into the kiss, making it long, languid, and passionate.

Her heart slowed and her body began to cool. Luke slipped off her and pulled the quilt over them. His hands slid from her breasts to her legs. They were sensitive hands, hands that could build things, fix things, hands that had held her in anger and in love, hands that touched so many lives, including hers.

The clock on the bureau chimed. Clara waited for it to complete the music of the clock in Westminster Abbey before counting the hour. Annie Pearl had given her the clock for her birthday last year.

Three o'clock. Luke slept quietly next to her. She listened to his even breathing as she lay in his arms, and through the window she could see the snow falling. How many inches were on the ground now? Luke shifted, his arms tightening around her. How much longer? she wondered. How long before he woke and left? She knew tonight had been a last. Too many tongues wagged in the valley. When she met people, she knew they talked about her. She could hear the sudden silences when she walked into a crowded room. Hushed whispers followed her like a shadow.

She snuggled closer to Luke, taking his hand and holding it to her breasts. The shadows would all be there in the morning. Tonight she'd be thankful for what she had.

Something inside him was changing, Luke thought. He cradled Clara to him. He'd fallen in love with her. She hadn't been awake when he'd told her, yet he could feel the bonds between them forming, growing strong. He'd have to declare for her soon. Wouldn't that cause Miss Emily a good laugh. The old woman had been right all along. Clara was the woman for him.

"If you don't get some sleep, you'll never be able to stand up in front of your class tomorrow."

"How did you know I was awake?" Clara asked. She rose on her elbows and faced him.

Luke ran his hand around her, grasping her buttocks. "Because you've moved this against me three times in the last five minutes." Luke laughed. Sitting up, he turned to her, his smile gone. "What's keeping you awake?"

Clara looked away. "I was thinking."

"About what?"

"Forbidden subjects."

"There are no forbidden subjects," he told her, although he knew there were. "What is it?"

Clara laid her head on her pillow. "When you were married . . . what was it like?"

Luke let his breath out through his nose. Peg. He'd known that sooner or later he'd have to discuss his relationship with her. It was only fair. He knew Clara must be wondering how she compared to his wife.

"Are you asking what our days were like or . . . our nights?" He waited for the shock to register on her face. He wasn't disappointed. For a moment he let her wallow in indecision, then he began to speak. "When I met Peg, her eyes were like fire. I'd never seen anyone like her before. She did everything properly. I felt clumsy around her, and it took me weeks before I'd even speak to her. I'd fallen in love before I knew what had hit me. We married against her father's wishes. He wanted a banker or a doctor for his daughter, not a common laborer who worked with his hands." Luke looked at his hands, examining them as if he could step outside his body, and Clara took them in her smaller palms.

"They are wonderful hands," she said. "They can translate dreams into reality."

"We built a small house and set about trying to make a living and have a family . . ." He stopped. "After two years, Peg told me she was going to have a child. I was happier than any man had ever been. We set up a nursery and spent most of the year making things for the baby. Then the baby came. I knew something was wrong: It took too long, and no one would talk to me. All they wanted was more clean sheets and hot water. At daylight, they let me see her. She was so pale and so weak, she could hardly talk. She told me she loved me and I promised her I'd always love her, that no one would ever come between us. She died then."

Clara was speechless. He'd told the story so poignantly, she wanted to cry. She felt as if she had known Peg, as if she had been a close friend and now she was dead and no one could ever talk to her again.

"Luke," she began, adjusting the sheet and looking directly at him. The blanket covering her slipped to her waist. "When someone is dying, we often make promises."

"I know."

She took his hand. "After they're gone, we can't take our words back. Rationality returns and no one would expect us to keep those kinds of promises. Peg knows you loved her and that you'll never forget her."

"I understand that."

"You do?" Clara stared into the candlelight.

"Yes." He bent forward, took her face in his hands, and kissed her tenderly. "I intend to take you to Miss Emily Hale's tomorrow and make a declaration for you, Clara Elaine Winslow."

Clara stared at him, stunned.

"Luke, you can't do that." She sat up, pulling the sheet around her.

"Clara, what's wrong?" His eyebrows knitted together in concern. "I thought you'd be happy."

She was happy. No, she wasn't. She didn't know what she was. Luke didn't know how happy he could make her, but there was no solution for them. She couldn't let him do this—not when he wasn't doing it for the right reason. He didn't love her; he was trying to protect her, and she couldn't let him, even if it meant returning to Virginia.

"Have . . . have you . . . have you heard the talk?" she asked.

"I've heard it."

"You're declaring for me to protect me from the gossip going on."

Luke hesitated long enough for her to recognize the truth.

"I admit the thought crossed my mind, but I'm not in the habit of declaring for a woman to save her reputation."

"Then why now? Why didn't you offer this when we decided to pretend?"

Luke grasped her arms. "I wasn't in love with you then. I am now."

Clara stuck a yardstick in the snow next to the school entrance. Twenty inches were covered before it reached the ground. She found that the path to the school had been cleared. Luke must have done it before he'd left in the early hours of the morning.

Inside the room was warm. A fire blazed in the potbellied stove. Reverend Reed and three of the church deacons stood warming their hands.

"Morning, ma'am." Reverend Reed touched the

brim of his hunting cap which covered his ears and ringed his face with fur. Clara thought he looked like a colored Santa Claus.

"Gentlemen," she said. "I didn't know you were here."

"It's our job to keep the roads clear around here," he told her. "The school is part of our duties."

Clara felt as if the walls were closing around her. Luke had to have left footprints in the snow. She wondered what they had made of that? Had he known they would come?

"Your path was already clean when we got here. You don't have to do it yourself anymore," one of the deacons—Chucky Boy's father—said. "We'll take care of it."

Relief spread through her. They thought she'd been out early enough to shovel her own walkway. "I'll remember that."

"The children should be here soon and we've got miles to go . . ." the pastor paraphrased.

"Thank you, gentlemen," she said. They filed out as Martha came in. She beamed this morning, as she had every morning since the committee had agreed to give her the job. Martha helped her lay out the school books and find the right map for the geography lesson.

The younger children showed up minutes before the bell. Clara opened the door to find them pouring out of a sleigh driven by the town blacksmith.

"Picked them up for ya," he explained.

Clara thanked him as the children jumped down

and began a snowball fight which, by the look of them, had started earlier.

As the sleigh turned to leave the older grades appeared, smiling and cold as they passed her on their way inside. When everyone was settled, her thoughts went to the small village. She supposed a little snow meant business as usual. It also meant helping out. She was surprised at how the community banded together to make sure the valley ran smoothly. On the farm, life had been self-sufficient, as though each family lived on separate islands connected by small bridges. When help was needed, there was a path to get there; but unless something dire happened, each one worked without the other. Out here, there was only one island, with all the farms consolidated into one. Everyone had a job and did it to keep the valley running. She supposed it was necessary since the weather was so harsh. A slight mistake and a person could die.

Martha spent part of the morning replacing pants and dresses and drying socks in front of the stove. Even with the ride to school, the children hadn't been able to resist playing in the white powder. Nearly all of them were wet somewhere, and they found it hard to keep their attention on learning how to add and subtract or where the states of Tennessee and Georgia were located when they wanted to be outside throwing snowballs.

With so little sleep the night before and Luke's comment reverberating in her brain, Clara couldn't keep her mind on history or arithmetic either.

Martha, proving herself a jewel, came to her aid. She'd set the lesson to music and taught the children the names of the forty-five states in song. Clara smiled at the cleverness of her ploy and the enthusiasm of the children in learning it.

By October, the routine was established. Each day Clara would work with groups of students, teaching subjects at their level while Martha reinforced the previous lessons. Martha excelled with the younger, slower children. She proved to be patient and willing to repeat concepts over and over until they learned them. When that failed, she resorted to music, which Clara knew she liked better than the standard forms of teaching. And because it worked, Clara had no reservation about her using it. The object was for the children to learn. The method didn't matter.

The children settled into a form, too. Chucky Boy continued to regale the class with his antics; Joanne Wilson, who'd been on the top of the grade roster, stayed there; Wendell and Mike Carver had a healthy rivalry going, and Alice Mildred remained quiet and timid.

She hadn't seen Luke in almost three weeks, but Martha told her he'd been called away to repair storm damage. Before he'd left her, Clara had managed to convince Luke to hold off saying anything unless they were both present. Thankfully, that was the tradition in the valley. Each party needed to be on hand for the declaration, which generally took place at a church social. Since Luke wasn't a church-goer, he wanted to declare for her at Aunt Emily's.

The repairs wouldn't last forever. One day he'd show up unexpectedly, and then she'd have to find a way to prevent him from doing something that would make him hate her for the rest of her days. In the past few weeks she'd accepted and rejected a dozen solutions to her dilemma.

"Is there anything else, Clara?" Martha pulled her coat on, preparing to leave.

"No." Clara had been so absorbed in her thoughts she'd forgotten the young girl was in the room. "I'll see you in the morning."

"All right." She turned to leave, pulling a grey-wool hood over her head. At the door, Martha looked back. "Oh, I almost forgot, Miss Emily asked if you could come to dinner tonight."

Clara froze. She wondered if Luke had said anything to her aunt. He'd promised to wait, but had he?

"Tell her I'll be there."

Martha left with a smile. If Clara hadn't been so wound up at the invitation, she might have noticed the small changes in Martha—the lightness in her step, the way she smiled and almost danced about the room.

"It's probably just an innocent invitation," she told herself. "After all, you haven't been back there since you moved." It was natural, she thought, for her aunt to want to see her. There was nothing to be apprehensive about.

By the time Clara had dressed in one of the reconditioned satin-and-lace gowns and pulled her hair into a melee of curls at the crown of her head, she'd convinced herself this was just one of Aunt

Emily's frequent dinner parties. The dress was royal blue and made her feel good with its puffy sleeves, tight waist, and sleek skirt. Looking in the mirror, she was amazed how much she resembled her aunt.

The number of wagons parked outside the boardinghouse told Clara her aunt *was* indulging in her favorite pastime—entertaining. Light spilled from the many parlors, giving the house a festive glow. Men and women laughed and talked in the halls and seemed to take up every available amount of floor space. Clara had a sudden realization that her aunt might be throwing a party. She clenched her teeth. Luke would not do this to her, she thought, smiling as Reverend Reed passed her on his way to the smoking room.

Where was he? She searched the room, hoping she didn't look too obvious. If he were planning to make a declaration tonight, she had to derail it.

"Martha," Clara called, a bright smile splitting her face. Martha's feet danced down the stairs.

"Another beautiful dress!" The girl openly admired the gown. "One day I'm going to have clothes like yours." Clara spun around, showing Martha the way the short train draped the floor.

"Have you seen Luke, Martha?" Clara didn't try to hide the anxious note in her voice.

"Not since I came in." Martha glanced over her shoulder, and Clara followed the tilt of her head. Young Frank Crabtree leaned awkwardly against the doorjamb. Frank had a reputation for being a very serious young man. He went to the engineering college and planned to blast through the mountains and build roads that would allow people to travel without the hazards they had to face today. Luke had introduced her to Frank, and the young man helped Luke when he was home. Clara wondered why he was here tonight. School was in session. Shouldn't he be away? Suddenly, she remembered her conversations with Martha.

"Is that—him?" Clara whispered.

Martha nodded, staring at the floor.

"He came home to see you. That's a good sign."

"He's home visiting his family," Martha objected. "Miss Emily invited them to dinner tonight."

Clara knew her aunt. If she invited them to dinner, she was more than likely practicing her matchmaking craft. Martha didn't know she was probably a pawn in a well-orchestrated scheme led by Emily Hale. She hoped she was right. Martha wanted it that way; Clara could see it in her eyes. If she were right, maybe the old woman wouldn't have time to think about directing her niece's life.

"He came home to see you, Martha." Clara gave her a confident nod. Martha was turning from girl to woman; her black hair shone and her face glowed with a light that could only come from being in love. She smiled and walked toward Frank.

Clara went back to her thoughts of Luke. Did her face shine like Martha's? Dashing the thought, she looked around again. She had to find him, find out what he'd told her aunt.

"Cla-ra."

Hearing Luke sing her name, she turned, ready

to grab Luke's arm and force him into the kitchen for a few well-chosen words; but when she saw him at the top of the steps, her mouth dropped open. He was dressed in a black suit, its coat falling just short of his knees, his shoulders broad and commanding, and a pristine white shirt with a black tie contrasted with the golden coloring of his tanned skin, robbing her of the ability to speak. Luke walked casually down the steps, coming to a stop directly in front of her, where he placed his index finger under her chin and closed her mouth.

Clara jerked her head as if snapping out of a dream.

"I guess, by your reaction, buying this suit was a good idea," he said.

Clara knew he was teasing her, but she couldn't argue with him. He looked wonderful! Better than wonderful. Then sanity returned. Luke had bought a new suit. Aunt Emily was giving a dinner party, and most of the valley's prominent citizens were present—Reverend Reed and his wife, Doc and Mrs. Pritchard, Antonia Morrison, the owner of the valley's general store, Frank Crabtree's family; the list went on and on.

She was convinced Luke had broken his promise. "Luke, you haven't—"

"Clara, you're here!" Her aunt came forward, embracing her as if they hadn't met in years. "And Luke . . . so glad to see you." She took both their hands. Clara knew he'd told her. She threw him a look that said *you promised*. "Now that you're here, we can go in to dinner."

Being pulled along by her aunt, Clara wondered

if she had used the singular or plural form of the word "you're."

Dinner didn't go well for her. She kept waiting for someone to make a toast and salute her and Luke on their declaration. All through the meal, she kept glancing at him, hoping to get a sign that he knew something was about to happen. Deliberately, she thought, he avoided making any eye contact.

It wasn't until Aunt Emily rose and ordered coffee for the parlor that Clara breathed any relief. As they filed out of the dining room, the men went their usual way, Luke included, to the smoking room and card parlor, while the women retired to the other rooms. Martha and Frank, she noticed, went toward the back of the house where the kitchen was located. Clara sat in a winged-back chair near the double doors away from the main part of the room and accepted a cup of coffee.

"Clara, we asked Emily to invite you here tonight," Mrs. Davidson began when everyone had a cup.

Clara kept her face still. She had thought she was safe, that nothing about Luke and his desire for a declaration would transpire this evening, but she had been wrong. Was this how it happened— the men in one room, the women in another?

"We, the committee, wanted to talk to you."

Looking about the room, Clara noticed eyes drop or turn away from her. "Committee?" she inquired.

"The school board committee."

Her gaze darted to the women present. The pastor's wife had been speaking to her. Antonia Morrison sat next to her aunt on the opposite side of the room. Doc Pritchard's wife and Mrs. Davidson faced her from two wing-backed chairs near the fireplace. Marlene Carter, who reminded Clara of Janey Willard and ran the general store with her husband, sat near Aunt Lucy.

Letting her breath out on a long sigh, Clara noticed that her heart beat an erratic rhythm in her chest. She was going to lose her job. She'd have to return to Virginia in disgrace.

"We don't mean to pry into your life," Mrs. Reed continued, her voice quiet as if she were talking to a person who'd confessed a grievous sin. "You're an example to the children. They like you, imitate you. We only want them to have the best guidance."

"Mrs. Reed—" Clara spoke in the same tone. "—what are you trying to say?"

"Well, my dear." She avoided Clara's direct stare by training her gaze on the cup she held. "It has come to the attention of the committee that you and Luke Evans . . ." She trailed off.

"Don't stop," Clara said, her anger backing up and making her voice barely audible. "Just what has come to your attention?" She looked around the room, her eyes focusing on Antonia Morrison, the accusation in them clearly apparent.

"Clara, you and Luke did stay all night in the hills." Marlene Carter set her cup on the table next to Aunt Lucy. She glared at Clara as if she were staring down a patron whose bill was overdue at the store.

"That's right, Mrs. Carter." Clara gave her a smile so sweet it could rival maple syrup. "Would you have suggested we kill ourselves in the dark? Would that have been better than waiting for sunlight?"

"I didn't mean it that way . . ."

"Just how did you mean it?"

Clara wanted to call her a dried-up old biddy, but she held her temper as close as she could.

"I mean . . . I mean . . ."

"Leave the child alone," Aunt Lucy said. "She ain't done nothing the rest of you ain't done, or wished you had."

Clara saw the smile that lifted her aunt's lips before she quickly recovered and replaced the humor with a solemn look.

"Aunt Lucy! This is serious. It involves the school and the children," Mrs. Carter told her.

"Don't involve anybody 'cept Luke and this here child, if you ask me. If I was her, I'd throw ya'll out of my parlor." She flung her thin arm in the air and chewed on her toothless gums.

"Where is Luke?" Clara wanted to know. She threw a look over her shoulder. No one was there. She heard deep-throated voices coming from the room down the hall. "Is he going through this same kind of court?"

"We're not here to discuss Luke," Mrs. Carter went on. "The fact is, you and Luke has become . . . compromised, shall we say?"

"No, we shall not say." Clara scrunched her mouth and eyes in tiny little circles, an exact imitation of Mrs. Carter. Removing the cup and saucer from her knees, Clara stood up. "What's going on here? Have I done something that the children are talking about? Have I done anything to destroy my dignity or their trust in me? Or is it the small-minded women in this room who are injecting something horrible into a night in which Luke very possibly saved my life?"

"You tell 'em, honey." Aunt Lucy slapped her hands in approval.

Aunt Emily and Antonia Morrison were unusually quiet. Why didn't her aunt come to her assistance? Why didn't she fight for her as she'd fought the committee to get her here? And what was Antonia Morrison up to? Clara would have thought she would be the one spearheading this discussion.

"Clara," Doc Pritchard's wife cut in. She had a compassionate look on her face. "The night in the hills isn't the only reason for our concern."

Clara stood up straighter.

"There are the baseball games."

"The children loved the games, and most of the adults did, too," she defended herself. "Your son *and* daughter played in nearly every encounter. The games won't do anything to harm the girls. It will make them stronger and better able to get along with other people."

"We're not debating the fact that the children enjoyed the games. What we see is that you and Luke . . . in front of the children . . . well, you act like you want to declare for each other."

"We don't." Clara answered a little too quickly.

"And there's the matter of Luke's horse in your shed all night long." Mrs. Carter jerked her head up and down as if she'd slapped the final trump card on the table.

Clara's ears burned so hot she thought they would erupt into flame by spontaneous combustion. Someone *had* noticed that Luke spent the night with her. "I suppose you want to know if Luke spent the night with me?"

"If it was me, I'd a slept with him," Aunt Lucy chirped. "Honey, if I was just fifty years younger, he could park his buggy in my stable any night— daytime, too, for that matter."

"Aunt Lucy," Mrs. Carter said, "we're trying to get something done here."

"Now *that* I can tell, Marlene Carter." Aunt Lucy sat forward in her chair. For a ninety-year-old she was suddenly years younger. "What you're trying to do is get into business that ain't none of yours. Why don't you leave this child here alone and go eat some more of them sweet cakes you been stuffing in your mouth? I know this is your fifth one."

Aunt Lucy had put Mrs. Carter squarely in her place, and the merchant's wife sat back in her chair, her hands cradling the dessert plate that held three of Aunt Emily's petit fours.

"We're not trying to pry into your personal life, Clara," Mrs. Pritchard continued. "What we're trying to say is that maybe you should rethink your position as schoolteacher for the valley."

Fear lunged at Clara's throat. Her hand went to her breasts. "Are you saying I'm fired?"

"There's another solution." Antonia Morrison looked clearly at her. Clara wondered what she was up to. Although her only comment of the evening sounded as if she weren't part of the group trying to chastise her but on a different path, Clara didn't trust her.

"What's that?" Aunt Lucy asked. All eyes turned to look at the vessel of moral conduct. "Spit it out, Antonia. . . . Never knowed you to hold your tongue."

Clara froze at what the woman staring at her could say.

"If Luke declares for Clara, then they can get married in the spring."

"No!" Clara refused. "I can't marry Luke."

"Why not?" Aunt Emily asked.

"She can't marry anybody. She already has a husband."

Clara whirled around to face the man in the doorway.

"Wade!"

Eighteen

It can't be morning, Clara thought. She was still
alive. She wanted to be dead. Why hadn't she died
during the night? Her eyes were puffy from crying.
Thank goodness it was Saturday and there was no
school, although, after last night, she probably
didn't have a job any longer. No one would have
sent their children anyway.

She had left Virginia with high hopes for a better
life, yet all she'd done was make a mess of everything. Pounding the pillow, she pushed her face
into the softness and cried muffled tears until her
body seemed spent of moisture. Getting up, she
splashed cold water in the bowl and washed her
face. She held the wet towel to her eyes, hoping
it would take away some of the redness and make
them appear less as if she'd been crying; but looking at herself, she knew she couldn't fool anyone.

She dressed quickly and went to the kitchen.
Wade sat at the table, a coffee cup and the remains
of breakfast in front of him.

"Morning," he greeted.

"Wade, I'm sorry." She didn't seem to be able
to find any other words to say to him. His appear-

ance last night had stunned more than her. While Aunt Emily had sat there quietly feeding her enough rope to force her to marry Luke, Wade's comment had effectively closed the shaft on that idea. Mrs. Carter sputtered and choked on her cake. The only people in the room with a voice had been Aunt Lucy and Mrs. Davidson, who had said nothing prior to Wade's arrival.

Half of the double space the doors took up had been blocked by Wade's frame. He had worn his Sunday suit and looked tired from days of traveling. This morning, he looked no better. Yet Clara thought he looked better than she'd seen him in years. The grey in his hair didn't seem as prominent and the lines in his face seemed more character defining than etched by time.

"I guess we ought to have a talk, Clara-girl." Wade called her by the name he'd used since she was fifteen.

In the six years they'd been married, they had talked very little. "This must seem pretty confusing to you," she offered.

"Not especially," Wade replied. "I've been expecting it."

"You have?" Clara came fully into the kitchen and poured herself a cup of coffee.

"I knew it was coming when you said you wanted to go to that teachers' college over in D.C."

"Why did you let me go?" She came around the table and sat down. Luke's paper rose stood between them in the jar.

"I couldn't stop you. It was time, Clara-girl." Wade's big hands grasped the cup, and Clara thought of Luke's hands. They were big and rough from work, but different from Wade's. Luke's hands made her body ache with need; his calloused palms over her body turned her to liquid fire. "You were growing into a woman. You needed to be around other young people. My sister was the closest woman to your age, and when she died, you were alone."

He surprised her with his insight into her feelings. She had thought Wade only worked, ate, and slept. She hadn't envisioned him thinking about his own needs, much less hers.

"Do you mean you knew I'd . . . expected me . . . to meet someone?" Clara took a drink of her coffee.

"I suspected it would happen."

"But we were married."

"Clara-girl, we've never been married, not in the real sense of the word. You don't know what marriage means. I was married to Mabel. She gave me two sons; and when she died, I needed someone to care for the house and the boys. You came along 'cause your daddy and ma died. If it hadn't been for the busybodies at the church, we could have gone on without having to satisfy their moral code." He stopped and stared at her. "And you wouldn't be in this mess you're in."

"I suppose I'll have to return to Virginia. I doubt they'll let me teach after this."

"Is that what you want?"

Clara gulped her coffee. "I don't know what I want." She was lying. She wanted Luke, but he'd never speak to her again. She wondered where he was and what he thought of last night. When she all but ran from the parlor, she hadn't seen Luke. Somehow, in the back of her mind, she'd hoped he'd come to the house, burst down the door in a rage, and insist that she marry him. But the night passed into daylight without further incident.

"Do you want to be married to me?"

She had never expected such a question. "I *am* married to you."

"No, Clara-girl. We said some words in front of a preacher. We signed a paper, but that doesn't make us married."

Clara shivered. She'd only felt this apprehensive once before, and that had been in the barn when Ian had attacked her. "Wade, are you in love with me?" she asked fearfully.

"No," he said.

"Do you think you could ever be in love with me the way a man loves a woman?" Luke's image rose in her mind as she asked the question.

"No," Wade answered.

"Then why do you want to change our relationship?"

"You're no longer a fifteen-year-old child, Clara-girl. You're a woman and I'm a man."

"Wade, when . . . when my parents were . . . killed, I didn't know what to do. I thought I was supposed to marry you even though we were . . . you were . . . I was so young. I didn't know what my daddy had meant when he'd told me to go with you."

"Did you ever wonder why we were such good

friends—your daddy and me? Why he had you send for me just before he died?"

Clara shook her head. She had never heard Wade speak like this. She had often wondered how her father would even know a man like Wade. For them to be friends enough for him to ask her to send for him when he lay on his deathbed was still a mystery.

"I bet you didn't even think we'd know each other." Wade laughed, voicing her thoughts. "A man who could read Homer and Euripides to his daughter, but would also spend time laughing with the hospital janitor."

Clara's eyes opened wide. "You met at the hospital?"

"The day you were born. I cleaned the floors then, and your daddy had been there all night long waiting for you to get born. He was dead tired. When you finally screamed your first sound, he was so happy we could hardly keep him from waking up the entire ward. I took him to my place that night—a single room in the city. It was dark and dirty and smelled like the beer garden it was over. He came there often, later, and we talked about everything under the sun, but mostly he talked about you."

Wade had a faraway look in his eyes. He wasn't in Montana. He was back in New York in a dingy little room where a friendship had been forged.

"When you were three, I met Mabel and we moved back to Virginia. Your daddy would write me long letters. Mabel would read them and answer them for me. He told me once, when I asked him why he wanted to be friends with me, that we had the same soul."

"What does that mean?"

"I didn't know at the time. He said every time a baby was born, it got a soul from God. But sometimes God made people share them. It didn't matter that your daddy used his hands to soothe away pain and suffering and I pulled boll weevils off cotton plants; we were alike. We both knew what we wanted to do, what we were suited for, and liked it. We didn't have to mask our feelings or defend our choices. It was enough to just be who we were."

"Do you think my daddy wanted me to marry you?"

Wade shook his head. "He sent you to me for protection and I've tried to provide that."

"You've succeeded, Wade." Clara got up and looked out the window. The snow covered the ground as far as she could see. The road lying in the distance had black ruts in it where the sleigh and carriage wheels had run. The mountains were snow-covered and majestic. "Look how I repaid you. I ran away and got myself into a mess. I expect the committee to show up soon and ask for possession of the house."

"Clara-girl, you're still young. You've got most of your life ahead of you. This is only a small skirmish, and you can still win if you want to fight."

Clara turned back. "What do you mean?"

"I mean you have choices. You can come back to Virginia with me. We can change our relationship and have a real marriage, if that's what you want. But I don't think it is."

Clara shook her head. "Wade, you're like another father to me. I could no more be your wife than I could . . ." She couldn't think of anything to say.

"Suppose you weren't married."

"But I am—"

He raised his hand, stopping her from continuing. "Suppose you weren't, would the young man marry you?"

"Not after this." She hung her head. "It doesn't matter anyway. After he hears about last night, and the way news travels here he's bound to know by now, he'll never speak to me again."

"Don't go deciding what other folks will do. Now, would you marry him?"

Clara waited, staring at Wade. She didn't want to hurt him. She'd lied enough since leaving him, and she'd found one lie led to more and more. She was through with lying. "Yes," she said. Wade's reaction wasn't what she'd expected. She'd thought he'd appear hurt, but to the contrary, he looked relieved.

"Then there's only one thing for us to do."

"What's that?" Clara frowned. She'd never been this confused when talking to Wade. He was usually straightforward and quick to the point, using words to a minimum. Today, he appeared to be leading her, testing her for answers as if this conversation had both a direction and a purpose.

"We can have our marriage annulled."

* * *

Sparks flew as Luke threw another log into the fireplace. The red glow of the burning wood lit the room and turned his shirt a wine-red. He sat back on the sofa in Ellen's living room and stared at the flaming logs as if they could answer his questions.

Married! He couldn't believe it. The news had hit him like an avalanche. His entire body had frozen as solid as Lot's, but instead of a pillar of salt, he was a block of ice. Leaving the mantel, he paced the floor, disoriented, unsure whether he should sit down, try to sleep, or ride his horse until they were both too tired to do anything, feel anything.

That was it! He felt. He didn't want to feel. When she'd arrived, he'd told himself not to let her get to him, not to let her smooth skin turn his head, her cotton-soft hair give familiarity to his hands, but he'd ignored his own voice and let her in. Then, like a vampire, when his heart was in plain view, she'd sucked his blood. And he'd liked it, even offered it to her. He pounded his fist into the palm of his hand. Where was she? He had a mind to go find her, find them both, her and the man who was her husband.

Luke crossed the room again. Picking up a piece of wood, he turned toward the fire before realizing he'd already thrown a log on it. He dropped the wood back in the bin next to the hearth and crossed the room again, his mind wandering as aimlessly as his feet.

"I waited through a prairie fire in Kansas and a snow storm in Wyoming to get this carpet. If you cross it one more time, I'll send you to Massachusetts to personally purchase a new one."

Ellen clutched her green-velvet robe close to her body. Her hair was tangled, the ends wrapped around pieces of cloth that stood out like bent branches.

"I suppose I shouldn't ask how you're making out." She glanced at the pillow and blankets folded neatly on the end of the sofa. Luke had asked to sleep there for the night, but he hadn't slept at all.

"Did I wake you? I didn't mean to make any noise."

"You didn't wake me. I haven't been to sleep," she told him. "I've been listening to you pacing up and down."

"I'm all right, Ellen. There's no need for you to worry about me."

"I *am* worried about you," she told him. "I'm also worried about Clara."

Luke's shoulders went back. He clenched his jaws tight to keep from saying something too tender for Ellen's ears.

"Put yourself in her shoes for a moment."

Crossing his arms, he turned toward the glow of the fire.

"Why do you think she ran away and came here?" Luke didn't answer. "What kind of life do you think she had back there, married to a man old enough to be her father?"

"But she was a—" Luke stopped. Clara had been a virgin. He had known that, but the knowledge had escaped him while he'd wallowed in his own misery. Pain ripped through his chest at the remembrance of how he'd changed that condition. He could still feel her soft body, naked against him as she slept in his arms; he recalled the way she squirmed and stretched when she woke.

"Clara didn't tell me much about her life back East, but I have the feeling she had few friends and worked all the time. Her days were taking care of a house, children, cooking, and cleaning; and each day she walked ten miles to go to school, then the same ten miles home."

Luke could only stare. "Why?"

"Fortitude, perseverance, a thirst for knowledge, a wish to escape to a better life." Ellen's stare was direct. "She's married to a man fifteen years her senior, and she's been married since she was fifteen. School represented a way to be with people her own age. Luke, remember your own days at school. Weren't they some of the happiest times of your life? Didn't you have plans for the future, things you wanted to do?"

Luke frowned, remembering the talk and beer gardens of Philadelphia, the other students he'd met, people who even today he could call by name.

"Don't you think Clara thought of those things? She was a young girl. Young girls think of pretty dresses, parties, and dancing with handsome young men. But Clara was already married. What did her future look like? When she ran away, how did she know you would be part of that future?"

"Are you saying it's not her fault?"

"No, she should have told us the truth."

"If she had, she never would have been hired to be the schoolteacher."

"She knows that. It was one of the reasons she lied and, once here, she had to continue the lie."

She could have told him, Luke thought. He'd told her he loved her. They'd made love, incredible love. He remembered how she'd made him feel, how his insides had melted. He couldn't imagine never feeling like that again. He'd wanted to declare for her and he would have last night if Wade Pierce hadn't showed up before he'd gotten the chance.

"Ellen, what am I going to do?"

She didn't answer, and Luke knew she wouldn't. She couldn't tell him what to do. This was his problem, his and Clara's and Wade's. Whatever happened, he had to make his own decision.

"Walk the rug some more," Ellen said. "I'm sure you'll find a way. I have to go to work now."

With Ellen gone, Luke resumed his relentless walk up and down the carpet. How could there be a solution? Clara was married. She was not available. Her husband would take her back to Virginia, and he'd never see her again.

Luke sat down. He'd been here many times. He'd built this room from the ground to the roof and yet he found it strange. He stared into the fireplace, but did not see the flames. He saw Clara's face. She faded in and out, smiling, laughing as if she were already a memory.

Clara's petticoat caught on the saddle horn as she tried to get down from Red Wind. She yanked at it, but it held fast. Too excited and in too much of a hurry to take the time to loosen it, she ripped it free. Her legs were freezing from the raw wind and improper clothing. When she'd left Ellen's, she'd been in too much of a hurry to worry about changing into her riding pants.

"Luke," she called as she quickly opened the door and went inside Clem Kincaid's cabin.

She searched for Luke, but he wasn't in the main room. She turned about, looking in every corner for him, but he didn't answer immediately. Still, Ellen had told her he was headed for this place.

"What are you doing here?" Luke asked. *"How* did you get here?"

She looked up. He stared at her from the bedroom door. "It's amazing what you can do when you have a purpose." The trail had been hard. Many times she'd had to walk instead of ride Red Wind. She wouldn't tell him how many times she'd fallen in the snow or how long it had taken to get to the cabin. She'd had to get to him, and that thought had kept her going.

"I guess you ought to know about that," Luke said flatly.

He was still dressed in last night's suit, minus the coat, which was thrown haphazardly across a chair. Clara took her own off and threw it on top of his. The black tie he'd tied into a perfect bow was missing and his shirt stood open at the neck, an erotic tease to her senses. She could see he hadn't thought of changing clothes either.

"You've found me." His voice was as stiff as his back. "What do you want?"

"You're angry with me." Clara couldn't help

teasing. So much had changed in the last twenty-four hours, she didn't know whether she was going crazy or about to jump for joy.

Luke looked down at her, his eyebrows raised, his eyes piercing. "I'm free!" she burst out.

"Free of what?"

"I'm not married. At least I won't be for long. Wade is releasing me from my promise."

Luke's expression changed. His granite-hard exterior chipped a bit. "What are you talking about?"

"Six years ago, I promised to love, honor and obey. We didn't love each other, but we had to marry to satisfy gossip. Today, we decided to have our marriage annulled. Wade is going back to Virginia. He wants to marry Miss Picket."

"Slow down, Clara." He came into the room. Clara watched him duck under the doorjamb, then he stood in front of her. "You're not making sense."

Clara exhaled deeply. She was so excited. "Come on." She took his arm. "Sit down. I've got so much to tell you."

Clara, feeling as if a huge weight had been removed from her shoulders, virtually danced across the room. Luke sat on the end of the sofa while she perched on the armrest. Her head was so light, she knew she'd get hysterical and begin to laugh again if she didn't calm down. Taking another deep breath, she forced herself to relax.

"My parents died two days before my fifteenth birthday; then Wade came and took me to his farm, where I took care of his boys and house. Talk started there the same as it did here, and before long Wade said we had to get married. I had no-where else to go. The house in New York was gone, and I had no money to return to the school I'd attended before my parents died. So I married him."

"Did you know what you were doing?"

Clara shrugged. "I thought I did. Where Wade lived, people married young. Many girls my age already had one or two babies. And none of the church women thought anything of my marrying him, except Miss Picket. Even then, she might have thought it wasn't a good idea, but she never said a word."

"What about the other girls? The ones you met at the finishing school. Were they marrying at fifteen?"

Clara shook her head. "Most of them came from very good families."

"The daughters of doctors, lawyers, prominent citizens in the community," Luke teased. She was glad his attitude was changing; when she'd first entered the cabin, she'd thought he would throw her out.

"I know I'm one of them. Anyway, the others talked about boys most of the time we weren't studying. When I think of them now, they were so silly. None of us knew anything about life, about how hard it is to live and work and support a family. Wade worked hard from sunup to sundown. He rarely complained, and I've never known him to be sick. He took me in and cared for me as if I were one of his children."

Clara slid off the arm of the sofa.

"Luke, I felt like one of his children. He never slept with me or even attempted to . . . to make advances to me."

Luke nodded. He knew she'd been a virgin. He'd told her that in this very room what seemed a lifetime ago.

"He offered to take me back to Virginia to be his wife."

Luke's eyebrows went up.

"I refused." She cut off any protest he might have offered. "We decided to have our marriage annulled. The really good news is Wade's going to marry Miss Picket." The smile Clara had greeted Luke with came back to her.

"Who is Miss Picket?"

"Oh, I forgot, you don't know." Clara giggled. She felt girlish. "Miss Picket lives on the next farm. She helped me with the children while I went to school."

"Children?"

Clara wasn't surprised to see his eyebrows raise. She'd become used to the gesture whenever something annoyed him.

"They're Wade's children—twin boys. Of course, Wade's sister's children, they lived with us, too."

"You have four children?"

"Wade's boys, Stephen and Wade William, were only five when I came to live with them. They don't even remember their real mama. And the girls, Lisa Rose and Mary Rose, were born three and four years ago. Wade's sister died, and they had no one but us to take them in. They're so cute,

Luke. You're going to love them when you see them."

"They're here?"

"Wade brought them. It's probably the last time I'm going to see them." Tears welled up in her voice when she thought of not seeing them grow up. "They're all leaving on tomorrow evening's train." Clara pushed away the sad thoughts that overpowered her when she thought of the children. "The point is, Wade's offered me my freedom, Luke. Now you can declare for me."

Luke hesitated a long time. His stare made her uncomfortable.

"I don't think I will," he said.

"What?"

Luke's face was straight and serious. Clara's stomach plummeted. How could she have read him so wrong?

"At least not until you've gone through the hell you put me through last night." Luke's mouth trembled and finally broke into a smile, then a laugh. Then he dragged her into his arms, twisting her around and placing her on his lap.

"I love you," Clara confessed.

"Not half as much as I love you."

Nineteen

"Mommy! Mommy!" Mary Rose's high-pitched voice greeted her as she and Luke entered the boardinghouse and a three-foot-tall ball of energy ran toward her. Clara caught and lifted her into her arms, kissing the top of her forehead. She swung around. Luke stepped back.

"Where've you been?" Mary Rose asked. "We've been waiting all day."

"Come on, Lisa Rose," Clara opened her free arm. Lisa Rose was the younger sister. She looked past Clara to Luke before moving. Clara hugged her to her side. Carrying Mary Rose and holding onto Lisa Rose, the group entered the parlor. Lights brightened the room. Clara set Mary Rose on the floor and sat down, a child positioned herself on each side of Clara.

"Why they both named Rose?" Aunt Lucy asked from the same position she'd occupied the night before. "Did you run out of names, what with using them up two at a time?"

Clara couldn't help laughing. "Actually, they're named after their grandmothers."

"Girls, I want you to meet a friend of mine.

This is Mr. Luke Evans. You'll never believe what
he does."

Luke stood near the door. She had sat in the
chair next to where he stood only last night. It
seemed like years ago. Her life was so different
this evening than it had been at this time the day
before.

"What?" Lisa Rose questioned.

"He builds people houses . . . and they have
bathrooms on the inside."

"Why?" Lisa Rose asked.

Luke laughed almost despite himself.

"Where are Wade William and Stephen?" Clara
asked.

"Zeke took them and Wade into Butte to send
a telegram. They should be back soon. It's already
dark." Aunt Emily moved the curtains aside and
checked the outside path. "They've been gone a
long time. I wonder what's keeping them?"

"Quit worrying, Emily," Aunt Lucy scolded her.
"They'll be here soon."

Luke studied Clara, relaxed and giggling with
the girls next to her. She looked happy, happier
than he'd ever seen her. Lisa Rose laid her head
in Clara's lap, and Clara stroked the child's hair.
She'd want children of her own, Luke thought. It
was only natural. Why shouldn't she?

He didn't. He thought of his own child. His son,
whom God had only let live a mere ten days. He'd
buried the small bundle in a short grave next to
his wife. The pain seized him again, and he tightened his fist at the harshness of having to relive
it. He needed to talk to Clara. There were things

they needed to agree on, to understand before he declared for her. He never wanted children, never wanted them to die and leave him heartbroken and empty.

It was too late for him to resist a wife. If he didn't marry Clara, the pain would still be there, and it would be more painful without her in his life now that he had let himself love her. Children, however, were another story. He didn't need to ask for more pain. If he lost Clara in childbirth, it would kill him.

"Mommy says you can do magic." He hadn't seen either girl move, yet a black-eyed child waited eagerly for him to perform.

"I don't do much," he told her, then he looked at her hair. "What's that?" he asked.

The child looked behind him. "Where?"

"Here." Luke pulled a flat square box about an inch around from behind one of her braids and presented his open palm to her.

"Wow," she said, pulling the box open. "Look Mommy, it's candy."

"Is it?" Clara acted surprised.

Lisa Rose's eyes widened, but she didn't move from Clara's embrace as Mary Rose pulled a piece of chocolate from the box.

"Can I eat it?"

"Of course you may," Clara affirmed, correcting her grammar.

"Just a moment." As the child moved Luke stopped her. "What's this?" He pulled another box from the other braid. "This one must be for Lisa Rose."

Mary Rose smiled, taking the white box from his open hand. She went back to Clara, passing the second box to her sister.

Aunt Emily looked out the window again and turned back to the room. Piano music started in the distance. Lisa Rose's attention was immediately turned to it.

"That's Martha," Clara explained to the girls. "She plays the piano. Why don't the two of you go in and listen to her."

Lisa Rose hesitated, leaning closer to Clara. Mary Rose started for the door.

"Go on, Lisa Rose. Martha will show you how to play and let you sing."

Clara got up and walked with them to the door. When they were gone she slid the double doors together. Aunt Emily and Aunt Lucy sat expectantly waiting for whatever explanation she was ready to give. Luke moved to the fireplace. "I married him after my parents died," she began, then related the whole story, leaving out nothing, not even her talk with Wade this morning and their agreement to annul their marriage.

Each woman listened without comment. Luke was the one who worried her. He prowled about the room as if something were wrong. It had started when they'd left the cabin. He'd been uncharacteristically quiet on the ride down the mountain, but she'd attributed his preoccupation to the snow and their inability to determine exactly where the path was.

"Why didn't you tell me this?" Aunt Emily asked when she finished speaking.

"I couldn't. Since I'd deceived you all these months, I didn't know how to tell you I was married. You'd fought for my appointment. You'd given me a place to live. If I'd told you, then you'd have been obligated to let the committee know, though it didn't seem to matter, since Mrs. Morrison was out to get me sent away from the day she met me. She spread the story to the committee, and her gossip culminated in last night's . . . meeting." She wanted to call it last night's *court,* but held her temper.

"What story?" Aunt Lucy asked. "Antonia talks a lot. That woman's always got something to say, but she ain't told me nothing about you."

Clara stared at the old woman. In one of her few bouts with reality, she looked totally lucid and in full possession of her faculties.

"She didn't," Aunt Emily confirmed. "Of course everybody knew about the hills. With so many people living in the house, it was impossible to keep them from talking about you two being together all night, no matter the cause. But Dora Davidson saw Luke ride up to your house. I suppose she kept vigil until he left."

"Now that woman's no better than a black widow spider. You can't trust her," Aunt Lucy said.

"Aunt Emily, last night we talked about Luke declaring—"

"Clara." Luke stopped her. He gazed through the lace curtains at the front path. "Miss Emily, are you expecting Doc Pritchard?"

Luke slid the double doors apart as Doc Pritchard rushed through the glass-inlaid front door. Martha stopped playing, and she and the girls gathered in the hall. Miss Emily and Clara stood up. Two boys, about eleven, flanked the country doctor. They could only be Stephen and Wade William.

Doc Pritchard surveyed the room before letting his gaze settle on Clara.

"Mommy!" one boy called. Doc Pritchard put his hand on the boy's shoulder. He looked at him a moment, then pushed him forward. He rushed to Clara, hugging her around the waist and bursting into tears.

"Stephen, what's wrong?" Clara tried to pry the boy's arms from around her, but he wouldn't let go and continued to sob. Then the other one came forward. He didn't cry, but his chin trembled as he fought the attempt. The girls came in and stood staring.

"Where's Wade?" Clara asked.

Doc Pritchard looked uncomfortable. "Clara—"

"He's dead, Mommy," the other boy shouted as tears covered his face. "He's dead! He's dead! He's dead!"

Clara's face turned ashen. Luke thought she was going to faint. He rushed to her, detaching the child and pushing her down into a chair. As Stephen protested, he let him kneel next to her and go back to hugging her waist. Wade William he pulled to his own waist. Martha held the girls by the hand.

"I tried, Clara. It was too late. He went too fast."

"What happened?" she whispered. Her throat sounded raspy.

Doc Pritchard took off his coat and sat in front of her. "I'm not sure. The telegraph officer said he suddenly screamed as if he were in some pain. He clutched his head, and then he fell to the ground. He was already gone before anyone got to him."

"Wade's never been sick."

"Did he have any medical problems?"

"Nothing more than an occasional headache. I'd see him take a headache powder now and then, but he never saw a doctor."

"How long was he having headaches?"

Clara shrugged. "As long as I knew him."

"Didn't he know headaches are usually symptoms of something else?"

"Wade was a simple man. He only knew about the earth, growing things, and going to church. 'God and the ground,' he used to say. 'They are the only things man really needs.' "

"What do you think killed him, Doc?" Luke asked.

"I suspect it was his pressure. It got so high that it just burst. I won't know for sure without an autopsy."

"I have to take him home." Clara spoke almost to herself. "It's what he would want. I'll bury him next to Mabel. He loved her."

"I think everybody better stay here tonight," Miss Emily said. "Martha, will you get the girls ready and put them in bed. Put them in Clara's

old room. I'll take the boys. Aunt Lucy, you can
help me. Luke, you stay with Clara."

Clara was numb. She felt the weight of Stephen's
arms leave her as Doc Pritchard lifted him and
carried him away. The boy continued to sob softly,
but did not protest leaving. Wade William followed,
Lisa Rose and Mary Rose each kissed her on the
cheek before Martha led them out.

Alone, Luke gathered her in his arms and sat
back on the sofa. Hot tears spilled from her eyes.
She couldn't believe it. When she'd left him this
morning, he'd been alive, looking forward to going
back to Virginia and marrying Miss Picket. Now
he was dead. It was unfair.

Luke rocked her gently, stroking her hair. She
slipped her arms around him and cried herself to
sleep.

Miss Emily came back down the stairs, but
didn't come into the parlor. Luke didn't attempt to
move Clara. She'd slept in his arms before and he
liked holding her, as if she were a child and
needed his comforting. He hadn't known his heart
could get as full as it did whenever he was around
her. How was he going to make her understand
they could never marry?

Pain pounded in Clara's head when she opened
her eyes. Where was she? For a moment she didn't
remember anything. Then she recognized Luke's
room. She was in his bed. Quickly she turned to
the other side, but it was empty. She didn't know
if she were relieved or disappointed. Why was she

here? Where had Luke slept? Closing her eyes, she
gave herself up to the moment. She could smell
Luke's scent on the pillow. It was heady and took
her problems away, and she allowed herself to stay
there until she could no longer avoid getting up
and returning to the real world.

Holding her forehead, she pushed herself up and
memory came flooding back to her. Wade. How
could he have died so suddenly—and from what?
Headaches didn't kill people. Women died in childbirth or from infection or disease. All Wade had
ever done was work hard and care for his family,
Clara included. The least she could do was care
for him now.

Clara pushed her legs out from under the covers
and stood up, discovering that she wore one of
Martha's nightgowns. Finding her own clothes laid
out on a chair, she dressed and washed the night's
dreariness from her eyes.

"Mommy?" Lisa Rose's head popped around the
door. The child's voice was soft and questioning,
and she did not smile.

Clara went to her, stooping to the floor and pulling her into her arms. "Good morning, sweetheart." She tried to appear happy and normal.
"Have you had something to eat yet?"

"I'm not hungry." Her thumb started for her
mouth, then she remembered and put it in her lap.
Clara had spent many days breaking Lisa Rose of
the habit, but she still reverted to the comforting
pattern of thumb to mouth each time she felt unsure.

"The boys say Daddy's dead. What's dead mean?"

"Where are the boys?"

"Downstairs."

"Maybe we should all have a talk." Clara got up and took the child's hand. In the dining room she found the other children. Three bowls of oatmeal and three full glasses of milk sat in front of them, but only Wade William's bowl seemed to be less full than the others. Each face looked solemn, as if tears lapped at the surface and any word would have them spilling down their faces. Clara sat down at the head of the table and took the girls onto her lap.

"We haven't had a family meeting in a long time," she began.

" 'Cause you ran away," Stephen blurted out.

The words hurt her, but she deserved them. She was afraid the children might have thought they'd been the cause of her leaving, though if she could have brought them with her, she would have.

"I did run away, Stephen, but it had nothing to do with you," she assured him. She looked about the room. "It had to do with me."

"Is that what Daddy did?" Lisa Rose asked as she burrowed against her shoulder, while another pair of dark eyes eyed her intently from beneath a tangle of curls.

Clara hugged her closer and reached for Stephen's hand. "Wade died," she said. "It means that God called him to live in heaven with him."

"When will he be back?" Lisa Rose asked.

"He's not coming back, you ninny," Stephen said.

"I'm not a ninny." The girls reacted as one in retaliation, but Clara grabbed their hands. "Not now, children. We have to stick together right now." Clara was surprised at how close she was to tears. "Your father loved you more than anything in the world. I know he wouldn't have chosen to leave you without telling you why. He had no chance to talk to you or he would have. We'll have to get along without him the best way we can."

"How are we going to do that?" Wade William asked. "Who's going to run the farm?"

Wade William, the oldest twin, must have been born practical. When Clara had first met him, at six years old, he'd told her there was no need for her to unpack her trunks since she had more clothes than the closet could hold. He'd think of stockpiling for winter and saving money to replace farm equipment as soon as new equipment was bought. Wasn't it like him to think of running the farm?

The farm had been the last thing on Clara's mind. What would happen in Virginia hadn't seemed important. Her only thought had been that the children were now her responsibility and that they would stay with her. They had no other relatives. Only Clara, and Clara couldn't go back to the farm. She had a job here in Montana, and—if she were conservative in her spending—they could all live very well without the farm. The children could go to school and maybe do something more than grow up and work the same land their father had and his father before him.

"Wade William . . . Mary Rose . . . Stephen, I teach school here, and I have a house with many rooms. You can all stay with me, go to school and grow up here." Clara waited uneasily for their reactions. Wade had only died yesterday, as suddenly as blowing out a candle. How could she expect them to easily accept the upheaval of their young lives?

"Won't we ever go home?" The girls lifted their heads at Stephen's question.

"I'd hoped you'd want to stay with me and make this your home."

"We have to stay somewhere," Wade William said. "What will we do with the farm?"

Clara almost smiled. Wade William was a natural leader. When he spoke, the others usually agreed with whatever he said. "We have to go back to bury your father," Clara said. "Then we'll return here and you'll go to school."

"Won't we have chores?" Stephen screwed his face up.

"A few," she admitted. "We have a lot of snow to clear in the winter. We don't have much equipment or many animals to take care of yet. In the spring, I suppose we can plant a garden."

"What about Miss Picket? She's taken care of us since you left, and Ian Watson and Andy Boatwright?"

A cold chill ran through Clara at the thought of Ian Watson. She never wanted to see him again.

Miss Picket was a different story. She would be devastated by the news of Wade's death.

"You'll be able to say goodbye to them before we leave."

They seemed to accept what she said, but Clara knew the next few weeks were going to be hard. Taking Wade home to Virginia, talking to Miss Picket, deciding what to do with the farm and the children—all this would have an effect on them. Her own life had changed completely when her parents had died. She'd have to make sure these children never felt alone and abandoned as she had felt. She was now responsible for their lives.

"Clara, they're not your children." Luke glared at her from one side of Aunt Emily's parlor.

"I'm responsible for them." She went toward him, keeping a tight rein on her temper. She wanted to yell.

"Why? Why can't they go to a relative or the woman Wade was going to marry?"

"They don't want to go to her. They want to stay with me. The girls have never known another mother, and Stephen and Wade William were too young when their mother died to remember her."

"That's not any reason you have to suddenly become the mother of four."

"What do you suggest I do, Luke? Send them to an orphanage? Or should I leave them on the side of a road?"

"You know that's not what I mean."

"Then say what you mean."

"I don't want children."

"And you don't want a wife, either. I've heard this song before, and I don't think I care to hear it again."

"You won't have to." Luke grabbed his jacket from the back of the chair and left her standing in the room alone. Seconds later, Clara heard the door slam. Collapsing on the window seat, she watched him mount his horse and ride away. She stared blank-eyed through the window. The snow was all but gone due to the warm chinook winds that had come in a week ago and stayed. They were due to go away, and more snow would come. The children would like that.

What would happen now? she wondered. Luke was the most bullheaded man she'd ever met. She couldn't abandon the children; she loved them. She'd been happy when Wade had told her they were here with him, and she'd rushed to see them immediately.

After re-uniting, being separated from them would tear her apart. She knew how it felt to lose a parent, to be young and alone in the world. The children needed a stable life, and she could give them that. She'd hoped Luke would grow to love them, too. He was so good with all the children in the valley, and they loved to see him. Hadn't he coached the baseball team, done magic tricks for the little ones, and always had a sweet ready for them?

Somehow she'd known this would happen. Luke had told her how Aunt Emily had tried to get him married for years. She knew he was using the children as an excuse, even if he didn't. He'd become so used to putting up barriers that he didn't even know he was doing it.

Luke needed time, just as the children did. Maybe it was better for them to spend some time apart. Luke could examine his feelings for her and decide if he really loved her. The children could become accustomed to their new home and the loss of their father. And as for her, she could get used to not having Luke around—in case he decided he couldn't take her and her ready-made family. She'd be leaving on the evening train to take Wade back. Luke would have plenty of time to think about what he really wanted . . . and so would she.

Twenty

Martha waved from outside the train window as the Northern-Pacific pulled into Butte. Clara was glad to be back. Being able to see Annie Pearl and James had been a tonic for her system, but the funeral arrangements and subsequent burial had taken a toll on her energy. With all the neighbors coming in and out, it had been hard to keep the children from falling into depression.

Being here meant a new start for them. Time and distance would make them forget after a while. The young ones would forget soon. Stephen had cried at the funeral, but Wade William worried her. He had been in the telegraph office when Wade had died; and throughout the entire ordeal, he had never showed any sign of grief, just his sense of practicality. Clara knew he was walling his feelings inside as Luke had done.

Thoughts of Luke perked her up. Had he missed her? Had he come to see her return? Clara searched past Martha and saw her aunt and Antonia Morrison. Even Zeke was there, but Luke was absent.

Hiding her disappointment, she gathered their

belongings and ushered the children off the train.
Martha hugged and kissed her, and so did Aunt
Emily and Zeke. Even Antonia Morrison broke
into a smile for her and the children. It meant a
lot to Clara that the children were made to feel
welcome.

"Do I still have a job?" she asked when Zeke
had stored their luggage and everyone was in-
stalled in the carriage. The road was bumpy and
snow-covered, and the girls' eyes were so wide
Clara thought they were going to burst.

"The committee thought, in view of the children," Antonia began, "and since you were so re-
cently widowed, that retaining your position would
be acceptable."

Clara's heart soared. Other than her thoughts of
Luke, her job at the school had been a source of
anxiety since she'd boarded the train in Washington's Union Station.

"Do I have you to thank for this?" Clara stared
directly at Antonia.

"Yes," Aunt Emily told her. "Antonia refused to
have them levy their own moral judgments on you.
She told them—"

"That's enough, Emily."

"Thank you, Mrs. Morrison."

"Call me Antonia."

"Thank you, Antonia," she said. "What's been
happening here since I left? How did Martha do
with the teaching?"

"Martha did fine. She did so well we're thinking
of giving her her own class," Aunt Emily teased.
Martha beamed.

"Have the Crabtrees been back for any dinners?" she whispered to the young girl.

"Apparently young Frank Crabtree has invited Martha to a college dance."

"Martha, that's wonderful!" Clara leaned over in the carriage and hugged the girl who'd become her friend. "When do you go?"

"A week from Friday. Miss Emily ordered me a new dress, and she's letting me and Frank's sister Amanda go alone."

"Good," Clara told her. "It's nearly a new century. It's time women learned to travel alone."

Aunt Emily and Antonia Morrison laughed. "Aren't you going to ask about Luke?" her aunt asked.

Clara stiffened, but tried not to show it. "How is he?"

"He been up in those hills since you left."

"What's he doing up there?"

"I don't know. The snow up there is deeper than it is down here."

Clara knew that. When she'd made the trip to the cabin the day Wade had agreed to annul their marriage, the trail had become more and more difficult the higher she'd gotten. Looking outside the carriage, she could see high mounds on the sides of the road. At Clem Kincaid's cabin, the drifts were probably up to the roof.

"He probably needs some time alone. There isn't much work for him while there's snow on the ground." Clara provided an excuse for Luke's absence, remembering her time in the cabin with Luke. She didn't think that great a happiness could ever come again. Luke was against marriage and children, and she now represented both of those vices.

She touched Mary Rose's braids. Whips of hair had come loose. She could never have decided to do anything other than keep the children. Luke hadn't ask her to choose, but the implication had been there. She'd hoped in the last three weeks he'd changed him mind, but his absence at the train station told her she'd lost him forever.

The morning after returning to the valley, Clara went back to school and resumed her role as teacher. Antonia Morrison had agreed to watch the girls while Clara taught, and the school gained two additional students in Wade William and Stephen.

Winter continued. Snow piled up on top of that already on the ground, and Luke did not return from his self-imposed exile. At the first sign of spring, the roads in the valley turned to rivers of mud, but the children arrived in the sleigh drawn by the blacksmith and the inhabitants of the valley conducted business with little notice or inconvenience. Clara found herself washing socks and shoes and cleaning pants before she went to bed each night. It gave her something to do to keep her mind off Luke. That and the letters from Annie Pearl.

Today, Zeke had brought her a missive so exciting that she could hardly contain herself from rushing to deliver the good news to Martha.

Luckily, the family was invited to dinner tonight at Aunt Emily's and she could give Martha the news then.

"Why do I have to wear this? It's too tight around my neck," Wade William complained, pulling at the collar of the suit she had insisted he wear. He was growing too fast for his clothes and she could see his point, but this was the proper method of dress for young men.

"You look wonderful," Clara told him.

"I don't want to look wonderful. I want to put on my other pants and stay here."

"Wade William, it would be rude to not accept an invitation from someone who has been so good to your family."

"Aunt Emily wouldn't mind. There are always so many people there, she wouldn't miss us."

"I'm sure she would miss you."

As soon as everyone was ready, Clara herded them into the wagon her aunt had loaned her and she sat next to Wade William as he drove them to the boardinghouse.

They were greeted like old friends who hadn't seen each other in a long time. Aunt Emily embraced each of the children. Wade William and Stephen winced as she squeezed them, but the girls vied to be picked up and held.

"Is Martha here?" Clara asked as she helped the children with their coats.

"She's still in her room."

"I want to see her."

"Go on up. I'm sure she won't mind."

Clara nearly ran up the stairs. She knocked on

Martha's door and swung it inward. Martha stood, trying to see her reflection in the small mirror, and Clara could hardly speak. She looked wonderful. Her hair had been swept up and pinned. Over her left shoulder, two curls lay on the walnut-colored skin that disappeared at the square collar of her dress. It was a dress that showed off the promise of womanhood.

"I hope Frank has seen you in that," Clara said.

"I wore it to the dance he took me to last winter."

"He'll be home soon. Spring has arrived, and school will end in a month."

"I can hardly wait." Martha grinned.

"Well, when you write him again, here's something you can tell him." Clara handed Martha the envelope that had come for her that afternoon.

"It's addressed to you," Martha objected.

"Read it."

Martha pulled the single sheet out and opened it.

May 1, 1900

Dear Clara,

I finally heard from the publishers in New York. I forwarded the music you sent me last winter to my friends at the New York School of Music. They thought so highly of the style and arrangement that they offered to buy it.

Enclosed is a check for $10.00 for Martha Ames. They asked if she has any other music which they can publish. If she does, the address

*she should send it to is on the bottom of this
letter.*

*I wish I could be there when you tell Martha
the good news. Please extend my congratula-
tions.*

> *Your friend always,*
> *Annie Pearl*

Martha read and re-read the letter. Then she
pulled the check out of the envelope. Clara expected her to jump for joy. Instead, she sat quietly
down on the bed.

"It's real," she said.

"Martha, they liked the music."

Martha looked at her. "They won't take it away?
This isn't a joke?"

Clara shook her head, and suddenly Martha reacted. She jumped up, grabbing Clara, dancing her
about the room and shouting "it's real" over and
over.

"Clara, they want my music," she said, as if
Clara didn't know the contents of the envelope.
"They sent me money, Clara. A check. And they
want more. Did I say that?"

Clara nodded, letting Martha enjoy the moment.
She'd never seen the girl so alive. It was good to
know she could be so happy.

"Martha, there's something else." The smile on
her face kept the girl from losing her joy.

"More good news."

"Annie Pearl plays the piano, too. She knows
many people in publishing. She has agreed to have

you go to Washington and live with her family while you attend college."

Martha didn't say a word. She stood across the room, her hands to her chest. Clara knew her heart was in her throat.

"I can't go away," Martha said.

Clara knew why—Frank Crabtree. It was the same way she felt about Luke. She hadn't wanted to leave him, either, but she had and she was getting used to not seeing him. "Don't refuse too quickly. Think about what it could mean to the rest of your life."

"But . . ."

"Frank?"

Martha stared at her toes, something she did when she was unsure how to answer.

"Frank will be in college, too, Martha. You'd be writing him letters the same as you do now. Talk about it with him when he comes home. You don't have to answer Annie Pearl right away. The invitation remains open until you accept or refuse it. In either case, you've sold a song, you've got a check, and you've got an invitation."

The smile on Martha's face couldn't be described.

"I think I'll write him right now. Tell Miss Emily I'll be down in time for dinner."

"I will."

Clara closed the door as Martha sat down at her desk. She was pleased for the young girl and wanted to share her good news with the most important man in her life. Luke's image loomed in front of her. How she'd like to see him.

At the landing, in front of the huge stained-glass window, Clara turned to descend the final set of stairs and stopped immediately, barely able to keep her feet from faltering. Luke stood alone at the bottom of the stairs. She blinked, refusing to believe—as Martha had the check—that he was real. Her heart pounded at the sight of him.

Luke looked up the stairs. He couldn't move or say anything. He'd hoped his reaction to seeing her again would be different, but he stared at her like a love-starved teenager. Her dress was green, as brilliant as the trees on a bright spring day. God! she looked good in green. She looked good in everything and without everything.

Luke stopped his train of thought. He could no longer think of Clara as his. She had the responsibility of four children, and he'd vowed to never have any again. Of course, he amused the kids in the valley, but that was temporary. There was no way he wanted to take up with any on a daily basis. He didn't want to be captured by their innocent charm and begin to love them, only to have some disease claim their lives.

Clara took a step forward and began to descend the stairs. She walked slowly, like an African queen attending a ceremony, and Luke couldn't take his eyes off her. She was different. Some of the innocence had left her, and she was confident and relaxed; no longer did she have that frightened look in her eyes. On the last step, she stopped. Her small frame stood eye to eye with his, and he could feel the heat of her body. Barely a foot of space separated them. Luke didn't want anything to separate them. He wanted to slowly peel the green dress from her brown body and kiss every bit of skin it covered.

He'd missed her. In the cabin she'd filled his daytime thoughts and his nightly dreams with erotic frustration, but nothing prepared him for reality. He wanted to put his hands up and take her waist, lift her the one step to the floor, and kiss her into submission. Instead, he stepped back and let her descend the final step without his assistance.

"How was the winter, Luke?"

She knew where he'd spent it. That was no surprise to him. Didn't everyone in the valley know? But was she aware of how lonely the winter had been? Could she be aware of everything he did and thought as he was of her?

"It's spring now," he said. "Time for flowers . . ."

"And baseball."

He hadn't been about to say that, and he stopped because he'd almost pulled a flower out and presented it to her. The motion was natural and almost completed before he thought about it and pulled back.

"And baseball," he finally confirmed.

She smiled then, and Luke's insides turned to candle wax. He'd better go in to dinner or once again he'd give the people of the valley reason to dismiss Clara Winslow Pierce.

Offering her his arm, he escorted her to the table, seating her reverently, then took a chair as far from her as he could get—which turned out to be next to Wade William.

Luke didn't know how he was going to get through dinner. Wade William immediately began to ask him questions about building houses—how he began, what came first, even what kinds of nails he used to hold the posts together. Wade William's questions filled his evening, and he had little time to dwell on Clara. Still he was aware of every movement of her head, the sound of her voice when she laughed or spoke, each time she took a drink from her glass or set it on the table.

"Luke . . . Luke."

He heard his name and discovered Miss Emily staring at him. She had one of those looks on her face that only he recognized.

"Luke, Clara is ready to leave. Could you take her home please?"

No! he wanted to shout at her, but noticed everyone looking at him. Not tonight. But tonight he was too vulnerable and let the old woman manipulate him. Sometimes he could strangle Emily Hale! She knew he wouldn't be able to refuse with a roomful of people staring at him.

"Aunt Emily, I can see myself home," Clara protested. "It's not far, and I can come back tomorrow and pick up the children."

"Nonsense," she said, as usual overruling other people's wishes at will.

"There really is no need. I have the wagon. I can just as easily come back tomorrow."

Clara got up and kissed the old woman on the cheek.

"That wagon needs a wheel strut and the brake stick doesn't work. Zeke will fix it tomorrow, and we'll bring the children back. Now, Luke, take Clara home."

Luke stood up. "I'll get the wagon." He knew there was no use arguing with her. He might as well do as she asked and be done with it.

When he pulled the wagon to the front of the boardinghouse, Clara was waiting on the steps.

"I can see myself home, Luke. Aunt Emily was only trying—"

"I know what she was trying to do," he said sharply. "Come on. I'll take you home and she'll be satisfied."

The wind cut through her as Luke helped her into the wagon. He wrapped a rug around her legs and climbed in next to her. The short ride was accomplished in silence, and Clara thought back to their first trip into Butte. Emily Hale had sent her on that excursion, too, and Luke had treated her as if she had the plague then and he continued his silent disapproval now.

Clara endured the ride in silence. Why was he punishing her? She'd tried to tell him she could take herself home; she'd also tried to explain that the children could have come home with her, but Aunt Emily had pushed her protests aside, telling her how much she wanted to get to know the children. And Wade William, even in his suit, had been swayed by images of sweet cakes and homemade ice cream. Clara had papers to correct and tests to make up. Aunt Emily had readily agreed she should go home, and then she'd summoned Luke and directed him to take her.

Luke pulled the wagon to a stop in front of the house. Climbing down, he turned to help her. Clara put her foot on the wheel, and the brake stick gave. The wheel jerked, and she lost her balance and pitched into Luke as she fell. He absorbed her weight, stepping backwards, then took several steps trying to regain balance. Finally he stopped, holding her against him.

She looked up, and wild sensations shot through her when she realized how close his mouth was to hers. Clara had wished for this moment. Since she'd come back from Virginia and found him gone, she'd hoped he'd return and want her. He held her close, and Clara gripped his arms. She was shameless.

Linking her hands behind his head, she pressed her mouth to his. She felt Luke resist. His hands on her waist pushed her back, and she knew in a second he'd break contact with her. Fighting for one last moment, Clara pushed her hips against him, opening her mouth and sliding her tongue through to the recesses of his mouth. Her hands on the sensitive parts of his ears made him groan, and in seconds he lost control over his resistance and his arms banded her like tight belts. Grinding her hips against him, he wedged her into the well of his body which fit only her form.

Clara's hood fell back as Luke lifted her and kicked the door open. He closed it as he set her down and pressed his back to the cathedral carved portal. Clara was hot, burning up with the fire

Luke created. Shifting her arms, she let the cape-like coat slip from her. Free of its bulk, she went back to Luke, skimming her sensitized fingers over his face, his ears, his hair. Luke's tongue danced in her mouth as he pushed her away only enough for the coat to pool at her feet.

Something gripped her, a sensation she'd held back. A giant emotion that refused to be harnessed any longer ripped through her being and made her a woman in his arms. She knew Luke felt the change because his passion deepened. Clara thought her neck would snap with the force of Luke's kiss, and her nerve endings reached a fever pitch as his hands skittered over her arms and down her back.

The lack of oxygen made her light-headed when he slid his mouth to her neck. Clara had to have Luke tonight. If no other night in her life, tonight she couldn't let him leave her. She'd waited the entire winter; she'd slept alone thinking of him, dreaming of his huge body plunging into hers. She wouldn't deny herself tonight.

Taking his hand, she led him to the darkened bedroom; and when she closed the door, they stared at each other, the hunger between them as visible as the rising hills at dawn. Clara crossed the room, her hands reaching for the buttons on his coat. One by one she released them, then pushed the fabric over his shoulders until it slid down his long arms and fell to the floor, his suit jacket and shirt following. Tender fingers rode over his hair-roughened arms to entwine with his.

Luke found it almost impossible to stand still.

He'd never had a woman undress him. Clara was hesitant at first, but her continued progress gave her confidence. Her light touch drew flames wherever she made contact with his overly susceptible skin, and her open mouth pressed into the middle of his chest. The pleasure which racked through his body was as close to heaven on earth as Luke thought he'd ever get; she was rapidly pushing him over the edge. When her hands went to his belt buckle, he groaned loudly. Pushing his hands into her hair, he discarded every pin, threading and combing through the silky-soft mass as if he might die from the pleasure of its touch. He kissed her forehead, her ears, her cheeks.

Turning her around, he undid the buttons on her dress. His fingers fumbled, but the green dress quickly blended with his black-and-white suit. Clara stood before him with only her chemise and petticoat for cover. Her face, aglow in the semi-darkness, offered him trust and love. With exquisite tenderness, he kissed her mouth, pinning her hands to the physical evidence of his need for her. Clara massaged him, slipping her hands over his bulge with a knowledge inherent to women.

He cried out in pleasure, begging for the torture to stop. He could endure it no longer. Walking her backward, he took her to the bed, but Clara stopped at its edge. Slipping his pants over his hips, she extended her hands down his legs as far as they would reach, which was far enough for Luke. With lightning speed, he stepped out of his shoes and pants and then finished undressing

Clara. He placed her on the bed—his body hard, erect, ready—and tried to be gentle, tried to make her time as pleasurable as she made his, but it was a battle he didn't think he could win.

Luke covered Clara's smaller body with his massive one. He kneed her legs apart and entered her, the fever driving him forward. The rhythm between them was immediate, fierce, and primal. He was caught in a web of golden strands—imprisoned but impassioned for his jailer.

He listened to her sounds—the whimpering and moans of pleasure. She writhed beneath him as if pulling him deeper into her was her only purpose on earth. His own climax gripped first at his stomach, then spiraled throughout his entire being, grabbing at his core and holding him in its grip. He worked with Clara, worked to find it, hold it, and keep it going until they shared that plane where light exploded into blinding color.

Clara's scream blended with his yell as he called her name and collapsed in a mass of arms and legs. Clara breathed raggedly, drinking air in huge gulps. He could feel her heart beating and see the rapid pulse in her neck as the moonlight spilled into the room and across her glistening body.

"Luke," she whispered.

"Shh," he told her. "Sleep now."

With a satisfied smile, she snuggled into his arms and closed her eyes.

Luke held her long after her breathing told him she had fallen into a contented sleep. He, too, should have slept, but his mind was too active, too

awake. What had she done to him? Why was it
that no matter what he told himself, the moment
she stepped into the room, he gravitated to her as
if to a magnet? He gave Emily Hale credit for
having thrown Clara at him, but he hadn't had to
catch her. He could have stopped this long ago,
but the truth was he didn't want to stop it. He
wanted Clara as he'd never wanted any other
woman. She was brave and strong and willing to
face anything.

She'd taken hold of her life in Virginia and
changed it for the better. Even her act of running
away, in her innocent eyes, had been a way of
changing her life. She wasn't one to look back
or dwell on the past. Clara looked to the future—
for the children as well as for herself. A twenty-
one-year-old providing for four young children
had to be the most courageous thing he could
think of.

Luke wished he were more like Clara. When Peg
died, he had reverted into himself, burying his life
with her and his dead child. Even Miss Emily's
efforts to snap him out of his delirium had had
little effect on him. Until Clara. Now he could
think of nothing but her.

He pulled her closer. She was warm and soft,
and the smell of lilacs did crazy things to his equilibrium. He kissed the top of her head. He'd have
to leave soon. He had to get back to the boardinghouse before the parlor games ended and the
women went to bed. He'd only hold her for a few
more minutes, hold her as he'd dreamed of holding
her during the long winter in Clem's cabin. Some

days he had thought he'd go crazy with longing, now he knew going on without Clara would kill him.

Twenty-one

Clara stretched languidly. Luke was gone. She hugged his pillow, taking in his scent. If only she could have stayed there all day! But she had work to do—even though she could only think of Luke and their night together. Giggling, she wondered if this were what a "brazen hussy" felt like. Turning onto her back, she took Luke's pillow with her as if she were pulling his hard body onto her own. She couldn't even tell Annie Pearl how Luke made her feel. Only he knew how wild and uninhibited she could be. Clara had never thought she could act that way. She'd undressed Luke, run her hands all over him, wherever she felt like, without any shame or guilt.

Giving in to her desire to stay in bed, Clara closed her eyes, needing to dream a little longer. When she opened them again, the sun was high in the sky and the clock was counting out the hour. It was eleven o'clock.

Where were the children? She couldn't possibly have stayed in bed this long! Throwing the covers back, she shivered as the cold air touched her naked body. Grabbing her robe, she pushed her arms into it and went to stoke the fire. When the embers had grown into a full flame, she washed and dressed.

It looked sunny and cold outside, and the trees stood straight as they reached toward the sky, telling Clara there was little wind to further cool the air.

When she'd had something to eat and the children had still not arrived, she began to worry. It wasn't far to Aunt Emily's and, with the warmth of the sun, the ground wouldn't be as muddy as it had been from the melting snow and rain of the past days. Putting on her boots and coat, she went outdoors. Was it her imagination or was the sky bluer today? The trees looked greener; the air smelled fresher. *Everything looks different when you're in love.* Clara heard Janey's voice in her head. Today, even Janey couldn't make her cross. She *was* in love, and everything did look different.

Clara kicked the loose dirt from her boots onto the porch before she opened the door to the boardinghouse. Inside it was quiet, too quiet when four active children should have been underfoot.

"Hello," she called. "Anybody here?"

Clara hung her coat on the rack by the door as Martha came down the stairs.

"Good afternoon, Clara."

"Hello, Martha." There was a change in the young girl, too. Happy herself, Clara recognized her own sense of joy in Martha's countenance. "Where're Aunt Emily and the children?" she asked.

"She took them with her," Martha said.

"Where'd they go?"

"To take Luke his lunch." Martha couldn't have known the impact her words would have on Clara. "She said if you came by you should come out to the site."

"I'll go right over." Clara picked up her coat and Martha pulled the back up so Clara could slide her arms inside.

Clara walked happily behind the boardinghouse and toward the building site. She could hardly wait to see Luke again. All their problems of the winter seemed to have melted with the coming of spring. Clara decided that spring was her favorite season and that it would remain that way forever.

She passed the point where the warning flag had been. It was absent today, indicating that she could proceed safely. She heard the children laughing before she saw them. Over the rise in the hill she saw the house. Luke had completely walled it with wood and angled out the windows. The part facing her was the new section that had been the reason for the dynamiting last fall. It would be made up almost completely with long rectangular windows that stretched from ceiling to floor. Clara could imagine sitting beside the glass panes with the sun warming her or spending a warm summer evening staring at the stars. She smiled at the thought of having Luke sit with her.

A loud laugh brought her attention back to her mission. Aunt Emily sat at the picnic table facing her. Luke had his back to her. Wade William sat next to Luke on one side while Lisa Rose sat on the other. Stephen occupied the same bench as Aunt Emily. The only one she didn't see was Mary Rose.

Scanning the area her smile suddenly froze. She spied the child on the ladder leaning against the structure. She was a third of the way up the ladder leading to the flat roof.

"Mary Rose!" she shouted causing everyone to turn toward her, then to follow the line of her vision. Luke was quickly out of his seat and striding toward the child. Clara ran, obstructed by her skirts and petticoat. When she reached the child Luke had her in his arms. Clara grabbed her, making sure she was all right.

"Mary Rose, you scared Mommy to death. Don't you ever, ever do that again."

She hugged the child to her breast, her heart beating like a tom-tom.

"Clara, I'm sorry," Luke apologized behind her. "I didn't know she was on the ladder."

"It's all right," Clara said. "She's all right." She glanced at him. Sweat popped out on his brow and his face looked pale. His fair coloring and the summer-darkened skin he'd lost during the winter months made him appear ill. Clara thought Luke needed more comforting than the child in her arms. She wanted to embrace him and let him know everything was all right. She reached for his hand, and Luke squeezed hers, holding it a little longer than usual before dropping it when Aunt Emily came up.

"Maybe I'd better take the children back now," she said.

"That's a good idea," Luke agreed. "Maybe it's best if they stay away while I'm working."

"I'll go along with that," Clara said. It was impossible to keep an eye on them all the time. They were inquisitive about everything, asking question after question and investigating on their own when answers weren't enough. Clara gathered both of them into her arms and held them close.

"Zeke ought to have that wagon fixed by now anyway." The old woman took the girls' hands before going back to the picnic table. While she repacked the picnic basket, Clara turned to Luke.

"Clara." Luke reached for her and her fingers tingled at his touch. "I'm sorry."

"I know you are, Luke. It wasn't your fault," she reassured him. "They're a handful. That's just the way children are. You never know what they'll get into. But just to be on the safe side, I'll keep them away from here."

He nodded, his face still pale.

"She didn't fall, Luke," she said gently. "She's not John." Clara remembered the brother who'd fallen under the wagon wheels. "She's going to be all right. She's not going to die." Clara felt his brow. Even in the cool air he was sweating. He brushed her hand away.

"Don't bring them back here," he said brusquely. "And maybe it's a good idea if you don't come back either."

"What?" A coldness ran through her at his words. "You can't mean that. After last night—"

"Last night should never have happened."

"Are you saying you're sorry it did?"

"Clara, I've told you how I feel. Today was a perfect example of why I don't want children."

"Luke, she's all right." Clara spoke slowly. "You

can't go on thinking every child will die by falling
off something or developing a fatal disease. If that
were true, there wouldn't have been a baseball
team and half my class wouldn't have survived a
sleigh ride down the hill."

"Those are my feelings," he said adamantly.

"Are they, Luke? Can you really tell me you
don't love the children of this valley? That you
wouldn't climb into those hills to find one of them
if he were lost? That the chances of their surviving
to man or womanhood is less than the length of
one fall?"

"A fall killed my brother and I buried my son."

"But nothing happened to Rose. She's fine. She
has no bruises, no cuts, not even a loss of appe-
tite."

"Just keep her away from me, Clara. Keep all
of them away."

Clara stared at him. She didn't know this man.
She'd been more intimate with him than with any
other man on earth, but she did not understand
how he could be so stubborn.

"I feel sorry for you, Luke Evans," she said
sadly. "You have the capacity to be a loving father
and husband, yet you run hot and cold. One minute
you're a tender, sensitive man, and the next . . .
I'd like to knock some sense into that thick head
of yours."

"That will be all for today." Clara dismissed her
class. "Don't forget final exams begin on Monday."

Clara sat down as the noise level in the room

rose and the children filed out, joyful that the next two days would be free of any learning requirements. Placing her hands to her temples, Clara massaged her head. It pounded with tension and lack of sleep.

Three weeks had passed since she and Luke had argued. Clara found it difficult to sleep and even more difficult to keep her mind from wandering to him. Why was he so bullheaded? It had to be more than his brother's dying so many years ago and losing his wife and child. Luke was a strong, virile man; she knew that firsthand. For him to spend his life without a wife and children was unthinkable to her.

"Clara."

She looked up at the sound of her name. Martha stood in front of her desk.

"I've had a letter from Frank," she said. "I told him about your friend's offer and college."

"What does he think?"

"He thinks it's a great idea." Martha beamed. She was so happy, she seemed to glow, and Clara wished her own life were like Martha's. Everything was falling into place for the young girl: She had a young man whom she loved and he was in love with her; she had an offer of college in the East, a place she wanted to see; she had a music publisher paying for her compositions. Life was being good to Martha.

"Martha, that's wonderful," Clara enthused. "I knew he'd think that. Frank Crabtree strikes me as a very practical young man."

"He says he'll finish school a year before I do and maybe we can think of being married then."

"Married?"

"Yes, isn't it the most wonderful thing you've ever heard of?"

Clara left her desk and hugged Martha. "It's the best news I've heard today," she said. "Have you told Aunt Emily?"

"Not yet. I wanted to tell you first."

Clara was honored she thought enough of their friendship to give her the news before anyone else.

"I want to let Miss Emily know at dinner tonight," Martha went on.

"She'll be pleased, Martha. You're like a daughter to her. She'll be glad you're going to school; and when you graduate, you'll give her a reason to plan a wedding. She'll do everything she can for you."

"I know," Martha whispered. "I'd better go now. I want to wear something pretty when I tell her, and Mr. and Mrs. Crabtree are coming to dinner."

She turned to leave.

"Martha, I have an idea. Would you like to wear my blue dress?"

"The one with the Gibson Girl look?"

Clara nodded. Martha stared at her, speechless. "It should fit you," she encouraged. "And it's a great dress for your good news." Clara took her arm and led her to the house.

Martha tried on the royal-blue satin-and-lace gown and was so pleased by how good she looked that Clara packed the dress immediately and sent

Martha home. The young girl was happy enough
to pull Clara's low spirits up.

She waved a cheery goodbye, then remembered
the girls. She had to pick them up at Antonia's.
Wade William and Stephen, who'd left when the
class was dismissed, usually showed up in time for
dinner; she didn't worry about them. Every child
in the valley was blessed with a mother in every
household, which—from a child's point of view—
might be considered a curse. But at least Clara
could rest assured her boys wouldn't get into
trouble without having someone close at hand to
correct them.

He was there again. Each day, as soon as the
school bell rang signalling the end of classes, he'd
show up. Luke could almost tell time by his arrival. So far he hadn't done anything but stand and
watch. Luke didn't like having him here, but he
had no real reason to make him leave. Near supper
time he'd disappear, and Luke would finish up for
the day and go to the boardinghouse.

Luke thought the boy was like Martha. He
wanted to talk to someone, but couldn't figure out
how to begin. He'd heard Wade William hadn't
shown any emotion at his father's death or at the
funeral. In the weeks since he'd returned, Luke had
sat next to him at dinner and found that the child
talked incessantly, but he never mentioned Virginia
or his father. Luke should have sent him home.

The only thing that *did* bother him about finding
Wade William at the edge of his property was that

seeing the child made him think of the mother—
Clara. Luke was down to thinking about Clara only
once in every second, so shooing Wade William
away would accomplish nothing.

She would fade in his memory. He knew that.
Peg had. He couldn't remember her face, and his
brother was only a name on a stone in the valley
graveyard; even his parents' images were no longer
clear.

"What're you doing?"

He jumped at the sudden intrusion of Wade Wil-
liams's young voice. The boy was behind him,
standing close enough to touch, yet he'd never seen
him move.

"I'm about to set this window." Luke looked at
him. He sized up the window and the equipment
around it as if he were deciding how best to frame
the glass in his mind.

"How do you do that?"

Luke had told Clara to keep them away; but here
was Wade William asking questions, and he
couldn't tell him to go. So he said, "See these
grooves?" and pointed to the double-well indenta-
tion in the window frame.

Wade William nodded.

"You set these little metal clips inside them."
He dropped the casement holders into the two bottom grooves. "Then you slip the glass into the top
first. When it fits into the top, drop it into the
bottom casement and it holds it in place." Luke
demonstrated at he spoke. "This holds the glass
in the window."

"That little piece holds this big window?" Wade

William's head fell back as he eyed the six-foot single piece of glass.

"It holds it in place so you can use your hands to put the putty around the edges." Picking up his tray, he spaded the putty and showed the child how to mold it around the window. "This holds the glass permanently in place and acts as an insulator to keep the cold and rain out."

"Oh," Wade William said.

Luke hid a grin.

"Are you going to put all these windows in?"

"Yeah," Luke said. "Do you want to help me?"

The twelve-year-old's eyes opened as wide as his mother's when she was surprised. Luke had begun this venture alone and had planned to complete it without anyone's help. It had been his dream, but now he realized it had been an outlet for his anger at Peg's dying, at his parents' dying. Building had been therapy for his failing memory, a monument to the dead—but it no longer symbolized an end to life. It was a house. When it was done, he'd live here. He loved the land, the hills in the distance, and the work he'd put into it; but he no longer needed solitary labor to cover over the scab of pain left by the death of his wife and parents. Wade William needed the therapy more than he did. Giving him something to do might help him exorcise the pain he was struggling to hide.

"Do you mean that?"

Luke nodded. "Think you can lift that piece of glass?"

* * *

"Wade William, where have you been? And look at you." He was covered with dirt. His clothes and hands were filthy.

"I'm hungry," he said.

"Go wash up. You're late for supper."

Wade William rushed off. Where had he been? She'd noticed that he looked happier; his face, covered with dust, was bright and animated.

The other children had adjusted to their new life with ease. The girls loved Antonia Morrison, who spoiled them rotten. Stephen had made friends with some of the boys in school and enjoyed playing with them. Wade William was the one she worried about. Until tonight, he'd maintained his control, kept his feelings to himself, and done whatever was expected of him; but he hadn't shown the healthy signs of healing. Tonight he was changed, and she wondered what had been the catalyst.

Just as Wade William joined them at the dinner table, a knock came at the door.

"I'll get it. Stephen, say grace and you all begin to eat," she instructed as she set her napkin on the chair.

"Luke!" Shock gripped her as she opened the door. He was covered in the same dirt and grime that had enveloped Wade William.

"Wade William was with me. I thought you ought to know."

"Come in," she invited.

"I haven't had time to clean up yet." He looked down at his work clothes.

"Wade William was even dirtier when he got

home. And we do have water. You can clean up here."

Luke shrugged and stepped into the room.

"It's Mr. Luke." Clara heard Stephen whispering behind her.

"The boy came to the building site today. I asked him to help me. I thought you'd want to know where he'd been."

All four siblings inched across the floor until they stood close to her, listening.

"Thanks for telling me."

"He's going to come each day, after school, and help." Clara glanced at Wade William. "Is that all right with you?" he asked.

"He won't be in the way? I know you said—" She studied him closely.

"As long as he does his homework and chores around here, I'd welcome his help."

"Then it's all right with me."

In a fit of uncharacteristic exuberance Wade William sailed across the room and caught her in a bear hug that brought tears to Clara's eyes. She put her arms around Wade William and reached unconsciously for Luke's hand. Almost without thinking, he closed his fingers around her palm.

"Thank you, Luke." Her voice was a raspy whisper.

"Luke, why don't you stay for supper?" Wade William asked, and Stephen and the girls voiced their approval.

Luke glanced at Clara, but she didn't need to answer.

"You can wash up in there," she said.

* * *

What was he doing here? Luke dried his face
and hands. He wished he had a clean shirt to put
on, but he'd come straight from the building site
following an attack of guilt. His instructions to
Clara had been to keep the children away from
him. It was only fair to explain that he'd asked
Wade William to help out.

Now he was in her bedroom . . . the room
where he'd held her naked body against his . . .
where he'd made love to her. His body reacted,
turning hard at the thought of what she could do
to him.

Folding the towel, he hung it on the rack and
returned to the kitchen. Everyone stopped talking
when he entered the room.

"Over here, Mr. Luke." Wade William had saved
him a seat next to him—at the head of the table,
directly across from Clara.

Luke sat down. At first, no one said anything.
Everyone looked at him wide-eyed and surprised,
as if they hadn't expected him. Luke adjusted his
chair, embarrassed. "Did I do something wrong?"
He looked at Clara.

"No." She shook her head. "When we were in
Virginia, Wade would sit there," she explained.
"His clothes were often dirty while the rest of us
were clean. I guess it's the shock of seeing you in
his place."

Luke looked about the table. He made eye contact with each of the children.

"I know you all loved your father," Luke said.

"I know you miss him a lot. At times you forget he's gone and expect him to come in from the fields and sit down. There's nothing wrong with that. No one can replace your dad. When my dad died, I thought he was going to come back. I blamed him for leaving me, because I needed him to talk to, to teach me things. And I needed to tell him I was sorry."

Wade William whimpered next to him. Stephen's eyes were misty, but the girls looked straight at him, as if they were trying to understand what he was saying.

"Then I remembered," he went on. "I remembered something he'd told me long before he died. He'd said that death wasn't final. It meant we couldn't talk to each other, but he would always understand how I felt and when we were reunited, I could tell him in person."

"Did he want you to die, too?" Stephen asked.

"No, he wanted me to know that he understood there were things we say that we don't mean. And that he would always be with me, even though he was in heaven and I was here."

At Luke's last words, a silence fell over the room as each child digested his words.

"Shall we eat?" Clara whispered, picking up a bowl of rice and spooning it on a plate.

Clara was surprised at how well the meal had gone after its heavy beginning. Wade William had led most of the discussion, telling them about the house he would be helping Luke build. Luke had handled sitting in Wade's place at the table well by explaining how death could hurt the living. Clara was proud of him and hoped the healing process would begin now.

"Would you like coffee?" she asked Luke when everyone had finished eating. They'd spent a long time at the table and it had been so pleasurable that Clara didn't want it to end. Luke nodded, rising with her. "Why don't you go into the front room?" she urged. "I'll bring it in."

The children followed him as if he were the Pied Piper. Clara cleaned up the dishes and made coffee. When she entered, Luke was pulling a silver coin from behind Stephen's ear, Lisa Rose was curled up in his lap fast asleep.

"Would you teach me how to do that?" Stephen asked excitedly.

Clara set the tray on a low table.

"Mom do we have any books on building?" Wade William searched her bookshelf. He'd found a project he liked and couldn't wait to get started on it.

"I don't think so. We can try the library in Butte," she told him.

"Do you want me to take her?" she asked, reaching for the sleeping child.

"She's fine."

Clara stared at him for a moment, then resumed her position by the coffeepot. It was strange that a man who said he didn't want anything to do with children was always around them. More surprising was the girls' display of affection for Luke. They had each other for companionship and tended to be reserved in the presence of adults they didn't know well.

Pouring a cup of coffee, she added three sugars and a dollop of cream before handing it to Luke. He slid his fingers over her hand as he accepted the cup, and Clara's eyes flew to his; but the contact was broken when he moved the cup.

"I have plenty of books, Wade William. You're welcome to read mine," Luke offered. "I'll bring one tomorrow."

"Thanks, Mr. Luke."

"I know you're all having a good time, but you have to get ready for bed now." The boys surprised Clara by not arguing, and Stephen got up quickly and kissed her on the cheek.

"You *will* remember to teach me the magic tricks," he pressed as he passed Luke.

"I'll remember." Luke stood, shifting the close-lidded girls onto the sofa, and shook Stephen's hand.

"See you in the morning," Wade William said.

"I have to get the girls to bed." Clara accepted a sleeping child from Luke and the contact between them weakened her knees. She had to concentrate on holding Lisa Rose. "Drink your coffee. I'll be back in a moment." She left the room quickly, not daring to meet his eyes.

The girls went down without a peep, not even waking when Clara changed their clothes. So much evening activity had worn them out, and they were fast asleep when Clara blew out the lamp. The boys waited for her to come into their room.

"I like Mr. Luke," Stephen told her. "He's really good at magic."

"Yes he is," Clara agreed.

"Do you think he'll come again?"

"I don't know."

"Will you ask him? He likes you, Mom. I can tell."

"He likes us all, Stephen." She wanted to jump on the remark, but Luke had warned her not to see him or bring the children near him. He'd allowed Wade William to help out, but that didn't mean he wanted anything more to do with her and her children.

"He likes you best. When he looks at you, it's different. It's like when Daddy used to look at Miss Picket. Like he wants to marry you."

Clara dropped down on the bed. Her knees wouldn't allow her to stand. "Stephen, I don't think Mr. Luke wants to marry me."

"I do," Wade William said. "He looks at you all the time. Tonight even, his eyes never left you when you were in the room. While you were in the kitchen, he kept looking over his shoulder, hoping to see you."

"You're imagining this. Mr. Luke is a very nice man who's letting you help with his house, Wade William. Maybe he'll teach his magic tricks to Stephen. He's grateful that we invited him to dinner, nothing more."

"I think there's more." Wade William refused to let go of the conversation. "Grown-ups don't notice us kids unless we're in the way. I looked at Mr. Luke tonight and saw that even when he was doing tricks or talking to us, he kept looking at you."

"So, Mom," Stephen urged, "invite him to dinner again. I like him."

Clara agreed, kissing him and straightening his coverlet. She pulled the blanket around Wade William's neck and kissed his forehead. "Good night," she said and blew out the lamp.

Luke stood when she came into the front room. "You were a hit with the children tonight," she said. "They want you to come back to supper again."

Pouring herself a cup of coffee she sat across from him.

"I enjoyed tonight, Clara."

"You say that as if you hadn't expected to."

"I hadn't."

Clara withheld comment. For some reason, she thought he was about to tell her a secret, one that he'd kept from everyone—including himself. She waited for him to continue.

"I don't remember them, Clara," he said, looking at the floor.

Clara didn't think he meant the children.

"Every day I think of them. I try to see their faces, but they aren't there. She's fading in my memory. I can't get a clear picture of her in my mind. Whenever I think of her, I can't quite see her. I need photographs just to remember what they looked like. I promised, Clara." He lifted his gaze from the carpet to her. "I told them I would always love them and remember them. Now I can't. Nothing is clear in my mind."

Clara moved closer to Luke. She sat on the sofa directly next to his chair.

"Luke, that's normal," Clara told him.

"Normal? I was married to her for over three years. I loved her. How can I not remember what she looked like?"

"Luke, you're alive. Each day new experiences change you. Peg remains the same."

"That's all the more reason I should know what she looks like."

"Memory doesn't work that way. It closes the pain of loss. The pain fades along with clear images. You can remember her hair color, her eyes, her smile."

"Yes, all those things, but not all together."

"And you're afraid that in time you won't even be able to recall those things."

"How did you know?" He frowned.

"I felt the same way about my parents. I was closer to my father than I was to anyone on earth. Yet I can't see his face anymore. I know he had a mustache and my mother had long black hair, but I can't make their features crystal-clear unless I look at their wedding photograph. I think it's part of growing. We keep growing, getting older, living, doing what we have to, need to. They don't. As everybody around us changes, it becomes more and more difficult to remember the people we don't see."

"But I loved them. I never thought I'd forget them."

"You haven't forgotten them. You've stopped

grieving, that's different. It means you're ready to go on."

"Live again?"

She nodded. "For me it happened when I decided to fight for my education. And, of course, when I made the decision to leave Virginia. It was time to live again, to be responsible for my own life. I love my parents the same. That hasn't changed. Just as you probably love Peg." Clara paused.

Irrationally, she wanted him to tell her he was in love with her. She knew he wouldn't do it, but she hoped.

"Peg wouldn't want you to live alone forever. I know she was a wonderful person. It wouldn't be like her to hold you to that promise."

"You're very old for your years, Clara."

"And you're wise for yours," she told him. "What you said to the children tonight was better than anything I could have told them. I think they are beginning to heal."

"Especially Wade William."

"Why him specifically?"

"He's been coming to the building site every day. He'd only stand and watch. Today was the first time he spoke."

"I appreciate what you're doing for Wade William. He's still a child; but with his father gone, he thinks he should be the man of the family. Letting him help you will give him a skill and an expression for his anger."

"Clara, you're doing a wonderful job. You're a good mother."

She wanted to tell him he was a good father, too, but the night was easy and calm. If she mentioned it, he'd close up and the truce they'd unconsciously established would be destroyed.

They sat in quiet, comfortable silence for a while. Clara finished her coffee and offered Luke another cup.

"I'd better go now." Luke rose, and Clara did, too. They each stopped, staring directly at each other.

"Will you come again?" she asked. She told herself it was for Stephen's sake, but she knew that wasn't entirely true. "Stephen wants to learn the magic tricks."

"And you?"

"I . . . I'd . . ." She couldn't voice her thoughts.

Luke surveyed the roof. A sea of black tiles stretched before him; yet he knew that with the portion of blonde pine behind him, it would remain uncovered until his next shipment arrived. He didn't know how long that would be. He'd hoped to finish the roof before the summer festival, but that didn't look likely now.

The days continued to lengthen, giving him more light each day, and with Wade William's help, he had made excellent progress. The boy was surprisingly capable. Luke looked up. It was about time for him to arrive. There he was, walking fast. Luke was glad he liked coming. Their afternoons together reminded him of the times he'd spent with his father, only now he was in the role of the adult.

That was enough for today, he thought. Climbing down the ladder, he reached the bottom just as Wade William crossed the yard.

"Do you want me to help on the roof?"

"We'll let that wait. I'm almost out of tiles." Luke dipped water from a bucket and drank it straight from the dipper. "Want some?" Luke offered the dipper to Wade William.

"No, thank you." He always used such good manners. Luke could see Clara's influence in the way he and the other children acted. Wade William appeared different today. He was hesitant, as if he had something on his mind. Luke wondered if he wanted to talk.

"Is there something bothering you?" he asked, leaning against the table that held the water bucket.

"May I ask you a question?"

"Sure," Luke said, wondering when Wade William would trust him enough to open up. He'd thought last night at dinner he would break down and cry, but he'd tightened his jaws and refused to let the tears fall.

"Mom said your parents are dead."

"That's right."

"Did they die when you were a boy?"

Luke turned to Wade William, but the boy averted his eyes. "No. I was married when they died."

"Oh," he said.

"I was just as angry, Wade William. I felt deserted, as if they'd left me alone, and I didn't know how to act. You probably feel the same way." Luke offered him a lead.

"I feel—" he stopped, his voice thick with unshed tears.

Luke didn't press him, but gave him time to get his thoughts in order.

"I feel like I'm not doing anything right."

Luke sat down on the table. He touched the space next to him, and Wade William swung back onto the seat. "Has Clara—your mother—complained?"

"She wouldn't. It's just that I'm . . . I'm supposed to know how to—" His voice cracked.

Luke put his arm on Wade William's slender shoulders, and the child dissolved in tears. He wanted to be a man, thought it was expected of him. He let go of the grief then, and the tears poured from him. Luke knew it was good for him; he was young enough. There was no one else to witness his tears, and Wade William knew he could count on him to keep his secret. Letting go of the dead was part of learning to live. Clara had taught Luke that.

Wade William pulled away, drying his eyes with his shirt sleeves.

"No one expects you to be anything more than be a twelve-year-old, Wade William. You're supposed to do just what you're doing. No one expects you to be able to run the farm or break horses or work in the mines. They love you. The only thing they expect of you is for you to love them back."

"That's all?" He squinted as he looked up at Luke.

"That's all." Luke smiled. "Now how about we finish the parlor floor?"

"All right," Wade William agreed. "What about the roof?"

"It'll wait."

By the time Wade William left, he was covered with dirt but had a large smile on his face. He had worked as if he were exorcising the demons from his soul. Luke knew he wouldn't always be that way. In fact, he expected a marked change in the boy the next day.

He grinned at how eager Wade William was to learn. He was a wonderful child, confident most of the time and willing to do anything over and over until he got it right. He reminded Luke of himself.

The last few weeks had been better than he'd thought possible. He hadn't expected to want the boy around, but Clara had been right. Washing his hands, he wasn't surprised to find his thoughts straying to Clara. They always did. She'd seen his natural love for children and told him he wouldn't be able to live his whole life without the fulfillment of a family. Sure he'd fought her, and she'd probably even known he'd done it unconsciously. With Wade William coming each day and Stephen so proud to show him his accomplishments, he'd grown attached to them.

The girls would clutch his hands and curl up on his lap. He enjoyed their naps against his shoulder and their constant stream of questions. He didn't think he'd mind seeing them each day, being a part of their lives.

He wanted to be a part of Clara's life, too, although he'd refused her dinner invitations in a vain attempt to put his life back as it had been before she'd come to the valley. He should have known it would never be the same again. The festival was only a week away. He'd talk to Clara then. He knew he'd have the opportunity to be alone with her. Even if he did nothing, Emily Hale would make sure her dinner went to him. Luke smiled at the thought. There was a time he'd have wanted to strangle the old woman; now he looked forward to her manipulations. With him and Miss Emily both trying to get Clara married, the brown-skinned beauty didn't have a chance.

Twenty-two

The annual summer dance and dinner took place every year on the last Saturday in June. The valley went into planning for the event a month in advance, and no one seemed to discuss anything else. School was officially over until fall, and Clara was free to help out with any of the preparations.

Aunt Emily had volunteered her to work with the children for the program section. The children had been practicing three songs for months to be ready for the event that would take place in only a few more hours.

In the meantime, she'd made the special meal for Aunt Emily. Why she had to do it, she didn't know. Her aunt had a kitchen staff, but she'd told her they were so busy that they wouldn't be able to prepare the basket she needed. Clara agreed, understanding that the old woman had something else in mind.

"Do you think Mr. Luke will be there early?" Stephen asked. "I want to show him my new trick."

Stephen had been practicing pulling a coin out of his sleeve for weeks. Since the night Luke had

come by, Clara hadn't seen him. Wade William
worked at the building project, and a couple times
Stephen had gone over to learn a new magic trick.
Luke hadn't accepted any of the invitations to dinner she knew the boys had extended, and Clara
was beginning to think he'd retreated into his private world. Wade William and Stephen came in
each night with animated stories of what he'd
taught them and what he'd said. They were developing a bond with Luke that she hoped worked in
both directions.

After that night when they'd talked so openly,
Clara had thought he, too, might begin his healing
process, but she wasn't sure any longer. Like the
children, she was looking forward to seeing Luke
today. Maybe she could tell how he was doing
without having to ask.

Wade William and Stephen had helped her prepare and, once she was ready, they left to find
their friends. The girls were with Antonia, leaving
Clara to enter the church grounds alone.

"Clara, thank goodness you're here," Mrs. Reed
greeted her. "Let me help you get these things over
to the tables." She immediately hoisted the heavy
bowls of food and carried them to the tables set
up for the day.

"Is this the basket for the lottery?" Dora Davidson didn't give her a chance to answer. The woman
had been barely civil to her since the incident in
Aunt Emily's parlor. "I'll put your name on it."
Clara didn't know anything about a lottery, but as
long as she was labelling the basket, Clara would
be able to find it to give it to her aunt.

"Mommy! Mommy! They got clowns." The girls clutched her skirt. "Look! shouted joyously. Clara saw the town black Pritchard dressed in baggy pants and Doc Their faces had been painted with huge s hats. their hair was bright orange. She laughed, and lighted as the children.

Antonia joined them, and the day was full of puppet shows, madrigals, and general fun. Luke performed a magic show, with Stephen assisting him. The boy surprised everyone when he produced a coin he'd concealed in his sleeve. The crowd of children was astonished, and the smile on Stephen's face showed his pride. Clara and Antonia sat on a front-row bench, a child on each lap.

Luke took a red scarf from his pocket and showed it to the audience, first the front then the back. He folded it into sections and stuffed it into his closed hand. When he opened the hand and snapped the scarf open, it was white. The children applauded and clapped their hands to their faces in wonder. Even Clara was amazed by his illusions.

The show went from scarves to bouquets of flowers, linking rings, and disappearing coins. Stephen ended the program by performing his other mastered trick—pulling a single rose out of thin air and presenting it to his mother. Clara accepted the flower. It reminded her of the paper rose she had in her kitchen, the one Luke had given her.

When the show ended, Clara stood and looked around. For a moment she caught Luke's eye, but

his attention w~~...~~ quickly captured by her second
son. ~~...~~ara." She looked over her shoulder, a
"Hello for Ellen. "Are you enjoying the fes-
sp~~...~~

"I didn't expect it to be so large," Clara told
her.

"The whole of Butte turns out for this. It's the
only place to sample all the different foods and
see native costumes from around the world. The
mines close down today, and tonight there will be
fireworks."

"Here, let me take the girls." Antonia linked
hands with the little ones. "We're going to go
watch the swans."

Clara relinquished the children and watched as
they happily threaded their way to the pond.

"Since no one is in town, I suppose there was
no need to open the restaurant." Clara resumed her
conversation.

"Exactly," Ellen said, not the least disappointed.
She looked over her shoulder at Luke who was
breaking down his props. "And how are things going with Luke?"

Clara began walking. She didn't want Luke to
hear her and she felt uncomfortable under his
stare. "Ellen, I think he hates me," she whispered.

"Why?" Ellen glanced at him again.

"He came to supper a few weeks ago. I thought
he'd come back. I've invited him, but he's steered
clear of me since. I'm not what he wants, Ellen.
I'm a woman with children, which is exactly what
Luke doesn't want in his life."

"I don't believe that. He's in love with you. When Wade came, he was so upset I thought he was going to ruin my rug with his pacing."

Ellen nodded and stopped to say hello to several passersby. Clara waited until they were alone again. "I think his pride was hurt. I'd lied to him and everyone else. He was going to declare, but then Wade showed up."

"Clara, you never told me that."

The two women walked and whispered like sisters.

"I couldn't have let him, Ellen. I knew about Wade, even if he didn't."

"Well, you're free now and there's nothing to prevent you two from finding each other." Ellen stopped and stared at her. "Is there?" she asked.

Clara shook her head. "No, I have no other husbands with which to shock the valley."

Ellen laughed. "Let me have a talk with Luke."

Clara grabbed her arm as she started to reverse direction. "Don't do it, please. He has to decide on his own. I don't want anyone to play matchmaker for us."

"Lottery time . . . lottery time," a husky voice boomed.

"Excuse me, Clara, I volunteered to help with this." Ellen kissed her cheek and rushed across the grass.

"Lottery time!" The shout came again, and people gathered in front of a platform where Reverend Reed presided. Clara migrated to the edge of the crowd, noticing that Luke and Stephen continued to pack away props, oblivious to the proceedings.

"Come on in." The preacher used his arms to draw the crowd toward him. "I know this is the one event of the day you've all been waiting for."

Clara spied Martha Ames and walked over to her. "What happens here?" she whispered.

"It's a dinner. The men donate money to have their names put in the lottery basket along with the name of the woman they want to have dinner with. The woman cooks a meal, and the two of them share it."

"Did you make a dinner?"

"Yes, Frank donated for my dinner."

"Oh my God!" Clara suddenly remembered what she'd done.

"What's wrong?" Martha asked.

"The first dinner." The pastor cleared his throat dramatically and held a bowl of paper tags in front of one of the valley's most prominent citizens— Emily Hale.

"I cooked a dinner," Clara whispered to Martha.

"That's all right. Who donated for you?"

"Meg Collins and Dan Forest, Jr." Reverend Reed's voice carried to the back of the crowd. A wave of applause followed the announcement, and Meg and Dan came forward to claim the basket.

One by one, the happy couples accepted their baskets and went off to enjoy their meals, and Clara held her breath against the inevitable. There was a chance that Luke had donated for her, but she doubted it. Since their impromptu dinner three weeks ago, he hadn't spoken to her. She doubted he'd arrange for her basket without her knowledge, but Aunt Emily would have—enlisting Antonia as

a co-conspirator: Antonia would take the girls and
Aunt Emily would provide meals for Wade William and Stephen.

Then the pastor linked her name with Luke's,
and Clara's heart fell. The applause which had accompanied each name was mingled with gasps of
surprise and knowing nods. Clara had hoped
against hope she was wrong and that the meal
she'd prepared at her aunt's request would not
show up in this auction, but there is was, blue-
gingham cloth and her name in block letters,
printed no doubt by Dora Davidson.

Scanning the crowd, she saw Luke coming forward. He took the basket and came to her. "Where
would you like to eat?" he asked, his voice non-
committal.

Clara didn't care. She didn't want Aunt Emily
interfering in her life anymore. If she and Luke
were to have any kind of relationship, even friendship, they had to accomplish it on their own, without her intervention.

Clara followed Luke past the picnic tables where
everyone else had taken seats to a place on the
grass. He opened the basket and took the tablecloth
out. Spreading it on the ground, he faced her.

"Luke, I didn't do this."

"But we know who did." His voice sounded as
if he were in on Aunt Emily's joke.

"You don't have to eat with me. You can go now
if you want to. I know you don't like being around
me."

He walked across the grass, stepping on the
blue-and-white cloth he'd spread on the ground. He

came so close Clara had to look up to see him. "How do you know that?" he frowned.

She wanted to move away. He was too near; she could feel the heat he generated. Her hands were close enough to touch him, yet she stood her ground. "I'm not Peg."

Luke frowned. "I don't expect you to be."

"You do. You open up sometimes, and I'm vain enough to think it's only with me; then you push me away, remembering that I'm not the woman who bore your child and died." Clara took a breath. "I'm another woman and one with children. Well, Peg's dead, Luke, and I'm not, but I can't be like her."

Tears gathered in her throat. She stopped talking, turning away to regain control. When she had, she turned back. "I'm going to talk to Aunt Emily tonight. I'll let her know I don't wish to be part of her game anymore. You can crawl back into that shell you've erected and die with Peg. The rest of the world will go on without you."

Impulsively, Clara reached up and kissed him gently on the mouth. "Goodbye, Luke." Before she could change her mind and stay, she ran away, leaving the party behind her.

She ran aimlessly, desiring only to get away from Luke and his unreasonable attitude. She ran, hoping she could leave the love she had for him in her wake. She ran for the love she'd never see fulfilled, and she ran for all the happy couples taking their meals and enjoying each other's company.

Stopping, Clara slumped against a tree. She gulped the air as if it were liquid and she could fill her lungs with its life-sustaining nectar, then she let the tears come. Hot streams of water flowed from her eyes at the death of something that had never had life. Like Luke's child, who'd died within days of birth, their love, too, would die without having time to flourish and blossom into the kind of love that sustains a lifetime.

Finally, spent and tired, Clara looked up. Aunt Emily would wonder where she was. Thank goodness the children's choir didn't sing until the evening meal. Clara stared at her surroundings. Where was she? She laughed ironically. She was at the building site. The house was nearly done.

She walked tentatively toward it. All the windows were in place. The door had been hung, and the bricks in one wall were nearly completed. It was a magnificent house. Clara could see Luke in every brick, in every square joint. He'd put his love into this house, she thought. So much of him was here. With the part he reserved for his wife and child, and the amount here, there was none left for anyone else—nothing for her.

Taking a deep breath, Clara lifted her gaze to the mountains in the distance. "I suppose this is one of those times in life when everything changes," she told them. Luke had expressed in his words and actions so many times that he didn't want her around, that it was time she took her own advice and got on with her life. She had four children to care for. Their futures would have to take precedence.

With one last sweeping glance, Clara headed toward her own house. Something fell behind her, and she jumped at the explosive cloud of dust that billowed up. A broken tool box lay on the ground. She froze, a strangled cry escaping her lips. Wade William was on the roof.

"Wade William?" She paused. What was he doing up there?

The boy didn't answer. He gripped the middle chimney with both hands, a look of terror spreading across his face. Shaking free of the fear that rooted her in place, Clara called to him. "It's all right, Wade William. I'm coming. Don't move."

The child was afraid. He'd climbed the ladder not knowing how high up he would be, and now he was too frightened to come down. Clara grasped the middle rungs of the ladder that leaned against the three-story house.

"Hold on, Wade William. Mommy's coming. Everything will be all right." She spoke calmly, hoping to keep him from panicking.

Clara hopped onto the partially black-topped roof. Her dress stuck to the pitch, and on her hands and knees she crawled over the tiles, her progress slow.

Remembering her own encounter on the roof and Luke's telling her he hadn't wanted to frighten her, she didn't touch the boy once she'd neared him.

"Wade William," Clara said.

His eyes were terrified. Clara wasn't even sure he knew who she was.

"I'm here, Wade William."

He sniffed, making animal noises with his mouth.

"I want you to take my hand."

He shook his head violently, clinging to the chimney and pressing his face into it.

"Just one, sweetheart. One hand. Put yours in mine."

"I . . . I . . . can't," he sobbed. "I'll . . . fa . . . ll."

"Mommy won't let you fall. Take Mommy's hand."

He glanced at her. Clara forced a smile of encouragement, and he loosened his grip slightly, then squeezed his eyes closed and grabbed the chimney again.

"Wade William, I'm going to come closer."

"No-o-o," he pleaded.

"I won't touch you. I won't do anything you don't want me to do."

Clara inched closer until she could put her hand on his shoulder. She rubbed it comfortingly. "Give me your hand. We'll get down together."

"I'll . . . fall."

"I'll hold you. You won't fall."

The boy only grasped the bricks tighter. Clara reached for his hand, covering it with her own. She didn't try to move his fingers, and after a moment she took her hand away. By repeating the performance several times, she let him know it was possible to let go and not fall.

"See what Mommy's doing, Wade William? You can do this. Just take my hand."

He hesitated, indecisive. Then he let go and gripped her hand. Clara let her breath out. Icy fingers crushed her bones together. "Good," she said.

"Wonderful. We're all right. We're going to be all right." Her heart was beating fast. She was scared, too, but Wade William had trusted her enough to take her hand. She needed to free his other hand and then coax him to the ladder at the edge of the house.

Her back was wet with sweat, and the rough roof tiles had torn her skirt.

"All right, Wade William. I need the other hand. Let go and hug me."

He shook his head. "I'll hold you. You've already given me one hand. Let me have the other." It was a chore to keep her voice even, but he needed her to be strong, calm, and consistent.

Wade William eyed her fearfully, but with a strange mixture of trust. With a little more time, she felt confident he'd come to her.

"Your other hand," she said calmly, as if she were saying good night. "I promise we'll be all right. I'll get you to the ladder and then to the ground."

She reached out to him. Wade William's tears stopped, and he shifted toward her. Clara wanted to grab him, but stopped the impulse. The only movement she released was a nod of her head. Wade William let go and grabbed her around the neck in a stranglehold, and then Clara held him to her.

"I'm scared, Mom," he said, his voice higher than usual, his confidence gone. He was just a scared little boy.

"Mom won't let you get hurt." She waited for his shaking to subside. "Close your eyes, Wade

William. Don't look around. Put your head on my shoulder and keep your eyes closed."

She rocked him, rubbing his back as she had done when he'd been as young as the girls. If he'd been one of the girls, she could have rocked him to sleep and carried him down, but Wade William weighed eighty pounds. She couldn't even lift him.

"It's time we moved," she whispered in his ear, and his small hands gripped her tighter. Clara didn't say anything else. She slid backward, checking the location of the ladder, and whispering that Wade William should keep his eyes closed. He whimpered at the movement.

Clara continued, inch by inch, until they reached the ladder. She would have to get him to loosen his grip on her to climb down.

"What's going on?"

Clara almost dropped her hold on the child at the relief she felt hearing Luke's words behind her.

"Thank God you're here," she said. "Wade William is afraid of heights. I need help getting him down."

"The hard part is done, Wade William." Luke's voice was comforting. "We'll fly down these steps and kiss the ground, okay?"

The child said nothing. He kept his eyes squeezed tight and gripped Clara's neck hard enough to make breathing a labor.

"Let me have him."

She tried to loosen his arms, but Wade William held her in a death-grip. Each time Luke attempted to pull him away, Wade William cringed and choked her more.

"Wade William, you're going to suffocate your mother," Luke said, his voice stern. Clara would have been gentler, but the child loosened his grip.

Luke pried the small arms from Clara's neck, and put the boy on his back. Wade William didn't have to be told to hold on tight. Linking his legs around Luke's waist, he shook visibly. Clara wanted to go to him.

"We're going to start down now. Ready?"

Wade William remained quiet. Luke stepped onto the first rung and quickly went the rest of the way down.

Once on the ground, Wade William recovered miraculously. "Mom, I left my cap," he shouted from his safe position.

"I'll get it," Clara told him. She got up, leaning forward to compensate for the forty-five degree angle of the roof, but she didn't see the hat until she'd crawled to the untiled section of the roof behind the chimney. Waving it above her head, she grinned at the two on the ground, then—clapping it on her head—she modeled the flat-topped cap.

Wade William laughed.

"That's enough, Clara. Come on down," Luke ordered.

Clara recognized the tone in his voice. He was uncomfortable with her on the roof; she was too high up for antics. This time she'd follow instructions and get down. But at her first step, her foot flew out from under her. She hit the roof and rolled toward the edge. *I'm going to die,* she thought. She reached out, but found nothing to grab hold of. Her fingers raked the bare wood, and the grooved tiles cut into her lace-gloved fingers. As she went over the edge, she fought the air for a solid hold, and one hand caught.

"Clara!" Luke shouted. "Don't let go." He started up the ladder. "Go get help," he hollered back to Wade William. The boy's eyes were paralyzed as his mother dangled above him. "Go!" He ran in the direction of the summer party.

"Luke!" Clara screamed. "I can't hold on." The ground was three-stories below her. She swung her feet, trying to reach the side of the building, but the eaves were too wide. Even if her legs had been long enough to reach, she couldn't have held on. If she fell . . . He stopped that thought. She wasn't going to fall. He'd get to her in time. He had to.

The edge was steep. Luke climbed up to the roof and flattened his belly against the surface. *Hold on,* he prayed, crawling to the edge and grabbing her hand.

"Luke, don't drop me," she pleaded.

"I won't drop you, sweetheart." The angle was wrong, and he couldn't get enough leverage to pull her up. He was going to have to drag her to the side of the house so he could stand up and use the force of his legs to pull her over the surface.

"Give me your hand," he ordered.

"I'm falling, Luke."

"Give me your other hand." Clara wore gloves. They were too big, and she was slipping away from him. Sweat popped out on his brow. He squeezed her small hand, dragging her closer to him. "Take it," he commanded. Extending his hand, he balanced on his elbows, trying desperately to dig his knees into the roof tiles. He slipped forward, then rocked his weight back.

Clara reached for him. Her hand was inches short of his, and her glove slipped over her palm. Her feet flailed below her. She looked over her shoulder at the ground below, and terror filled her eyes when she looked back at him.

"Damn it, Clara, don't you dare fall. Now grab my hand."

She bit her lower lip and clutched at him, but missed. The glove slipped again. The sound of tearing fabric ripped at his sides. Only her fingers, attached precariously to his, kept her from falling. Luke was too afraid to say anything. Clara swung again.

Contact!

He let out his breath as he grasped her arm in a strong grip, but her fingers slipped through the glove and he lost control of her right hand. She still dangled over the edge, her back to the house. Her feet kicked at the ladder, which shifted, then settled into place. He felt himself pulled forward. It wasn't her weight that moved him, but the angle of torque that gave her center of gravity the greater leverage. Where was Wade William? Luke wasn't going to be able to maintain his hold much longer, and they'd both be killed.

"Clara, listen to me. The ladder. We need to reach it. You're going to have to catch my hand so I can swing you toward it." He didn't want her to know he couldn't pull her up.

She nodded and swung toward him. Their hands met, then Luke slipped forward. He stilled his movements. "Don't move," he said through clenched teeth waiting until his motion stopped. Silently, he thanked the Lord they hadn't plunged over the side.

Luke closed his eyes. One catastrophe averted. Now to the other. Forcing himself to breathe, he used all his strength to try to pull her up, but it wasn't going to work. She was going to have to help him. "Clara, I can't hold on like this. We need to get you to the ladder."

"All right," she said. Her voice appeared calm, but Luke understood her well enough to know that in the face of danger she steeled her emotions and aligned her wits to determine the best method of solving a problem.

Clara swung toward the ladder. Her feet reached for it—too hard. The ladder slid sideways and toppled to the ground. The resounding crash sealed their fate. Without the ladder, their chances of surviving were cut in half, and the force of the fall nearly made Luke lose his grip.

"I'm sorry, Luke," she apologized.

"It's all right. We'll find another way." His voice was more confident than he felt. Where was Wade William? "Clara, we have to work our way to the side, where I can stand and pull you up. This way we'll both fall."

Luke's strength was almost gone. He needed to rest his hands and his arms. "Listen to me carefully. . . . Do exactly as I say." His voice was commanding.

She nodded. Her eyes were trusting, but she was scared. He was too. If she fell . . . he blocked the image. She wasn't going to fall.

"I need you to grab the side of the roof and hold on—"

"I can't," she started.

Luke clenched his teeth. He didn't have time to argue. Her hands were slipping again, and her weight was dragging him toward the edge of the house.

"I need you to hold onto the eave. My hands and arms are getting numb. If I don't get feeling back, I'll lose my grip."

Clara nodded, but he saw the uncertainty in her eyes.

"It'll be all right, Clara." His heart thundered. "Can you do it?"

"I . . . can . . . try."

"Good." He liked that about her. Of course that was why they were in this position, because she'd tried to save Wade William alone. She should have called for help first. But he couldn't fault her. The boy was her child, and he'd have done the same thing in her place. "I'm going to pull you forward. When your hands get close enough, grab onto the side."

"All right." She checked over her shoulder.

"Don't look down," he shouted, startling her into returning her attention to him. "Look at me. Concentrate only on me."

Luke could feel the cords popping out in his neck as he strained to lift and pull Clara's weight to the edge of the roof.

"Okay," he told her. "One hand at a time."

Clara's right hand grasped the rough surface. Her feet searched for footing, but found none.

"Don't do that!" he shouted, then reined in his anger. "Just hang straight."

She nodded, her teeth biting hard into her lower lip.

"The other hand."

She checked with him without uttering a sound. Her eyes said everything. Luke saw her complete trust reflected there as she let go of his hand and grabbed the roof's edge. Her elbows straightened, and her head dropped from sight.

"Hold on, honey. It's going to be fine." Luke rubbed his arms. The skin was ripped and bleeding from scraping along the roof's surface.

"Luke," Clara called. "I'm going to move."

"Clara, no."

"Don't argue with me." Her left hand let go of its hold and moved a foot to the left before it gripped the roof again. The right hand followed in the same fashion. "Go higher on the roof and to the side. I'll make it there," she told him. It had been months since Clara had tried anything like this; she only hoped she still had the strength. Hanging from the roof was nothing like pitching hay in the barn. She had done that, and her arms had grown strong from work on the farm and carrying books back and forth to school. In the months she'd been in Montana, she'd been pampered, free of any responsibilities unbefitting a lady.

She moved her hands again. The pain from her

bleeding fingers was excruciating, and her grip was slipping. She couldn't wait for Luke to regain feeling in his hands; she had to get to the position he wanted her in faster than he could help her there.

With his heart in his mouth, Luke obeyed Clara's wish, following step by step as one ragged glove grasped the security of the edge and "walked" around the roof. When she was within a safe distance, Luke rushed to her. In a flash he grasped her upper arms, his grip so tight he knew it would leave bruises. Pulling almost straight upward, he lifted her until her knees came level with the roof and then dragged her forward. Dropping to his own knees, he hugged her to him. She was safe.

Clara collapsed against him, her arms hugging his midriff, refusing to let go. She was wet with perspiration, her heart a sledge hammer against her chest wall.

Luke pushed her back to look at her. He checked her arms and her bloody fingers, looked at her face and then her shoulders, then he hauled her into his arms and seared his mouth to hers.

Clara didn't know how long they stayed that way. She didn't think about the whole valley looking at them from the ground or that she and Luke had argued that afternoon only a few yards from where they were now. She was glad to be alive, glad to be in love with Luke, and glad to be in his arms. She touched him everywhere, her hands free to roam wherever she wished, just to know nothing had happened to him or her. She kissed his chin, his bottom lip, his eyelids. Touching him, confirming his presence and that they had both survived, took any inhibitions she possessed and dropped them to the ground.

Unmindful of the crowd gathering below them, Clara buried her face in Luke's chest and held him to her. She didn't ever want to let him go. If at no other time in her life, she needed him to know now that she loved him.

"I love you, Luke. I've loved you since the first day. Since I saw you hammering on this roof. I don't think I can stay here if you don't love me. I'll take the children and return to the farm."

"Be quiet, Clara," he told her. "Let me tell you I can't live without you. That if you'd fallen off this roof, I've have gone after you. You're my life. I love you. Without you, there's nothing."

Twenty-three

"Is Mr. Luke here yet, Mommy?" Lisa Rose asked from the door of Clara's bedroom.

Clara went to her youngest and dropped to the floor. "He said he wouldn't return until tomorrow," Clara answered. "I'm sure he'll come and see you as soon as he gets off the train."

"He's bringing me some candy for my birthday." Lisa's head bobbed up and down. "He said they have a big candy story in that Boat's man's place."

Clara smiled at her interpretation of the word Bozeman.

"Do you think he'll bring it to Aunt Emily's if we're not here?"

"I'm sure he will. Now are you ready to go?"

They were having dinner at her aunt's. The children looked wonderful in their new dresses and shoes. Clara, too, had bought herself a hat, a yellow felt one. It matched the yellow dress and made her happy just to look at it. She smiled at her reflection, remembering that day long ago when she'd had no money and had wanted the hat so badly. Now, she had income from the farm—Andy managed it for her back in Virginia—and she had a salary from her teaching.

Lisa's birthday was tomorrow, but tonight was like a celebration. Luke was working in Bozeman, and she would miss his presence, but the rest of her friends—Martha, Antonia, even Dora Davidson, who'd apologized for starting the vicious rumors about her and Luke—would be on hand. As would some of the children from the valley. Lisa would be surprised when they found balloons and paper streamers decorating the backyard.

"Where are Wade William and Stephen?" Clara asked.

"In the kitchen," came the ready response.

"What are they doing?"

"Stephen is practicing pulling chocolate candy out of Wade William's hair."

"Oh, no," Clara moaned, increasing their pace down the stairs.

In the kitchen she found Stephen, his hands filled with the chocolate squares she'd spent the last evening making.

"Stephen, no." She took the melting confection from him and got a wet cloth to wipe his hands.

"I told him he couldn't do it," Wade William said in his oldest-child manner.

"I can't leave you alone a moment without your getting into trouble," she scolded.

"Can I show my new trick at Aunt Emily's, Mom?" Stephen, not put out by her manner, asked.

Clara couldn't help giving in to his happy face. He was so proud of the tricks Luke had taught him, and he'd spent hours practicing the illusions.

It hadn't surprised Clara that Luke was patient and considerate and that he didn't seem to mind helping Stephen.

After the events of the summer party, Wade William helped Luke every day, but he had not ventured up the ladder again. Clara looked at her hands. It had been a month since the near-accident at Luke's house. Doc Pritchard had bandaged her hands, and Aunt Emily and Antonia Morrison had taken turns cooking for her and the children. Luke, his own hands and arms in bandages, had been almost always nearby. Her hands had healed, and there were little physical effects left of her trauma. She admitted that the idea of going up on the roof didn't sit well with her; but if she had had to do it, she was sure she could have.

"Ready, everybody?"

At the collective assent, they left the house and climbed into the wagon, Wade William automatically taking the reins. Clara often let him drive. The only time he abdicated was when Luke was with them.

"It's about time you got here," Aunt Emily said when the wagon stopped in front of the boarding-house. "I thought I was going to have to tie down some of these children." She reached up and lifted one of the girls to the ground, then the other.

She looked at both of them. "I think there might be some people over there you know." Aunt Emily pointed toward the side of the house.

"I don't see anyone," Stephen said, a frown on his brow.

Clara took his arm and shook her head. She didn't want him to spoil the surprise.

"Would you like to eat in the yard? We have a picnic table and everything."

The girls stared up at her, then started together for the side of the house. When they were at the corner, everyone jumped out screaming, "Surprise!"

Lisa Rose's hands went to her face. The yard had everything. Bright lanterns hung from strings around the perimeter. A huge wheel turned at one end of the yard, and Clara recognized the azoetrope. A line waited to view the pictures reflected on small, rectangular mirrors. It provided the illusion of moving pictures.

"Happy birthday, sweetheart." Aunt Emily bent down and hugged her.

"Look at all those presents," Stephen yelled.

Everyone took off running toward the table with boxes wrapped in bright-colored paper and tied with ribbons.

"Can we open them, Mom?" Stephen yelled to her again.

Clara shook her head. "It's Lisa's birthday."

A moment later they were all distracted by the other children and Antonia, determined to organize party games.

"Clara, would you go into the house and bring out the rolls? I left them on the stove."

Clara agreed, leaving her aunt and walking toward the steps. Speaking to everyone she saw, she felt right at home in the valley. No longer an outsider, she didn't think she could ever leave this beautiful country.

Inside the kitchen, she found the rolls exactly where they were supposed to be. The room was warm with the smell of bread permeating the air. She put the rolls in a basket before heading for the door.

"Where have I seen that hat before?"

Clara turned around, dropping the rolls on the table, and ran into Luke's arms. "When did you get back?"

"This morning," he said, his arms wrapping around her. He kissed her lazily. "I've been thinking of this for four days."

"Me, too," she told him, suddenly breathless. His gaze roved her face. "I like the hat." He leaned down, reclaiming her mouth. This time his tongue probed inside. Passion overtook them; and his arms, around her waist, tightened as he molded her to him. Clara wondered if she'd ever get used to the riot of emotions that speared through her body whenever he took her in his arms. Her arms linked behind his head. Angling her face, Clara leaned into his kiss.

Luke broke contact. "Do we have to stay for this party?" He kept her close to him.

"Luke Evans!" She feigned anger. "Lisa Rose would never forgive you if you missed her party. And Stephen is dying to show you his new trick."

"I guess you'll just have to wait for your trick." Clara saw the mischief in his eyes. Smiling, she remembered the young girl who'd first seen him. She wasn't that girl any longer. She had grown up and was in love with him. Clara considered the freedom love gave her. She was free to smile into his eyes, to kiss him and hold him, and to tell him her most precious secrets. She couldn't imagine her life without Luke.

He walked her to the door and down the steps. Clara went, completely forgetting her purpose in having come to the kitchen. Lisa Rose spotted him across the yard and threw herself against his legs.

"Mommy said you wouldn't be back until to-morrow." A small lip pouted its accusation.

"I came back especially for you." He scooped her up and kissed her on the cheek.

"Did you bring my candy?"

With exaggerated movements, Luke stuck his hands into his pockets, pulling the insides out. He unbuttoned his coat and looked in his vest pockets, and then the inside pocket of his coat. The girls looked on in wide-eyed fascination. The other children crowded behind them, recognizing that Luke was about to perform for them.

"Is this a new dress?" he asked.

Both girls shook their heads.

"They must be very special dresses . . . magic dresses."

"What's magic about them?" Stephen asked from the edge of the crowd.

He reached into a tiny pocket and pulled out a green scarf. Then the color changed to red as he tugged at it, and more and more colors flowed from the pocket of the new dress. Surprise and delight registered on everyone's face.

"It looks like that's all," Luke said, holding most of the scarf.

"No it's not," Mary Rose said and reached for the part of the scarf still in her sister's pocket. She gasped suddenly and pulled on the piece of gauze, delivering up a box with a large red ribbon tied like a rose.

"Candy," she shouted, and their young guests crowded closer.

"Where's mine?" Lisa Rose's face fell.

Straight-faced, Luke put his hands out in front of him. He turned his palms up and down. Then he balled his hands into fists and quickly turned them over, mocking a throw into the air. His fingers opened and inside was an identical box of candy, which he handed over with a bow.

"Thank you," she chimed.

The crowd applauded. Luke smiled and nodded at them. They dispersed as he came to Clara and slipped his arm around her waist. More by mutual agreement than plan, they walked around the boardinghouse and headed toward the path that led to the building site. The July sun warmed the afternoon, and Clara wrapped her arm around Luke and walked in companionable silence.

As the gradient changed, they climbed the slight incline and suddenly Clara stopped. "Luke, it's done!"

Before her rose a three-story structure of red brick with chimneys marking the four winds. Clara ran to the entrance. Before she opened the door, Luke caught her arm and pulled her back.

"I've got something to say before you go in."

She waited expectantly.

"When you first came here, you said this was a very big house."

Clara glanced at him. "I asked if you had a large family, and your face closed up."

"I was still hurt over losing what I thought was the only love of my life. Now I know that wasn't true. I suppose from the first I wanted this place to have a big family living in it."

Clara stepped directly in front of him. Luke's face was serious and nervous.

"I've been thinking about you and the kids."

"What about us? We're a large family, but we already have a house and I have a job and income from a farm." She grinned, teasing him.

"You're not going to help me with this, are you?"

Standing on tiptoe, she kissed his chin. "Not in the least."

Luke grinned. "I know one way you'll be forced to." His arms encircled her waist, and his mouth angled toward hers. He stopped a breath away from her. "Help," he muttered.

Clara melted into the kiss. He knew she had no resistance where he was concerned. Her arms went around his neck, and he squeezed her closer until not even air could pass between them.

"You're going to have to marry me, Clara," Luke whispered against her mouth. "If you don't, we'll set this house on fire from the sheer heat of reaction."

Clara moved against him. His groan told her he was hers and she was his and always would be.

"Is that a proposal?" she asked.

"I love you."

"I come with baggage," she reminded him.

He hugged her closer. "Yes," he breathed into her hair. "I couldn't love them more if they were my own." Shifting back enough to see her face, he said, "I know they'd like living here. They can each have their own room, and—"

"I'll marry you, Luke." Clara interrupted him. She knew she couldn't live without him, and the children loved him, too. "If we only had a house as big as Clem Kincaid's cabin, I'd marry you."

Luke kissed her, the force of emotion overtaking them. Scooping her up from the floorboards, he carried her over the threshold, his mouth never leaving hers. As he kicked the door closed, Clara silently thanked Janey Willard. One day she'd have to tell Luke about her.

Epilogue

Tears misted in Emily Hale's eyes. Luke stared at the woman who had become his aunt. Sitting regally in his front parlor, she stared at him. Luke never expected her to change.

"Don't cry. You've gotten your way in everything."

"Luke, how can you say that?" She smiled through the water in her eyes. "To tell you the truth, I never thought I'd see it." She dabbed at her eyes.

"Aunt Emily." He emphasized their relationship. "This was your primary goal the minute you saw Clara's name on the application."

"I admit I hoped, but I never thought for a moment . . ."

"Of course you did," Clara interrupted her. She stood in the archway. "You would have married us off as I stepped from the train." She smiled, then looked at Luke. "We'll forgive you."

Clara's hair glowed in the highlights of the setting sun that streamed through the windows that made up three of the four walls. Luke had built this room with her in mind. It was the reason he'd ordered so many windows, why he'd decided to clear more land and frame the perfect room for her.

"Give me my grandchild." Emily Hale opened her arms.

Clara came forward, the small bundle in her arms wrapped in a white blanket. Luke met her in front of Aunt Emily. He lifted the blanket and stared at his son. He was so small and so perfect. Luke had counted his little fingers and toes. He'd spent the first night watching him sleep, making sure he was all right until Clara had forced him to bed, assuring him the child would still be there in the morning. He couldn't explain the love that welled in him whenever he thought of the luck that had come into his life with Clara's arrival and the children. Lisa Rose and Mary Rose kept him busy with their endless questions and requests; the boys couldn't wait to help out at his building sites. He loved them all. He wanted to have more, many more.

Luke took little Waymon Evans from his mother and kissed his head. Then he laid the child in his great-aunt's arms. With all he had, he could afford to be generous. He understood her need to have a child in her arms, to know that her bloodline would continue long after she was gone.

The two of them watched the effect the baby had on Emily Hale—the tears in her eyes, the love on her face. Luke understood love. Aunt Emily had tried to tell him about it, but it was Clara who had showed him what it meant. She slipped her arm around him and looked into his eyes. They'd been married for over a year and her look still melted his insides. He knew it always would.

Dear Reader,

Clara and Luke touched many lives in their course to find true love. I hope you enjoyed reading *Clara's Promise* as much as I enjoyed the characters visiting with me for the past year. Their hopes and dreams became mine, especially in the building of the house. I, as well, searched for and moved into a wonderful house during the writing of this book.

I'd also like to thank those enthusiastic fans who sent me letters on my first book, *Whispers of Love*. Writing is a rewarding occupation and comments from readers are always appreciated.

Should you want to hear more about *Clara's Promise* and other books, I have a readers newsletter which I'll send to you if you include a business size, self-addressed, stamped envelope. You can write to me at:

P.O. Box 513
Plainsboro, NJ 08536

Sincerely,

Shirley Hailstock

IF ROMANCE BE THE FRUIT OF LIFE—
READ ON—
BREATH-QUICKENING HISTORICALS FROM PINNACLE

WILDCAT (772, $4.99)
by Rochelle Wayne

No man alive could break Diana Preston's fiery spirit . . . until seductive Vince Gannon galloped onto Diana's sprawling family ranch. Vince, a man with dark secrets, would sweep her into his world of danger and desire. And Diana couldn't deny the powerful yearnings that branded her as his own, for all time!

THE HIGHWAY MAN (765, $4.50)
by Nadine Crenshaw

When a trumped-up murder charge forced beautiful Jane Fitzpatrick to flee her home, she was found and sheltered by the highwayman—a man as dark and dangerous as the secrets that haunted him. As their hiding place became a place of shared dreams—and soaring desires—Jane knew she'd found the love she'd been yearning for!

SILKEN SPURS (756, $4.99)
by Jane Archer

Beautiful Harmony Harper, leader of a notorious outlaw gang, rode the desert plains of New Mexico in search of justice and vengeance. Now she has captured powerful and privileged Thor Clarke-Jargon, who is everything Harmony has ever hated—and all she will ever want. And after Harmony has taken the handsome adventurer hostage, she herself has become a captive—of her own desires!

WYOMING ECSTASY (740, $4.50)
by Gina Robins

Feisty criminal investigator, July MacKenzie, solicits the partnership of the legendary half-breed gunslinger-detective Nacona Blue. After being turned down, July—never one to accept the meaning of the word no—finds a way to convince Nacona to be her partner . . . first in business—then in passion. Across the wilds of Wyoming, and always one step ahead of trouble, July surrenders to passion's searing demands!

Available wherever paperbacks are sold, or order direct from the Publisher. Send cover price plus 50¢ per copy for mailing and handling to Penguin USA, P.O. Box 999, c/o Dept. 17109, Bergenfield, NJ 07621. Residents of New York and Tennessee must include sales tax. DO NOT SEND CASH.

HISTORICAL ROMANCE FROM PINNACLE BOOKS

LOVE'S RAGING TIDE   (381, $4.50)
by Patricia Matthews

Melissa stood on the veranda and looked over the sweeping acres of Great Oaks that had been her family's home for two generations, and her eyes burned with anger and humiliation. Today her home would go beneath the auctioneer's hammer and be lost to her forever. Two men eagerly awaited the auction: Simon Crouse and Luke Devereaux. Both would try to have her, but they would have to contend with the anger and pride of girl turned woman . . .

CASTLE OF DREAMS   (334, $4.50)
by Flora M. Speer

Meredith would never forget the moment she first saw the baron of Afoncaer, with his armor glistening and blue eyes shining honest and true. Though she knew she should hate this Norman intruder, she could only admire the lean strength of his body, the golden hue of his face. And the innocent Welsh maiden realized that she had lost her heart to one she could only call enemy.

LOVE'S DARING DREAM   (372, $4.50)
by Patricia Matthews

Maggie's escape from the poverty of her family's bleak existence gives fire to her dream of happiness in the arms of a true, loving man. But the men she encounters on her tempestuous journey are men of wealth, greed, and lust. To survive in their world she must control her newly awakened desires, as her beautiful body threatens to betray her at every turn.

Available wherever paperbacks are sold, or order direct from the Publisher. Send cover price plus 50¢ per copy for mailing and handling to Penguin USA, P.O. Box 999, c/o Dept. 17109, Bergenfield, NJ 07621. Residents of New York and Tennessee must include sales tax. DO NOT SEND CASH.